LEVEN THUMPS AND THE GATEWAY TO FOO

Leven Thumps

and the Gateway to Foo

Obert Skye

SHADOW ®
MOUNTAIN

For those who saw me slip through
and held their tongues—
your part in this is just beginning

Visit us at leventhumps.com

Library of Congress Cataloging-in-Publication Data

Skye, Obert.
Leven Thumps and the gateway to Foo / Obert Skye.
p. cm.
Summary: When fate brings fourteen-year-old Leven and thirteen-year-old Winter together, they discover that for mankind to continue dreaming, the gateway between reality and dreams needs to be found and demolished.
ISBN 1-59038-369-9 (hardbound : alk. paper)
[1. Magic—Fiction. 2. Dreams—Fiction. 3. Fantasy.] I. Title.
PZ7.S62877Le 2005
[Fic]—dc22

2004025103

Printed in the United States of America 18961
R. R. Donnelley and Sons, Crawfordsville, IN

10 9 8 7 6 5 4 3 2 1

Contents

Contents

Contents

"... it is a place where possibility is eternal; where scenery can change as effortlessly as dreams. There a being's view is shaded not by obstacle or travail, and *impossible* is a whisper spoken only by the souls who have just accidentally stepped in. It is a place where young children play in the shadows of Morfit, their voices a familiar melody, singing low in the wind, 'Step on a crack and Foo will snatch you back ...'"

The Beginning

It was at least forty degrees above warm. The day felt like a windowless kitchen where the oven had been left on high for an entire afternoon. Heat beat down from above and sizzled up from the dirt as the earth let off some much-needed steam. The sky had decided it had had quite enough, thank you, and had vacated the scene, leaving the air empty except for heat. No matter how wide a person opened his mouth that afternoon or how deep a breath was taken, there just wasn't enough oxygen in the air to breathe. The few remaining plants in people's gardens didn't droop, they passed out. And the flags that only days before had hung majestically on the top of local flagpoles no longer looked majestic, they looked like multicolored pieces of cloth that had climbed up and tragically hung themselves.

All this in and of itself was not too terribly unusual, but as the

heavy sun started to melt away an odd, wild, uncoordinated wind began to pick up. Not a northerly wind or an easterly breeze, it was a wind with no direction or balance. It was as if the four corners of earth and heaven all decided to simultaneously blow, creating what the local weather personalities in Tin Culvert, Oklahoma, called "beyond frightening." Sure, people could breathe, but now they were getting blown away.

Trees bent and writhed, whirling like pinwheels as the atmosphere pinched and pulled at them. Rooftops buckled and nature picked up huge handfuls of dirt and spastically flung them everywhere. Cats learned how to fly that evening, and any loose article weighing less than a car was taken up in the rapture of the moment. People locked themselves in their homes, radios on, waiting for someone to tell them everything was going to be okay, or for nature to do them in.

As dusk matured into night and just when those cowering in fear could stand no more, a darkness, the likes of which had never before been seen, began to ooze up from the ground and ink in the gray of evening. The hot windy sky quickly became a thick sticky trap. Animals that had foolishly taken shelter in trees or ditches began to suffocate as the heavy, plastic-like blackness folded over them. The wild wind swooped in from all directions to steal their last breaths and leave them dead where they once whined.

The blackness weighed down on everything. Porch lights burst under the weight of it. If the wind had been absent, a person could have clearly heard the explosion of almost every light and window in Tin Culvert as the fat, dark atmosphere let its full bulk rest upon anything glowing. Homes came alive with screams as front windows buckled and blew inward. Cars and mobile homes creaked under the force of darkness upon their backs. People cowered under tables and beds trying to escape the advancing crush.

Just when it looked like the end of the world had officially begun, the lightning started. Jagged stripes of blinding light flashed continually against the black sky. Anyone foolish enough to be standing outside would have been able to watch as the lightning moved with calculating accuracy, deliberately touching anything above ground level and quickly setting it ablaze. It moved sideways and upward. The sky became a giant blackboard with heaven scratching out its apocalyptic messages with lightning bolts.

Tin Culvert was dying, and this was the first night of the end of its life. Fate had set its course and was making certain to carry it out.

Even amongst the complete destruction and panic, a person would have had to be dead not to hear and feel the thunder that struck at exactly 10:15 that fateful night. The boom was felt as far as fifty miles away, and the entire sky fractured from light, scribbling one final message—"It is over!"

Lightning bled down on everything, touching and igniting any structure Tin Culvert had ever dared raise. People finally figured out that hiding was no longer a sensible option. Folks set out into the open, desperate to get away from it all.

In the chaos nobody noticed Antsel, a thin, aged man running across the ground at a terrific speed. Electrical static buzzed around him as he flew across the earth. The odd little man had traveled half the world to get to this spot and now, as the moment grew closer, his heart and soul surged. Fire raged up around him as he moved. His long beard curled and began to singe at the edges.

Lightning flashed in the tumultuous sky.

Antsel's stride became uneven, his face red with sweat and heat.

He ran in a pattern, away from the fire and as if he were trying to throw somebody off his trail. The thick gray robe he wore flapped in all directions as the wind became aware of him and started to work him over.

Lightning flashed again.

Antsel stumbled and fell as he looked toward the sky. His knees plowed into the earth as he ground to a halting stop.

Lightning flashed yet again.

Kneeling, he reached with aged hands into his robe and pulled out Clover, a small cat-like creature—the tiny being wriggled and spat angrily.

"Be calm," Antsel ordered, wiping sweat from his own forehead.

Instantly the small furry being relaxed. Clover's tiny body was covered with gray hair. He had leaf-like ears that were thick and wide, and his knees and elbows were as bare as any palm. He had on a tiny cloak that was the color of his fur but shimmered slightly under the light of fires.

"This is it," Antsel whispered with severity. "The shadows will soon be here. You know what you must do. It'll be some time from now, but he will be here, and the girl as well. Be patient."

"Only if you tell me to be."

"Be patient," Antsel insisted.

"I won't leave you," Clover whimpered.

"You *will* leave me," Antsel commanded.

"I will leave you," he answered.

"Now run!" Antsel shouted, setting the furry creature down. "Run!"

Clover looked at Antsel. "You will be proud of me?"

"Of course. Now run."

Clover spat and smiled. He jumped, shivered violently, and ran off on two feet, bucking oddly as he leapt, and was lost almost instantly in the dark. Antsel gazed after him. He knew the risk he took in putting so much trust in such a mischievous creature, but he had no choice. He turned and ran the opposite direction.

Lightning flashed.

Antsel slowed his pace, feeling his age and marveling over the fact that his heart had not yet given out. He reached into his robe and withdrew an object more important than any soul within a million miles could comprehend. Sweat poured from his neck and wrists, and he could feel his heart beginning to crumble. Antsel held the tiny seed up to the light of the surrounding fires and glanced at it one last time.

Lightning flashed again.

He placed the seed back in his robe and kneeled. He pressed his face to the ground and used his ability to see everything beneath the soil. Every insect, every particle. This was the perfect spot. He lifted his head and brushed the sweat from his eyes. He then began to dig. His old hands bled and trembled as he plunged them deeper into the dark, rich earth. Lightning struck continuously as fire after fire

ignited. The atmosphere began to relax, drawing in more oxygen to feed the flames.

Antsel paid no attention.

He had something to finish. He pulled the seed out again and pressed it down into the earth, then worked madly to fill the hole with the soil he had scraped out.

Lightning flashed, thunder crashed, and the howling of the wind increased.

He looked over his shoulder and shuddered. They were here, he could feel it in the wind. Antsel glanced at the ground, knowing that the fate of a thousand generations rested beneath only a foot of soil.

"Grow, Geth," he whispered. "Grow." Antsel patted the ground and dusted his palms. His job was done, and he stood with purpose.

Lightning flashed again, while simultaneously a sickened soul in another realm breathed a small dark army of shadows out over Tin Culvert. Sabine sat impatiently in Foo, breathing heavily and yet with control, letting his shadows twist down through the dark dreams of men and into reality. His castoffs were darker than the night, black. Like a perverted wind they swirled and billowed as they rushed across the fiery earth, laughing and screeching. Their white eyes and shrill voices gave their two-dimensional forms an eerie depth. Invisible to mankind, they swept the fiery landscape. They were not here to sightsee, however; they were here for a purpose.

Antsel knew the shadows had arrived. He couldn't let them find the spot. Running deeper into the night and far away from what he had planted, he wiped at his forehead with his heavy cloak and clutched his chest in agony. He would not last the night. He accepted this; after all, his mission was accomplished. The only thing he could do now was to run as far as possible away from the ground he had just touched. He pushed himself, darting to the right and turning a sharp left. His legs screamed in pain, and he could feel his heart pulsing up inside him like some sort of red-hot inflammation.

The moans of the shadows roared as they circled the burning town. Like a cyclone they twisted in tighter and mightier, their hollow eyes searching the firelight for the withered form of the old man they had been sent to find. The wind shifted and all together they lifted their heads and looked to the east. Nothing but flames and beyond that, darkness.

The winds shifted again.

Light from the fires reflected off a small hint of silver in the distance. The reflection vanished for a second only to spark up again even farther away. The shadows took notice. Something was running from them. Their restless forms turned toward the dark and flew.

Antsel ran. He could feel them coming toward him now and in a brief moment they were hovering over him, hissing and screeching. His old heart was making his stride short and almost pointless. Sabine's shadows swooped down and wrapped themselves around him, smothering his progress and slowing his gait even further. He pushed with his arms, waving the night away and struggling to go on.

It was no use: they had him surrounded and were pressing their hideous forms against him, moaning and gnashing their teeth. They circled him like a ring of plague. Antsel's purple eyes could faintly make out their inky outlines as they whispered wickedly.

He moved to the east but was stopped by the billowing of a shadow. He moved to the north and received a blow to the side.

Antsel was trapped.

"Where is it?" the shadows hissed. "Give us the seed."

His heart struggling to keep beating, Antsel wiped his eyes, put his palms to his knees, and tried to draw in breath. He straightened and lit an amber stick and lifted the firebrand to just below his eyes. The light from the stick glowed in a sphere around the gathering.

Antsel could see nothing but dripping darkness and thousands of shadows wildly circling him. They moaned, their white eyes even dimmer in the light of the amber stick. Nowhere in the sea of muted eyes could Antsel detect even a hint of mercy. He knew that somewhere in Foo, Sabine looked on with pleasure—his former friend no longer having any thought or feeling for anyone but himself.

Antsel's breathing was shallow and his heartbeat weak. The insistence of the surrounding shadows and the roaring of the fire in the distance seemed fitting to what he knew would be his end.

"Give us the seed," they hissed. "The seed."

"It is in Foo," Antsel gasped at them.

"You lie," they whispered back. "You lie."

"I—"

The shadows had no patience. Screaming, they leapt onto the old man. They clawed at him, searching for the object. Their hands ripped at his robe and body. Their mouths screamed and moaned as they tossed Antsel around like a rag doll. Antsel tried to fight back, but there were too many, and his strength and will were gone. The shadows thrust his face into the soil. Antsel could see everything. He watched the seed, though far from where he now lay, already begin to grow.

The shadows spun him once more and then withdrew with nothing.

Antsel lay on the ground moving only his lips. He murmured

weakly, committing his soul to rest and waiting for fate to tell him it was over. He stared up and could see the false face of Sabine in the thousands of shadows. His soul relaxed and his life slipped away.

The shadows began to moan. The seed had not been found. They knew too well that Sabine, the being who had cast them, would not be happy Antsel was dead. The shadows berated themselves. A few of them began to hiss, "Burn everything. Burn it!"

Antsel might have deposited the seed on earth. Sabine knew this, and even the remotest possibility of that couldn't be ignored. Most of the landscape was on fire, but a few pieces and parts were still void of flame.

"Burn it all," the shadows were now whispering fiercely. They all began to rise and laugh and dance, happy in their fury to carry out such a horrific thing. They swirled and scattered in a thousand directions to do Sabine's bidding. Some twisting together in a massive funnel cloud, they sucked up fire and dripped it down upon everything.

In the distance, far away from the heat and light, Clover stopped running so as to better cry. He stood to his full twelve inches and shivered. The fur over his body bristled in waves. His wet eyes viewed the flames as they devoured the entire landscape.

"Antsel," he whispered, his thin leathery mouth quivering. He wiped his blue eyes with the hem of his small robe, his leaf-like ears twitching to listen to the wind. He turned and continued running. Clover saw no reason to go back. Antsel was gone, and the journey had begun.

CHAPTER ONE

A RELATIVE OF FOO

THE BIRTH OF LEVEN

Who can say for sure what constitutes the perfect birth? Perhaps a mother, while playing cards and sipping lemonade, might simply hiccup, pat her stomach, and there in her arms would be a beautiful child, already diapered and pink-cheeked, looking up at her and emitting a soft coo. That wouldn't be too bad.

Or perhaps, while taking a nice ride up the coastline on a golden afternoon, a woman might tap her husband on the shoulder and say, "Look what I found."

Together they would peer into the backseat and there would be their lovely newborn buckled in a car seat and sleeping blissfully. A person could argue that that scenario would be perfect to a lot of people.

Well, Leven Thumps experienced nothing of the sort. He came

into the world like a delivery that no one knew what to do with and nobody wanted to sign for. His father had passed away in a tragic car accident only a week before his arrival, sending his mother spiraling down into a deep pit of grief and mourning. Her only hope was in knowing that the husband she had lost would live on in the son she was about to give birth to. Two days before the delivery her health suddenly began to deteriorate. She couldn't stand, she couldn't sleep, and she found it difficult to even breathe.

On October fifteenth, at 2:30 in the morning, Maria Thumps knew she was not long for this world. She called her neighbor, who came immediately and quickly drove Maria to the hospital. Maria had been inside the hospital for only five minutes when her son was born. The child had a head of thick dark hair and wise open eyes.

The doctor placed the baby in her hands, and for the first time in a while Maria smiled. "Leven," she whispered.

Maria's smile began to fade. Her face paled to a new shade of white. She clenched her eyes shut and began to struggle for breath. Her hands twitched and Leven rolled from her arms and into her lap. Every machine in the room with a voice immediately began to wail and frantically beep, and the lights suddenly dimmed. Doctors and nurses huddled over Maria, trying desperately to work a miracle. It was no use. A tall doctor picked up Leven and handed him to one of the attending nurses. She stepped quickly out of the room with the child, saving him from the scene and pulling him away from the last person on earth who would love him for some time. Two minutes later Maria Thumps closed her eyes, ceased her labored breathing, and passed away.

Leven lay alone in the hospital nursery for days. Every morning at 10:00 and each afternoon at 3:15, a different nurse would come in, pick him up, and hold him for exactly four and a half minutes. Other than that he was touched only when being fed or changed. The hospital staff whispered about what to do with him, waiting for the state to decide, but the wheels of compassion were slow to get moving. Everyone was holding out hope that a kindly relative or family member might be found and the little orphan would be taken away and off their hands. The hospital was already short-staffed and money was hard to come by, thanks in part to a dozen or so recent malpractice law suits the administrators had been forced to settle.

On the fourth day following Leven's birth, the prayers in his behalf were answered. Well, sort of. Contact had been made with a half sister of Leven's mom. Her name was Addy Graph, and at this very moment, she was on her way to the hospital from one state over and two states up.

She arrived that evening, bringing with her a violent rainstorm that battered the hospital. Addy pulled up in a dull-looking black car with only one headlight and a mismatched door. The car shuddered to a stop in the spot reserved for ambulances and Addy Graph got out. Addy was not a pleasant-looking woman. She was heavy-set and had a high forehead and no lips. Her flesh was pasty white, and the veins beneath her chalky skin were not only visible, they were bulging, as if there were too much thick blood coursing through them. She had a protruding stomach and skinny legs you felt sorry for due to the big ball of weight they were called upon to support.

She slammed the mismatched car door and held a newspaper over her frizzy hair as she cursed the weather and moved toward the entrance to the hospital.

As she walked away from her car, a little security guard with a whistle around his neck hollered out at her. "This is for emergency personnel only," he chirped. "You'll have to move your car."

Addy glared at him. "Excuse me?" she sneered, her neck veins bulging.

The short man cleared his throat. "No unauthorized vehicles allowed." He made a large circle with his arm, indicating the area. "Your car must be moved."

"Then move it," Addy snapped. She pushed past him and into the hospital.

The young woman at the reception desk did her best to welcome Addy, but her pleasant greeting was met with total disgust.

"I drive all day and then when I get here some Neanderthal with a whistle tries to tell me where to park," Addy growled.

"I'm sorry . . ." the young girl tried. "But we—"

"Stow it. I'm here to pick up a kid," Addy interrupted, dismissing whatever the girl was about to say. "His mother died, so I'm saddled with him."

"Saddled?" the girl asked, confused.

"Stuck with him," she snarled.

"So you want the nursery?"

"What I want and what I'm about to get are two different things, Sweety. I've already spent too much money coming to fetch this brat."

"I'm sure someday he'll be grateful," the girl said, trying to be kind.

"I'd take that bet, if I thought you were good for it," Addy sniffed. "Now where's the nursery?"

For a moment, the young girl considered pointing in the wrong

direction—thinking that might buy her some time to race up the stairs and rescue the poor baby that was going to be stuck with this piece of work. But she had to stay and answer the phone, so she simply pointed to the stairs and said, "The nursery's on the fourth floor, east wing."

"There had better be an elevator," Addy huffed.

"There is, just past the stairs."

Addy stormed off, mumbling and criticizing everything she passed. The elevator took too long to come. The inside of it smelled funny. The person at the reception desk for the nursery was curt. The nursery was cold. The floor was dirty. The staff was unfriendly.

By the time she finally laid eyes on the child she was completely out of sorts.

"That's him?" she almost laughed. "He's so small."

Leven squinted at her.

"He's just about the right size," the nurse on duty said.

"For what?" Addy sniffed.

"He'll be old before you know it," the nurse tried. "Babies grow so—"

"Thank you," Addy snipped. "I'm perfectly aware that babies grow. Do I need to sign something?"

The nurse was dumbfounded. Sure, all of the years she had worked there had made her a bit callused and bored. Babies were born every day, and it had long since ceased to be a miracle to her. She had seen everything. She once saw a baby born with two heads. She had even seen newborns come out laughing. She had also seen a dozen or so children be born and pronounced dead only to come alive again minutes later. She had seen a lot, but this loud,

vicious lady was uglier and meaner than anything she could remember.

"I'll get the doctor," the nurse said, biting her lip. She stepped away, leaving Addy alone with her new responsibility.

Addy eyed Leven coldly. She sniffed again and looked away. When she looked back he was still there. She lifted up one of his legs and looked at it. She touched Leven's head. She scowled. She put her hand on the baby's arm and gingerly lifted it as if it might be diseased.

She dropped the tiny arm, screaming.

A huge, hairy, grey ball scurried out from under Leven, circled over his stomach, and rolled back under him.

Addy screamed hysterically as she pushed back and away, knocking over an empty cart and sending diapers and baby shampoo everywhere. The shampoo bottles exploded all over the floor, causing Addy to lose her footing and fall hard onto her rear. Her rump seemed to pop as a loud rush of air escaped her screaming, lipless mouth. A small team of nurses and a couple of doctors rushed through the door wondering what could possibly be going on to generate so much noise.

Addy just sat there, screaming and pointing. The nurse, who had had the pleasure of talking with her just moments before, filled a cup with water and happily threw it in Addy's face.

Sputtering, Addy said, "A rat. There's a giant rat on that child."

The medical staff all looked at the baby. No rat. Leven was simply lying there with his eyes wide open and a serious look on his face.

"That's impossible," one of the doctors said. "There are no rats here. Besides, it wouldn't be able to climb into the cart."

"Maybe it fell from the ceiling," Addy offered.

Everyone looked at the ceiling. It looked okay, no holes or possible way for a rat to fall from it.

Two nurses tried to help Addy to her feet, but thanks to the soapy floor, they lost their footing and also went down. Their flailing limbs knocked the legs out from under one of the doctors, and he fell, taking two more nurses with him. Everyone scrambled across the slippery floor, reaching for something to pull themselves to their feet with. It took a number of tries, but eventually everyone was standing again.

Once up they all carefully worked their way over to the baby. One of the nurses picked him up and inspected him.

"I don't see a rat," she said.

"It's there," Addy cried. "I saw it with my own two eyes. He was huge."

One of the doctors loosened the diaper and made sure the supposed rat had not hidden in there.

"No rat," he declared. "I've worked here for twenty years, and I have never seen a rat."

"Well, I've been here for a little over twenty minutes and already I've seen one," Addy said meanly. "Give me the child so I can take him somewhere safe."

"There are a few papers we need you to fill out," the doctor informed her. "And we have some questions and information for you."

"Fine, just hurry. I have a long drive back."

Everyone left the room except for one nurse who was on her hands and knees trying to clean up the soapy mess while the baby slept. Neither she nor Leven noticed Clover as he once again slipped up over him and scurried back underneath. Smiling.

CHAPTER TWO

A Cold Wind Blows In

THE ARRIVAL OF WINTER

Amelia sat silently across the hall from the delivery room. She looked down at the baby in her arms, held her finger to the infant's thin lips, and softly quieted her. Amelia's meshing cloak hid them both from view and helped them blend nicely into the wall of vending machines on the fourth floor of the hospital. To anyone passing by, Amelia's head would have looked like a bag of chips, her body an assortment of candy bars and sodas. Amelia smiled at the baby in her arms.

"You're going to do great," Amelia whispered. "Remember, this is for Foo."

The child's green eyes widened at the mention of Foo as Amelia shifted and stood just a bit so as to have a better look into the

delivery room. It appeared for a moment as though the vending machine were stretching. Amelia could clearly see everything in the birthing room.

Unfortunately, things didn't look wonderful. As far as births go it looked rather sad. No father around—he had left months ago—and the mother of the impending child was not terribly happy about what she had gotten herself into. Amelia could see her embittered face.

Janet Frore was a square woman with an oval mouth and thick, wild eyebrows. Thanks to the research she had recently completed, Amelia knew the whole history of Janet's pathetic life. She knew Janet was a bitter person who saw nothing good in the world around her. It had been documented that Janet had smiled only twice in her life and certainly today's events would not elicit a third. Normally a stern and quiet person, Janet was at present ranting and screaming as a small army of masked doctors and nurses scurried around, performing their duties and trying to act calm.

"Push," Amelia heard the doctor order. "Push!"

Two pushes later, Janet's own screaming was drowned out by the wailing of a brand new voice ushered into this very old world.

The new child screeched as if it had been sent to earth to do just that. It put her mother's hollering to shame. Lights rattled and windows shuddered in the face of the unworldly wailing.

The new mother pinched up her cheeks and squinted as sweat cascaded down her face. The doctor tried to hand her baby to her, but Janet was plugging her own ears. Nurses scurried about acting busy, none of them wanting to be handed the wailing infant.

Amelia watched the doctor through the open door. He was begging the mother to hold her own child.

"I'm not holding her," Janet said, pushing back and waving the child away. "I don't want to hold her."

"Mrs. Frore," the doctor pleaded, "this is your daughter."

Janet looked at the small helpless child, her eyebrows wild. She twitched and rubbed her own forehead. "Maybe so, but I'm in no frame of mind to hold her. Take her away," she ordered.

Amelia tsked, she and the blond baby hidden beneath her cloak still blending in with the vending machines. Amelia could see the frustrated doctor wipe his brow. She figured he was probably wondering why someone had not helped him think through the decision to become an obstetrician.

Dr. Scott handed the child to a fat, happy-looking nurse named Pipa, who was the only nongrimacing person in the room. Nurse Pipa gently placed the child on a rolling table with high plastic sides. She clucked her tongue in disgust loudly enough to be heard and walked out of the room and down the hallway right past Amelia and the infant she was holding.

Amelia followed Pipa, the meshing cloak she was under making it look as though the wall was rolling in a wave behind the fat nurse. She slipped into the nursery after Pipa and moved into a far corner to wait.

Pipa bathed the newborn, gave her a couple of shots, and left the infant lying naked under the heat lamp. When she waddled out of the room, Amelia glided over to the newborn. She pulled back the meshing cloak to reveal her own face and the blond child she was holding in her arms. The cloak made the back half of her look like medical cabinets and a sink, while her exposed face had a lumpy nose. She wore thick glasses that made her piercing eyes look huge. She glanced over her thin shoulders and around the room. She was

not a pretty woman, but her countenance was bright, and she had a strong, determined look about her, like a mother protecting her child from bullies. Amelia leaned forward, put the blond child under the heat lamp, and picked up the baby Janet Frore had just given birth to.

"Come, child," she whispered to the Frore baby. "You'll be much better off where I'm taking you."

Amelia turned from the baby she held and looked down at the one she had placed. "Good luck, and remember," she whispered ominously, "don't touch him."

She glanced at the blond child one last time, pulled the cloak back over her face, and stepped out of the nursery—unseen, with the once-screaming newborn resting calmly in her arms.

Nurse Pipa returned and stared curiously at the little blond baby who was now lying there.

"I don't remember wrapping you up like that," she muttered. "I've got to stop working two shifts in a row," she said, shaking her head. She moved to the adjoining room to attend to her other duties.

The child lay there in the still room. She was a cute baby, with thick, white-blond hair, a pink face, and brilliant evergreen-colored eyes. She smiled and laughed softly as the clock on the wall ticked. She rocked her body, flexed, and sat straight up on her hind end. She wriggled out of the tightly wrapped baby blanket and touched the sides of her cradle. She looked about the room and smiled. Sure, she wouldn't exactly be loved in the home where she'd be living, and yes, what she needed to accomplish in her life would take many long years. But none of that mattered at the moment. She was here, and the journey for her had begun. She took in the room. She couldn't believe how differently things looked here. The realm she had just left seemed like a dream. The fighting and the desperation she had escaped in Foo felt more like a story she had heard than a situation she had lived through. The thought of Sabine's eyes and his hatred for her burned in her mind, but even now she could feel the memories dissolving and fading away. She knew her knowledge of where she had just come from would soon be gone. Somehow that didn't frighten her. What she was here to accomplish made any risk worth taking. She lay back down and gazed up at the fluorescent lights on the ceiling.

Nurse Pipa stepped into the nursery with a skinny nurse named Elizabeth. They stood together and let their eyes rest on the unwrapped child. The baby looked back at them, her green eyes seeming to focus on their faces.

"How'd you unwrap yourself?" Pipa questioned. "That's odd." She picked the child up, rewrapped her, and laid her back down.

"Oh, look at the smile on her," Elizabeth said with wonder. "That's sort of unsettling—she looks all grown up."

"All grown up," Pipa gently scolded, "don't be silly. She's got a little gas, that's all." Pipa rubbed the baby's belly and told her she was beautiful, gas and all.

"Look at those eyes," Elizabeth said. "I've never seen such a color. And they look so . . . knowing."

Pipa touched the baby's cheek and noted, "She feels a bit cold." The fat nurse turned up the heat lamp above the baby.

The baby frowned. In a few hours she would no longer know anything about her former self, and she was hot. She frowned again, the reality of who she really was beginning to slip farther away.

"Pity she's stuck with such an awful mother," Pipa whispered to

Elizabeth as they continued to look at her. "I have never seen such a bitter person."

"The woman just had a baby," Elizabeth defended. "Maybe she'll mellow a bit."

"Let's hope so." Pipa touched the baby's nose and smiled. "Will you be okay?" she asked in a soft voice.

"I'll be fine," the newborn answered.

Both nurses' jaws fell. Elizabeth dropped the towels and rolls of bandages she was holding.

"Did you hear that?" Pipa whispered in awe.

"I think I did," Elizabeth squeaked. "Ask her again."

Pipa touched the baby's nose again and with more interest than last time asked, "Will you be okay?"

The baby smiled, closed her green eyes, and slept.

CHAPTER THREE

Where Monsters Live

The Rolling Greens Deluxe Mobile Home Park was situated on fifty-five acres of Burnt Culvert's finest burnt soil. The town, once named Tin Culvert, had rebuilt itself following a devastating fire that had burned most of it down a few years earlier. No one really wanted to build over the actual charred parts, but Mr. Hornbackle, an Irishman with a bad knee and a soft heart, bought fifty-five acres of blackened land. He put in a couple of wells, laid out a few roads, and called it Rolling Greens Deluxe Mobile Home Park. Now it housed over one hundred and twenty mobile homes. Thirty-two of them were double-wides, and all the rest were singles, except for two RVs that had been allotted the tiniest of space to reside near the north end of the park, by the east leech field.

As soon as the park opened people began to move in and either upgrade or downgrade the area. Some residents planted trees. Some

put in lawns. A few built sheds or outbuildings. Some paved tiny slabs of concrete so as to have somewhere to put a picnic table and a barbecue. Others added awnings and outdoor carpeting.

Some, of course, did nothing.

Despite what residents did and didn't do, almost the entire park had sold out. Folks in the area were happy to live somewhere cheap. They were willing to put up with the surrounding scorched earth and the constant smell of smoke in the air. They didn't even mind that after a rainstorm their streets would run with what looked like tar. If a person could make his mortgage payment and still have money for food and entertainment, that was all that seemed to matter. To heck with the condition of the soil your home rested on if you could still afford to go to the movies every once in a while.

Strangely though, one lot in the Rolling Greens Deluxe Mobile Home Park had never sold. Near the far back at the edge where the park skirted up against a shallow creek bed there sat empty a single plot of land, and as hard as Mr. Hornbackle had tried to sell it, nobody wanted to buy it. That was somewhat surprising, seeing how it was situated in a relatively quiet area and had the only mature tree in the park growing on it.

People were interested, but something always came up to squelch the sale. For instance, while walking around the lot, potential buyers would stumble into deep sinkholes that peppered the ground. Or they would be put off by an odd smell that wasn't evident just one space over. Unusual weeds also grew on the land—weeds with sharp ends that seemed to have angry or defensive spirits. There had been a number of people poked or stabbed by the wild growth that spot of soil produced.

A ladies' auxiliary group that focused on community beautification

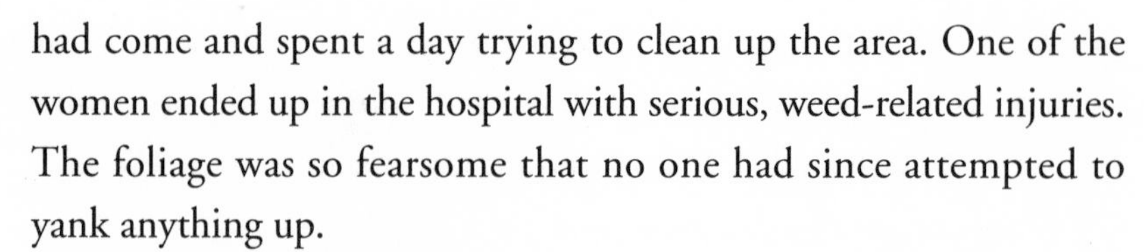

had come and spent a day trying to clean up the area. One of the women ended up in the hospital with serious, weed-related injuries. The foliage was so fearsome that no one had since attempted to yank anything up.

It was simply bad land.

Mr. Hornbackle had lowered the price of the lot until it was almost free, but land that comes with a foul smell, hundreds of sink holes, and weeds with an attitude is not all that desirable, even at a cut-rate price. So the lot had remained unoccupied, watched over by the lone tree, which grew quite well despite the seemingly poor earth in which it was planted. The tree produced huge leaves in the summer, and in the winter its thick gray bark was striking. It had hundreds of gnarled limbs that lifted and twisted in the most unusual manner and directions. It had come a long way from the seed it once was.

A true thing about seeds is that they don't always stay seeds. In addition, most seeds grow up to be something. Some become plants or trees that then go about producing more seeds. Some seeds get popped and eaten and . . . well, you probably have a pretty good idea of what happens to things after they get eaten.

Some seeds are dried, some are pressed for oil, and some simply end up in bean bags or as the rattle in a baby's toy. It's probably fair to say that the life and times of a seed isn't necessarily the most exciting thing in the world, but what the seed lacks in excitement, it makes up for in miracles.

It's a miracle that a tiny seed can change from a dot in your palm into a towering tree whose wood can be made into the home you live in or the paper books are printed on.

But the seed that Antsel had slipped from his robe and deposited

in the rich soil all those years before was not an ordinary seed. It was a transplant from the realm of Foo, a fantrum seed that contained the exiled soul of a great lithen named Geth.

The plot of ground in which Geth was planted might very well have remained unsold forever if it had not been for Addy and Terry Graph. They drifted into town like an unpleasant odor. She was loud and self-righteous, with a head full of perpetually bad hair. He was loud and usually soused. When they inquired about buying a lot at the Rolling Greens Deluxe Mobile Home Park, they were told by Mr. Hornbackle that the place was full up.

"Full up?" Terry snapped, obviously used to people finding or making excuses to keep him out of their neighborhood.

"No vacancies," Mr. Hornbackle insisted. "Except . . ."

"Except?" Terry questioned, suspiciously.

"There is one open lot, but I'm not sure it would suit you and your lovely family." Mr. Hornbackle looked at Addy Graph as she held an almost two-year-old Leven on her lap.

"That's not my family," Terry insisted. "I'm married to the woman, but the kid belongs to my wife's half sister who died. He doesn't even have our last name."

"I'm sorry to hear that," Mr. Hornbackle said sincerely.

"We've been tried heavier than most folks," Terry offered. "Now where's this lot?"

"It's unlivable," Mr. Hornbackle insisted.

"We'll see about that," Terry snorted, his lumpy nose and forehead growing red.

Mr. Hornbackle instructed the Graphs and their young burden to get into the cab of his pickup truck. He then drove them to the one open spot he had never been able to sell.

"It's not perfect," Mr. Hornbackle primed them as he drove. "The ground's not very good, and it's a bit overgrown with weeds."

"Oh, great," Terry whined, turning his bloodshot eyes to Addy. "I'm not spending my days pulling weeds someone else let grow."

"There's also a tree," Mr. Hornbackle pointed out.

"A tree," Addy sniffed sarcastically. "Did you hear that, Terry, a tree?" She rolled her puffy eyes.

Terry laughed, making an annoying gurgle in his throat as he did so. "Are there any other mobile home parks around here?" he asked. "My wife's employment is just up the street."

"I'm afraid not," Mr. Hornbackle said sadly, wishing he had never met these two. "The town is slowly rebuilding from a huge fire that came through here a few years ago. There are a couple of mobile home parks about fifty miles west."

"I'm not driving fifty miles to work each day," Addy declared. "You'll pull weeds before I submit myself to that."

"I'm not pulling any weeds," Terry whined. "Where's this lot?"

"Right around this bend," Mr. Hornbackle answered. "I'm sure you'll find it—"

Mr. Hornbackle's jaw dropped as he turned the corner and saw the lot. There at the end of the road sat 1712 Andorra Court, a spectacularly beautiful piece of land. The tree was lush and full. Around its base, the ground was covered with an array of dainty white and purple flowers. Chirping birds flitted in and about the leafy tree, which was illuminated beautifully by a shaft of brilliant sunlight.

"That's it?" Addy asked in amazement. "That's the unlivable lot?"

Mr. Hornbackle was too busy gawking in disbelief to respond.

"Just as I thought," Terry bit, wiping his lumpy nose on his

sleeve. "Holding out on us, huh? Well, it's not going to work. We'll take it."

"I don't—" Mr. Hornbackle tried to say.

"I said, we'll take it." Terry reached into his wallet and fished out enough for a down payment. "We'll be back next week with our home."

Mr. Hornbackle took the money, still gaping at the serene and beautiful lot that lay in front of him. Just yesterday the place had been nothing but weeds and darkness. Today it was a section of land he could have easily charged double or triple price for.

Mr. Hornbackle turned the pickup around and slowly drove back to the office. Once there he stayed in the truck as Terry, Addy, and the small child got out.

"Don't even think of leasing that out to anyone else," Terry warned. "We'll have you in court. Unlivable my eye." He turned and spat on the ground.

Mr. Hornbackle just stared, his mouth still hanging open.

CHAPTER FOUR

GETH

Fate was working splendidly. Geth stood tall, shading with his branches the newly parked trailer house of Leven. He stretched his trunk, creaking as he took on inches. Geth peeked with the tips of his limbs through the windows of the single-wide, looking for Leven. Terry and Addy had finally settled in, but there would now be some wait for the child to grow into his role.

Geth twisted the tips of his branches inward to look at himself. He was a long way from what he had been in Foo. Geth, you see, was a member of the First Order of Wonder. He was also a lithen, a rare species that travels and lives by fate. Lithens know little of fear or confusion because they let fate move them. A true lithen would think nothing of walking off a four-hundred-foot cliff because he would know that if it were his time, he would hit the ground and die. But if it were not meant to be, he would simply be picked up by the wind or rescued by a giant eagle. Lithens were fearless and honest to a fault. They were also the original inhabitants of Foo, given a sacred charge to guard the realm that gives humans the privilege of dreaming.

Geth had grown well where he was planted. At first a tiny shoot, he had emerged through the soil and into the blue sky knowing that there was plenty of time to grow as he waited to accomplish what needed to be done. But by the time he had grown two stories tall, Geth had discovered the power of his limbs. It had happened quite by accident. A family of birds had made themselves happy in his top branches, and he had simply *thought* about shooing them away. Well, no sooner had he thought it than his branches began whipping around, waving the birds off.

He also had the remarkable ability to see from every tip of his branches. He could see in front, in back, and on all sides continually. There was not a creature or person who could approach without him knowing.

By simply willing it, Geth could also extend his roots hundreds of feet underground, boring effortlessly into the earth to fill it with holes and pock marks. He could collect rainwater in these underground channels and use that water to produce wicked sprouts that sprang out of the earth like angry weeds. Geth knew all of these tools would be necessary for what was coming.

Antsel had known there was no way for Geth to return to Foo without help. He had been well aware that in order for hope to continue, Geth would need a bit of assistance on his return. Antsel also understood that there was only one person who could both bring Geth back and thwart Sabine's evil plan.

It was that person Geth was now watching over—Leven

Thumps. It was only a matter of time before Leven would be old enough to complete the task at hand.

Geth stood tall in the Oklahoma soil, growing stronger each moment, and behaving like the lithen he was. He had no worries, no concerns, and no panic. Fate had put him where he was, and if he did his part, fate would get him back home.

Geth uncurled the tips of his branches and gazed into eternity. The waiting had begun.

CHAPTER FIVE

FOURTEEN YEARS OLD

Terry and Addy Graph couldn't stand to hear Leven talk or fuss, so from the time he was a little child, they insisted he sleep in an old twin bed on the screened-in back porch of their trailer house.

Leven didn't mind. He liked sleeping outside by himself. He would listen to Terry snore or the neighbors argue and count stars and trace the long swaying branches of the huge tree in his yard.

His life was not charmed. He had no friends, no cousins, no grandparents, not even a single kindly neighbor who looked out for him or waved as he walked by. Terry wouldn't let him get a pet, and Addy insisted he stay away from other kids for fear that Leven would form some unhealthy attachment to some hoodlum who would only grow up and steal her good jewelry when he came by to visit Leven. So, for the bulk of his childhood, Leven had been alone.

All that changed one night in the middle of summer and during a low moaning wind storm. Leven got a surprise. He was fourteen now and so tall that his feet hung off the end of his small bed by a good six inches. His long dark hair was the color of rich mud and on the right side of his head there was a streak of brilliant white hair. According to Addy something had happened to him when he was four that had scared the pigment out of him. Addy claimed the incident had occurred when she wasn't around and that she had no idea what had transpired. "What business is it of mine?" she would always say. Leven couldn't remember any incident. He had tried to color the streak, but no matter what he did it remained bright white.

Beyond that, he had clear brown eyes, a straight nose, ears that protruded slightly more than most people's, and a large mouth that made him look a bit like a boy who had not completely grown into himself yet, which is what he was.

Normally, Leven wasn't scared of sleeping alone on the porch, but tonight he was a little spooked by the strange wind and the low noise it was emitting. As he lay in his bed he stared out through the screened porch. Leven was looking toward the home next door when he saw a thick patch of black swoosh behind the neighbor's place. It glided and seemed to be whispering something.

Leven sat up rail straight, his heart pounding, the back of his neck burning.

He squinted his brown eyes and tried to make out whatever it had been. His eyesight was awful, and his aunt refused to buy him glasses on the grounds that she thought it would make her look silly to be walking around with a bespectacled boy.

Another swath of black slid across the ground and brushed over the screen, whispering. The shadow turned, and tiny pinpoints of white stared at Leven from a dark, rat-like face as it glided by.

Leven scooted as far as he could away from the screen and back in his bed, willing whatever it was to go away. The black shape circled back, pressing up against the screen, its white eyes glowing.

"Find him," it whispered. "Him."

The shadow pushed against the screen and began to work itself in. Like black spaghetti it oozed through the mesh. That was enough. Leven leaped out of bed and began pounding on the door to the trailer house.

"Let me in!" he insisted. "Aunt Addy! Terry!"

The black shadow moaned and oozed some more.

"Aunt Addy!" Leven yelled. "Aunt Addy!"

Leven could hear movement and grumbling inside.

"What is it?" she hollered through the door.

"There's something out here!"

Terry and Addy kept the door locked at night so as to keep out burglars and prevent Leven from waking them up by using the bathroom or coming in too early. Those locks now turned as she unlocked the door to open up.

"This better be good," Addy threatened through the door. "I was applying my mask."

Over his shoulder, Leven could see the blackness seeping into the porch, hanging there like a stringy rag. It drooped, dripped, and then began to quickly retract.

The door opened. Leven turned to look at his aunt, his face white and his eyes frantic. He glanced back at the screen. The black swath was gone, but now Leven had his aunt to contend with. He half wished the blackness was back.

"Something was coming through the screen," Leven pleaded. "It was—"

"Where is it now?" she barked. Her face was green, thanks to a nighttime mud mask she was wearing, and her hair was sticking up all over the place, making her head look like a honeydew melon sprouting kinky hay.

"It's gone," Leven said sheepishly, his eyes foggy.

"I have a job," Addy hissed. "Do you think I can go to work tired and still keep my job? Do you?"

"No," Leven said. "I'm sorry; maybe I should sleep inside tonight."

Addy laughed. "I should say not. You're fourteen. Besides, this night air will do your imagination some good." Small flecks of dried green mud showered from her face as she spoke.

"Really," Leven begged. "It was coming in."

"Monsters don't come in through doors," Addy said impatiently. "They live under beds like that one," Addy added, pointing to the small, used bed that Leven slept on. "But don't worry, if there was one under yours it would have eaten you already," she said coldly.

"Aunt—"

"How many times have I told you, don't call me *aunt.* I am your mother's half sister." She slammed the door and locked it.

The wind moaned.

Leven looked at his bed. He looked at the screen door and quickly bounded across the porch and jumped back onto his mattress. He pulled the blankets up over himself and tried to think of something safe and comfortable. His short blanket was a clear symbol that his life had not been full of too many safe and comfortable things, so it took great imagination to conjure up something pleasant. He thought about his parents, whom he had never known. He thought about his mother, who had died giving him birth. He thought about his futile life and wished he could just fly away from it. Not on a plane or in a helicopter, but just by himself. He wanted to stand in the open prairie and lift off, up to the moon to soar between clouds and above houses. He had almost forgotten about the blackness that had visited him earlier when he heard a scratching from beneath his bed.

He stopped breathing so as to better panic.

Skritch, skritch.

Leven's heart stopped. Something was under the bed. He could feel the light vibration as it scraped away.

"Just go to sleep," he told himself. "Just go to sleep." He closed his eyes as tightly as he could. The back of his eyelids burned and white dots danced in the blackness.

Skritch, skritch.

It was still there. Leven thought about jumping off of his bed, but there was nowhere for him to go. The door to the inside of his home was locked, and the screen door leading outside had just been occupied by oozing black. He thought about trying to fall asleep, but he couldn't bear the thought of that happening now for fear that whatever was scratching would feast upon him as he slept.

Skritch, skritch.

"Who's there?" Leven whispered. The noise stopped. With the rest of his body pressed tightly against the wall, Leven moved his head to the edge of the bed and peered over. He could see nothing but floor. He pulled his head back onto his pillow and breathed deeply. Then he inched back to the edge and leaned over a bit farther so he could see under the bed. Nothing. He pushed his head down even more, the ends of his shaggy brown hair hanging and touching the cold floor. He gazed under the bed.

He was not alone.

Two big glowing blue eyes stared back at him. Leven pulled back so quickly he pushed the bed away from the wall and fell into the space onto the floor. Scuttling like a crab he backed into the corner of the porch, searching for anything he might use to protect himself. He grabbed a couple of rocks out of the bucket Addy kept by the back door for throwing at noisy dogs or cats. He crouched against the wall, facing his bed, ready to throw them at whatever was there.

The blue eyes under the bed blinked.

Whatever it was, it was clinging to the bottom of the mattress, its head hanging beneath it with its eyes staring out. It looked no larger than a small cat, but its shape was inconsistent with any animal Leven had ever seen. He thought about hollering, but he knew Addy would never come out now that he had already cried wolf once. The creature blinked and smiled.

"Hello, Lev," it said kindly.

"Excuse me?" Leven said in disbelief, amazed that whatever it was, was now talking to him.

"Sorry, for the scare and all." The creature's nose twitched. "Antsel told me to not do that."

"Antsel?" Leven asked.

"He was my burn before you."

"Your *burn*?"

"My assignment. We sycophants burn only for those we are assigned. It has always been our lot. I desired nothing but to serve him at that time."

Am I dreaming? Leven questioned himself, wondering if he had perhaps fallen asleep.

"Not likely," the little creature laughed. "Dreams are pretty and usually involve horses or rainbows or castles, or big—"

"I know about dreams," Leven interrupted. "Then who are you?"

"I am Clover. Clover Ernest." His blue eyes blinked. He let go of the bottom of the bed and twisted to land on two of the littlest feet Leven had ever seen. He strode out from under the bed with confidence. He stood like a human but with a body more like a cat. He had no tail and was about twelve inches tall and covered in gray hair everywhere except for his face and his knees and elbows. He had leaf-like ears, a wide, crooked smile, and wet, blinking blue eyes. His nose was straight but pointed to his right just a bit. He wore what looked to be a little silvery dress with a hood on the back. His fingers were as thin as twigs and as knotty as any pine a person might encounter. He was like no monkey, bear, raccoon, cat, or any other animal Leven had ever seen. The long hair directly above his eyes stood and wiggled whenever he spoke.

"What are you?" Leven asked.

"That all depends upon you," Clover smiled. "What do you want me to be?"

Leven looked closely at Clover; there was an aura about him that wasn't threatening and Leven wasn't afraid. He felt comfortable and relaxed just a bit. "How about being honest?" Leven said.

Clover sighed, his eyelids contracting. He motioned to a small stepstool Terry used to change light bulbs. "Do you mind?" he asked, wanting permission to sit.

Leven nodded.

"I can't believe they keep you out here," Clover said, hopping up onto the stool.

"It's not too bad," Leven shrugged.

"It's better than where you lived when you were first born. I'll give you that. That place was awful," Clover complained.

"You know where I used to live?" Leven said in amazement.

"Of course," Clover seemed to brag. "I was there, too."

"Under my bed?"

"Under your bed, in your dresser, your car, your yard, your bathroom—you name it, and I was there." Clover shook his head and smiled as if reliving a pleasant memory.

Leven stared at the creature in amazement. "Why?" he finally asked.

"I'm guessing you're a nit. Although I haven't seen your gift surface yet."

"A nit?"

"They're fairly common in . . . well, that's not important. What matters is that Antsel told me to stick by you."

"And you do whatever this Antsel says?"

"Of course; I'm a sycophant. That's what we do," he said nonchalantly. "But now, I'm *your* burn."

"I don't understand," Leven said. "I don't know any Antsel." He stood and looked at the locked door leading inside. He gazed at his bed. "I must still be asleep," he reasoned.

"Do you want me to agree with you about that?" Clover asked nicely.

"Only if it's true."

"You're not asleep. Nope, in fact, this is probably the beginning of a long sleepless night. It's actually the beginning of much more than that. But, for now, all that's important is that I'm Clover, or Cloe, or whatever. I answer to any of those. Of course, I would be

fine with you labeling me something else entirely." Clover paused to see if Leven was going to say something.

Leven didn't.

"I was assigned to Antsel hundreds of years ago," Clover went on. "He wasn't much older than you are now. A little shorter, though."

"Hundreds of years ago," Leven said skeptically. "How old are you?"

"I can't remember," he waved. "We sycophants live forever. There's only one way for us to die."

"How's that?" Leven asked.

"It wouldn't be very prudent of us to go telling folks that, now would it?" Clover grinned, and his blue eyes slanted as the corners of his mouth pushed up on them.

"I suppose not," Leven smiled, beginning to like the small creature. "So why are you here?"

Clover shook a bit and said, "I've been with you since birth. There have been few moments of your life when I have not been around. I slept in late a couple of years ago and you made it to school without me, but aside from that . . . "

"How is that possible?" Leven asked, more in wonder than in doubt. "How could you have been there for any of that? I've never seen you."

Clover smiled and looked around. "You want me to show you?"

"Sure," Leven answered, his brown eyes blinking.

Clover got up off his stool and brushed his forearms. He walked right up to Leven and asked him to hold out his hand. "Can you feel this?" he asked, touching Leven's right thumb.

Leven nodded.

Clover stepped back. His robe shimmering slightly in the moonlight, he looked like a doll designed for trolls to play with. Then he pulled his hood up over his head and touched Leven's hand again. Leven felt nothing. Not only that, he could no longer see Clover. Leven looked around the porch and glanced under the bed and into the corners.

"Clover?" he whispered, surprised to find himself hoping it had not all been just a dream. "Clover?"

Suddenly there he was again, sitting in Leven's lap. Leven jumped just a bit.

"How'd you do that?"

"I'm a sycophant," Clover said again. "It's what we do. Technically, I am a part of you, and I want nothing but to make you happy."

"I don't believe it," Leven said sadly. "Why would anyone . . . or anything . . . want to make *me* happy?"

"Ah, Antsel said you would be slow to believe," Clover smiled. "Leven Thumps, you are incredibly more than you believe yourself to be. I wouldn't be here otherwise."

"I've got to be dreaming," Leven said honestly. It was harder for him to believe that he was of value than it was to believe that there was a furry creature named Clover Ernest.

"You're not dreaming," Clover insisted, brushing his own ankles with his hands. "I've been here and I will be here for the duration."

"The duration of what?"

"Of our time," Clover said sharply.

"Why have I never seen you before?"

"Because you weren't supposed to see me."

"Why now?" Leven asked, flexing his shoulders as he leaned closer to Clover.

"Because time is running out and they are getting near."

"Who's getting near?" Leven said, looking around.

"I wasn't the first to show myself tonight, was I?" Clover asked, cocking his head to one side.

"You mean the blackness?"

"That blackness was one of Sabine's shadows. They have been looking for you for many years."

"Why?" Leven asked, as if he had just been told a joke. "Why would they be looking for me?"

"I can't tell you everything," Clover insisted.

"But I thought you had to tell me everything."

"I desire nothing but," he bowed.

"So tell me," Leven asked kindly.

"I was bound to Antsel first," Clover replied. "His wishes are still of importance to me."

"So what will happen if *they*, whoever they are, find me?"

"Nothing good," Clover whispered. "That's why we have to get going soon."

"Going where?"

"That's for Geth to explain." Clover jumped up onto the bed and made himself comfortable on Leven's pillow.

"Geth?"

"Yep," Clover said. "Pretty much the fate of the entire world is depending on it though." Clover yawned, and his small face scrunched up as he did so. He blinked and closed his eyes. "No pressure, though."

Leven simply sat there staring at him, with his wide mouth

hanging open. A few moments ago he was an unwanted child sleeping on the porch of his cold-hearted aunt's . . . his mother's half sister's . . . house. Now, he was a confused boy, talking with a stuffed animal that seemed to think Leven held the future of the world in his hands.

"You're kidding about all this, right?"

Clover opened his blue eyes.

"Do you want me to be?"

"I'm not sure," Leven answered honestly.

"Well, then neither am I."

Leven got up onto the bed next to Clover. His mind was racing a million thoughts per second. He couldn't focus his brain on any one thing. He wanted to fall asleep so that he could wake up and realize that all this was just a dream. On the other hand, he was afraid to close his eyes for fear of discovering that he wasn't what Clover was saying he was.

"Good night," Clover said softly.

"So I should call you Clover?" Leven asked in reply.

"Whatever you wish."

"Good night, Clover."

The leaves on the giant tree in Leven's yard rustled softly in the night breeze. Leven lay next to the furry, cat-like thing named Clover, trying to mentally digest everything he had just seen and heard. His head kept filling with self-doubts and odd pictures. For some reason his mind began to play images of a girl. She wasn't familiar to him, but no matter how he tried he could not get her face out of his head.

Clover complained about Leven's fidgeting.

"Sorry," Leven said. "By any chance is the person we're waiting for a girl?"

Clover laughed. "Geth, a girl?"

"Well?" Leven asked.

"No."

"I keep seeing a girl in my head," Leven said.

"Is she pretty?" Clover asked sweetly.

"No . . . I don't know. She's just there."

"Pay attention to her face," Clover yawned. "She might be important."

Leven didn't sleep a wink.

CHAPTER SIX

HAIRY SITUATION

Winter Frore had a hard life. Her mother, Janet, was not a good person. If you had a mom who continually taunted you, tripped you, talked poorly about you behind your back and negatively in front of you, drew mean pictures of you, the kind of pictures where your head looked small and your rear looked big, told lies about you, pointed at you in public places and ridiculed you, stole your things and broke your favorite possession by stomping violently on it, well, you'd call it a hard life, too. And that's the kind of life Winter had been dealt.

Winter had long, wild, blond hair and wide-set, green eyes. She had a small nose and rounded cheeks that made her look as though she were always about to blow out a candle or begin whistling. She had no friends and spent most of her time at the library, in the back corner, reading books about people with families and friends, or at

the very least, pets. She had felt alone for as long as she could remember.

The only positive in her life was a kindly family who lived in a yellow house with missing shutters and a red front door two blocks down from her and her mother. The house was home to Tim and Wendy Tuttle—a fun-loving, extremely brainy couple that loved having Winter around. Wendy Tuttle was a kind woman with big hips and long black hair that she always wore in a braid tied off with a yellow ribbon. Her husband, Tim, was a garbage man with a weak chin and big ears. His job, although not one esteemed by society, seemed desirable to Winter because he always came home with interesting finds—lamps that sort of worked, bikes with no seats or missing spokes, and furniture that didn't look half bad once it was repaired and painted. The Tuttles had two young boys named Darcy and Rochester. Darcy was eight and Rochester was six. Winter loved the Tuttles and their boys. They were an island in the sea of disdain and sadness in which she lived.

Winter's mother, Janet, did not like the positive influence the Tuttles had over her child.

"The world is not a happy place," her mother would always insist. "The Tuttles are giving you false hopes."

Janet forbade Winter from visiting them, but it was an order that Winter refused to obey. Whenever possible, Winter would sneak away from home to be with a family that loved her and was so completely different from her own.

Winter's mother, Janet, knew nothing about "love," unless you were talking about the love of self. She placed mirrors everywhere around the house, so she could catch frequent glimpses of herself. Janet would stare into the mirrors for hours, fascinated for some

perverse reason with her pinched, sour reflection and her bushy eyebrows and homely oval mouth, which she could never completely close.

Janet didn't talk unless she had something mean to say, and she thought only of the negative even if life was treating her fairly. The worry and bitterness she carried around had turned her into a sour, disgruntled person. She was a wrinkled prune of a woman with a heart no bigger than a raisin.

She had never caught on to the fact that the child she was "raising" was not the actual child she had given birth to. In all honesty, she had never looked at Winter long enough to realize how completely different from each other they were. The only good thing Janet saw in Winter was that the girl provided her with a huge, never-ending something to complain about.

The only time they ever spent with each other was at dinner. Janet insisted the two of them eat together, sitting at a table in front of the window so that any neighbors driving by could spot them being a family. Of course, when Winter and her mother did sit down to eat, Janet would do nothing but mumble and slobber over her heaping plates of food. As Janet would stuff her face, Winter would sit there with nothing but her usual dinner: a half dozen peas, which Janet had usually picked from her meal, a single crust of bread, and a spoonful of sugar-free strawberry jam—sugar-free because Janet had read once how bad sugar was for children.

Winter hated peas. She stared at them with her green eyes, wishing they were something else. They never were. She was equally unimpressed by the crust of bread, and she thought the jam always tasted funny. So she would usually roll her peas into the jam and sop

them up with the stale crust, all the while pretending it was something other than what it actually was.

Today, however, Winter was more disappointed than usual.

It was her thirteenth birthday, and she had been hoping that tonight she might get a full piece of bread or maybe a bit of broccoli. It seems strange that a teenager would want broccoli, but when you're hungry and sick of peas, odd things sound surprisingly good.

Winter considered her half dozen peas and sighed. She thought about the thirteen years she had been alive and hoped the next thirteen might be different. It had taken the doctors a lot of coaxing to get Janet to even take Winter home from the hospital. Janet had not wanted her, and she had been frightened to death of the responsibility. She felt as though Winter would ruin the lazy lifestyle she had done so little to achieve. So Janet had named her Judy—after the patron saint of desperate cases—in hopes that the child might grow up to serve her and make something good from what she thought was a *very* desperate case.

No sooner had Janet brought Winter home than odd things began to happen. For one thing, Winter was always cold. Janet could put her under a blanket with a heating pad for hours and the baby would still feel cool to the touch when she unwrapped her. Janet would also find Winter's bottle in the mornings, frozen over. And even though the first days of Winter's life were warm, on two separate occasions Janet had witnessed frosty breath coming from the child's mouth; it was as if she were standing out in the cold in the dead of winter, exhaling.

Resenting her daughter's demands on her, Janet referred to her as "a bad bit of winter." Over time, Janet was simply too lazy to say the

whole thing, so she shortened it to Winter, and the name stuck. It was almost as if fate desired her to be named that.

In the weeks leading up to Winter's thirteenth birthday, a strange, new feeling had begun to come over her. She couldn't quite figure it out, but it seemed as if she could feel the future coming toward her. She had no clear idea of what lay ahead, but she felt there must be someplace she needed to be, other than the spot where she now was. It was almost as if her life might have a purpose she had never discovered. She would have visions while wide awake—images of people and places she did not remember ever having seen before. There was a reason she was here, she just couldn't remember it yet. The thought both delighted and frightened her.

Winter stared at her peas while her mother slurped up her bountiful meal. Winter wished for plates filled with food and friends to share it with. She thought back to a daydream she had had just yesterday and the boy who had been in it. She thought of her neighbors the Tuttles and imagined them gathered around their table, eating and laughing. More than anything Winter wanted that for herself. She wanted desperately for the future that was coming to involve a real family.

Winter was so deep in thought she didn't realize her mother wasn't feverishly consuming food any longer. Winter looked up and found Janet staring at her. The silence was deafening, and the expression on Janet's face was one of complete horror. Winter hurriedly began to eat her small portion, figuring her mother was simply disgusted with her for not joyfully eating what she had sacrificed to provide her. It took Winter only a second to finish, seeing how a half dozen peas, a crust of bread, and a spoonful of sugar-free jam go down pretty fast if eaten frantically. Winter looked up again,

hoping her repentance would be enough to satisfy her mother. Janet looked even more horrified.

"I ate—" Winter tried.

"What is that?" Janet asked, pointing at Winter. "What's happening to your hair?"

Winter could hear clicking now.

Her mother jumped up from her chair and hollered. "Whatever trick you are trying to pull, knock it off this instant!"

Winter could not have been more confused. She looked around the room, wondering if perhaps her mother was speaking to someone other than her. Nobody else was there—just her horrified mother, and a strange clicking noise.

Winter lifted her hands to her hair and was shocked to feel movement and ice. She stood quickly and turned to the mirror that hung on the wall next to the table, the same mirror Janet had forbidden Winter to use for fear of her image ruining it. Winter didn't care about that at the moment. She looked into the mirror with her green eyes and gasped. Her long, wild, blond hair was floating and spinning everywhere. And even more astonishing, the mass of hair looked to be completely frozen, each strand clicking against the next as they moved in a pulsating motion. The light from the overhead lamp reflected off the frozen strands, throwing flecks of light all over the walls and ceiling like an uncoordinated disco ball. Winter turned to her mother, stunned and confused.

"What are you doing?" Janet whimpered, her wide-open mouth a perfect oval. "Stop it!"

"I'm not doing anything," Winter insisted. "I was—"

"Stop it immediately!" Janet ordered.

"I can't stop it," Winter pleaded. "I don't know how I started it."

Winter's icy hair spun wildly, the frozen strands lashing out and striking Janet on the forearm and face. Red welts instantly began to appear.

"Ahhh!" Janet screamed, scooting herself as far away from the table as possible. "Stop it!" she yelled. "Stop it!"

Winter looked at her wild-eyed mother. Janet was holding a fork and knife out as if to defend herself. Her wrinkly face was covered in food she hadn't had time to wipe off. Her bushy eyebrows were wet and stringy. Her hair was sweaty, and she shivered as if this were the end of the world and she were being personally invited to burn. The red welts upon Janet's face formed the backwards letters, D, A, B.

Winter's green eyes smiled. Her entire life she had been picked on and pushed around by her mother. This was the first time she could remember ever having the upper hand. But then the movement of her hair began to slow, finally settling in large, icy sweeps upon her head. The frozen strands began to melt and drip. A few strands, still swirling, flung water around the room, but in a few more seconds it was all over. Winter sat, her face dripping wet.

Janet wiped at the food on her face and dabbed at her greasy lips. She glanced out the window to see if anyone had witnessed what had happened, then stood and looked closely at Winter's hair, cautiously reaching out to touch it. Upon feeling the wet mess she jerked back her hand and made a disgusted face.

"Are you done?" Janet asked, her anger growing. Her dinner had been interrupted, and the portion she had been able to previously inhale would be difficult to digest, what with all the discomfort and commotion Winter had just caused.

"Was that some sort of prank?" she demanded. "Because if it is, it's not the least bit funny."

"It's my birthday," was all Winter could think to say.

Janet glared at her. "Your *birthday,*" she ridiculed, her nasty composure returning in full. "That's what this is? I give birth to you, keep you in this house for thirteen years, and you repay me with a childish prank?"

Her greasy mouth twitched angrily. "This food you ruined cost good money," she complained. "Do you think I love working at the post office so much that it doesn't bother me to throw away the hard-earned money I make?"

Knowing there was no right answer to the impossible question her cruel mother had asked, Winter sat without responding.

"Too clever to answer me?" Janet demanded, her mean, wrinkled face scrunched up into a sneer. "Well, let me tell you this. You will clean up this mess. You will wipe down every spot in this room twice. You will polish this table and make the floor sparkle. Or I will turn you over to the state to be dealt with properly."

Winter clenched her fists under the table, willing her hair to act

up again. She thought of everything cold she had ever experienced. She thought of the vicious delight she had experienced just moments before as her mother had sat, shaking in awe.

Nothing happened.

"I should take the strap to you," Janet snarled, "but my television show starts in three minutes." She stood up and looked at herself in the mirror. She studied the red welts on her face and could see what they spelled out. "I will deal with you later," she huffed, too angry to say more. She brushed up her brows, smoothed her cheeks, and stormed out of the room.

Winter sat there alone, her hair now hanging in wet ringlets from her head. She reached over to her mother's abandoned plate and stabbed a big piece of roast beef. She swirled it in the gravy and lifted it to her mouth, juice dripping across the table as she did so. Chewing, she closed her eyes and reveled in the flavor. She had never tasted anything so delicious. She helped herself to a few more bites, then lifted her glass and was astonished to find the water in it completely frozen.

"Odd," Winter said to herself, looking closely at her glass.

Defiantly, she grabbed one of her mother's drinks. Janet always insisted on having three full glasses of soda with her meals, and two of them had not been touched.

Winter drank one of the sodas down.

She smiled, stabbed another piece of roast beef, and contemplated what a wonderful birthday she was having after all. She was obviously much more unique and extraordinary than anyone had ever told her she was. Savoring every bite, Winter finished her meal and made her way over to the Tuttles, where Wendy was waiting with a small cake that was topped with a ring of thirteen burning candles.

Winter didn't hesitate at all before making her wish.

CHAPTER SEVEN

LIGHTNING STRIKES TWICE

Leven's male guardian, Terry Graph, was a short man with long arms and little education. He was mean and always looking for someone to blame for all his problems. He had deep-set eyes, a spongy nose, and a tiny, tight mouth that framed his crooked, yellow, rotting teeth.

Terry was a little man with no compassion or concern for others. Not much interested him aside from giving Leven a hard time. He didn't just holler and taunt Leven on occasion; Terry made tormenting Leven his full-time occupation. Terry particularly enjoyed verbally assaulting Leven when he came home from school, berating him for dawdling, failing to do his chores, or for anything else that might be bugging Terry at the moment. He also enjoyed hiding behind the door and jumping out at Leven when the boy walked

unsuspecting into a room. If Leven made a friend or had an interest, Terry made certain to squelch it.

In Terry's view, Leven was his greatest burden. He had never gotten over the resentment he felt the day Addy announced there would be another mouth to feed. From then on, he saw Leven only as a nuisance and a pest, and he had literally never said a single kind word to the boy. Leven was not a son, he was just an additional expense and a bother.

Terry never had steady work. He procured an odd job here and there, but what he earned was not enough to support a wife and a leftover child. He always blamed his lack of good fortune on the current president or on his seventh-grade shop teacher who told him he would never amount to anything—or, more easily, on Leven.

Terry's laziness meant Addy had to work to support the family. Her job was folding napkins for a small, posh napkin company called Wonder Wipes. The shop was located about five miles away from the mobile home park, and one of the selling points of the napkins was that they were hand-folded. The owners of the company made a big point of this, as though the fold of the napkin enhanced its capacity for absorbing spills or wiping a face. Fortunately for the company and for Addy, the Wonder Wipe napkin had become a real status symbol for those who could afford them. There was enough work to keep Addy away from home and busily folding napkins day in and day out.

Addy would get up, go off to fold, and come home too tired and worn out to prevent her husband from making Leven's life miserable. Once in a while she would pretend to stick up for Leven, but for the most part she ignored him and his needs. Leven's impression was that she was annoyed that he was still even there. She was a

worthless advocate who always had tired hands and the weight of her world on her shoulders. Leven felt she and Terry wouldn't mind if he were to simply run off and disappear out of their lives. On those rare occasions where she would defend or say something concerning Leven, it only made things worse.

"Leave the boy alone," she would yell while Terry was picking on him. "He ain't all there."

Terry would throw up his hands. "The boy needs discipline, Addy," he would slur, "and he's certainly not going to get it from the likes of you. Always working and away. Folding, folding, folding. Making me cook my own meals and live in a filthy house while you're folding some piece of cloth so that some uppity rich people can properly wipe their pampered faces."

Terry and Addy would argue until one was too tired to carry on or until Terry went out for some night air, which the three of them knew meant air that was at least ninety proof. Addy would then turn the TV up so loud Leven wouldn't dare speak, and he would wander off to bed on the porch or go outside to sit beneath the huge tree and wonder what he could do to make things better.

This was Leven. He was a tall, surprisingly strong, fourteen-year-old who saw things in a way that most kids his age didn't. He had not had a pretty life, and yet for some reason he didn't understand, he always felt there had to be something better. Things couldn't possibly be this bad forever. Sometimes, if Leven squinted his brown eyes and really concentrated, he could almost see, or at least pretend, that the existence he was living was only a prelude to something much more important. It was a feeling that continued to burn inside him, even as Terry tore him apart or as the rest of his life crumbled around him.

Understandably, Leven didn't smile much; but when he did he was a rather handsome kid. Older folks could easily pat him on the head and know that a couple of decent kids still existed in this world. He always wore Levi's and one of the free T-shirts Addy would occasionally get at work. As if making friends wasn't hard enough, imagine being a fourteen-year-old boy trying to impress his peers while wearing a shirt that says "Wonder Wipes."

To avoid ridicule, Leven would always wear the T-shirts inside out so the decal wasn't as noticeable. Of course this infuriated Addy, who thought it was a slap in the face to all the hard work she put in to support the family. So Leven had to remember to always turn his shirt inside out before arriving at school and reverse it before he got home at night.

Thanks to Clover, in the last few days Leven's life had changed dramatically. In Clover, Leven had found both friendship and an affirmation that something more was out there. Leven had learned a few things about Clover and where he had come from, but for the most part the furry little guy remained tight-lipped whenever it came to discussing the task and future that lay ahead of them.

"You have to tell me what's going to happen," Leven said as they climbed down through the rocks that lined the steep ditch at the edge of the prairie. "And if you're not from here, then where? Another planet?"

"Don't do this," Clover said, rubbing his own bare left elbow. "I am bound to keep the secret."

"How do I know that you're not just some made-up part of my imagination?"

Clover stopped climbing. His leaf-like ears fluttered. He looked at Leven as if he had been wounded.

"I'm sorry," Leven said. "I shouldn't say things like that."

"I would love to tell you everything I know," Clover explained again, "but I am bound. I can tell you this, though," Clover said, looking carefully around, "it's getting close."

Leven picked up a small rock and looked at it. "You've said that already. What's getting close?" he asked.

"I've been with you for fourteen years. Of course, I had to wait a while before you were born for you to get here. But I can tell now that the time is close," Clover affirmed, taking the rock from Leven's hand and looking at it. "During all those years I have known that someday we would go. And now I know that someday is near."

Clover reached into the front pocket of his robe. Leven was pretty amazed by Clover. He was, after all, a twelve-inch-tall furry creature with wet eyes and a huge smile who was supposed to serve him, but was usually too busy telling stories or marveling over rocks and leaves to attend to Leven's immediate needs. As interesting as Clover was, it was the pocket on the robe he wore that fascinated Leven most. Clover called it a void.

"My mother stitched it on when I was seventy-two," he had explained.

Void was a perfect name for the pocket, seeing how there appeared to be an endless capacity to it. Clover was constantly pulling things out of it. Books, small toys, an array of useful tools, and even a kite. And those were just the things Leven recognized. Clover had pulled out many things Leven had never heard of or could never have imagined even if he had tried. The pocket also held an unlimited store of food and candy. Clover was always chewing or sucking on some kind of weird treat he had apparently stocked enough of to last over all the years he had been here.

"Mupe?" Clover asked, holding out to Leven what looked to be a purple rock.

"What's mupe?" Leven asked.

"Just try it," Clover smiled. "Back home it's very popular candy."

Leven stuck the purple thing in his mouth and bit down. It tasted like honeyed, cooked wheat. It wasn't awful, but it wasn't candy. "This stuff is popular?" Leven asked in amazement.

"It's kind of fun," Clover said, skipping.

"What's fun about—?" Leven's mouth started to feel sticky. He tried to open it wide, but it felt as if his tongue were glued to both the roof and bottom of his mouth. At the same time his vision went weird. He could see in what seemed to be two different directions and a unpleasant odor filled his nostrils.

Clover was looking at him and laughing. "Wow! That was a strong piece of mupe."

"What do you mean?" Leven asked, talking out of the side of his head. He threw his hands up to his face and realized that his mouth was not where it had been. He touched his face frantically. He found his mouth on the side of his head where his right ear used to be. One eye was where the other ear used to be, and the other eye was underneath his chin. He yelled, and almost broke the eardrum of the ear that was in the hair right above his mouth. His streak of white hair had moved to the top of his right hand.

"Best I've ever had was an ear on my elbow," Clover said enviously. He looked at the wrapper. "Oh, this pack has 'Extra Feature Fission'."

"What do I do?" Leven hollered.

"It'll wear off in a moment," Clover said, as if disappointed.

"What's that smell?" Leven asked. "Where's my nose?" Leven

began to touch his arms and stomach trying to find his nose. He sniffed. "Oh, great," he complained. He sat down and hurriedly untied his left shoelace. He threw the shoe off and pulled off the sock. Leven's nose was sticking out from between his big toe and the next in line.

Clover was quite amused, "I wish I had a camera," he said, as if he were a parent, wanting to capture the image of a well-groomed son going off for the first day of school.

Leven was happy Clover didn't have one. He could only imagine how odd he must look. In a few moments, the effect of the candy slowly began to wear off. Leven could see his nose sliding up his leg and over his body as it migrated north. His ears sprang back into their places, and his eyes circled around his mouth and returned to their rightful spots.

"Am I normal?" Leven asked, feeling around to know for himself.

"Yes," Clover said sadly.

"Don't give me anything like that ever again," Leven said seriously.

Clover looked hurt. "I'm not the best sycophant," he admitted.

Leven couldn't stand to see Clover feel sad. "It's all right," Leven sighed, patting Clover on the head. "Besides, I'm glad you're around."

Clover smiled. "Me, too," he added sincerely, happy to move on to other subjects. He stopped, looked at his little right foot, pulled out a pebble from between his toes, and smiled.

"I'm sure whatever happens next, we'll be fine," Leven said.

"Let's hope so."

"I mean, I shouldn't worry with you around," Leven said,

setting Clover up. He wanted to see if he could trick Clover into telling him more.

"I'm glad you feel that way," Clover sniffed proudly. "It'll be fun."

"So where are we going again?" Leven asked, so casually that Clover fell for it.

"To Foo, of course. . . ." Clover caught himself, his eyes wide and frightened. "I mean, to wherever it is we will be going."

"Foo?" Leven asked. "Did you say Foo?"

"I didn't say anything," Clover denied. "I was just muttering."

"What's Foo?"

"Foo's nothing," Clover insisted. "I was talking about food."

"We'll go to *food* someday?" Leven said sarcastically.

"Right," Clover tried to say with conviction. "We'll get some food someday."

"Foo." Leven said to himself as he slid down a big rock and stepped across the shallow stream, avoiding the water. "Is it a building?"

"No," Clover adamantly answered, placing his small furry feet into the stream. The current was almost strong enough to pull him down. He braced himself and smiled, proud to still be standing.

"But is it—"

"I'll disappear," Clover warned, lifting his hood as if to put it on.

"Forget it, then," Leven quickly said. Leven couldn't stand it when Clover just disappeared. It was impossible to see or find him once he was gone. "Maybe you're not such a good sycophant after all. I thought you were supposed to do my bidding," Leven joked.

"I try, but whatever I do I just can't help thinking of myself a little."

"I don't see why you can't just tell me what's coming," Leven sighed. "You make it sound urgent, and then we spend our days doing nothing. I promise I won't tell anyone. It's not like I have anyone to talk—"

Leven stopped speaking due to the sudden appearance of Brick, the official school, neighborhood, and all-around-town bully. Standing next to Brick in the stream bed was Brick's pale, rich friend, Glen. The two of them had been out shooting cans and prairie dogs with their BB guns.

"Who you talking to, Skunk?" Brick laughed at Leven, making fun of the white streak in his hair. "Playing make-believe?"

Leven looked quickly to see if Clover was still in sight. He was gone. "I wasn't talking to anyone," Leven insisted, looking Brick in the eye.

Leven tried to move past the two of them.

"Not so fast," Brick sneered, holding out his arm to prevent Leven from passing. "This is our field. Me and Glen don't like it when others trespass. Isn't that right, Glen?" Brick asked.

"Can't stand it," Glen said meanly, pumping the lever on his BB gun. "I mean, what's the world coming to when just anyone can come onto our field?"

Brick pumped his gun, smiling cruelly.

Leven tried to keep going, but Brick jabbed Leven's shoulder with the barrel of his BB gun.

Leven grabbed his shoulder in pain. "It's not your field," he protested, a strange, confident feeling beginning to creep over him.

Brick jabbed Leven even harder. This time Leven stumbled, slipping on a rock and sprawling on his back in the water.

For as long as he could remember, Leven had been uneasy

around water. He frequently dreamed of drowning and often woke up in the middle of the night choking and gasping for breath. Now here he was, soaking in a stream after being pushed down by the barrel of a BB gun.

Brick and Glen laughed like they had never seen anything funnier.

Leven scrambled up out of the water. He was surprised. He wasn't mad, and he wasn't scared. In fact, he was remarkably calm. As he watched Brick laughing, thoughts formed in his mind. They weren't thoughts such as *I wonder what I'll have for lunch,* or *I think green is my favorite color.* They were thoughts so strong and so focused it was almost as if he could see the future. He pictured lightning coming down from the darkened, cloudy sky. And there, suddenly, was a bolt of it, striking the ground no more than a hundred feet away. The flash was blinding and the sound deafening, and Brick and Glen screamed and fell over on their backs in the stream bed.

Leven steadied himself. He looked at Brick and Glen cowering in fear and was amazed.

He envisioned another bolt of lightning, and once more a brilliant scratch of light shimmered and crackled just beyond Glen and Brick.

The sound shook the earth.

Their previous screams were nothing compared to the ones Brick and Glen were now emitting as they began scrambling on their stomachs up the bank and away from Leven and back toward the mobile home park. Leven envisioned lightning chasing them all the way home and, amazingly, that was exactly what happened. One after another, lightning bolts struck the earth directly behind them as they scuttled on their stomachs, crying hysterically and trying to cover their heads with their hands. They had both abandoned their BB guns and were scraping their knees and hands something fierce as they crawled frantically across the dry prairie.

Leven watched them squirm under the mobile home park fence. Astounded by what he had been able to do, he gaped after them in awe. He looked to the far distance, beyond the park and past the town water tower. He pictured a bolt of lightning and watched in wonder as it flashed out of the cloudy sky. "Unbelievable," he whispered to himself as the echo of it died down.

"Pretty neat," Clover said, suddenly sitting on his left shoulder.

"Thanks for leaving me," Leven half-joked.

"I knew you'd be okay."

"Did you know I could do that?"

"I didn't know *what* you could do," Clover said, climbing onto the top of Leven's head to get a better look at the now-vanished Brick and Glen. "They're not so tough." Clover shook a tiny fist in their direction.

"What do you mean you didn't know what I could do?" Leven asked, still in awe over what had happened.

"All nits have a gift. You know, fire, flying, burrowing. Some sort of freaky talent that sets you apart from everyone else—weird breed." Clover brushed the thick hair on his calves and sniffed, his leaf-like ears wiggling as he did so.

"Nits?" Leven asked, finding it odd that Clover would consider anyone else to be a weird breed.

"To be honest with you," Clover said, ignoring Leven's inquiry and climbing down off his head, "I had my doubts about you being the right one. I like you and all, but I was beginning to wonder."

"The right one for what?"

Clover stared at him and smiled. "Do you think every boy here gets a sycophant?"

"No."

"You have a purpose beyond any of these people out here. In fact, if you fail they're all pretty much toast." Clover picked up a rock that was about half his size and heaved it into the stream. He smiled at the splash it made.

"This is crazy," Leven said, frowning and brushing his dark bangs back. "I am just a kid who lives in Oklahoma and is bad at math. I can't save anyone or make lightning strike."

"You just did."

"That was a coincidence."

"Stop it!" Clover said forcefully. "Don't use those kinds of words around me." His ears twisted and shook.

"What kinds of words?"

Clover looked around. "There are no coincidences," he said sternly. "Sabine and his shadows would love you to believe that every small miracle you witness throughout the day is nothing more than a chance happening. But I know better. You should, too." Clover looked wounded.

"I don't know what I know anymore," Leven said honestly.

The two of them waded out of the shallow stream. Leven climbed up the rocky bank onto the flat prairie and gazed off to the north. Nothing but horizon and sky. He walked toward the Rolling Greens Deluxe Mobile Home Park and picked up one of the BB guns that Brick and Glen had dropped. He held it to his shoulder and pointed the barrel into the empty distance. He pulled the trigger and a weak puff of air shot out. Clover found the other gun and ran

it back to Leven. Leven waved it away, and Clover happily aimed it toward the sky and pulled the trigger. A little puff of air shot out and into the sky.

"Weird," Clover said. "Is that supposed to scare someone?"

"They're just toys," Leven answered, his thoughts elsewhere. "So, do these nits have only one gift?"

"Usually."

"And mine is to make lightning?"

"I guess," Clover replied, smoothing down his little dress-like robe.

Leven looked to the north again and tried to envision lightning striking.

Nothing happened. He turned and thought of it coming down to the south.

Nothing.

He could feel his thoughts were different this time. They weren't as clear or as focused as they had been before, when Brick and Glen were laughing at him. His mind wandered for a bit and then suddenly things solidified. He envisioned a huge hawk dropping from the sky, its talons extended, aimed right at Clover.

He quickly turned.

A huge raptor *was* swooping down right above Clover. Leven yelled at Clover to disappear and Clover did just that. The confused bird almost flew into the ground. Its talons brushed the earth as it pulled up and returned to the sky, turning its head to find any sign of the furry feast it had viewed just moments before.

"Clover?" Leven yelled.

"I'm right here," he replied, materializing on Leven's right shoulder.

Leven jumped. "I've told you not to do that."

"Sorry," he said casually. "How'd you know that bird was there?"

"I saw it before it happened," Leven answered, confused.

"Unbelievable," Clover whispered. "Your gift isn't *just* lightning."

"What is it then?"

"You're not a nit, you're an offing," Clover said almost reverently.

"What's an offing? Is that bad?"

"Oh, I wish Antsel was around to see this," Clover lamented.

"See what?" Leven asked almost desperately.

"I can't believe my burn is an offing," he said with excitement.

"What does that mean?" Leven asked, frustrated.

"You can see the future," Clover said enviously. "You have it in you to manipulate fate a bit. Offings can not only see the future, they can help make it turn out to their advantage. Your safety and dislike for those boys probably helped you pick that lightning's striking point. You have a great gift, Lev, an extremely rare gift. I know of only one other who has it."

"Who?"

"I can't say."

"I just saved your life," Leven pointed out.

Clover waved. "That bird couldn't have killed me," he said confidently. "I told you there's only one way for us sycophants to die."

"How?" Leven tried.

"I'm not falling for that." Clover smiled, his blue eyes squinting.

Leven smiled back.

"Imagine, little old Clover working for an offing," he went on. "I wish I was somewhere where people could be envious." Clover jumped off of Leven's shoulder and skipped along the ground.

Leven picked up both guns and put them over his shoulder. He followed Clover back across the field toward home. In the far distance he could see the tree that shaded his house. He thought of Terry and Addy and Clover. He thought of the turns his life had taken recently. He tried to draw his thoughts in, but it was no use; some gift, he couldn't see his own future.

Clover turned to Leven and smiled. "What are you thinking?" he asked merrily.

"I think it's time for us to leave," Leven replied, surprised to hear the words coming from his mouth. "We should think about getting out of this place."

"Good." Clover hopped. "I was thinking you'd never say that."

"So do you have any more of that candy?" Leven asked sheepishly, admitting that the stuff wasn't half bad.

"I told you it's popular," Clover smiled, taking another piece of mupe from his pocket.

Leven put the candy in his mouth and smiled from his palm.

CHAPTER EIGHT

Everybody Please Remain Seated

Winter's life was by no means going any more smoothly. She came home from school one day to discover that her mother had been fired from her job at the post office for throwing away a bag of mail she was too tired to sort. Since then Janet had decided she didn't want to do anything but watch TV for the rest of her life. So she lay on their worn orange couch, eating and eating and eating while watching shows about thin people doing things she was never going to do anymore: things like walking, reading books, or getting up for the remote themselves.

She was also done with being a parent. From that moment on, the most extensive parenting Janet provided was to yell loudly at Winter whenever she blocked her view of the TV set. Janet moved the refrigerator closer to the couch and fed the yard hose in through the window so she could get a drink of water whenever she felt like it.

It cannot be stressed enough: Winter was not in a happy place.

Things at school were no better. It seemed that no one wanted to be friends with an unusual-looking girl who had wild blond hair, wore tattered clothes, and was so introverted. Most kids saw Winter as nothing more than the perfect test case for their clever put-downs.

"Garbage-heap head."

"Frostbite."

Even the teachers were cruel.

"Now class," Mr. Bentwonder, her homeroom teacher, would say, "leave that skinny white thing alone. Only heaven knows the last time soap and water touched her."

Mr. Bentwonder was a big fat meanie. Sorry, but there's really no better way of saying it. His puffy face was as round as a melon, and his fleshy lips were always wet. He couldn't say a single thing without having to wipe them afterwards. He had eyes the color of dung and a nose that was pushed up so drastically at the end that students from across the room could tell that he needed to use a tissue even before he knew himself. He taught math by trade, and hate and ignorance by example. Unable to find a woman who was actually attracted to a homely man who couldn't say a kind thing and never did a kind deed, he had never married. True, there are people who are married to individuals who can't say or do anything kind. But in most cases, those individuals are not married to someone unkind who also has a giant mushy melon head, breath that always smells of liver, and perpetually has to have his mouth wiped by an elected student.

Mr. Bentwonder had been good for something, however—that one good thing being a comment he made that finally set Winter to thinking about getting away from the life she had been dealt.

It was during the middle of math class at Samuel Tolerance Junior High when Wendell Prattlemelt, the school kiss-up, raised his hand and told Mr. Bentwonder that he was sure there had never been another teacher as inspired and brilliant as he. Mr. Bentwonder had responded by expressing his conviction that there were few people who could match Wendell's intellect and stating how if every child were as perceptive as Wendell, he, Mr. Perry Bentwonder, might very well be the president of the United States, and the country would be much better off for it.

Then he boasted, "I am who I am, class, because I have made myself so." Mr. Bentwonder failed to mention that he had been born into a wealthy and privileged family and had been pampered his entire life. Nor did he explain to the class that he had gotten the job he now held only because his uncle was the principal of Samuel Tolerance Junior High. No, he left all of that out and smugly repeated, "I am who I am because I have made myself so."

His words triggered something in Winter's mind. It was suddenly clear. She would never be anything if she kept waiting for someone else to change things for her. The thought made her feel as though someone had flipped a switch and finally activated her soul. She sat still, listening to Mr. Bentwonder go on and on about poetry, and how it took a rare and sensitive mind such as his to actually understand it.

"What's in a name?" he drooled. "That which we call a rose by any other name would smell as sweet." He turned his mushy head so that young Patty Foote could dab his mouth. She did so and

smiled. "You don't just read poetry, you breeeeeathe it," he instructed.

"No one breathes it as well as you," Wendell Prattlemelt gushed. Mr. Bentwonder nodded and bowed slightly.

"Again, Wendell, what a *joy* you must be to your parents," he cooed.

Winter snickered. She just couldn't help it. Wendell a joy? Mr. Bentwonder breathing poetry? It struck her as funny, and she couldn't keep from laughing.

Mr. Bentwonder looked up and over his spectacles toward her.

"Excuse me?" he said indignantly. "Does something strike you as funny, Miss Frore?" Flecks of spittle flew from his fleshy lips, and the ever-accommodating Patty Foote reached to blot his mouth.

"No, sir," Winter replied, her green eyes unable to hide her mirth. "I just . . ."

Winter laughed again.

The class went silent. No one had ever laughed at Mr. Bentwonder, unless he had made it clear they were supposed to. Now here was Winter, laughing at him, twice. His forehead reddened and Patty went in for another dab. He brushed her away and heaved himself to his feet.

"I have never," he huffed. "Never, never," he puffed. "Never have I been burdened with such an insolent and disrespectful pupil."

Wendell smiled as he watched Mr. Bentwonder work his ponderous way through the desks and toward Winter. Winter just sat there, her gaze locked on the floor.

"Poverty is one thing," he went on, gesturing to Winter's old clothes and disheveled appearance, "but even in poverty one ought to show respect to those who are attempting to help her." The desks

were positioned too close together for Mr. Bentwonder to fit through. He began pushing and shoving students out of the way. Some students frantically moved to get away from him as he waded closer to his prey.

His voice was menacing. "I have given you my time and my attention, and you have returned to me spite and ingratitude . . ."

Winter tried to control her feelings, but as she sat there in her desk, with her classmates scurrying out of the path of the threatening Mr. Bentwonder, a powerful feeling came over her. Her body burned, and she was afraid to look up for fear of losing the sensation. She would have kept her eyes averted from her oncoming teacher if it had not been for the screams and cries of her classmates.

She looked up and marveled at what was happening. An expanding circle of silvery ice was flowing out from where she sat and filling the room. As from the epicenter of a frozen earthquake, waves of ice rippled out and away from her, arresting and suspending everything in their way.

Winter smiled and the avalanche of cold increased.

She watched as Wendell turned to run. The silvery frost caught his left foot, keeping him right where he stood. Wendell screamed and cried as ice crept up his leg and over his body, eventually immobilizing him completely. Suddenly fearful, Mr. Bentwonder turned to lumber for the door, but cold tapped him on his big, cowardly back. He turned to look, and in an instant he was one of the fattest and least aesthetically pleasing sculptures Winter had ever seen.

Those who had not yet been frozen tried to wriggle out of their desks and escape from the room, but Winter wouldn't have it. She simply shook her head, and at once, the entire rest of the room was frozen solid. Students had their arms out and in mid-stride,

motionless in place. Desks and walls glistened and shined. The fish tank at the front of the room was a solid block of ice. No clock was ticking, no computers were humming, nor was Mr. Bentwonder prattling. The frost-filled room was completely quiet.

Winter was amazed. The only things unfrozen were herself and her desk. She stood, gathered her books and put them into her backpack, then walked to the front of the room, stopping only twice: once to snap Mr. Bentwonder's tie in two, and once to touch the fish tank. When she did, the water in the aquarium melted instantly, and the fish resumed swimming. Winter felt better. The fish had never done anything cruel to her.

She walked to the frozen door and touched it, and it warmed. She pulled it open and walked out. Now suddenly seemed like as good a time as any for her to escape her unhappy life. She had been contemplating running away, and she was smart enough to know it would be wise for her to be gone by the time Mr. Bentwonder and her class thawed. She knew they would defrost soon, and when they did they would be cold but none the worse for wear.

It was time for Winter to go.

"Excuse me?" a strong male voice said, interrupting Winter's flight down the hall. Winter jumped and put her hand to her heart. She had been so deep in thought that she had not noticed Principal Helt walking toward her.

"Why aren't you in class?" he demanded.

"I'm running an errand for my teacher, Mr. Bentwonder," Winter lied.

"Mr. Bentwonder?" the principal questioned. "My nephew? I would think a man of his intellect and breeding would be sufficiently prepared not to need children scurrying about for him."

Principal Helt took Winter by the arm and pulled her back toward her classroom. It was not a smart move on his part. Winter closed her eyes and let the feelings she had experienced only moments before return.

"We can't allow—"

Mr. Helt was stopped cold. Winter opened her eyes to see him open-mouthed and frozen solid. She looked up and down the empty hall and then opened a janitor's closet door right behind him. She slid him inside, taking care not to break off an arm or finger, closed the door, and continued down the hall and out into the open. She had walked out these doors hundreds of times, but today it felt different.

She was free.

"I am who I am because I made myself so," she said aloud, looking toward the east and feeling as if she had been this strong once before but just couldn't remember where or when.

It was a good feeling.

When Winter reached her house she climbed into her room through the window so as to not bother her mother, who was watching TV. She collected some money she had been saving and packed a couple of outfits. She wanted to stop and tell the Tuttles she was leaving, but she knew they would try to talk her out of it. She also knew that it would be too heartbreaking for her to have to say goodbye. She felt better after telling herself she would be back to see them again someday. It wasn't all that believable. Winter pushed those thoughts aside. She had something to do, and whatever it was, she couldn't let anything stop her. She climbed out her window one last time.

Winter walked straight to the bus station and up to the ticket

counter. She looked at the schedule and tried to determine which destination would be the best. After some time her eyes fell upon a place that felt perfect! It was the next step and she knew it. She gave the big lady behind the glass forty-two dollars and bought a bus ticket to someplace away from where she now was.

"Are you traveling with your parents?" the ticket lady asked suspiciously.

"Alone," Winter answered. "I'm going to see my grandmother," she lied. "Those are my parents over there." Winter pointed to a couple sitting on a bench, two ordinary people with their noses buried in magazines. "They've come to see me off."

The large lady realized she had invested enough of her time in this funny-looking girl's business as it was. "Here's your ticket. The bus leaves in forty minutes." She pointed. "It will pull up right there at that rear door."

Winter thanked the woman and walked off in the direction of the couple she had pointed at. Just to be safe she stopped in front of the man and woman and asked them the time. The woman smiled at Winter and gave it to her.

"Thank you," Winter said, her evergreen eyes shining for the first time in a while. "Is this seat taken?" she asked, pointing to an empty place on the bench beside them. The woman shook her head and Winter sat.

"Traveling alone?" the woman asked.

"For the moment," Winter replied. "I'm going to visit my grandmother," she lied.

"How nice," the thin lovely woman said. "And how brave of you."

Winter shrugged.

"When I was your age I would have never traveled on a bus alone," the woman tisked. "I clung to my mother until I was out of high school. Your parents must think you're really responsible."

Again Winter shrugged.

"And modest," the woman added, referring to Winter's quiet nature.

Winter stifled a laugh. Her mother didn't even know she was missing, much less care about her. Her entire life she had been confused and lost. It was as if she didn't know who she was, and she had constantly felt as though she didn't belong where she was. Sometimes she would have memories or see things that seemed so unusual they scared her. Now this morning she had turned her whole class into ice cubes and it had felt normal. It had felt like something she was expected to do—like something she had done before.

She thought about how rude it had been of her to just walk away from her house without telling her mother where she was going. Winter wondered if she could freeze things she couldn't directly see. Now felt like a good time to find that out. In her mind she pictured Janet's water hose frozen solid. Although she couldn't see it, Winter could feel it work. She smiled. It would be a small reminder to Janet of her child.

"Well, you just stay by us," the lovely woman said to her, pulling Winter out of her thoughts. "Our bus doesn't leave for an hour. How about yours?"

"Thirty-five minutes," Winter reported.

"There, then," the woman smiled. "You won't be alone."

Winter smiled back, knowing that "alone" was exactly where she was headed. For some reason, however, that didn't frighten her. It

just seemed as if she had been there before. Winter glanced at her ticket and whispered the destination.

"Oklahoma."

She had never wanted to go there before. She was both determined and incredibly uneasy. Something bigger and scarier than she could clearly understand had begun.

CHAPTER NINE

SABINE'S RANT

Foo was changing. As the history of mankind had advanced, the dreams and desires of those on earth had become darker and more selfish. This darkness had changed Foo. In the beginning Foo was a secret location the heavens had created to give imagination and dreams their own place to flourish without restraint. It was a world that existed within the minds of all men and women, made possible by the boundless potential that lies within each of us. But over time the beauty and magic of Foo had begun to erode, as some of its inhabitants became poisoned by the increasingly selfish and perverted dreams of humans and the destructive idea that the dreams of those in reality were not their concern.

Sabine had grown powerful by the rank wishes and sordid desires of men gone wrong, and he wanted out of Foo. He knew the time was finally coming. The skies in Foo dimmed dramatically as

the dreams of man grew ever darker. He had selfishness on his side. He had done very well to stir up the inhabitants of Foo. Now it was crucial for him to find the gateway out. Foo and reality could never be one if there was no way to move between them and bring the two together.

Sabine thought of little else besides this gateway. The Council of Whisps still fought against him, but as soon as they were properly dealt with his only resistance would be in not knowing the direction to lead his followers out of Foo.

Sabine was not a happy being, but he knew of two things that would bring him great joy. One was discovering the gateway, and the other was locating the only one who could stop him: the missing link and the only person alive who could destroy the gateway before Sabine could find it and bring his dark legions through it into reality.

Sabine's to-do list was short, but difficult.

He stood by the window, shifting and creating shadow after shadow, each instantly trying to flee his dark presence, only to realize it couldn't completely operate on its own. As each new shadow materialized, Sabine would blow, sending it through incoming dreams into reality. He would feel the shadows as they floated above the earth, undetected by all those living. He would call them in from time to time and berate them for not being able to accomplish such a simple task as finding the single human on earth who could destroy everything.

Through the window Sabine could see Jamoon thundering closer. Jamoon was a rant and one of Sabine's most loyal confederates. Sabine withdrew from his position to welcome his visitor.

Jamoon entered Sabine's lair like a swirling storm—blowing

through the doors and down the long corridor into the grand hall. His thick black robe billowed as he strode across the room. Sabine was seated at the far end of the room in a chair made from the hide of a large roven.

Jamoon bowed and Sabine nodded.

Rants were a strange breed; often only a half of each one was ever recognizable. They were beings in constant change, one half human and stable, the other half whatever someone in reality was currently dreaming. As a breed, rants were typically easy to control. The main cause of their condition was that they were easily influenced and manipulated. They were offspring of nits who didn't have the character and fortitude to just enhance the dreams and imaginations of those on earth and then move on. Instead the dreams overcame the rants and stole half of their personality and individualism.

Rants were not happy or stable beings.

At times being half a dream can come in handy. For example, if your right arm is injured and your left arm is currently that of a surgeon. Or if you just don't have the strength to open a new jar of potch, and one half of you becomes a weight lifter with an iron grip. But say you are down at the Dripping Trough, trying to enjoy a guys' night out, and suddenly your entire south side becomes a beautiful ballerina that some child on earth is dreaming of becoming. That would make things a bit awkward. Because of just such a scenario, most rants wore long black cloaks that covered their entire unstable bodies and hid the truth of whatever half of them might be at the moment.

"Remove your cloak," Sabine demanded. He liked to see exactly what he was dealing with.

Jamoon dropped his cloak to the floor. He was tall and strong, with a right arm and leg in top physical condition and cloaked in a smaller robe. The other half of him at the moment looked to be an astronaut.

Sabine didn't smile. To a rant a smile was the most insulting thing you could show them. They felt certain all smiles were aimed at their ever-changing second halves.

"News?" Sabine asked.

"You have our support," Jamoon said solemnly. "We stand waiting in the shadows to flee Foo."

"Excellent." Sabine twitched. "And what of the gateway?"

Jamoon's left side spoke out of turn. "Houston, we have a problem." Jamoon then began to tremble . . . not out of fear, but due to the transformation he was suddenly undergoing. The astronaut part of him began to pucker and boil, then the image ran together and dripped slowly to the floor. Obviously little Bobby back in reality no longer wanted to be a spaceman. As the image dripped away it was filled in with that of a seven-foot-tall basketball player. Half of Jamoon instantly began to dribble a ball and sweat. It was easier for a rant to become half of something that was close to his same size. But since Jamoon's right half was only 5'10" and his left half was now seven feet tall, it looked particularly odd. The dribbling and the height were distracting, but Sabine, ever the evil diplomat, refrained from smiling.

Jamoon ignored the gyrations of his left side and continued as if nothing was happening. "We have found no indication or clue as to the location. We are searching as fast as we can for the gateway, but we have so little to go on."

"Intensify your search," Sabine insisted, ignoring Jamoon's left half. "Your very happiness is dependent upon it."

"Pass it here, I'm open!" Jamoon's new left side hollered.

"I understand," his stable half replied. "What of the whisps?"

"*I* will take care of them," Sabine said. "Soon they will no longer be a problem for us."

Jamoon bowed and Sabine waved him away. Jamoon slipped his cloak back on and ran quickly from the room as if driving down a basketball court and going in for a dunk.

CHAPTER TEN

A Marked Target

With every mile Winter traveled away from her home, she began to feel more and more at peace with her decision to leave. It was as if she were doing exactly what she was destined to do. As she rode the bus toward Oklahoma, the image of a boy she didn't know began playing in her mind. For some reason Winter had never experienced dreams while sleeping. She figured that was because of her awful life. She did occasionally have visions during the day. Her eyes would glaze over and she would see things. Lately, she had seen a lot of Leven Thumps. She had no idea who he was or what purpose he might have in her life, but she knew she needed to find him. Each time his face would flash into her mind, a voice within her head would whisper, "Don't touch him."

The warning was so troubling and confusing, that the first time Winter heard it she had been unable to sleep the next night, but

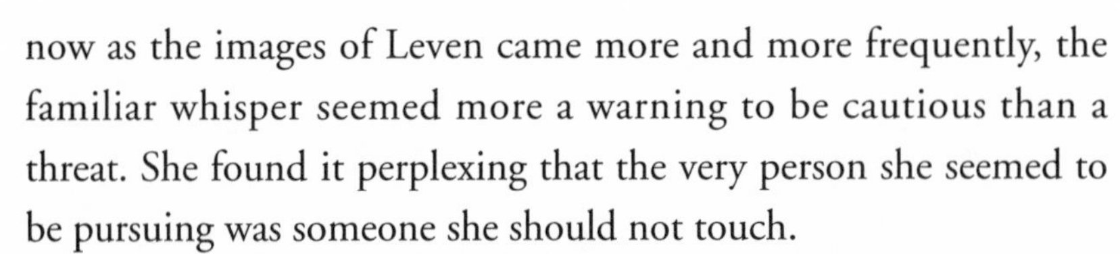

now as the images of Leven came more and more frequently, the familiar whisper seemed more a warning to be cautious than a threat. She found it perplexing that the very person she seemed to be pursuing was someone she should not touch.

Winter arrived in Oklahoma early in the morning, unsure of just what to do next. Her wonder was answered by a poster on the wall of the bus station. It read: "Visit Burnt Culvert: Site of the State's Worst Lightning Fire." Winter thought two things: one, Burnt Culvert could use a new ad campaign, and two, that was where she needed to go. She was happy to learn that Burnt Culvert was only an hour away. She found a taxi and asked the driver to take her there.

"Site of the state's worst lightning fire," the driver said, confirming what the sign had proclaimed.

"Is it a big town?" Winter asked.

"Depends on what you think is big," he smiled. "It's bigger than where I come from, but that's not saying much."

"Do you know if it has a junior high school?" Winter asked.

"It does," he replied. "If I remember right, it's the home of the Fighting Ashes."

"Can you take me to the school?" she asked.

"Sure," he smiled. "Are you starting there?" he asked, having no problem prying into her business.

"No," Winter replied. "I just need to pick something up."

The driver dropped the flag on the meter and pulled out.

Winter knew what she was looking for was there in Burnt Culvert, but as they drove she heard the voice whisper again in her head, "Don't touch him." Still puzzled, she looked to see if someone else might be in the backseat with her.

Winter was very much alone.

ii

The softball hit Leven squarely in the back of his head. The pain was immediate, and he could see stars and hear laughter. Leven was not a big fan of lunch break.

"What's a matter, Skunk?" Brick called out. "Can't catch with the back of your head?"

Leven turned and saw Brick laughing. Brick's long skinny face was scrunched up, nearly pinching his little pea-sized eyes shut. His fat knees stuck out from under his shorts and were knocking together as he and Glen laughed it up. Brick had the personality of a pit bull—he picked on and chewed up anyone who got in his way or was a threat to his ego. And since he had the smarts of a week-old doughnut, almost anyone qualified as a threat to his intelligence. Brick was a large child who in reality should have been in a class two grades up, though his intellect best qualified him to attend classes two grades down.

Leven pointed to the sky and said, "Lightning."

Both Brick and Glen immediately stopped laughing.

"Ahh, forget about him," Brick said, momentarily scared. "He's not worth it."

Leven just stared at them, wondering why they took so much pleasure in picking on him. He had never said an unkind word to them or hurt them in any way, but from the moment he had started middle school, Brick and Glen had singled him out and made him the target of their animosity and hatred.

Leven looked around the field. Students were everywhere—peers of all shapes and sizes, yet for some reason Leven was Brick's favorite person to pick on. Leven wasn't the heaviest, or the shortest, or the

tallest, and his brown eyes were as average as his grades. Maybe it was the bright white streak in his hair that had drawn their attention. Something like that was hard to hide. He kept his hair a little longer in hopes of it helping, but that only made the streak more prominent. To most of his school he was "Skunk." Leven got no credit for what he didn't do: he didn't pick his nose or laugh like a mule or cry when picked on. And he was always careful to wear his Wonder Wipes T-shirts inside out. None of that mattered; Leven stood out and probably always would. Imagine the attention he might have gotten if people knew he had Clover always clinging to him.

Brick picked up the ball he had just thrown at the back of Leven's head and turned—he and Glen laughing it up as they left.

"They're just a couple of bullies," a voice from behind Leven said. "Not tough enough to fight their way out of a cobweb."

Leven turned to see who was speaking to him. It had to be someone with no knowledge of what Brick could do, to say something so bold. A girl with messy blond hair and an angry expression on her face was staring back at him. She had her hands behind her back. Though Leven knew they had never met, he thought he recognized her. She gazed at him with her deep green eyes.

"Excuse me?" Leven asked.

"They're bullies," she sniffed, pulling back her wild hair.

"You might want to keep your voice down," Leven whispered. "Brick would be plenty happy to verify what you're saying." Leven looked closely at her. "Do I know you?" he asked.

"I don't think so. My name's Winter."

"I'm Leven," he replied, reaching casually to cover his white streak with his hand.

"Lev," Winter said reflectively, shortening his name, like Clover often did. "That sounds right," she added. "And don't ask me how, but I think I already know you."

Leven stared at her, his mind trying to make sense of what she was saying. She was a different-looking girl. Her strong features would have made her easy to pick on at his school. He half hoped she had come to enroll so that he would drop to second in the pecking order. She had on faded jeans with flared bottoms and a thin blue shirt with a pocket in the front and long loose sleeves. She was either really cutting edge and wearing hip retro clothes, or she was poor and wearing clothes so outdated they were in style again. Her eyes stood out against her light-colored skin and long wild blond hair—they were large and looked like wells of deep green water. She was about four inches shorter than Leven, but the shoes she was wearing made her look no more than three.

"I think I know you, too," Leven finally spoke.

"Weird, isn't it?" Winter responded, appearing relieved to know she wasn't alone in her thoughts. "Us seeming to know each other and never having met, I mean."

"Do you go here?" he asked, nodding toward the school.

"No," she answered.

Leven was captivated by Winter's green eyes, and he gazed at them as he might have looked at a treasured object. As he studied her face, his head cleared and his brown eyes burned gold. Leven had tried many times since that day in the field to see the future again, but had never succeeded. Now all of a sudden it was working again. In his head he saw himself and Winter running. He blinked his eyes and shook his head, puzzled by what he had seen.

"So you're here because . . ." Leven let his question hang, hoping she would complete it for him.

Winter laughed just a bit and shrugged her shoulders. "I think I'm looking for you," she said shyly. "Is that odd?"

Leven smiled. "It would have been a few weeks ago, but it's no odder than some of the things that I've been through lately."

They were silent for a moment.

Winter could hear the voice in her head whispering fiercely. "Don't touch him." She looked at Leven, noticing his straight nose and strong brown eyes. She could see a cautious determination buried deep beneath his somewhat insecure exterior. He seemed to be fighting himself to stand tall and slouch at the same time. His shirt was on inside out, and he had an unusual streak of white hair on the right side of his head. "Don't touch him," the voice warned again.

Normally Winter would have had no problem obeying the warning, but for some odd reason she was drawn toward Leven, as though he were a piece of home or an emotional oasis.

"So what do we do now?" Leven asked, the two of them continuing to look at each other.

"I was hoping you could tell me."

"I can't tell you anything except that I knew something was coming," Leven said. "I think that something is you."

"And I think I've been looking for you."

Leven laughed. "Disappointed?" There was a brief awkward silence.

"I don't think so," Winter said, dipping her head shyly and keeping her hands behind her.

"I guess—" Leven started to say, but he was interrupted.

"Hey, who's the broom with hair?" Brick sneered, breaking into their conversation. He and Glen had grown bored of playing ball, and in their boredom they had spotted their favorite victim, Leven, talking to a skinny girl with wild hair. It was too good to pass up.

"New girlfriend, Skunk?"

"Knock it off," Leven warned.

"Oh, Skunky's unhappy," Brick teased. "Maybe we should help cheer him up."

Leven looked around for someone to help—no one was there. No teacher was *ever* there. The schoolyard was full of kids running and screaming, but as usual, no teacher was on duty. There never was. A big kid with a bat was chasing after a smaller boy. Two girls were playing in the mud and getting dirtier than any student should ever be allowed to get, and the entire seventh grade was taking turns drawing chalk outlines around the bodies of students who were posing as dead and sprawled out on the asphalt.

Sterling Thoughts Middle School was not exactly the best school to send your child to. It was a forgotten school where teachers with no backbone or gumption were sent to teach. Its principal was a noodle of a man who hid out in his office, making occasional announcements over the speaker system and hoping the students would leave his car alone.

Leven's eighth grade teacher was a tall woman who had experienced a nervous breakdown at a different school, so she had been transferred here to bide her time until retirement. All she did was sit behind her desk, begging the students to stop hitting each other and pleading with them to please open their books. Discipline was a rarity and, unlike so many of the other kids, Leven couldn't stand it. He craved order in his life and yet he couldn't find it at any point.

Now here were Brick and Glen, threatening to rough him up once again, and there was not a single adult around to intervene.

Leven thought of lightning—nothing. He tried to kick his gift into gear and still nothing.

"No one's going to help you, loser," Brick sneered. "The sky's clear."

Leven looked to the sky for a brief second, and in that instant Brick swung and punched him squarely in the gut. The air whooshed out of Leven, and he bent forward, holding his stomach. Brick grinned.

"Leave him alone," Winter snapped, stepping up next to Leven, her arms by her sides. "Are you all right?" she asked, looking at Leven over her shoulder.

"I'm fine," he wheezed, embarrassed, his eyes now on Brick.

"That didn't look like a very strong hit," Winter said firmly, making fun of Brick's punch. She stepped closer to the bully.

Glen "Ohhhhed" seriously.

Only one person had ever stood up to Brick, and that person was Nervous Todd. He had been just plain Todd previously, but ever since the lesson Brick had taught him he had been nicknamed "Nervous." He spent his days sneaking around, hiding in corners, and trying to make himself inconspicuous, for fear of saying or doing anything to ever upset Brick again.

"What did you say, you smelly piece of trash?" Brick asked, stepping closer to Winter and smacking his right fist into his left palm. A small crowd gathered, hoping to witness something exciting.

Winter leaned close to Leven. "Want to see something cool I can do?" she whispered.

Leven looked at her, wondering if she was crazy. Before he could

think further of it, Brick lunged out to attack. He got about a foot from Winter before he was stopped in his tracks by his feet turning to solid ice.

"What the—?" he yelled, looking down at his feet. The ice rose slowly, like quicksand in reverse, climbing up his legs and toward his waist. He reached down and tried to pull his legs up but they wouldn't budge. Glen stepped back, eyes wide and mouth hanging open in wonder.

"Help me!" Brick ordered. "Give me your hand!"

Glen inched farther away. Winter looked at Glen and blinked. Glen was suddenly a solid ice sculpture.

Winter turned back to Brick. He was staring at Glen and whimpering. The ice inched up his legs and frosted his fat bottom. He pounded at it, screaming, trying to break it apart. Leven looked on in both astonishment and fear.

"Make it stop!" Brick yelled at Leven. "Help me!"

Leven moved toward Brick as if to help, but Winter motioned him back. The ice continued to migrate north, covering Brick's chest and neck and inching toward his head. The students who had gathered to see a fight were in shock over what was happening and from seeing Brick cry.

"Help me," he sobbed. His arms were now frozen stiff. "Help!" he cried. "H—" the ice covered his mouth, silencing him as it crept over his nose, past his panicked eyes, and then capped him off completely.

Everyone stood there with open mouths, in disbelief. Leven gaped at Winter.

"Did you do that?" he whispered.

"I can't stand bullies," she said.

"Will he be okay?"

"Sure," Winter said, seemingly not overly concerned.

Some of the students had run back into the school and retrieved a few teachers to come and see what had happened. You couldn't retrieve just one or two teachers at Sterling Thoughts Middle School, you had to get five or six before they would have the nerve to come out and investigate. A handful of them crept cautiously out of the building, looking scared. A few students pointed in the direction of Leven and Winter.

"Let's get out of here," Leven said nervously, his brown eyes alive.

"I was just waiting for you to say the word," Winter said, smiling. It is amazing, the amount of confidence a person can have when blessed with the ability to freeze things.

Leven reached to grab Winter's arm and guide her back around the school.

"Don't touch me!" she said sharply, drawing back.

Leven pulled his hand away, looking confused.

"Just don't touch me," Winter said again, this time a bit softer.

The teachers running toward them hollered and ordered them not to move. Leven and Winter did just the opposite, sprinting away, running around behind some portable classrooms, skirting the pond, and topping the small hill where students often met to fight with one another at the end of the school day.

"Where are we going now?" she asked.

"I'll tell you when I know," he yelled back.

Winter smiled, happy to finally have someone besides her calling the shots. They turned a street corner and worked their way back behind a record shop and a shoe store.

"How did you do that?" Leven asked. He was out of breath and stopped to catch it.

"I don't know how," Winter answered, breathing hard and brushing her stringy hair back out of her face.

"She's a nit," Clover said, unseen but not unheard.

"Who said that?" Winter asked, confused.

Clover materialized and smiled. Winter stepped back just a bit, her green eyes wide.

"It's okay," Leven said. "It's just Clover."

Clover leaped from Leven's head onto Winter's shoulder, smiling. "You don't know this, but I think I might know you," he said happily. Winter smiled back. "If so, you were taller before," he added.

"Really?" Winter said, tentatively touching Clover on the back of his head. She slowly began to pet him as if he were a cat. Her smile made it obvious just how delighted she was.

"Sure," Clover purred, his eyes closing slightly. "But we can reminisce later. I think the time has come for us to go," he said, suddenly serious and shrugging Winter's hand off of him.

Leven looked at Winter. Something was finally happening in his life. He felt different than he had felt only moments before. It was time for him to step away from his past and walk into his future.

"I just need to get a few things from my house before we go," Leven replied.

"Well, hurry," Clover insisted. "I've been waiting years for this to begin."

"I can't wait till I know what we're even talking about," Winter laughed.

"Me, too," Leven said seriously, looking at Clover.

"I'd tell you if I could," Clover smiled. "But I was told specifically not to be the one to break the news."

"So tell Winter, and she can tell me," Leven tried.

"I would still be telling Winter." Clover disappeared.

"So, you could—" Leven was stopped by the school gym teacher, Coach Tally. He had been out having lunch when he spotted Leven and Winter running off. A lover of the hunt, he had hidden behind the shoe store and jumped out, and he was now holding Leven by the ear.

"Where are we off to, Thumps?" he asked, his crew cut bristling in the sun. "You should be on campus." Coach Tally was heavy, kept his hair cropped short, and had a perpetually red face. His breath always smelled of garlic.

"Nowhere," Leven said in pain, his ear being stretched to its limit.

"Nowhere's the other direction," Coach Tally yanked.

Winter was just about to turn the belligerent man to ice when Clover came up with an idea. He materialized, sprang from Leven's head, and like lightning hurled himself into the face of Coach Tally, cramming himself into his open mouth. Coach Tally let go of Leven, gagging and choking as Clover began to slip down his throat. He threw his hands to his neck and tried to squeeze Clover out. His eyes bulged, and his face was the color of fire. As Clover meshed into his body, becoming one with the coach, Tally emitted a loud belch and looked desperate and confused. Clover twisted the big body and stood up straight. The coach stared, bug-eyed, at Winter and Leven. They in turn stared back, not knowing what to make of him or what had just happened.

"Now where was I?" Coach Tally said, sounding like himself but with the inflections of Clover. "Oh, yes, Foo."

Under the influence of Clover, Coach Tally pulled a piece of chalk out of his pocket. The coach kept it there to draw circles on pavement, in which he made students stand until they, as he said, "developed character." Coach Clover began to draw on the outside wall of the shoe store.

Leven and Winter were dumbfounded.

"Listen closely because I am only going to say this once and even then I am going to deny having said it." Coach Clover looked around as if to make sure nobody was near. "There is a space between the possible and the impossible—a very real place called Foo." He drew a big circle. "It is a place your mind enjoys keeping from you, yet it is as real as a thick patch of goose bumps or as any strong nagging notion. It exists within the minds of everyone, because without it there would be no room to dream or hope. It was created at the beginning of time so mankind could aspire and imagine. It is an entire realm hidden in the folds of your mind."

Coach Clover was talking with great excitement. Spit was flinging everywhere. He again looked around to make sure no one could overhear what he was saying.

"As real as Foo is, however, it is not easy for someone to get there," he went on. "You can't plan a trip and call your travel agent. Most people who enter Foo do so by accident."

Leven looked around as if confused.

"Pay attention," Coach Clover insisted, tipping a bit. He was having a hard time balancing such a big body. "Now, someone interested in things other than themselves might have, at one point in their lives, noticed that all sidewalks and street corners and roads are

not the same. Some are wide, some are narrow. Some are made of concrete while some are brick or stone. The world is covered with thin, dirt lanes and wide, expansive stretches of asphalt, all of them designed to lead someone somewhere and most of them connecting and crossing evenly, straight, and just as they were planned. There are, however, roads and lanes that are not quite so uniform—street corners and crossings that don't match up as they should. Whether they were designed poorly or constructed by people too lazy to do a perfect job, it doesn't make a difference."

Leven and Winter looked down at the ground they were standing on. It looked all right.

"If you stand between two connecting lanes that don't match up quite right, while the temperature is divisible by seven, and the universe sees fit to fire off a couple of shooting stars, you will get quite a surprise—quite a surprise indeed." Coach Clover spat. It wasn't an impressive spit. The saliva just barely cleared his lips, then sort of drizzled down onto Coach Tally's chin. The big body began to sway back and forth. "The mind will snatch you up instantly and take you to Foo." From the way Coach Clover was teetering, it was obvious that Clover was having a hard time managing such a heavy body. He leaned up against the shoe store to keep his balance.

"How does—" Leven tried to ask.

"Save all questions to the end. Take Gladys Welch, for example." Coach Clover used his chalk to draw a stick figure of a woman on the side of the building. "She was an innocent woman who was simply walking her child on a hot August night when she unknowingly stepped upon the very spot where East Willow Road and Juniper Way haphazardly meet. Who knew that twenty years earlier, when John Packer and Timmy Lance were pouring that sidewalk, that they were unknowingly creating an entrance to Foo? John was in a hurry to meet up with his girlfriend, and Timmy wanted the day to end so he could play a little pool before going home. They had rushed through the job, ignoring the plans and doing a halfway job. Their sloppiness resulted in a less-than-perfect street corner and a potential portal to Foo.

"It wasn't Gladys's fault she stopped to calm her fussy child right there on that particular corner. Likewise, it could be argued that she was simply going about her business when she looked up at the dark sky and spotted a shooting star streaking across the black, like chalk across a newly inked blackboard. Before she could make a wish, however, she was gone, swept into Foo."

Leven and Winter remained silent and amazed.

"Nobody ever saw Gladys Welch again. The papers went on and on about how tragic it was—her disappearance, that is. A young mother taking her child for a walk just up and disappears, the helpless baby left on the corner of a public street alone and scared. Some speculated that Gladys Welch had been murdered; others assumed she had simply abandoned the child; a few suggested she had been abducted by aliens. But no one knew the truth, which is that Gladys had been taken to Foo."

Leven and Winter stood there with open mouths.

"These are the evidences and thumbprints of a place and force nobody knows to worry over or actually even wonder about. No one knows to be careful or to step lightly, but their lack of knowledge doesn't change the fact that all over the world there are street corners and intersections that don't quite match up or evenly meet. And if the heavens have you in their sight, they just might take you before your time and send you, in interim, to a place called Foo."

Coach Clover drew on the wall what looked to be a big raisin and a square sun, when in reality it was supposed to be a brain and a gateway.

"There is no place on earth that even begins to compare with the realm of Foo. In the beginning it was a perfect place set up so there would be room for all those who were born on earth to dream, an area the brain created to hatch the dreams and imaginations the logical, physical world would deem impossible."

"Amazing," Leven whispered.

Clover just couldn't manage the big body any longer, so he decided to wrap it up.

"In conclusion, sycophants are a blessing to us all."

Coach Tally began to quake and teeter. His body was doing the wave. A large lump rose in his throat, and he suddenly expelled through his open mouth the agitated Clover, who landed in Leven's hands. Coach Tally crumpled into a big pile of human on the ground.

Leven and Winter stared at Clover.

"What was that all about?" Leven asked.

"Is that true?" Winter asked in awe.

"I don't know what you're talking about," Clover sniffed. "I didn't say anything."

"Unbelievable," Leven whispered, his brown eyes glowing. "Foo's a real place?"

"My lips are sealed," Clover declared.

Coach Tally began to twitch and groan. Leven led Winter at a quick pace to Leven's house. Addy was at work at the napkin factory, and Terry wasn't at home. He was most likely down at the corner bar telling the waitress his troubles. Leven had planned on gathering a

few things to take with him, but he soon realized he had little to gather. He threw on a thin hooded sweatshirt and shoved some extra socks into his pocket.

As he exited the house the wind was blowing fiercely, causing the huge tree in his yard to sway and violently bend. Small branches were breaking off the limbs, and it looked as if the gigantic trunk might be wrenched out of the ground. Leven gazed at the wind-whipped tree, realizing he might never see it again, and was surprised to experience a feeling of sadness.

He said good-bye to the writhing tree and empty house and he and Winter walked away. As they did so, the wind ceased.

"So you can freeze things?" Leven asked Winter as they headed toward town.

Winter nodded.

"Anything?" Leven asked.

"I think so," she smiled.

"Well, Lev can see the future," Clover bragged, materializing in the hood of the sweatshirt Leven was wearing. "He's an offing."

"You can see the future?" Winter asked, amazed.

"Sort of," Leven answered.

"And," Clover went on, "he can change the future."

"Really?" Winter said as if she didn't exactly believe it.

"I think so," Leven said. "If the timing's right, or if it's necessary, I can make things turn out in a way different than they might have."

"That's pretty cool," Winter smiled.

"Pretty unpredictable," Leven smiled back. "I think I'd rather be able to freeze things whenever I wanted."

"We all have our strengths," Clover said, trying to sound wise.

Winter and Leven looked at him and laughed.

"So where should we go?" Winter asked. "How do we get to this Foo place?"

"I say we head downtown," Leven answered. "Let's find someplace to practice your freezing and my manipulations while we figure out where we're going."

Both Leven and Winter looked at Clover as if to prompt him to speak.

"All right, I think I can let you in on one more thing," Clover said, looking around nervously.

Leven and Winter stared at him.

"We're looking for a person named Geth," he whispered. "He knows the way."

"Geth?" Winter questioned.

"Yes," Clover answered seriously. "He's the only one who knows what's next. He'll find us."

"That's all you can tell us?" Leven asked. "Geth? Can't you take over Winter and tell me more?"

"No way!" Winter gasped, covering her mouth with her hands.

"I think I've said enough for one day." Clover said, then disappeared.

Leven and Winter walked at a fast pace toward town. Leven wished he had a better idea of what his future really was to be. At the moment all he sensed was a new purpose, mixed with equal amounts of panic and uncertainty.

CHAPTER ELEVEN

Taking an Ax for the Home Team

The morning was different from usual on Andorra Court. Yes, the sun rose and the night faded. Sure, the paper boy came by flinging papers. A few automatic sprinklers turned on and off, and Mrs. Pendle stuck her ratty morning head out of her front door. She looked around to see if anyone else was out, then waddled quickly out to get her paper, wearing nothing but the tattered robe her husband had begged her for years to throw away.

As usual nobody saw her.

Actually, that's not completely true. The giant fantrum tree, which possessed the soul of Geth and stood in front of Leven's house, saw her—just as he had seen her every morning for so many years. He had seen everything that had happened there at 1712

Andorra Court—the ends of his branches gazing at all times in hundreds of directions and places.

Geth breathed and shook his leaves as if the wind were pushing through him. He shivered again, knowing the time had finally come. He was strong enough and Leven was gone. He had tried to stop Leven from leaving, or at least get his attention, but the boy had walked off.

At first Addy and Terry had made no mention of Leven not coming home that afternoon. But eventually Terry began to complain about what a stubborn and careless child Leven was to stay away when there were chores to be done. Addy took an hour off of work to both grocery shop and circle around Leven's school to see if he was there. Exhausted, she finally gave up the search and went home and argued with her husband about him finding a job, so she could take a break from folding.

Geth saw it all.

It was not a coincidence that in the afternoon, three quarters of Leven's house was shaded by Geth. Fate had put the Graphs' mobile home right where it sat, and now fate was going to take the next step. As Mrs. Pendle read her horoscope and drank her prune juice, the giant tree in her neighbor's yard was implementing a plan.

Geth would have preferred fate to have matched him up with Leven before the boy left, but what was done was done. Fate needed a little help, and it was now up to Geth to get to Leven. Of course, it's not easy for a tree to just walk down the street and get on its way. Trees have rules they are bound to obey simply because the earth feeds them. There are, however, ways to accomplish things when the need gets desperate, and Geth had been preparing and practicing for just such a situation.

The morning got brighter. Addy's alarm clock rang, and she rolled over and hit the poor thing harder than was necessary. It fell from the nightstand and softly bounced on the shag carpet. Addy sat up and moaned. All that folding had given her carpal tunnel syndrome, and her wrists were hurting like crazy. She felt cheated out of a life of luxury and resented the necessity of having to work. She was sick of it. She picked up the clock and looked at the numbers. Her face was pale green from her dried mask, and her hair, as usual, was a mess.

"A woman of leisure shouldn't have to get up before ten," she grumped to herself, her tongue feeling thick in her dry morning mouth. "Look at him," she added spitefully, glancing at Terry as he lay next to her, unshaven, mouth agape, snoring loudly. He had his knees pulled up to his chest and one arm hanging off the opposite side of the bed—every fifteen seconds or so his left leg would quiver.

Addy had finally had enough. "Get up!" she said, suddenly angry and whacking him on the chest with one of her sore arms. "Get up. I'm sick of it. You need to find a job." The mask on Addy's face cracked.

Terry grimaced and motioned for her to leave him alone.

"Get up!" Addy snarled. "Now!"

"I'm tired," Terry complained. "There's no work out there for me."

"Paul Brogan got a job last week. A good job with benefits," Addy informed him. "That job could have been yours."

"No use talking about it now," Terry whined. "He got the job and I didn't."

"You weren't looking," Addy snapped at him. "Now get up and go look."

"I will this afternoon," Terry said, closing his eyes.

Addy got up and moved around the bed to the closet, making as much noise as possible. She opened the closet door and pushed the hanging items to the side.

Addy's actions got Terry's attention. His right eye popped open; it was sunken and red like a pitted cherry.

Addy pulled out the two brown boxes that sat on the floor of the closet.

Terry's left eye opened; it matched the right.

Addy pulled back the carpet and lifted up the loose board that was hiding Terry's secret drinking money. She had known it was there for years, but figured it was easier to let him have his secret than to have him constantly begging her for money.

Terry's mouth opened. "Hey!" he hollered, jumping out of bed and grabbing for the money she had just snatched. "How'd you know? . . . that's my money."

"Wrong," Addy smirked. "It's *my* money. I earned it and I'll

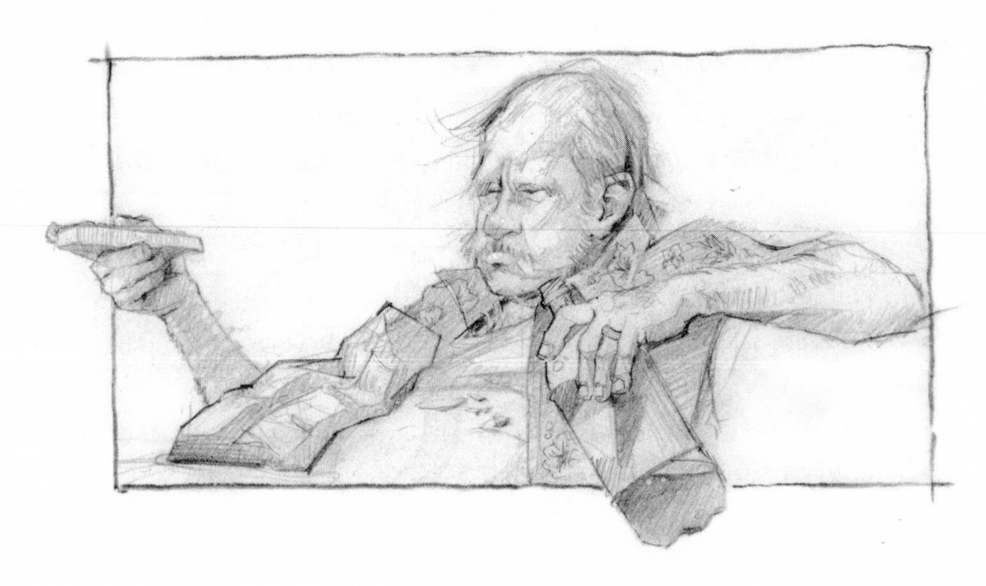

keep it." She stuffed the entire wad deep down the front of her nightgown.

"All right," Terry panicked. "I'll go look for work as soon as I can. I promise." His eyes were opened wide and his mouth sagging. His mushy nose glowed.

"You'll look *now*!" Addy screeched, the veins in her neck bulging.

"Now?" Terry repeated sadly. "But it's early. I can't just be expected to—"

Addy stamped her foot and glared.

"I can't believe I'm treated this way in my own house," Terry complained.

Addy pushed her hair back behind her square head and smiled coldly. "I'll give you the money back as soon as you've found a job."

Terry gaped at her helplessly. Addy smiled even wider.

"Fine." Terry stamped off to the bathroom to pretend he was getting ready for the day. He sat down on the toilet and began to think. This was not the morning he had planned. He rubbed his stubble of beard with his hand and tried to think harder. Sure, he could have spent his mental energy wondering how to find a job, or where the best place to begin looking for work was. Instead, however, every thought was directed toward simply getting that money back so he could blow it as soon as possible at the local bar. Just thinking about looking for work was making him thirsty.

Terry might very well have gone on for hours thinking about the money and growing even thirstier if it had not been for the unexpected tapping on his backside as he sat on the toilet.

He sprang immediately off the seat, screaming and slapping blindly at whatever had touched him.

He yanked his pajama bottoms up and turned to look at the toilet. There, wriggling out of the bowl, like some giant bark snake, was one of Geth's humongous tree roots. It pushed up out of the bowl like a huge serpent, writhing in the air. Terry's jaw dropped. He rubbed his red bloated eyes in complete disbelief. Then, as if to prove it was really happening, the root swelled and the toilet burst, sending water and shards of porcelain everywhere. Terry threw his hands up to cover his face as he cowered against the bathroom door, still not believing what he was seeing.

"What's going on in there!?" Addy yelled from outside the door. "What was that noise!?"

Roots came slithering out of the faucet and drain in the sink, reaching out toward Terry, stopping him from saying anything besides, "Heeeelp!"

The bathroom floor creaked and buckled upward as a huge root pushed up from below the trailer house. Terry fumbled for the door, screaming, wanting nothing more than to get away. He pulled open the door and came face to face with Addy. She was staring at him, her puffy eyes and green face creating a sight almost as frightening as the surreal scene behind him.

"Just what do you think you're doing?" she scolded. "If you've made a mess in—"

Before Addy could finish her sentence, Terry whipped past her. A thick wet root sprang up from beneath the floor, caught him by the ankle, flipped him across the bed, and slammed him into the wall. The whole house began to lift and sway. Addy stumbled. She was horrified and screaming at the top of her lungs. Had Mrs. Pendle stuck her ratty head out her front door at that moment she would have seen the giant fantrum tree surging and pushing the

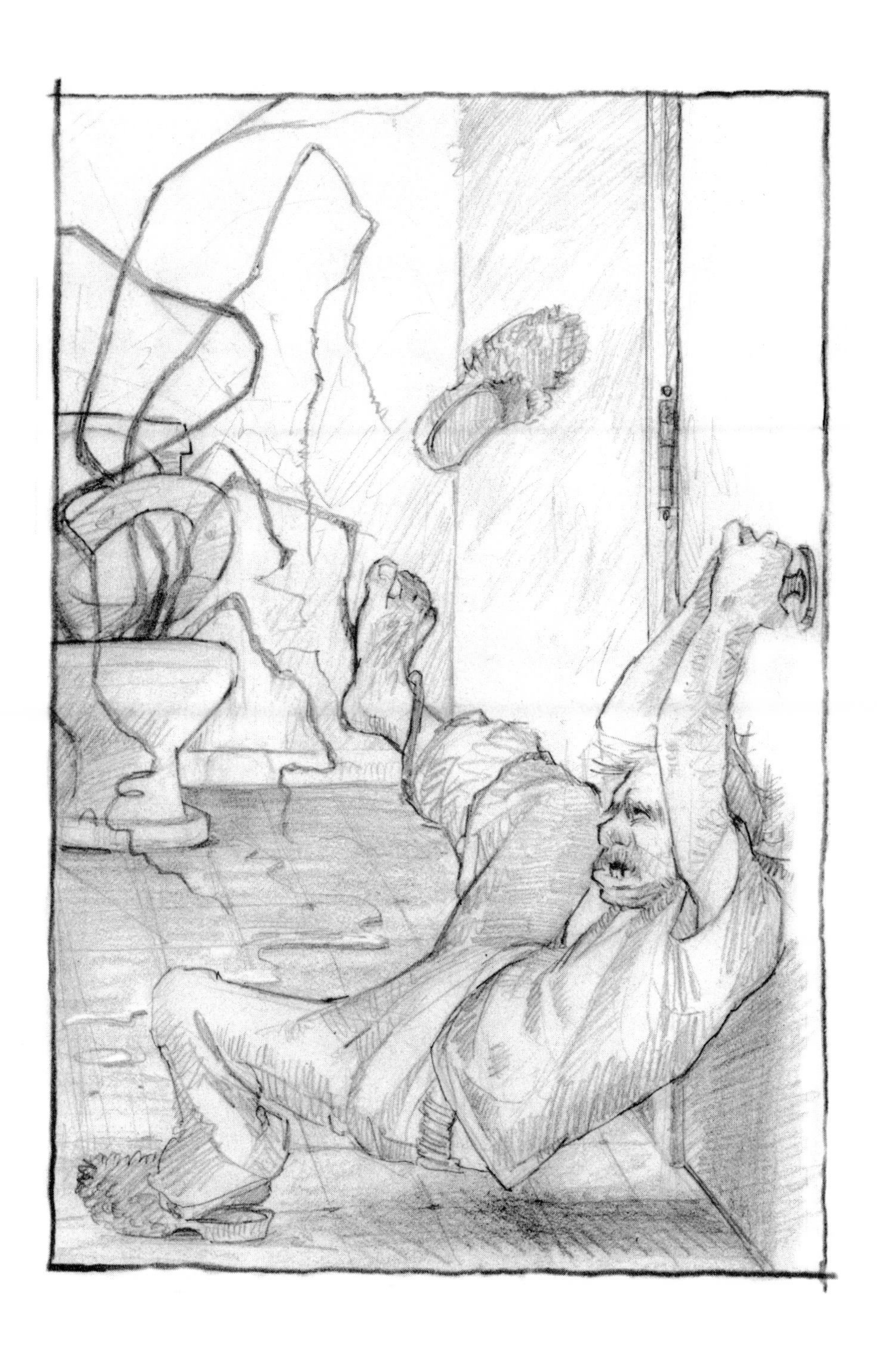

entire house up from beneath, its roots writhing and thrashing like the tentacles of a crazed octopus.

Terry ran for the window. Addy ran for the door. Both were stopped by thousands of tiny hairy roots that latched onto their feet and lifted them into the air and began whipping them around on the mattress.

Trees don't normally smile, but at that moment anyone could have seen the grin on that tree from miles away. The mattress whipping wasn't actually necessary, but Geth felt they deserved some payback for the way they had treated Leven.

After Geth had had his fun, his tiny roots pulled Terry and Addy off the bed by their ankles and dragged them screaming out through the back window. They were whipped about, spun in the air, and dropped with a thump at the base of the tree. Roots were sticking out of every window and door of the trailer house, waving madly.

Before Terry could free himself and run for help, the roots stopped wiggling and began to quickly withdraw, slithering back through the windows and doors and down through the floor of the trailer home. The entire place creaked as it settled back into a crooked, slightly-off-the-foundation position. In a few moments all the roots had disappeared.

Breathing hard, Terry looked at Addy.

"Did you see . . . ?"

"I did," she said, breathing just as hard and fanning her green face. She pushed her frizzy hair out of her face, wailing. It was at that moment she first noticed the bright red ax lying on the ground near her. She hadn't realized they owned an ax. She wiped at her tears. "I don't want you looking for work today," she finally managed to say.

"I told you I shouldn't—"

"I want you to get rid of this tree," she interrupted. "And do it now. It's never been right. Chop it up, sell the wood, and then you'll have the money." Addy worked herself up off the ground and stepped over to the ax. She picked it up, examined its blade, and carried it over to her husband.

"Now?" Terry whined.

"Now!" she almost screamed, thrusting the tool at him.

Terry stood up and tested his knees. He looked back at the house. Through the bathroom window he could see one root still sticking up out of the broken toilet. Suddenly it shivered and water flung off of it as it quickly retracted.

"I don't think my drain snake could fix that," he mumbled to himself.

Terry hefted the ax and moved toward the trunk of the tree. He was really thirsty. He drew the ax back and swung. The blade cut deep into the trunk, as if the tree had relaxed to let the ax slice deeper. Addy was almost impressed with Terry's strength; Terry actually was. He pulled the ax back and whacked again. A chunk the size of a football flew out and landed at Addy's feet. At this rate Terry would have the thing down and chopped up by early afternoon.

Terry smiled.

Geth stood there, taking every blow.

Trees don't really enjoy being cut to pieces. Some recognize their place in the world and accept it bravely, but few would actually provoke a human into chopping it up. Geth had done just that.

Whack!

Geth closed his leaves as darkness began to push upward into his trunk and through his branches. Geth could feel his bark pulling away and beginning to separate from the body of wood. His foliage

trembled with each blow. The air was becoming black and only bits and pieces of the surrounding scenery were clear anymore. The sky smeared and started to slide to the ground as pain made his thoughts dark.

Terry went at the tree with all his force.

Geth swayed. He was dizzy. Standing tall was quickly not becoming an option.

"Timber!!!" Terry shouted, taking one last swing. The ax sliced deep into the remaining trunk and got lodged. Terry began to violently jerk and wiggle it. As it pulled free, Geth, tipsy from destruction, leaned to the east and toppled, his remaining strand of trunk snapping loudly. The huge tree crashed down next to the rear corner of the trailer house, cracking the roof and crumpling a section of wall. It settled with a whump.

Terry looked at the tree lying there. His house was damaged, but still livable. "Stupid tree," he spat. Addy turned and went back inside. She had napkins to go fold.

The giant tree was no more.

CHAPTER TWELVE

DIVIDE AND CONQUER

It is a grand thing to be a stately fantrum tree that stands tall and oversees the world around it. With its massive structure and lush foliage, such a tree can be justifiably proud. Oh, there are a few drawbacks to being a tree. Birds give you no rest with all their constant flittering, chirping, and nesting; kids love to shoot at you with BB guns; and lovers invade your space and wreak indignities on you by gouging their initials into your bark. But those disadvantages are bearable.

There are the more serious drawbacks like, say, death. For example, when a tree is turned into firewood for burning or used to make furniture for sitting. Trees in our world know nothing else. They are born, they live, and then they die. The most they can hope for is to be transformed into the front page of a really historic

newspaper edition, or to be shaped into a cane for an important person, or to be made into a polished banister of some huge mansion.

The giant fantrum tree that Terry chopped down and dismembered had aspired to be something much greater than a chair or an ottoman. Geth knew very well what he was doing when he permitted Terry to take him down. Now it was up to fate to take Geth to the next step.

Terry loaded up the wood and hauled it to a lumberyard two miles from the mobile home park. He drove it there in his beat-up old truck, licking his lips the whole time.

Terry was thirsty. Very, very thirsty.

The owner of the lumberyard, Frank Welt, at first had no interest in acquiring such green wood, but when Terry explained how thirsty he was and said how little he was asking for the load, Frank gave him twenty dollars, and Terry was on his way.

Frank sorted the wood, pulling out the largest pieces and piling them under a tin-roofed shelter. He tossed the twigs and smaller limbs onto a heap of scrap he had drying.

Normally there's not much need to be concerned about what happens to a tree once it's been downed. It's a sad thing to lose a tree, but the loss is generally only temporarily mourned. A chunk of this tree, however, was worth tracking. Six inches beneath its bark, in its trunk, next to its lowest branch, was the heart and soul of Geth. And whereas the ax might have killed the limbs and body of the tree, the heart was still faintly beating in this piece. Geth was not done for yet.

"Lousy drunk," Frank said to himself. "Destroy a beautiful tree so that you can wet your tongue. Pathetic." Frank ran his gloved hand over the wood he had just bought and moved to go.

"Frank," Geth whispered, amazed that his reduced size allowed him to vibrate enough to actually make a noise.

Frank wheeled around, looking for whoever had spoken to him. He saw only open sky and his empty lumberyard.

"Frank," he heard again, this time more loudly and a bit deeper.

"Hello?" Frank yelled.

"Frank," the wood whispered back.

"Who's there?" Frank said, bewildered, knowing nobody was around but him.

"Frank . . ." Geth's voice faded.

Frank looked at the pile of green wood Terry had just delivered. He stepped closer and pushed aside a few of the large pieces, half expecting to find someone buried in the pile. No one was there.

"I must be crazy," he whispered. "I'm the one who needs the drink."

He looked more closely at a section of the tree's trunk. It was a piece about a foot and a half in diameter and two feet long. Protruding from it was a two-inch stump of a thick branch, and almost all the bark had been scraped off it. As he studied it, the chunk of wood appeared to inflate then deflate itself, almost as though it had inhaled then exhaled.

Frank rubbed his eyes, then picked up the piece of wood and held it in his hands. It was warm, and when he squeezed it, his fingers made an impression, as though it were made of clay. The wood reshaped itself as soon as he let go.

"Whoa," Frank whispered. "Odd."

A large truck pulled into the lot and honked, and Frank motioned the driver over.

"I'm here for the Tatum load," the driver hollered.

"I've got it all ready for you around back," Frank replied, nodding toward another shed.

The driver pulled ahead, and as it passed him, Frank tossed the whispering piece of wood into the open bed of the truck.

"One less thing for me to worry about," Frank said, dusting his hands and heading toward the office to get the forms the Tatum driver would need to sign.

ii

Tatum, Inc. was a manufacturer of a variety of products. The company had its hand in plastics, wooden toys, and handles for yard tools. They also had a division that produced indoor fans and one that molded outdoor chairs. Their best-selling item at the moment was a portable grill that flipped the meat for you. They also made rugs, manufactured doll body parts, and were the North American manufacturer of seven types of garden hoses.

They were diversified; a small arm of their business even manufactured wooden paint stirring paddles, popsicle sticks, and toothpicks.

It was into this division of the company that the driver brought the heart of Geth and the rest of the wood from Frank's lumber yard. He backed the truck up to a large metal vat and dumped the load.

Geth buzzed. In order to complete his mission, his heart had to stay intact. He was concerned about being reduced to pulp and made into paper. But he was powerless to resist what was happening. It would be up to fate to take it from here and work him into a position where he could find Leven.

A man with big arms picked up the section of Geth's trunk and heaved it into a rotating bin. Geth tried to call out, but things were moving so fast and there was too much noise. The bin tilted, and its contents were spilled into a vat of liquid chemicals. Geth bobbed around in the smelly mix until he was hooked with a long stick and dragged into an oven. Everything was black and the grinding of loud motors vibrated the building.

The chemical solution Geth had been thrown into was cold, and the heat of the oven was at first welcome, but it soon became unbearably hot. Geth felt as though at any moment he might spontaneously burst into flame. Just as he was ready to give up and turn to ash, he was hauled out of the oven and dumped onto a speeding conveyer belt. Machines whirred, clanked, and screamed around him in the darkness, and he heard the ominous sound of wood going through a grinder. The conveyor belt abruptly ended, and the heart of Geth plummeted down into the grinder. In an instant he was devoured by the blades. The lights in the factory surged and dimmed a bit. One of the workers commented on how that had never happened before and then simply went on with his job.

The rest of the day played out routinely for the workers at the Tatum toothpick factory. The new toothpicks were boxed up and stacked onto pallets and put onto trucks that would deliver them to surrounding states. For the workers, it was an ordinary day. Life just went on.

But Geth was down.

CHAPTER THIRTEEN

Realizing You Have Nothing

You may wonder what a messy-haired girl, an obscure boy, and a chopped up fantrum tree have to do with one another, and in doing so you would be justified. Typically a person wouldn't associate one with the others. A psychiatrist might grow concerned if he or she were to show you an ink blot shaped like a tree and you were to respond, "Young boy," or "Messy girl." But thanks to fate, these three were about to become entwined. Weaved together like a rug that humanity was about to unknowingly wipe its feet on.

It's difficult to know where you belong when the soul isn't even aware of what its options are. You can easily picture yourself behind the wheel of a fast car or lying on a sandy beach because you have seen pictures of or witnessed such things. But how can a person see himself somewhere his mind has refused to show him?

This was the situation Leven was in.

His entire life he had been told where to go, where to sit, where to stand, what to say, how to act, who he was, and who he was not. Now, fate was finished keeping Leven in complete darkness, but the boy still couldn't picture his future. Clover had hinted at Foo, but it seemed like a fable being told by a pretend friend. And Leven had a bigger problem that he was even less aware of.

Sabine was searching for him.

Sabine didn't clearly know it was Leven he was after, but he lusted to find the one who alone had the power to destroy his plan. He couldn't leave Foo to find that person himself, but he had an army to help, thanks to the dark shadows he cast. Sabine's horrid thoughts and evil desires consumed him. In his hatred and greed he had become completely dark in the head, sicker than any being had ever been in Foo, which is quite an awful accomplishment, since over time some pretty foul people had accidentally stumbled into Foo. In fact, a *number* of notable criminals and thugs had made their way into the realm. But even the worst of them paled in comparison to Sabine, who knew nothing but wickedness and rage thanks to an unknown force that controlled him. So profound was the evil within him that the very shadows he cast loathed him and desired to escape his presence.

Of course they could never do so—a shadow cannot exist without a master to cast it. These shadows were a legion of diverse, inky images—short, tall, fat, and thin—desperate, dark, whispering images of Sabine, frantic to escape him, but destined to remain captive to his will. And day by day, minute by minute, Sabine's shadows multiplied, an army of darkness that was ever growing.

Sabine's shadows could do things no other being had ever been able to do. Most remarkably, they could slip in and out of Foo

effortlessly and at any time. Because they were shadows, they were able to insinuate themselves into the dark dreams of men and emerge in reality. Sabine simply had to exhale, and his slavish minions would swoop over the earth, penetrating the minds of any who entertained selfish or conspiring thoughts. A quick intake of breath, and the dark images of Sabine would come back with a swoosh to the being who cast them. So invasive were Sabine's shadowy legions they had the power to affect both those in Foo and those in reality, whomever Sabine sought to harm.

Every morning when he awoke, Sabine would step to his balcony, which looked out over the Fundrals of Foo. He would gaze down with evil satisfaction upon the gathering of his shadows, a gathering that stretched endlessly across the base of Ardion, awaiting his directions. Then he would exhale, sending his envoys out of Foo and into the dark dreams of mankind.

His shadows swept the earth, spiraling down through the dreams of mankind, searching for the one soul who had the power to ruin Sabine's plan—the one soul who could destroy the gateway before Sabine could find it and go through it himself into reality.

Of course, his shadows had been looking for the wrong thing. Sabine had figured that the descendant of the gatemaker would be a grown man—a strong, wise being who could single-handedly step into Foo and destroy Sabine and his evil intentions.

You may doubt their existence, for the shadows of Sabine are not easy to spot, unless you are connected to Foo. But even for those who know nothing of Foo, it is possible to catch a glimpse of them. You can see the shadows searching even now. Watch when a car goes by. See how the light flashes off the chrome, reflecting things so

quickly that the normal eye can't take it in? If you are perceptive enough you'll see the shadows in those flashes.

Observe when someone waves her arm and her silver watch glistens. The shadows are there. If someone flips a coin, you'll see how it catches the light in its rotations but how quickly darkness extinguishes the glimmer. It is in these twinklings that the shadows of Sabine can be observed in their earthly flights. These are the fleeting evidences to those who know that the battle continues—the battle in which Leven and Winter were now very much involved.

The two of them had escaped their horrid lives and now were on a quest, searching for a person or thing named Geth. They had spent an entire day down by the river, hidden behind a thin line of trees, experimenting with their gifts. Winter had her ability down. She was able to freeze anything she chose: water, trees, even an abandoned car. Once the object was frozen, she needed only to touch it and it would thaw.

Whereas Winter had full control of her ability, Leven was struggling to manage his. He felt as if fate kept intervening, keeping him from manipulating the future. If he concentrated really hard he could get his brown eyes to burn gold, but unless the timing was just right, he couldn't clearly see what was coming. The best he achieved was envisioning an older boy crossing the street and being struck by a bicyclist. Leven had concentrated like mad, causing the cyclist to look up at the last moment, swerve around the boy and run instead into a parked car. It was a neat trick that left the boy intact but the cyclist shaken.

After spending a full day practicing, they slept that night under a bridge and woke up cold, hungry, and miserable. They arose and began searching the streets for Geth, a search that seemed futile since

they had no idea what this Geth looked like or where he could possibly be.

Clover was of no help. All he did was repeat over and over, "Fate will work it out. We'll find Geth."

Clover's repetitive mantra got old fast and, out of patience, both Leven and Winter finally told him to keep his thoughts to himself. He responded by pulling his cloak over his head and disappearing. In all likelihood, however, he was probably perched on top of Leven's head.

The town of Burnt Culvert wasn't much to look at. There was an older downtown section where the burned-out shells of a number of buildings still leaned or rested. A giant charred wall stood all by itself. It was scorched and covered with spray-painted messages and drawings. There was a park in the center of town that had green grass and a small Chat-n-Chew Snak Shack near the playground. Some of the buildings on Main Street had survived the fire and been cleaned up years before to give the town an all-American feel. It was really the only stretch of Burnt Culvert that looked put together. The city had installed some antique lampposts and, depending on the season, a variety of colorful flags were hung from them. At the moment all the flags on Main Street were black with orange jack-o'-lanterns stenciled on them. Surrounding the business district on Main Street were the residential areas.

Leven, Winter, and Clover would have been able to live for a while off the money Winter had brought with her. But for some reason that was still being argued, Clover had thrown away Winter's purse. That left them broke, hungry, and homeless. Oh, and a bit fed up.

"So do we just keep walking?" Winter asked Clover as day two

was coming to an end. "It's getting dark, and I thought this Geth was supposed to find us."

"Well, tonight could be the night," Clover said from the top of Leven's head.

"You said that last night," Leven pointed out.

"Fate will work it out. We'll find Geth," Clover repeated, which made Winter wonder again if she hadn't ought to freeze the little pest. She had threatened to before, but he had told her that because he was a sycophant, her gift wouldn't work on him. She wondered if that were true.

The October night was cold, and there was an ominous feeling in the air. Leven wondered if he would not have been better off staying at home and dealing with his miserable life instead of taking on the task of saving the world. At least he would have had a bed to sleep in.

"What do we do now?" Winter asked as they walked down Main Street for the four hundredth time. "Shouldn't you be telling us where to go?"

Clover shrugged. "I'm here to get you back, but I think Antsel would be upset if I started making the decisions. I only know that fate will lead us to Geth."

"Geth, Antsel, Foo," Winter muttered. "I don't think anyone is coming for us."

"Can I bite her?" Clover asked Leven, upset that she was bad-mouthing Antsel, his last burn.

Leven shook his head.

"We've been walking all day," Winter complained. "We've gone down every street and block in this city. We haven't eaten and we're broke."

"Well, it's not my fault that you can't manage your money," Clover countered.

"You threw away my purse," Winter huffed.

"I thought it was an enemy."

Leven listened to them arguing. The night was dark, and the stars in the sky were not strong enough to shine through the orange glow of the street lamps. Leven squinted and could see the neon lights of a diner down the way. His head cleared, his brown eyes burned gold, and in an instant he could see the future. His gift was working, and as usual he had little control of it. He saw Winter and himself sitting at the counter of that diner with nothing in front of them on the counter. He saw an old man beside him and an old woman walking out. He thought for a second. Lights shot across his view and Leven could feel his thoughts physically touching the woman's mind. He suggested she hand the nice-looking children some money. Leven finished manipulating the future and shook his head, returning to the present.

"I thought I saw it breathe," Clover argued, his voice bringing Leven even farther out of his thoughts.

"Purses don't breathe." Winter sighed.

"Maybe not here," Clover said.

Leven stared at the diner down the street.

"Are you okay?" Winter asked him.

"I'm fine," Leven replied. "Let's go get something to eat."

"But—" Winter said.

"It's okay," Leven smiled. "I've worked something out."

Clover stuck his tongue out at Winter one last time and flipped his hood up.

"It freaks me out when he vanishes," Winter complained. "He's probably sitting on top of my head making faces."

"Let's eat," Leven repeated, feeling an urgency to move toward the diner. "And besides, he's my sycophant, so he's most likely on my head making faces."

"So, did you see someone feeding us?" Winter asked as they walked, sounding as if they were animals in a zoo.

"Not exactly."

"Not exactly? What does that mean?"

"It means I helped fate a little bit."

Winter looked skeptical. "That's a nice trick. When it works."

Leven nodded. "Well, if they forget to give us ice in our drinks, you can work a little of your own magic."

They entered the diner and sat at the counter where Leven had pictured them sitting. They were studying the menu when an old woman stopped on her way out of the diner and handed Winter a twenty-dollar bill. The woman had a puzzled look on her face but said the meal was on her.

"I'm glad you're on the good side," Winter said, commenting on Leven's ability to manipulate fate, and now looking at the menu with renewed interest. "I think I would have made her give me more than twenty dollars." Winter reached to pat Leven on the shoulder but stopped herself. Leven noticed her pull back.

"So, what exactly happens if you touch me?" Leven asked. "Do I explode or something?"

"I don't know," Winter said, blushing just a bit. "But I'm pretty sure it's not good."

"How can you know that?" Leven asked. "Maybe that's what's

holding us back." Leven reached over as if to touch Winter on the arm.

She drew back. "Don't!" she warned, loud enough that the man sitting next to them looked over.

Leven pulled his hand back, and Winter smiled to show that it was all in fun.

"The thing is, I don't think it's a joke," she whispered. "Something bad will happen."

Leven shrugged, too hungry to care at that moment. He turned from her to concentrate on the menu. He tried to focus, but his thoughts kept circling around the room and back to the old man sitting next to him. Once again his gift was acting up. There was nothing unusual about the old man. He probably had children and grandkids who loved him, but that didn't exactly do anything for Leven.

Leven's eyes burned gold.

The old man took a bite of sandwich.

Leven's thoughts raced and pulsated. He could see the whole diner. He could see the area outside the diner. Lights flashed and buzzed in his mind. He could see Winter, and once again his thoughts raced and settled in on the old man sitting right next to him.

"Can I take your order?" the waitress asked Leven for the third time.

"Lev," Winter prompted. "She wants to know what you want."

Leven shook off the feeling he was having and focused on the menu. "I'll have the open-faced roast turkey sandwich in butter gravy. And a large glass of milk."

"All right," the waitress said, walking off.

"What were you doing?" Winter questioned. "She asked you three times what you wanted."

Leven would have answered her, but his mind was wandering again. In his thoughts the old man was getting up. He saw him throw some money down and flick a toothpick from his mouth onto the floor.

Leven came out of his thoughts and looked at the old man sitting there. He watched him finish his sandwich and begin to pick his teeth.

"Excuse me," the old man said to Leven. "Could you please pass me another napkin?"

Leven reached for the napkin dispenser and tried to pull one out, but the napkins were packed so tightly it was a struggle to remove even one. He pushed on the dispenser and the silver napkin holder jiggled. Light reflected off of it as it moved and as the glint disappeared Leven thought he saw something in the flash. It was a face, black and hollow. He quickly pulled his hand from the dispenser and glanced to see if anyone was behind him. A thick wisp of black slipped silently out through one of the windows of the diner. Leven would have spent a few moments being frightened, but the old man interrupted him.

"Could I have a napkin?" the man asked again, nicely but still needing a napkin.

"Sure," Leven fumbled. "I'm sorry, I thought I . . . Do I know you by any chance?" Leven asked politely, confused by what he had just seen reflected in the napkin holder. He handed the man a napkin.

"Not that I know of," the old man smiled.

The waitress served Leven's and Winter's drinks and gave them

place settings as the old man stood up. He put down some money, flicked the toothpick he had been using onto the floor, smiled and nodded at Leven and Winter, and left the diner.

"What was that about?" Winter whispered.

"I kept seeing him in my thoughts," Leven said, confused.

"He was sitting right next to you," Winter laughed. "Now you need visions just to know who's sitting by you?"

Leven shook his head. "It wasn't the future," he added. "It was something about the scene." Leven picked up his glass of milk and drank it down in three gulps.

There had been something about that man.

CHAPTER FOURTEEN

I Can See Clearly Now My Head Is Gnawed

Leven was halfway right, there *had been* something about that man, but it wasn't the man himself: it was the small sliver of wood he had used to pick his teeth and then discarded on the floor.

Fate had taken Geth from being a giant tree that stood proudly in the Oklahoma soil to a toothpick that had been loaded into a tiny, clear, plastic toothpick holder on the counter of Tina's Diner. Geth, of course, couldn't see anything; his world had been dark ever since Terry had taken an ax to him. Fate had left him little to work with, only his heart.

He was okay with that. After all, he was alive. He could feel pieces of himself missing, pieces that the machine had shaved off

and distributed to other toothpicks—toothpicks too dead to know what they had.

At the moment Geth was crowded into a pile of hundreds of other toothpicks who were as dead as wood could be. He shook internally and his toothpick body vibrated. The vibration caused the toothpicks around him to move slightly. He vibrated some more and made a little more room for himself. He then began to work his way downward toward where Geth hoped the opening of the toothpick dispenser would be. He felt no real urgency in getting picked next, but he knew of no other way to get out and find Leven.

As he vibrated his way down, a strong wave of understanding rippled through his thin body. Geth could *tell* that Leven was nearby. He couldn't see Leven, but he sensed his presence. He wiggled more frantically through the other toothpicks, rolling himself down toward the little plastic roller with the notch in it. He could feel the weight of the other toothpicks as he settled deeper into the pile, each shift making it harder for him to move.

He rolled again and felt the base of the container against his backside. The notch was filled with another toothpick. He wiggled his end and was able to wedge himself between the other toothpick and into the notch. He had no breath to catch or nerves to calm, but he was jittery. No sooner had he claimed the notch than the small plastic barrel rolled, and Geth popped out of the dispenser and into the fingers of someone. Geth thought for a moment it might be Leven, but he could tell almost instantly the old hands holding him did not belong to Leven Thumps.

Geth felt something pinch him on one end as his other end was jammed between two hard surfaces. He could feel moisture and a tongue.

The old man rolled the toothpick to the side of his mouth and let it rest with just the tip sticking out. Never had Geth felt more useless. It was one thing for a lithen to travel by fate while he was strong and mobile, but it was a whole other thing to trust in fate when he was the size of a sliver and had no real way of doing anything.

The old man rolled the toothpick with his tongue. He pinched the end again and pulled Geth out. He bit down on the top of Geth and turned him just a bit.

Geth's mind exploded, and pain jolted his tiny frame. He felt his mind waver and then as if he were having a vision, light began to seep in. The old man bit again and again—more pain, and even greater light.

Geth saw colors, deep rich colors, and bright lights. He could see the old man's tongue and teeth and bits of food. He was rolled over and stored in the side of the mouth again. The tip sticking out this time was the end where the teeth had perforated him, leaving a hole, and the light was almost blinding.

Geth could see! He saw the diner and the counter and the back of what looked to be a young boy's head. But from the angle he was on, Geth couldn't make out if it was Leven or not.

Roll me, Geth thought as loud as he could. *Roll me.*

The old man rolled the toothpick in his mouth and there, much to the great joy of Geth, was Leven. Sitting next to Leven was a messy-haired girl who had her face down over her plate, eating.

The old man leaned over and asked Leven something. Leven responded, looking confused and concerned. The old man took some napkins from Leven. He blew his nose, which created some terrible turbulence for Geth and was incredibly uncomfortable.

Then he stood, tossed some money on the counter, and flicked Geth out of his mouth.

Geth tried to fall in such a way as to land on Leven, but he couldn't make it happen. He tumbled and fell, light flashing and swirling as he dropped. He hit the floor, bounced, and partially rolled into a crevice between the floor and the metal base of the counter. His eye was wedged into the crack and he couldn't see anything. He tried to roll himself so he could peer up and out toward Leven, but he couldn't budge. He couldn't hear and he couldn't see.

ii

Leven had never tasted anything better. The open-faced turkey sandwich had been hot and smothered with rich gravy. It had been so delicious he began to think about manipulating fate so as to get himself another one. He thought about the old man who had been sitting by him earlier. As Leven savored the deep-fried, honey battered onion rings dipped in ketchup, he wondered what the connection might be between the old man and Geth. He grabbed a napkin for himself and thought about the hollow, shadowy face he had seen earlier in the polished surface of the napkin holder. He closed his eyes and remembered the black vapors that had tried to invade his sleeping porch on the night he had first met Clover.

His mind cleared and his eyes burned gold. He could see the diner from outside. He could see the door open and the counter he was sitting at. He could see beneath the counter and the stool he was sitting on.

Leven leaned over and looked down at the floor. Nothing. He used his toe to kick at a toothpick that lay up against the base of the

counter and noticed a dime by Winter's feet. He leaned down and picked up the coin.

"Can you make wishes on dimes?" he asked Winter. "Or is that just on pennies?"

Winter hadn't said much because she too had been reveling in the meal they had been lucky enough to procure. She had ordered a roast beef sandwich with creamy horseradish sauce and thick homemade French fries. She had also ordered a big slice of chocolate cake and a foamy root beer that came in a mug shaped like a cowboy boot.

"We couldn't have wished for better food," Winter said, as she came to the end of her meal.

"Unbelievably good," Leven said, smacking his lips. "What now?"

"You're the decision maker," Winter pointed out.

They both finished eating. Leven gave the waitress the twenty dollar bill, and she gave him one dollar and seven cents back.

iii

The pain came out of nowhere. One moment Geth was lying there wedged in the crevice, then the force of Leven's kick ripped him out of the space he was in and slammed him up against the metal footing that anchored the counter to the floor. On the end of the footing was a sharp piece of metal edging. The metal tore into Geth, splintering one side of his body and causing him excruciating pain. Geth lay there wishing for death and realizing he had no chance of getting to Leven now. He tried to roll over to better see where he was and realized he was more mobile than before. He

glanced down at his left side where the hurt was so strong, and saw what had happened. The strength of Leven's kick had shaved Geth an arm—a sliver he could bend and move like a real appendage. He pushed away from the footing and rolled back under Leven's stool. He could see Leven's feet and felt his soul soar at the possibility of finally connecting. He pushed off the base and put his newly formed arm to his side so as to roll more efficiently.

He stopped just under Leven's feet.

Leven's right shoelace was hanging low enough that it was almost touching the ground. Geth pushed himself up to it and lay on his backside to try and reach the dangling lace with his new arm.

He could almost touch it.

Leven shifted, and the lace dropped down even farther, touching Geth's body. But before he could catch hold of it, Leven stood up, whipping the lace away, and walked off.

Geth wanted to scream, but that's hard to do when you have no mouth. He wanted to run after Leven, but that too was impossible. He felt like crying, but as any self-respecting being knows, there is no dignity in a crying toothpick.

Geth watched Leven and the girl go through the diner doors and out into the dark and windy night.

iv

Leven stopped just outside the diner and bent down to tie his shoelace, his dark hair blowing all over in the strong wind. Of course, it was nothing compared to what the wind was doing to Winter's hair.

"So what was up with that old man?" Winter asked, trying to hold her hair down.

"I have no idea," Leven answered. "I just kept seeing a close up of him. I thought for a second he might be Geth."

Winter frowned. "I'm beginning to think we made a mistake. It's pretty hard to feel like you're making progress when you don't know where you're going."

Clover appeared, clinging to the front of Leven's shirt. "So where's my food, you guys?"

"I thought you said you'd take care of yourself," Leven said nicely, feeling sorry he hadn't even thought of saving some for Clover.

"Sure, I grazed off the plates of everyone else in there, but it still would have been a nice gesture for you to save me some of yours."

"We need to find a place to sleep," Leven pointed out, ignoring Clover.

"There's always the bridge again," Winter sighed.

"This is beginning to feel hopeless," Leven admitted.

Clover vanished, and Leven and Winter turned toward the river.

V

Geth knew what he needed to do. He was useless in the state he was currently in. Fate had given him vision, and fate had caused Leven to kick him in such a way as to create an arm. Geth knew now that in order for him to get anywhere he needed to make a few more changes to himself. Without some work, he would be dead. He lay on the floor wondering what the best way to do that would be.

He closed his eye and thought.

After a few moments he rolled to his left side and pushed off into the walkway of the restaurant, where the heavy foot traffic was. Waitresses and waiters and customers were walking back and forth, going about their business with no concern for the small sliver of wood underfoot.

It was now up to fate again.

A teenager with green hair and heavy shoes was the first to unknowingly kick Geth. He skidded across the floor and came to rest next to a booth a heavy woman was currently trying to work herself out of. The woman's high heel on her left shoe came down on the bottom end of Geth. His vision went momentarily black, as pain stronger and more massive than he had ever felt ripped through his body. He could see stars, and stars circling around those stars, and moons and lightning. He was half glad he didn't have a mouth for fear that his scream would have garnered a lot of attention. The woman moved off, leaving Geth there on the floor, writhing in pain. He looked down at his crumpled end and winced. He would have taken some time to feel sorry for himself, but the waitress who had been serving the large woman stepped up to the booth to see how much of a tip she had earned.

There was no tip.

The waitress stamped her foot in anger. "Well, thanks a lot," she muttered, hoping the stingy customer might look back and see her making a nasty face.

Geth might have been slightly interested in the entire exchange, if the waitress's stomp had not come down on the upper part of his thin body. He was now one tiny bruise. He rolled beneath the bench so he could recover a bit before going on.

"Ohhhh," he moaned.

Geth instantly stopped moaning. Noise had come out of him. "Amazing," he whispered. He couldn't hear what he was saying for lack of ears, but he could feel the sound within his head.

He lifted his left arm to the small hole beneath his eye that the stomping waitress had caused. He had a mouth. He looked to the bottom half of himself where the pain was still strong. The high heel had split his lower half perfectly. He moved his newly formed legs. Geth breathed hard.

He pulled himself up, and stood, took two steps, and smiled. Fate had worked him over pretty well. Geth wasn't done yet, however. He spotted the sharp point of a screw sticking out from the base of the bench.

"I can't stop now," he said to himself.

Geth took a deep breath, closed his eye, and smacked the side of his head into the tip of the screw. The pain was horrific, but nowhere near as bad as the high heel had been. Geth wobbled and felt lightheaded as noise rushed into him.

He could hear.

He whacked the other side of his head on the screw to make another ear and then worked on boring out a hole to smell with. It wasn't actually fun, but the results were miraculous. He could hear, he could smell, and he could walk. Geth tried to jab a hole for a second eye, but he could bang his head only hard enough to make a shallow dent—not a deep enough hole to see out of. Knowing what he had to do, he walked to the far underside of the bench, turned, and ran full speed toward the screw tip.

Now you might not think what Geth was doing too heroic or amazing. But if you had been under that bench and had watched

that toothpick run valiantly across the floor and hurl himself face-first into the end of a sharp screw, you would have been quite impressed . . . or fairly mortified.

Geth was screaming in pain, but he now had two eyes, one a little lower than the other on his skinny toothpick face.

A family who had slipped into the booth above him heard the tiny screaming and assumed it was a mouse. The mother jumped up on top of the bench, and the father got the manager, who insisted they must be mistaken. The diner was rodent-free and would they like to keep their voices down and enjoy a complimentary piece of pie for their troubles? The family accepted the offer, but moved to a different booth.

Geth caught his breath and looked around. He could now see well. Even with one eye located slightly lower than the other, he had a full range of sight. He opened and closed his mouth and smiled. He bent his legs and jumped. He flexed his arm. He had only one and it was a bit stiff, but he would now be able to fend for himself. He stuck his head out from under the bench to see if the coast was clear. It had not been long since Leven left, and with any luck Geth could get out of the diner and catch up to him.

The door of the diner was closed, and Geth could see no opening around it. He watched a couple of people come in and he figured it was now or never. He bolted out from under the bench and sprang across the floor as the doors were swinging to a close. He sprinted harder and jumped just as the doors were shutting.

He didn't make it. The doors came together, closing tight with him wedged between them. All the pain and agony he had endured from being stepped on and split apart and poked and gouged were nothing compared to what he now felt. He tried to scream, but he

couldn't open his mouth. Trapped as he was, he couldn't move his arm or legs or see anything. He was just a squashed toothpick caught about an inch off the ground between two gigantic, heavy metal doors.

It was a full six minutes before someone walked out of the diner and Geth was able to drop to the ground and roll out to freedom. He was in such agony he could barely move, but he knew if he stayed in the pathway he would only get beaten up further. He crawled into the grass just to the side of the door and flopped over onto his back. He looked up at the sky and wondered what in the world he was doing.

He began to laugh.

Geth was not a toothpick. Geth was the last heir of the great realm of Foo. He was a king and a leader. He was crucial to the well being and survival of all mankind. Yet here he was: a beaten up toothpick, tossed to the side of a diner, in the middle of nowhere.

He thought of those back in Foo and how they would react if they could see him now. He thought of his enemies and the joy they would have knowing the state he was in. He thought of Sabine and the satisfaction Geth's plight would give that dark figure. His body hurt. Being trapped by the door had crushed every bit of him, but it had also given him total mobility. Fate was too good to him.

Geth closed his eyes and fell asleep in the grass.

CHAPTER FIFTEEN

RUN FASTER

Leven and Winter walked toward the tree-lined river. In the darkness they made their way carefully through the woods and came to a dry rocky patch of bank. The still night air was cold and clammy.

"That old man has something to do with us," Leven insisted, still puzzled over the feelings he had experienced at the diner.

"How are we supposed to know who we are even looking for?" Winter asked in frustration.

Clover had been riding in the hood of Leven's sweatshirt. He showed himself and smiled at Winter. "You'll know." His nose wiggled.

"Why do we need him?" Winter questioned, gesturing toward Clover.

"He knows the way," Leven said.

"This is ridiculous," Winter moaned. "We've wasted—"

A rustling in the woods shut Winter up. Leven put his finger to his lips. A sudden wind blew and again there was the noise of something moving amongst the trees.

Clover disappeared.

"Hello?" Leven asked the wind.

A low moaning commenced.

"Something doesn't feel right," Winter whispered.

No sooner had she said the words than the trees around them began to bend inward over them. Dark vapors soared through the trees and swept low over their heads, whispering.

"You see us, you see us," the shadows whispered.

"Run!" Leven yelled.

It was a silly thing for him to say. Winter was already sprinting off through the woods with Leven frantically dashing after her. Branches scratched and whipped at them as they fled, while the dark shadows swarmed around them, encircling their heads and penetrating their noses and mouths.

Screaming in terror, Winter came to a sudden stop, with Leven right behind her. He looked to see what had stopped her and gasped.

The dark shadows were gathered in front of them in a tall, hissing spiral. Beneath the swirling mass, the ground suddenly erupted, heaving up a gigantic mound of rocks, dirt, and twisted foliage. Rising out of the fractured earth, a huge shape emerged. Shaking dirt and tree branches off its massive head and shoulders, it grew as big as a building—with a thick, wide body, like that of a bullfrog. It stood on four sturdy legs with thick scales covering its belly and its white eyes burning over a cavernous, wet mouth. A layer of rocks and dirt covered its back.

The beast breathed, showering mud and rocks on Winter and

Leven. The blast stung Leven's bare arms, and a gob of smelly mud filled his right eye.

The beast bellowed, snorted, and moved toward Leven and Winter. The shadows laughed hideously, hissing and screaming.

Winter and Leven backed away from the beast, eyes wide, their hearts in their mouths, and their minds spinning. Leven was quaking with fear almost strong enough to cause him to simply give up and be swallowed just to be done with it.

The beast bellowed again, giving Leven the courage to move.

"Get into the trees!" he yelled.

Winter and Leven ran back into the trees. The beast lumbered after them but was stopped by the heavy growth. It screamed and again spewed mud all over. Leven and Winter ran even faster as mud clods showered around them. The shadows were nowhere to be seen.

"Stop!" Winter yelled as they came into a clearing.

Leven was happy to oblige. His lungs were burning and his legs about to give out. He bent over with his hands on his knees, sucking in air.

"It can't run any farther," Winter gasped. "I think the trees stopped it."

Leven lifted his head and squinted into the darkness. He couldn't see a thing. "What *was* that?" he wheezed.

"Like I know?" Winter said. "It—" An ominous rumbling noise caused her to stop talking. "Oh, no," she whispered.

The noise was coming from the direction of the beast, and it was quickly getting louder.

Leven squinted into the darkness. A huge mound of earth was rolling toward them. The trees and foliage above it lifted and lowered as it came closer. As the burrow exited the woods, the ground broke open, and the beast they thought the trees had stopped erupted out of the earth once again. It looked much bigger and more angry than it had before.

Leven's mind spun as he tried to think of something to do. "Freeze it!" he yelled, remembering Winter's gift. "Freeze it!"

Winter trembled and closed her eyes. Ice began to build over the beast's ankles and on its scaly belly. He pitched and swung his massive head wildly, spewing clods of mud from its mouth in every direction. Ice quickly encased him, sealing his angry mouth and silencing his hideous roars.

Leven looked at Winter in awe. "Unbelievable," he breathed.

Winter was about to accept the compliment when a loud sizzling noise began to come from the huge block of ice. The beast beneath the icy cage groaned and shook violently. The ice covering him exploded with an ear-splitting crack, hurling huge chunks and shards of ice everywhere. Leven barely had time to cover his face before he was struck in the side by a heavy piece of ice that knocked the breath out of him. While trying desperately to breathe, he could see Winter lying unconscious on the ground.

The monster was now ice-free, and angrier than ever. Leven closed his eyes and tried to see the future. But he was no better at managing his gift now than before. He couldn't see anything but fear.

Hoping to manipulate fate into destroying the beast for him, he willed the beast to be gone. Nothing. The beast lumbered closer. Leven's mind cleared and he could see a possible solution. The solution involved him picking up Winter. He looked at her as she lay there and remembered her voice warning him not to touch her. He shook the warning off and bent over to pick her up.

The instant Leven touched Winter, there was an explosion that stunned him and made his ears pop. The world began to spin. The air around him appeared to melt and drip downward, and the landscape became smeared, as though a giant hand were being dragged across a still-wet portrait. Shooting stars traced crazy patterns in the sky, and big dots of burning light rose and fell on the horizon.

Then, like a spinning coin settling, things began to revolve more slowly and finally ceased moving entirely.

The beast roared again. Leven had no time to contemplate what had happened. He slid his arms under Winter and strained to lift her. Straightening, he looked into the white eyes of the approaching beast and shifted Winter in his hold. He turned and ran as fast as he could, through the trees and out onto the open prairie, praying his plan would work.

The monster stomped madly, hesitated for a moment, then plunged into the earth and began burrowing after them. Carrying Winter in his arms and trying to run was exhausting. Her weight was breaking Leven's back. His shoulders ached and the muscles in his arms were burning. Leven shifted Winter and pushed forward faster.

Winter began to stir. Still dazed, she looked up at Leven as he ran.

"What are you doing?" she moaned.

"Saving you!" Leven's heart and legs ached as his mind tried to calculate how much farther he needed to go.

Oklahoma is a relatively flat state. No Alps, no Rockies. If you rolled a ball in most places of the state it would stop eventually, due to there being no slope. There was, however, a cliff just to the east of Burnt Culvert. It was a sheer drop-off that towered over the vast prairie far below. It was a site where long ago, Native Americans used to drive huge herds of buffalo over its edge. The buffalo wouldn't see the drop until it was too late, plummeting by the hundreds to their deaths below.

It was toward that cliff that Leven was now running, his arms and shoulders screaming with pain from carrying Winter and his legs going numb. He pushed on across the prairie, listening to the rumble of the burrowing beast behind him. Leven peered into the darkness. He couldn't see, he was exhausted, and he was leading a giant dirt clod to a cliff that would more than likely kill him and Winter before it killed the beast.

The earth directly below him began to rise, and Leven struggled to keep his balance on the hurtling mound that had caught up to them. It was as if he were surfing a gigantic, speeding dirt wave. He teetered, trying to stay on top of the burrowing monster as it rushed forward. Leven peered ahead and prayed that his memory and calculations were correct.

"Get ready to fall!" he hollered to Winter as he held her, the rumbling of the earth so loud he had to yell.

"What?" Winter screamed.

Leven didn't have time to answer. He shifted Winter in his arms, closed his eyes, and leaped sideways off the mound of speeding

earth. He hit the ground hard and lost his hold on Winter, who flew out of his arms and rolled away.

The giant burrowing creature was caught by surprise. Before it could adjust for Leven's departure and change its course or slow down, it hurtled through the wall of the cliff and out into space, hundreds of feet above the prairie floor below.

Leven and Winter crawled as fast as they could to the edge of the cliff and looked over. The beast traveled beautifully through the air, arching past the quarter moon and dropping to burst violently on the hard ground far below. Even with Leven's poor eyesight he could see the tremendous explosion of dirt and debris of monster.

Leven rolled over onto his back and tried to catch his breath. Winter sat up and began to assess how many injuries she had.

"Do you think that killed him?" she asked, pulling dirt and twigs from her hair.

"Let's not stick around to find out," Leven said, getting to his feet.

Clover materialized and Leven shook his head in amazement.

"Where were *you?*" Leven asked.

Clover ignored the question. "That was impressive," he glowed. "Only an offing could have pulled that off."

"Yeah, well, thanks for the help," Winter complained. "The first sign of trouble and you disappear."

"I couldn't help it," Clover explained. "If the shadows had seen me, we would have been in an even bigger mess."

"Do you know what that was all about?" Leven brushed off his knees and his backside.

"Ah," Clover waved. "It was just an avaland, and a huge one, I might add. I'm sure Sabine's shadows set it free."

"Sabine's shadows?" Leven asked. "Is that what I keep seeing? Who's Sabine?"

"I can't say," Clover insisted.

"Of course not," Leven complained.

"Let's just get out of here," Winter sighed, looking toward the black sky. "I don't like this prairie, it—" Winter stopped mid-sentence. For a moment Leven thought she had seen something else alarming, but she just stared at him.

"You touched me," Winter whispered, her eyes big with the realization.

"I had no choice," Leven apologized. "You would have been eaten, or buried, or muddied."

"Muddied?" Winter smiled slightly.

"I don't know what dirt monsters do," Leven said, flustered, the white streak in his hair bright under the partial moon. "I had to pick you up. Besides, nothing really happened. The air just—"

"Listen to him," Clover said admiringly. "Nothing happened. You shot an avaland out of a cliff," Clover bragged. "Don't sell yourself short. That was very im—"

"I was talking about touching Winter," Leven clarified.

"Oh," Clover said.

"I hope we're not in too much trouble." Winter said, looking worried.

"I guess we'll find out either way," Leven added.

Clover disappeared, and the two of them made their way past the trees down to the river and over to the bridge. They were only just beginning to understand the magnitude and danger of what was ahead. It had been quite a night.

CHAPTER SIXTEEN

Picked Out of a Crowd

The shadows were not stupid. They were the castoffs of Sabine and his darkness, but they were not without wit and cunning. At the moment they were angry and desperate. They had been looking for Leven for some time and still nothing. Their problem was they were looking for a grown man with a crown and a scepter, not an obscure kid with bad eyesight and a white streak in his hair.

Okay, they were a little stupid.

Sabine had not been sleeping well. He could feel the pace of things ratcheting up. He could sense his shadows were close to capturing the prize, but he could not get a clear picture of what that prize was. He had exhaled and bidden his shadows to stop holding back. He had willed them to feel the air, the dirt, and the wind in an effort to discover who they were after.

They had assembled and descended in full force to do their master's bidding.

They had identified a few "persons of interest" whom they felt compelled to investigate—an old man in Germany who had an odd aura, a prince in Saudi Arabia with a look about him, a Canadian with a dark visage who appeared to draw the shadows in, a retired couple in Florida that might have magical powers, a woman in Mexico who was hiding something, and a young boy in Oklahoma who could see shadows. Each of these individuals had aroused Sabine's suspicions.

In his evil quest, Sabine instructed his shadows to fall upon each of these persons and observe his or her reaction. The shadows had conjured up avalands and telts as an ordeal for each. Confronted by these apparitions, the German cried, the Arabian cowered, the Canadian fainted, the Florida couple locked themselves in their double-wide and trembled, and the woman in Mexico tried to put a curse on them. Only the young boy in Oklahoma had thought his way through and escaped his ordeal.

Sabine dismissed them all except the boy. It is not easy to escape an avaland. He doubted Leven was the one only because he was so young, but upon further thought Sabine decided the boy's age might be the perfect deception. He sent his shadows once more. They spiraled out of Foo, locating the boy as he slept and invading his mind. Sabine could instantly tell that this was the heir of the Gatemaker. Someone or something from Foo had touched this child. That touch had left a mark on the dreams of Leven, which were different from the dreams of any other human. He clearly had a connection to Foo, and he had been touched by a nit.

Sabine roared. The only possible way for Leven to have been

touched by a nit was for one to have made it out of Foo through the gateway.

Sabine raged and breathed every last shadow down upon the boy as he slept, penetrating Leven's dreams. They screeched and whispered and hissed, filling Leven's head with a cavalcade of dark images calculated to convince Leven that he was worthless, without merit, and insane to take even one more step on the journey he had begun.

"Go home, go home," the shadows whispered. "Impossible. Impossible," they hissed.

Sabine's dark shadows were more powerful and dangerous than a whole herd of avalands could ever be. All night long Sabine's demons tormented Leven, filling his brain with frightening images and feelings of inferiority and hopelessness. They ceased afflicting him only when the first hint of light surfaced in the morning and Sabine inhaled, summoning his shadows out of the recesses of Leven's now-darkened brain and back to Foo.

CHAPTER SEVENTEEN

DIRTY ROTTEN

Winter awoke to the sound of Leven tossing and moaning. She had slept under the opposite side of the bridge, where there was more room. Now he was awake. She could see him crawling out from under the bridge and looking around. His hair was a mess and he had a lost and vacant look in his brown eyes—as if someone had stolen his personality as he slept. He had scratches on his arms and face and a big bruise on his left cheek. She looked at herself and observed the nicks and cuts she had suffered in their flight through the trees and in her fall from the beast.

She sat up. "Where are you going?" she hollered to Leven.

Leven squinted, looking over at her. "I'm going back." He pushed his dark bangs away from his face.

"Back where?" Winter asked, crawling out from under the

bridge and assuming he was referring to the diner and the intriguing old man they had met there.

"To my house," Leven said dully.

"To get something?"

"No, I'm done, Winter." He looked ashamed. "This is not how it should be," Leven said. "We have been wandering the streets with nothing to show for it. This isn't right."

"What about last night?"

"What about last night?" Leven questioned. "Oh, yeah, we almost died," he added sarcastically. "So you can freeze things and I can see stuff. How do we know that everyone else can't do those things?" Leven rubbed his forehead and winced as he touched one of his bruises. "I'd trade my gift for the possibility of not ever getting beat up by dirt again." He shook his head. "We're fooling ourselves."

"It's different and you know it," Winter said sadly. "I can feel it, Lev. I found you. You're supposed to do this."

"Do *what?*" he asked. "I can't do *anything*. I'm nothing but an orphan who has no family and no friends. I live on a porch because those who know me can't stand to have me in the house. I got a C in math, a B in English, and a C-plus in science. I am average, unwanted, and of no use to anyone. Now I'm supposed to believe a furry ball . . . "

Clover materialized sheepishly on Leven's shoulder.

" . . . when he tells me I can save the world? Come on, Winter, this is crazy." Leven looked distressed, as if the words he was saying were painful to expel. The shadows had convinced him well. "I wish I were dreaming so I could just wake up and have it all over with. I can't make this better."

"Well, if you leave now you don't have to worry about ever dreaming again," Clover said, brushing his forearms.

"What's that supposed to mean?" Leven said, trying not to look directly at Clover.

"If Foo falls, it's over for all of us."

"Foo?" Leven said, shaking his head. "I don't believe in Foo. I don't believe in *you,*" he said, pointing toward Clover, "and I don't believe in you," he said, looking at Winter. "I'm sorry," Leven added, "I guess I don't believe in me."

"Lev . . ." Winter tried.

He waved her off. "There is no way the world could be dependent upon me. And if by some chance it is true, then we're all in big trouble." Leven turned and began to walk off. He stopped, lifted Clover from his shoulder, and set him on the ground. "Stay here."

"I can't," Clover said sadly.

"Don't you have to do what I say?" Leven asked.

"In theory," Clover shrugged.

"Then I order you or command you or whatever the strongest instruction I can give you is, to stay away from me. Stay with Winter, understand?" Leven said sadly.

Clover looked hurt and confused.

Leven was gone.

ii

Geth could not believe how bright the sun was. He opened his eyes to find it almost directly overhead, burning like a celestial bonfire. He rubbed his eyes with his left arm and sat up. He could hear birds singing and see people walking in and out of the diner he had

escaped from the night before. He shifted in the grass and stood. His entire tiny body ached. His final slam in the door last night had been fate's most brilliant move. After that impact he was now flexible and much more mobile then he could have ever imagined. He could bend at the waist and even twist his top half to look around.

He gazed at his single arm and wished for fingers. They didn't appear instantly, but he felt confident that before too long, fate would hook him up with digits of his own. He also put in a silent plea for another arm.

Geth moved away from the grass and over to the gutter. An old man hosing down the sidewalk was creating a nice-sized stream of water, and a small piece of paper came floating by. It seemed too fateful for Geth to ignore. He did his part and jumped off the curb and down onto the paper raft.

He sloshed back and forth as the little scrap of paper danced over small ripples and twisted around a corner. A child crossing the street stepped into the gutter, creating a splash that showered the raft and flooded Geth's eyes. He wiped away the water and could see a culvert into which the water was flowing at the end of the street.

Geth lay back on the paper and enjoyed the ride as his little craft swirled through the culvert and bobbed along toward the river. Eventually he got caught up in a tangle of leaves and trash. Geth abandoned his raft and dove into the current, letting it carry him further. Using his single arm to guide him and kicking his legs, his light little body was swept along in the cool water.

He imagined he looked quite impressive.

The culvert eventually emptied out onto a large cement spillway. Geth skimmed along the bottom as the shallow stream of water

thinned to a trickle. Twenty more feet and Geth could feel the cement rubbing against his belly. Five feet later the stream of water was so diminished that Geth no longer floated, he dragged. He pulled himself out of the trickle of water and looked into the sun. He shook his legs and wiped off the tip of his head.

"What now?" he asked himself. He was standing in the bottom of a huge cement cistern with sides too high for him to climb and the sun beating down. A few dark clouds in the distance drifted closer.

Geth followed the miniscule string of water as it dribbled down toward the end of the waterway.

"I could use a little help," Geth said aloud and to nobody in particular. "I mean, I'm all for doing my part, but being a toothpick is not exactly the greatest confidence builder."

He reached a metal grate where the trickle of water fell into a deep, dark hole. A big pile of trash had gathered at the opening. Geth climbed to the top of the heap and looked down. After a few seconds of thought he stepped through the grate and blindly jumped into the darkness, anxious to see where fate would take him. He squeezed his legs together, tucked in his arm, and held himself rigid to look more like a traditional toothpick. Down he dropped into the musky, dank-smelling darkness, landing legs first and impaling himself almost body deep in the soft mud at the bottom of the hole. Due to the pressure of the foul smelling muck, he couldn't move his arm or even wiggle his legs. He couldn't speak, and he could see only a little bit from his slightly higher right eye.

Geth was stuck.

iii

Winter walked slowly down the road. She had no money, no direction, and no idea what she was going to do. She knew perfectly well that Clover was sitting on her head or clinging to her back or holding onto her leg, so she didn't feel completely alone, but she did feel completely helpless. To make matters worse, the once-blue sky was quickly filling with clouds.

"What do we do?" she asked.

"I don't know," Clover answered, the direction of his voice making it obvious that he was holding onto her leg.

"You're supposed to be helping," Winter said.

"I'm only supposed to make sure Lev makes it safely to Foo."

"Well?" Winter said.

"Well, this is just a minor setback," Clover insisted.

"*Minor setback?* This is a disaster. How can you return Lev to Foo if you don't even have him?" Winter's green eyes burned.

"It's not all my fault," Clover said, still invisible but climbing higher up Winter. "You were assigned to him as well."

"What?"

"You were . . . oh nothing," Clover said quickly.

"Show yourself, Clover."

"No."

"Clover Ernest, you show yourself this instant," she demanded.

"No."

"Listen, Clover, I am in no mood to goof around," Winter insisted. She stopped and began turning as if to spot him. "I have come all this way and have had nothing but trouble. Now you're saying I'm 'assigned'?"

"I talk too much," Clover admitted. "I shouldn't have said anything."

"If we're going to get Lev back I have got to know what's going on." Winter stopped, turning in an attempt to see Clover. She was a bit dizzy.

Clover materialized on her right shoulder. "I guess it won't hurt to tell you a few things."

"Good. To start with, who am I?"

"I'm not totally sure," Clover admitted. "All I know is that Antsel said there would be another to help lead Lev back to Foo."

"And that's me?"

"I think so." Clover scratched his head. "It's obvious from that ice trick you can do that you are a nit. It seems sensible that they would send a nit to help Lev back."

"And why's that?" Winter questioned.

"Nits are extremely loyal," Clover explained. "They stay true to their purpose no matter what."

Winter was silent as she thought. Dark clouds continued to pile up in the sky.

"That's a compliment," Clover pointed out. "Of course Sabine's a nit, and, well, he didn't exactly stay loyal."

"So there are others like me?" Winter asked.

"Of course," Clover said. "Thousands."

"Thousands," Winter whispered.

"Nits are those humans who are born on earth and stumble into Foo by accident," Clover explained. "As they adapt to Foo they take on a certain and unpredictable trait. You must have liked ice. It's a popular talent."

"So I've been to Foo before? I'd think I would remember that."

"Let's just say there's way more to you than you currently know."

Winter smiled. The thought of there being more like her was a revelation. And that she had some special purpose was exciting. "We have got to get Lev back," she said strongly.

"Maybe we should find Geth first," Clover suggested.

"So who is this Geth?" Winter asked.

"Well . . . since I already blew the secret," Clover said, bending over to brush his ankle hair, "I guess it wouldn't hurt to tell you." He cleared his throat, then said, "Geth was cursed by Sabine and brought here by Antsel so he would not be destroyed. Last I heard, he was a seed."

"But, who is he?"

"He is the last heir and king to the Order of Wonder. He is also one of the few who knows where the gateway to Foo is."

"You came through. Don't you know the way there?"

"Antsel kept me hidden," Clover said. "The fewer who know, the safer it is."

"So why does Geth need Lev? Why does he need any of us? Can't he just go back himself?"

"Antsel didn't tell me everything," Clover said sadly. "I'm just a sycophant. But from what I heard while hiding out on the ceiling and eavesdropping in Antsel's room all those years ago, Lev is of some major importance as well. I think it has something to do with him being related to someone important."

"So we have to find Geth," Winter said seriously.

"I've been saying that for a week," Clover pointed out.

Winter shook her head. "Do you have any idea where he could be?"

"Well," Clover said, "he *is* a king. Are there any castles around here?"

Winter was highly discouraged.

iv

Geth struggled in the mud. It was of no use. No matter how hard he wiggled or strained he couldn't pull himself out. The foul smell of the storm drain was almost nauseating, and if he had not been a lithen he might have figured himself for dead. But, seeing how he was a lithen and had great faith in fate, he simply closed his eyes and waited.

He had been asleep no more than a couple of hours when the rumbling began. Geth could hear the thunder tearing up the sky outside and above him. In a moment the sky opened up and proceeded to squeeze every bit of moisture out of the heavy clouds. Rain fell like cats and dogs and then tigers and elephants. Water poured off roofs and down rain spouts, running into the gutters and quickly turning the streets into wide, wild rivers. A small dog was washed away, a car was spun around, and store fronts all along Main Street were flooded as the deluge increased. Storm drains were quickly filled to capacity and water surged through them like a runaway train through a tunnel.

Geth just waited.

He could hear the distant rush of water, and then all at once the hole he was in was flooded, the water crashing down on him in a thunderous wave. The muck around him loosened and he could feel his legs again. He wiggled as the torrent of water cascaded over him, and suddenly he was loose and being carried along in the flood in

the darkness. Using his one arm, he tried to steer himself, but it was no use. He folded up and let the water take him.

The weight and volume of the water was tremendous. He was flying. It would have been fun had he had any control, but he was being tumbled along and banged into the walls of the culvert, and his mouth and eyes were filled with water. Just as he thought the buffeting would never end, he shot out of the culvert and floated into the middle of the flooded Washita River. The swollen river was foaming and rushing along. Geth pointed his legs and let the current carry him. Gradually the roaring water carried him near the far shore, where he bounced against some rocks and finally came to a welcome stop in a patch of long grass.

The raging river continued to churn past him—water huffing and spitting as it pursued its wild course downstream. Geth stayed there in the tangled growth, marveling once again at how effective travel by fate was.

V

Winter huddled under a storefront awning, wondering if the rain was ever going to stop. It looked like heaven had literally tipped and was spilling torrents of moisture down. She dashed to the next corner and waited beneath a shelter at a bus stop. No one was out. Here and there she could spot a face pressed against a window, gazing out in awe at the deluge, but for the most part, she was it. A huge truck roared down the street, parting the water like a great ship, hurling it up on the curb and drenching her.

Winter was miserable.

In fact, she was as ready as Leven to give up. She didn't need

shadows filling her head with doubt as she dreamt. She possessed plenty of doubt all by herself. She had seen and done some amazing things in the last while, but it all seemed for naught.

They had accomplished nothing.

Clover's revelation that Winter was assigned to Lev had left her immediately uplifted, but now even that little bit of truth seemed stupid and unbelievable. Big deal. Nobody in their right mind would send a girl like her to take care of anything. She had no experience and no potential. She hated to be a baby, but there beneath the bus shelter, she began to cry. She figured the tears would camouflage well in this weather.

Her jeans and shirt were soaked. She didn't think she could possibly be more uncomfortable. It seemed as if everything she had ever endured or survived was now a big knot, pushing up inside of her, pleading to be let out.

"I can see you crying," Clover said softly, not showing himself.

Winter wiped at her eyes. "I'm not crying," she insisted.

"It's all right," he said. "Things are sort of bad."

Winter wept. The rain had nothing on her.

"Maybe I should show you something." Clover said.

Winter didn't respond; she just kept crying. Clover materialized, hanging on her arm. She was so used to him showing up in odd spots she didn't even flinch. He climbed to the top of her head and wiped his feet in her hair as if cleaning his shoes on a welcome mat.

"Watch the street," he said.

Winter looked at the street. It was filled with water up to the top of the curbs, flowing wildly. No cars were in sight. She wondered why Clover would tell her that, but before she could question him or complain about him using her head as a doormat, he jumped

from her head down into the road. He landed in the rushing water, and his body seemed to dissipate and flow outward, painting the entire street with color and images. Clover was gone, but Winter was mesmerized by what she could see. Reflected in the water, she saw a countryside with an amber sky. The water surged. A moon and a river appeared, framed by a brilliant white braided rainbow.

Winter stared.

She could see a tall woman with straight red hair and strange animals circling around her. What she saw was not Oklahoma or anyplace on earth. What she saw was a bit of Foo. The oddest thing about these scenes was that they were not peculiar to her. She recognized them. She had seen them before.

She saw a tall, dark man on a horse-like creature, surrounded by shadows. She saw the turrets of Foo and the crowds of beings gathering to fight for what she was somehow a part of.

The water rose and flowed on, the images moving down the street with it. She stared at them until they were completely gone.

"Does that help?" Clover asked. Once again he was back on her shoulder and drying his hair with a towel he had pulled from his pocket void.

"How'd you do that?" Winter asked.

"We sycophants are pretty good at a lot of things," Clover smiled. "I'm not bragging, I'm just telling the truth."

"The tall man on the horse thingy," Winter said somberly. "I recognized him."

"I thought you might," Clover whispered. "That's Sabine. I know this all seems pointless and I'm not exactly the perfect traveling companion, but what we are hoping to stop is real and terrible. I promise."

Winter was silent for a moment. The clouds thinned and the rain softened a bit.

"We've got to find this Geth," she finally said with determination.

"That's what I've been—" Clover stopped himself and smiled. "I know we do."

"We'll find Geth and take him to Lev," Winter said firmly, trying to convince herself she could do it.

"Perfect," Clover cheered.

"I just don't have any idea where to start looking," she admitted.

"Fate will help," Clover assured her.

Winter smiled at Clover. There is nothing like the joy of having a conversation with a twelve-inch-tall, furry sycophant. She was still scared and unsure of herself, but she had seen something amazing in those watery images. It made her more frightened, but also considerably more hopeful. She pictured Sabine on the horse and shivered. He was part of this, she knew that. She stepped across the street and over to the park.

With the rain letting up a bit, a few people and cars began to make their way through the streets again.

CHAPTER EIGHTEEN

A Little Disappointed

In some ways Geth had simply moved from one mess to another. No matter how hard he tried, he could not free himself from the tangle of grass near the side of the river. The swollen stream was calming a bit and the sky had cleared, but his body was knotted into the growth, and he didn't have the strength to break loose.

But he didn't panic. Not Geth. He relaxed and tried to enjoy the moment. His mouth was just above the water line, but as the water moved it would splash into his eyes and ears and mouth, making things look, sound, and taste wet. He halfway wished he were still a tall tree with the ability to stretch and push his roots around. He missed being able to see from every angle and hear sound from beneath the ground and from the sky.

He missed a few things, but lithens never yearn for what was or what could have been. There's no point in it. There is no moment

more precious than the exact moment they are living. And that exact moment has a lot to do with how future moments play out.

Geth bobbed up and down in his watery nest. He closed his eyes and tried to whistle with little success. A fat fish came careening down the way and pushed through the grass at the edge to scratch its belly on the growth. The weight of the fish pushed Geth all the way under. He sprang right back up. The sun touched the top of his head and felt warm.

He was almost content.

In fact, if it weren't for the entire future of mankind depending on him and Leven getting back to Foo, Geth wouldn't have minded a bit just living out his days there attached to that grass.

A young girl walking down the edge of the river stopped on the bank near Geth. She was alone and eating a piece of fruit. From where he lay, Geth couldn't see all of her, but what he could see looked familiar. As she stood there eating fruit, a small, grey sycophant materialized on her shoulder. Geth was speechless. He had seen Clover many times before while standing in Leven's yard as a tree. Geth's mouth hung open as he listened to Clover and the girl.

"So I can't even have one bite?" Clover asked Winter.

"You've already had twelve whole ones," she laughed.

"I would have had more if that farmer hadn't caught us borrowing from his tree."

Winter took a few more bites then tossed the core of the fruit toward the river. Geth could see it coming straight toward him. The core bounced off his head, leaving bits of fruit clinging to him. He looked up to see Clover disappear and Winter begin to walk farther downstream.

"I would have eaten that core," an invisible Clover said.

"Sorry," Winter smiled. "I forgot that you'll eat anything."

"What a waste," Clover complained. "There was still fruit . . ."

They were far enough down the river that Geth could no longer hear them. He wrestled with the grass, trying desperately to get free. He had to get to that girl. But the hold of the grass was too strong for his single arm to break.

A huge fly landed on Geth's head and began to nibble at the small bits of fruit stuck on him. Geth waved it away. Not intimidated by a toothpick, the fly flew back and continued to graze on the top of Geth's head. This time he didn't wave it away. He bent himself over as far as he could, pushing the top of his head toward the center of the river. The unsuspecting fly licked and bit the top of him, buzzing and spitting.

Come on, Geth thought. *Come on.*

No sooner had he thought it than a huge fish leaped from the water and engulfed the fly and the top half of Geth. The fish thrashed his head about, breaking the grass and tearing away with both the fly and Geth in his mouth. The fly buzzed madly, thrashing around in the closed mouth, desperate to get free. The poor fish couldn't properly swallow the pest because the toothpick was poking into its lip and making swallowing near impossible. Geth pulled and kicked, the fish rocked and twisted, the fly buzzed and vibrated. The large trout finally opened its mouth slightly, and Geth was freed. He skimmed across the top of the water until a wave flung him into the air and sent him flying up onto the wet, grassy shore.

He stood and cleared his eyes, marveling at the creativity fate was demonstrating. He wasn't sure if he'd been flung past Winter or if he still needed to go farther. The question was soon answered. He glanced back up the bank just in time to see a foot coming down

directly on top of him. He tried to scream but there wasn't time. Winter's heel smashed him into the muddy bank as she walked right over him.

Once again Geth was stuck.

His top half was sticking out, but as he waved and hollered, his small voice was not loud enough to be heard over the sound of the still raging river. He watched Winter walk farther and farther away.

"Amazing," he said to himself. "So close."

"Amazing is right," a voice above him said.

Geth tried to look around but he could see nothing.

"A talking toothpick," the voice added. "That has to mean something."

"Who's there?" Geth asked, with no fear in his voice, only curiosity.

No one answered.

"Hello?" Geth tried.

No reply, just the sound of water rushing by. Geth looked off toward Winter. She was now almost out of sight, but suddenly she stopped. She stood still for a moment and then turned to look back in the direction she had just come. Geth couldn't tell if she was speaking or not, but in a moment she began walking back. Geth smiled. As she got nearer he could hear her voice.

"A toothpick?" she questioned loudly. "You saw a toothpick?"

"A toothpick," Clover said enthusiastically. He was still invisible. "Like one of those things you dig at your teeth with," he explained.

"I know what a toothpick is," Winter said. "But what would that have to do with us?"

"Antsel said to look for signs."

"A toothpick is a sign?" Winter said, mildly amused but also frustrated.

"It was talking," Clover insisted. "How many talking toothpicks have you ever met? It's there just beside that rock." Winter knelt down and began to carefully probe the ground with her hand.

"Hello," Geth spoke up.

Winter shifted her gaze from the spot she was searching and looked directly at Geth.

"Hello?" she said tentatively.

Clover let just his blue eyes materialize. "I was following behind looking for smooth rocks and I just heard him talking," he explained. "I thought a talking toothpick was worth investigating."

"I'm a bit stuck," Geth offered.

"Sorry," Winter apologized for not helping him out sooner. "Can I just pinch you?"

"Why not?" Geth said pleasantly. "You just stepped on me."

"I did?" Winter said surprised. "I'm so sorry."

"No problem, I'm glad you did," he replied. "Seems to be exactly what fate needed," Geth added as she placed him on her palm and studied him closely.

He was a thick wooden toothpick with light waves of grain running vertically up and down him. He appeared to be split down the middle on the bottom half, giving him two thin legs. He had one splinter of an arm and a pointed head. His face was a pattern of randomly scattered holes. He had a large right eye and a slightly smaller and lower left eye—the right one being circular and the left having a slant. He had a tiny hole for a nose and a big notch missing for a mouth. He gave Winter a lop-sided grin.

"I'm glad the grain of the wood runs vertically," Geth joked. "Horizontal stripes make me look fat."

Winter smiled, genuinely delighted for the first time in a long while. She had no idea what she held in her hand, but it was at the very least highly intriguing.

"Weird," Clover said, his eyes gazing at Geth.

Winter took it all in—floating eyes, talking toothpicks, no big deal.

"So what are you?" she asked.

The toothpick bowed slightly. "My name is Geth. I—"

Winter snickered while Clover's blue eyeballs bulged.

"Sorry," Winter apologized, "I thought you said your name was Geth."

"That's correct," Geth stated.

"But you're not *the* Geth, are you?" she asked, a bit of panic in her voice.

"I'm not sure what you mean."

"He's not *the* Geth," Clover tried, his eyeballs looking at Winter. "Geth is a great king. He's wise and handsome with golden hair and an infectious laugh and and . . . well, he's tall."

Geth laughed. "I know I must look foolish, but I *am* Geth. I was brought here from Foo by Antsel in the condition of a seed and was buried from Sabine with the express purpose of bringing Leven back to Foo."

Neither Winter nor Clover was laughing now.

"You're a toothpick," Clover said, materializing completely. "You're supposed to help us? No offense, but I think I could do a better job than a toothpick."

"Please say you're not really who we are looking for," Winter said seriously, all laughter gone.

"I am who you're looking for," Geth affirmed. "You must be the soul who was brought here to bring Leven back. I am the heir Leven needs to succeed."

"Lev already has hair," Clover pointed out. "Besides, there have been plenty of bald people who are successful," he added. "My father—"

Geth smiled. "I mean *heir.* As in lineage and rulers."

"Oh," Clover sniffed, patting his own hairy head.

"I know my shape isn't exactly impressive, but I can get you back," Geth said confidently. "Where is the boy?"

"Well," Clover cleared his throat. "It seems that Lev gave up this morning and returned home."

"Then we've got to give him a reason to go on."

"And you propose we do that by showing him a toothpick?" Winter asked.

The toothpick straightened itself. "I am the rightful heir to Foo," he stated. "I am also a lithen of the highest Order of Wonder, and I know there is nothing that can stop me from making it back to Foo with Leven. Fate will make it so."

"Oh, yeah," Clover said. "This has disaster written all over it."

Winter wiped her eyes and stood tall. Her clothes were still slightly wet and completely uncomfortable.

"I'm sorry if I disappoint you," Geth said softly to her. "I can only promise you that I am who I say I am and that I know how to get back to Foo."

Winter smiled at him weakly. "Then we should go," she said bravely.

"What?" Clover complained. "He's a toothpick."

"I'm tired of walking around," Winter complained. "Besides, if *I'm* a part of this then surely a toothpick could be capable enough. Let's go get Lev."

Clover shrugged. "Makes sense to me."

Winter slipped Geth into her front shirt pocket. "Is this all right?" she asked him.

"Perfect," Geth smiled, holding on to the top edge of her pocket with his one arm and gazing out.

Winter turned and headed in the direction of Leven's house.

"You might want to hurry," Geth said.

Winter looked worried.

"But don't fret about it," Geth added. "Optimism is our best ally."

Winter tried to smile. It's not that easy, however, to be optimistic, when you are taking directions from a toothpick.

CHAPTER NINETEEN

LIFT, HUCK, AND LISTEN

Leven was disgusted with himself. He had turned his back on the two people—well, one person and one whatever Clover was—who believed in him. No matter how he looked at it, he had left Winter and Clover high and dry. He couldn't help it. His head was so clouded with confused thoughts and self-doubt he could hardly stand straight. And now, thanks to the rainstorm that had just ended, he was soaked. His dark bangs were matted against his forehead, covering his right eye.

"It doesn't matter," he said to himself. "There's nothing I can do about any of this." The empty words didn't make him feel any better about giving up. He tried to walk tall, but it felt like the entire world was pushing down on his shoulders.

He rounded the turn in the road and spotted his house in the distance.

The first thing he noticed was the missing tree. The stump sat there like an ugly bone jutting out from the surface of the earth. He noticed Addy's car was not in the driveway and that the house looked askew and a bit more beat up than he remembered. One corner of the roof in the back was crumpled as if it had been crushed. And there were wood chips everywhere.

"I shouldn't be here," he whispered to himself.

Leven did not want to return home, but he had nothing else. He hated wandering the streets and having to sleep on the ground. Defeated, he sat down on the tree stump. The grass around it was long, and a few birds off to the south were chattering at each other.

His mind cleared and his eyes burned gold. His gift was flaring up. He could see Winter in his head. Lights and shadows swirled through his brain. Winter was walking swiftly and with purpose. She said something to someone and smiled. Leven couldn't remember if he had ever seen her smile that widely when he had been with her. She looked different, too: her green eyes were beautiful and her blond hair wasn't as wild as he remembered it.

Leven's thoughts suddenly darkened.

Winter appeared much happier without him. He was not surprised. Leven knew he was a problem, not an answer. That had been the pattern of his life. He had just seen the future and he now knew that Winter and Clover could get along just fine. They didn't need him. Leven rubbed his eyes and sighed loudly as if expelling air from his toes.

"Who's there?" Terry yelled from inside Leven's old house.

"It's me," Leven said with little enthusiasm.

"Where have you been?" Terry demanded. He stuck his head out

one of the trailer's open windows. It was obvious he had just gotten up.

"I got lost?" Leven tried.

"Lost? How dumb do you think I am?"

Leven prayed Terry wouldn't make him answer that.

"Your aunt spent an entire afternoon looking for you. She missed over three hours of work. Set us back something fierce."

"I'm sorry."

"We're all perfectly aware of that," Terry whined. "Now get in here and clean this place up."

Leven stood and walked up to the front door. He stepped inside and almost gasped at how messy everything was. It was as if they had done nothing but eat and litter during the two days he had been gone. A strong, unpleasant odor was coming from the kitchen, and trash was everywhere. Half-eaten plates of food littered the living room. Though he had been forced to sleep on the porch, Leven had always been the one in charge of cleaning the inside of the house. Terry pushed through the trash to stand right in front of Leven.

"See this mess?" Terry pointed, his ugly mouth drawn down into a sneer. "You did it. How do you expect us to teach you anything if we do your chores for you? Well, I'm sick of it. You have fifteen minutes to clean it up."

"Fifteen minutes?" Leven asked incredulously. The mess he saw in front of him would take a lot longer to fix than that.

"Fifteen minutes, or I'll make sure you regret showing your face around here again."

"So you cut the tree down?" Leven asked forcefully.

"Excuse me?" Terry said sarcastically. "Did I say it was special question time? Fifteen minutes! I'm going out for a drink." Terry

pulled his dirty baseball cap over his greasy hair and left the trailer house, slamming the door as he went out.

ii

Leven was still cleaning two hours later when Addy came home. Terry hadn't returned yet. Addy came in the door, threw her keys and purse down, and started complaining about the weather. Then she noticed Leven.

"What are *you* doing here?"

"Just cleaning up."

"Well, hurry, the place is a mess."

That was it. No "Hello." No "We've missed you." No "Good to see you." Just, "Hurry, the place is a mess."

Addy noticed Leven was wearing his Wonder Wipe shirt inside out. She began to bark at him. "Embarrassed about what I do? Too good to promote what feeds us? Maybe you would like a shirt made of gold?"

"I don't want a gold shirt," Leven insisted. "I just put it on wrong."

"I work all day to support . . ."

Addy stopped yelling to listen to the slurred singing of Terry as he made his way home. He fumbled with the door handle and stumbled into the house. He looked around at the filth that was much less than when he had left, but still quite a mess.

"What have you been doing?" he demanded. "I can barely see the carpet."

"I'm cleaning as fast as I can," Leven defended. "It's just—"

"Well, it's not fast enough," Terry interrupted, spitting flecks of

saliva into the air. "Come here," he slurred. He hadn't shaved for a few days, and with his scraggly beard and dirty clothes he looked like a bum.

"I'll keep going," Leven promised, picking up even faster.

"Don't you back talk to him," Addy snarled. "You take a vacation and come back with a smart mouth."

"I wasn't—"

"Come here," Terry stormed.

Leven had made a gigantic mistake. He should never have returned. He had been a fool to think he could just step back into the awful life he had always had. Now as Terry raged and Addy helped, Leven knew he was in trouble. He looked toward the front door, trying to gauge if he could make it out or not. Terry noticed.

"Going to make a run for it?" Terry mocked, his beady eyes red and hateful. "You'll never make it, Skuuuunk."

Addy stepped next to the back door, blocking any escape.

"Come here," Terry muttered fiercely. "I'm going to scare the rest of your hair white."

Leven began to back away.

"You should have stayed lost," Terry spat. "I think it's time to teach you the lesson your aunt never let me."

"I'm not his aunt," Addy said disgustedly.

Addy wasn't a compassionate woman, but she was less likely than Terry to hurt someone. There had been many times during Leven's childhood when Addy had stopped Terry from striking Leven or imposing his strength on him. At the moment, however, it didn't seem as though Addy had any intention of holding Terry back. She had experienced a difficult week. The hand-folded napkin market was soft at the moment, and the company she worked

for had laid off one of the fastest and most expensive folders they had, leaving Addy with over three times her normal workload. Her wrists would swell to the size of cantaloupes every afternoon from all the repetitive movement, and her carpal tunnel pain was killing her. She had come home each day a monster. She was tired of her job, tired of Terry, and tired of not being pampered and taken care of like some of those ladies she saw on TV. In short, she was spent, spoiled, and selfish, and had no more will to control Terry or feel for Leven.

"I'm his mother's half sister," she grumped.

Terry moved closer. Leven tried to clear his mind to see if by some chance he couldn't manipulate himself out of this. He couldn't see anything except the image of Winter walking and smiling.

Leven was sick about the mistake he had made in thinking he could come home.

iii

Winter was feeling better. She was still not completely confident that a toothpick was the answer to all her woes, but for the moment they had direction. That direction was north toward Leven's old house. Clover was so excited about going to get Leven that every few seconds he would materialize on a different place on Winter, shiver happily, smile, and disappear again.

Geth rested in Winter's shirt pocket as they traveled. The city wasn't huge, and they had only been five or so miles from Leven's old neighborhood, but it was slow going thanks to there being no straight shot there. They had to make their way across the river, through neighborhoods, over fences, and around businesses. Just at

dusk they reached the entrance of the Rolling Greens Deluxe Mobile Home Park.

Clover materialized. "I can't wait to see Lev."

"We just saw him earlier today," Winter said.

"Seems longer," Clover sighed.

"Are all sycophants as dedicated as you?" Winter asked.

Clover smiled, shook his whole body, and disappeared again.

The Rolling Greens Deluxe Mobile Home Park had over forty-five streetlights, but only nineteen of them worked. It took time and effort to change the bulbs, so when they went out they stayed that way. That left the area pretty dark at night. A few homes were lit up, and the occasional working streetlight helped to give outlines but no real detail to the scenery.

"I'm not sure how to say this," Winter began. "But I'm not terribly confident Lev will even want to come with us."

"He'll come," Geth said confidently.

"I don't know."

"It's fate." Geth was as wide-eyed and smiley as a toothpick can get.

Winter had never met anyone so self-assured as the little toothpick. She knew she could pick him up and snap him in half with minor effort. Or she could toss him into a fire and he would have no way to save himself. Still, he pushed forward and talked as though he had every capability and advantage at hand.

"I hope you're right," Winter said.

They turned the corner and Winter could see Leven's home. The curtains were closed and glowing over the windows. Winter had never met Leven's family, but the things Leven had said about them made it perfectly clear what kind of people they were.

As they got closer to the house they could hear yelling coming from inside. Terry was shouting at Leven. Winter hurried to the window and peeked through a gap in the curtain. Leven had his back to the opposite wall, and Terry was standing in front of him, shouting and rolling up his own sleeves. From where Geth was pocketed, he too could see clearly what was about to happen.

"We've got to stop it," Geth whispered, looking around quickly. He spotted the tree stump he had been severed from less than a week before. "If I remember Antsel right," Geth said to Winter, "he told me you were a nit."

"I think I am," Winter said, unsure.

"What's your gift?" Geth asked.

"I can freeze things."

"Perfect," Geth said. "I'm going to need your help. Set me down on that stump. I want to see if I can still work my old roots."

Winter took three giant steps and placed Geth on top of the tree stump. He lay down, face up, and oozed slowly into the wood.

Inside the house, Terry was screaming even louder.

iv

Leven had never seen Terry this bad. He was cursing and ranting and coming toward him with fire in his red-veined eyes. He spit as he spoke, rage dripping from him like sweat. All the events and tragedies and disappointment and failures of Terry's life had come to a heavy boil. He rolled his sleeves farther up, his mind focused on nothing but teaching this brat a lesson he would never forget.

Leven tried to open the window behind him, but the cheap clasp broke off in his hand. Terry smiled a wicked, lazy smile. He

drew back his fist and swung, stumbling under the forward motion and missing Leven completely. He righted himself and tried again, but the house rocked, and Terry lost his balance and had to grab onto a nearby chair to keep from falling.

"What the . . ." he muttered.

The house rocked again. Leven was as frightened as Terry. Addy grabbed the kitchen bar and hung on. The house shook, tilting to the west at a steep angle, and Terry flew into the wall. Leven dropped to the floor and tried to crawl upward toward the door. The house leveled out and began rising. It twisted and shook as it rose, tossing everything inside around like bingo balls in a bin. The mess that had been there before was nothing compared to how things looked now, with cupboards and cabinets bursting open and expelling their contents all over the rooms.

The front door blew inward and a thick root shot through and toward Leven. It wrapped itself around his waist and yanked him outside, all while the home rising higher and higher. Addy wasn't just screaming anymore, she was exploding with noise. The fear on her face would have elicited mercy from Jack the Ripper. Terry was still bouncing off walls and trying to right himself somehow. Two more roots shot into the home and twisted around both his and Addy's ankles. The frantic couple clawed and scratched at the floor, fighting to keep from being pulled out, but it was no use: Geth had them.

With all three of them extracted from the trailer, Geth kept the house suspended high above its foundation. Winter looked over at the stump where Geth lay. He looked back at Winter. She wasn't certain, but she could have sworn Geth's little wood hole was smiling.

"Freeze the house!" he commanded her.

Winter looked at the house hovering high above her and panicked.

"The whole thing?"

"The whole thing!"

Winter closed her green eyes and concentrated. She saw the house as ice and it was that simple. She looked up to witness the entire mobile home as one shiny block of ice. Terry and Addy, who were still being dangled by their ankles up in the air, screamed in fear and disbelief.

Geth looked up at Winter. "You might want to plug your ears," he said, "but I happen to like the sound of breaking ice."

Geth retracted some of his roots and the entire home plummeted swiftly to the ground. A fabulous rushing noise was followed by the complete destruction of the house Leven had lived in. The single-wide shattered into a million frozen pieces. Ice flew everywhere. A few shards blew out two of the neighbor's windows, and a dog across the street got a massive surprise welt as he was sneaking up on a cat. Geth was right, the sound was spectacular, like the explosion of a blimp full of fine china. Winter reached down and touched one of the bigger chunks. The ice instantly began to thaw.

Geth lowered Terry and Addy none too gently onto the very spot where their house had once stood. He also set Leven down and retracted all the roots completely back into the earth. Then he pushed himself up and out of the tree stump and Winter put him back in her pocket.

"Amazing," Winter whispered. "Absolutely amazing."

Winter walked over to Leven, who was standing in complete shock. The house was shattered into a million tiny pieces. He scuffed some of the frozen debris with his toe.

"I think that was my bed." Leven tried to smile.

Terry and Addy cowered on the ground in fear, as neighbors cautiously approached to investigate what had happened.

Leven looked at Winter. "What are you doing here?" he asked.

"Saving you," she answered. "Are you ready to go now?"

Leven looked at Addy and Terry. She was bawling and he was sniveling. They were both trembling. Leven wanted to say something nice, but all that came out was, "I'm done cleaning."

Addy glared in horror.

As Winter turned and began to walk off into the dark night, Leven paused for a moment, looking at the two people who had been most rotten to him. He wasn't quite ready to leave. He gazed at his shivering guardians and the ring of concerned neighbors who had gathered.

"What happened to your house?" Mrs. Pendle asked, holding her tattered bathrobe closed at the neck.

"The tree . . ." Addy began.

"It lifted up . . ." Terry stammered. "And then . . . my house."

They went blubbering on as Leven slipped back behind the crowd of people and off toward Winter. She was a few hundred feet ahead, whispering to the toothpick in her pocket.

"Should I introduce myself to him now?" Geth whispered to her.

"I think maybe you should wait until morning," she whispered back.

"Fine by me," Geth said, slipping down further into her pocket.

"How did you do that?" Leven asked, as he caught up to her. "I mean with the tree and the—"

"I'll tell you later," Winter said quickly. "Right now we need to find a place to sleep. We have to leave early in the morning."

"That was amazing! I've never heard a sound like . . . leave to go where?" Leven asked.

"The gateway," Winter replied.

"Gateway to where?"

"To Foo."

"You know where it is?" Leven asked.

"Geth does," Clover said, materializing with his arms around Leven's head.

"Clover!" Leven smiled. "I can't believe you both came back for me. Especially after what I said."

"It's forgotten," Clover waved.

"Good," Leven said. "Because I am so happy to see you guys."

"Let's hope you feel that way after you get some sleep," Winter said seriously. "You have a tendency to change your mind in the night."

"So you know where Geth is?" Leven asked, remembering how awful his dreams had been and wanting to think about anything else.

"Sure, he's—" Clover tried to say.

"We'll see him tomorrow," Winter interrupted, giving Clover the eye.

"I can't believe you found him," Leven said as they exited the mobile home park. "So he's going to take us to Foo?"

"In a sense." Winter's green eyes blinked.

"Unbelievable, so Clover was right. He was waiting for us?"

"Well, not exactly. I'll tell you everything later," Winter promised.

Leven stared at her, thinking about his life and what an amazing turn it had taken. Last night he was chased by the earth, today he saw a tree lift and shatter his old house.

"Unbelievable," he said again, still wondering how a person like himself could even be involved in all of this.

"I'm glad you're back," Clover whispered to Leven.

"I only left you this morning," Leven smiled.

"Still, it wasn't the same without you."

They worked their way through town and down toward the river. The night deepened to a rich black and in the far distance a pack of coyotes yipped mournfully. Leven and Winter had a lot ahead of them, and not much time.

CHAPTER TWENTY

FURY BY DESIGN

Sabine walked swiftly down the halls of Morfit, his rat-like features twitching. Those nearby scurried to be nowhere near wherever he was actually going. Few dared question his motives or reasoning anymore. Well, a few dared, but those few were separated from their loved ones and shipped to the far borders of Foo to live out their lives harvesting gunt—a very unpleasant job, to say the least.

Sabine was darker and more powerful than ever. He had created a true division in Foo, feeding off the most troubled dreams and stirring up the hearts of any who would buy into his plan to return to reality. Thousands and thousands of beings were now sold on the idea of Foo and reality coming together. They wanted to see who they had been taken from and live the impossible in the physical world. Of course Sabine was overlooking one crucial fact—that fact

being that what he was preaching would eliminate every dream on earth and ultimately cause Foo to collapse. If even a fourth of Foo were to abandon their fate, the dreams and imaginations of those in reality would cease to exist and hope would be lost to the human race. Fate took in who it needed to keep the dreams of man alive. If the population of Foo dwindled, those on earth would ultimately vanish. The wise in Foo knew this. They understood their purpose to be sacred and took their responsibility and roles seriously.

Sabine wanted none of that. He wanted to be able to slip in and out, so he could rule both reality and Foo. He foolishly believed he could have it all.

Sabine waved his hand, and the guards standing in front of the door stepped aside. He walked through and into the grand chamber. It was one of the largest caverns in Morfit. In the center of the room was a lengthy wooden table. Every seat around the table was occupied, except for the large one at the head. Sabine took his place and sat with a flourish.

"The full moon of Lant," he bowed, wishing them well, Foo-style.

Morfit was as tall as a mountain and as wide as any prairie on earth. A castle of rock, it stood next to and towered above the Lime Sea beside it. It was a work in progress, a place that constantly grew, thanks to the labors of those in Foo who sought peace in the aftermath of their own misdoings. If a person or being in Foo did something they felt was wrong or unbecoming a member of a realm of endless possibilities, they would dig up a stone wherever they stood and carry that stone to Morfit. There they would place the rock carefully and walk away without their burden. Long lines of people with stone in hand, working their way toward Morfit, were a common

sight these days, stacking rocks upon rocks, building the mountain of Morfit.

Morfit had not always been so imposing. In the beginning, Morfit was only a small scar in the ground. Now, as the dreams of men on earth grew darker and the division in Foo was creating fear and jealousy, Morfit expanded hourly. The castle of rocks reached to the thick upper sky, creating an imposing mountain filled with caverns and passages. Beings of all forms and desires hid among the caves and tunnels formed by the sins of those in Foo.

Morfit, by virtue of its size, had become the center of Foo. Those who met in council did so there, as well as those who established the changing laws and sat to hear disputes. The dreams of man could not penetrate the structure, making it an off-limits area for dream enhancement and a safe ground for personal thought.

Sabine considered those around the table in the grand hall and smiled broadly.

"We hope this will go smoothly," a council member spoke, addressing him.

"*I* trust it will," Sabine humbly affirmed. "*I* have come to make amends," he announced.

The members of the council looked at each other skeptically.

"*I* have been out of line and am in need of your forgiveness," Sabine continued.

A murmur went around the table, then ceased. The council members were shocked but seemed to like the direction the discussion was going. They had gathered to rebuke Sabine and put an end to his scheme to merge Foo and reality. As much as whisps longed to be whole, they understood that were Foo and reality to merge,

they, along with the dreams and imaginations of all mankind, would vanish.

"So your thoughts have changed?" the lead council spoke, his voice betraying his surprise. "You have created this division and now you feel differently?" he asked with disbelief.

Sabine nodded. "*I* was wrong. *I* see now that the path *I* was on is futile."

The room was dead quiet, which might have been expected, since all the men and women who sat on the council were pretty much dead. They were whisps, void of soul and life, a rare aberration and a unique breed in Foo.

Sometimes those on earth who step on a mismatched lane or sidewalk don't make it all the way to Foo. Or a better way of putting it is that they don't make it *completely* to Foo. Those beings only partially arrive and are robbed of only a portion of their presence: their bodies and souls remain on earth, feeling lost and confused, while Foo receives only a hollow likeness of them.

These oddities are called whisps. They have no real substance, but they can still think and react, while passing through objects as though they were ghosts. Whisps are worthless dance partners and of no help when you need to move a large object or want a push on the swings, seeing how they can't touch or react with anything physical.

Having no substance, they are valued only for their thoughts. So it is that they serve in Foo as members of governing councils and boards. They aren't indestructible, however, and Sabine was tired of those he had to answer to. He was fed up with procedures and the shifting logic and rules of Foo. Sabine thirsted for absolute power and personal glory. He wanted out of Foo so he could better control

reality. If dreams and hope were the casualties of his quest for control, so be it.

"*I* thought *I* knew what was best." Sabine's voice was thick with pretended emotion and remorse. "*I* know now that *I* have been wrong," he lied.

The council members were very pleased and flattered. They were also unaware that Sabine was setting them up. The biggest weakness in a whisp was his or her inability to resist a compliment. They normally had the ability to think clearly, but the moment someone complimented them on their two-dimensional hair or their intellect or anything else, they lost their ability to reason.

"You have served Foo in a most pleasing manner," Sabine continued. "It is your example and wise decisions that have helped *me* recognize *my* misbehavior."

Everyone in the room nodded in complete agreement.

Sabine removed the hood from his cloak, signaling his shadows to come in. A number of them filtered into the room, each of them carrying a small, polished object. The shadows were of different sizes and shapes, but each was a warped and flat reflection of Sabine. Each found a place near a council member and waited.

Sabine nodded, and his shadows displayed to the council members the tiny round objects they held in their hands. Some of the whisps were reluctant to look at what the shadows held.

"Do not be concerned," Sabine smiled. "Please," he gestured broadly, "these are merely gifts from *me* to you. *My* way of saying *I* was wrong."

"What are they?" one asked skeptically.

"Soul stones," Sabine replied, casually.

There was an audible, collective gasp, then the room fell silent. Sabine could not have uttered two more powerful words.

It had been rumored since the first whisp entered Foo that somewhere in the realm of Foo there existed an object that could make a whisp whole. "Soul stones," they were called, and possessing one, a whisp would be transformed from an empty, two-dimensional image into a whole being who could touch and run and experience a complete life in Foo.

To a whisp, nothing was more sought after and wondrous than a soul stone.

"Soul stones," they whispered reverently. A few tried to touch them, but their hands went right through.

Sabine smiled amiably. "These were not easy to come by, friends. But your forgiveness of *my* misbegotten behavior seems to have merited them. It is *my* pleasure to present them to you."

The whispering intensified. The possibility of their being whole clouded their judgment and suspended all caution.

"If you would like, *my* shadows will open them for you," Sabine cordially continued. "In a mere moment you will be whole for the first time."

Ecstatic chatter and excitement filled the room. A number of whisps wobbled as if faint. Others stood trembling in front of their assigned shadows, fidgeting and wringing their hands in joy.

Sabine gestured with his right hand, and the stones split open. A deep, red glow, mesmerizing and brilliant, oozed out of each one, then tantalizingly began to withdraw. The whisps gazed in awe and wonder. They reached forward, captivated by the hope of becoming whole and unable to resist. As their ghostlike hands touched the glow, they were suddenly sucked in toward the light.

For a moment they assumed it was a part of becoming whole, but a few quickly realized what was really happening. They should have known better. It had seemed strange that Sabine would admit his wrongdoing when he had been so arrogant in the past and so close to victory at the moment. It seemed unlike him to apologize when he had for so long resented the restraints imposed on him by what he often called the *wretched* Council of Whisps. His humility and cordial behavior were entirely out of character, but the hope of becoming whole had caused the entire group to go daft. They had thrown caution to the wind, and now they were paying for it with their thin lives.

The only way to get rid of a whisp is to suck it up. That is why whisps are so horribly frightened by vacuums. Their substance is so thin that a simple sucking can draw them in. And if they are drawn into a small enough space they can be trapped. If a whisp is compacted to the size of a pea, it then has enough substance to prevent it from simply slipping through the material that is holding it captive. More than one child in Foo had tormented and teased a whisp by chasing it with a vacuum outside the steps of Morfit. Whisps weren't fond of children.

Sabine, of course, wasn't looking to simply torment and tease. Sabine wanted the whisps gone for good. His cruel genius was in creating a vacuum small enough to fit into a polished stone.

Sabine laughed scornfully as the whisps writhed and screamed while being sucked into the tiny rocks. Some cursed him and others cried, knowing they had been tricked to death. The black shiny stones glowed as they consumed the images of all the whisps.

In a few moments it was over.

The shadows closed the tiny rocks and placed them on the

now-unoccupied giant table before them. Sabine looked at the pile and waved his shadows away.

Nobody could intentionally kill another being in Foo. You could hit your worst enemy in the head with a club, and it would have no effect. If someone *intentionally* pushed you off a cliff you would simply land at the bottom unharmed. If, however, someone *accidentally* bumped into you and knocked you off a cliff, you would fall to your death. That was an interesting fact of Foo that had prevailed ever since the realm had come to be.

Sabine, however, had found clever ways to kill and rid himself of those who opposed him. He had placed Geth's soul in a seed and set the crows loose on him. Now he had successfully trapped the Council of Whisps in the rocks, but he still needed some unsuspecting and innocent victims to finish the job for him.

He looked at the stones and with his power turned them into ice. Sabine too was a nit, endowed with the same gift Winter possessed. He collected the frozen rocks in a wooden box and handed them to Jamoon, who had been standing guard outside the door.

Sabine smiled. "See that these are given to the children out in the far field," he ordered.

"Yes, Your Perfectness," Jamoon bowed.

"Let them practice stick with them," Sabine suggested. "They may use them all. *I* don't want them back."

"You are so kind and giving," Jamoon added. "So kind and giving."

Sabine turned away, knowing that in a matter of minutes the entire council would be nothing but shattered rocks strewn over a child's playing field.

He stepped into the dark musty chamber off of the hall and

inhaled deeply. Shadows by the thousands rushed to him and swirled together into one dark spiral, humming and whistling vulgarly.

"We're here, we're here," they chanted. "We're here."

Sabine glanced and saw that something was not right with his minions. They were frightened and resisted his pull. Some whispered and cried as they told of Leven Thumps and how they had not been able to darken his dreams. Some reported that Leven was allied with Winter and a spirit they didn't recognize, but feared.

"What kind of spirit is with the boy?" Sabine demanded, the confidence he felt just moments before leaving him.

The shadows cowered, too frightened to speak. The shadows that surrounded Sabine were not only sinister, they were disposable. Sabine had gone through many. They couldn't escape the master who cast them, but he could will them to dissolve at any time he chose.

Sabine closed his eyes and clapped.

The dark spiral of spirits evaporated into nothing, each sending a piercing screech ringing through the chamber as it disappeared. Sabine moved in front of the tall window and drew the heavy drape back. Light flooded the chamber, casting Sabine's dark shadow onto the floor and against the far wall—a new, less intimidated shadow.

"What kind of spirit?" Sabine inquired of the newly cast dark patch. "What was the spirit like that your predecessors did not recognize?"

"It was strong," the sole shadow stated. "It was strong and familiar. It was unafraid. Royal."

"Royal?" Sabine whispered. "Did you hear mention of the name Geth?"

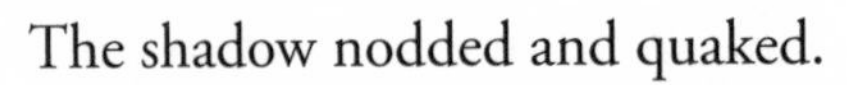

The shadow nodded and quaked.

"Geth is alive?" Sabine cursed.

Sabine turned and moved quickly. He walked in front of the window again, and a new, tall shadow formed to join the other. Sabine paced back and forth in front of the window, thinking, and a third appeared. By the time he had his thoughts about him, the room was filled with hundreds of new, dark forms of all sizes and lengths. They followed him out of the room, whispering eagerly, ready and willing to do his bidding.

Sabine had eliminated the Council of Whisps, but now he had Geth to worry about. He couldn't dwell on that. Those who would follow him would be much bolder, now that the council and their negative advice were gone. Sabine's followers needn't know that Geth still lived. Sabine shuddered and drew in breath like a rat. He *had* to find the gateway.

CHAPTER TWENTY-ONE

We Felt the Earth Squirm under Our Feet

Leven had barely fallen asleep when the shadows began their work. As deep as the night, they moved in from beyond, falling upon him, whispering, insinuating themselves into his dreams.

"You're worthless. Worthless," they hissed. "Fool. Fool," they howled.

Leven tossed and turned as they rolled over him and dived brazenly into his mind. Leven's eyes burned behind his closed lids, and his mouth was as dry as the entire month of July. He cried out and moaned, thrashing around madly in his sleep.

"He did this last night," Winter whispered to Geth as she sat beneath the bridge looking at Leven. "It looks painful."

"It is," Clover complained, appearing out of nowhere. "I can't sleep with him any longer. He's freaking me out," Clover shivered.

"It's Sabine," Geth said. "Leven has no control. Sabine's shadows have him by the dreams."

"That can't be good," Winter said.

"It's not," Geth replied. "But there is nothing we can do. We must let fate work its course. Your touch has changed his dreams. They are now marked with traces of Foo. They can find him in his sleep. At the moment it isn't such a concern. They know where we are. In the future we'll have to be more cautious."

"We could wake him," Winter suggested boldly, her own head beginning to throb.

"That is not a solution. It would only make Leven leave us now," Geth insisted. "It would not be wise."

"So we just sit here while a bunch of ghosts work him over in his dreams?" Winter complained.

Leven rolled completely over and cried out in fear. He tucked his knees to his chest and rocked back and forth, moaning. His eyes flashed open and were burning gold. They closed and he thrashed about again.

"I'm not doing this any longer," Winter insisted. "We need to start moving anyhow." She crawled over to Leven. Geth tried to stop her, but it's incredibly hard for a toothpick with one arm to hold back a thirteen-year-old girl who is actually tall for her age. So he just rode in her pocket, curious to see how fate would work this out.

Winter knelt beside Leven and touched him. His body was as cold as snow. She felt him shivering.

"Lev," she whispered.

He moaned louder.

"Lev, wake up, it's me," she said even louder.

Leven turned and looked at her. His eyes were black and in the whites of them she could see dark images floating back and forth. Winter gasped and drew back. Leven glared at her hatefully. He was not himself.

"I'm worthless," he whispered bitterly. "Don't you understand?"

"Let him be," Geth said. He—"

The ground shook.

"What was that?" Winter asked.

Geth stood as tall as he could in her pocket and looked around. The earth hissed. Winter turned to see the end of the bridge they were under lifting upward. The structure groaned and wailed as bolts sheared off and welds began to snap. Winter could see the ground rise and recognized what was happening.

"It's back," she yelled.

"Back?" Geth hollered.

In the distance Winter could see a gigantic mound forming to the left of her and another to the right. Two more heaved up behind her. She struggled to pull Leven up. He stared blankly at her as the entire earth seemed to mound up and take shape around them.

"Wake up!" Winter yelled.

Leven blinked dumbly. Clover materialized, clinging to the front of Leven, and took a little too much pleasure in slapping Leven awake.

"Wake up," Clover screamed. "We've got to get out of here!"

The end of the bridge heaved upward and began to roll toward them. Winter took Leven by the hand and pulled him to his feet, and the two of them began running. She bolted into the trees, dragging Leven behind her, just as the avalands rose out of the earth and

took full shape. There seemed to be hundreds of them this time, pushing up from the bottom of the river and covering the entire prairie like an eruption of gigantic, mutant groundhogs, beating their scaly chests and stamping their fat legs. They were spewing mud and raging.

Winter dodged trees and jumped over bushes with Leven in tow. At each step Leven became more and more conscious of his surroundings. He could see Winter pulling him and recognized clearly that they were in real trouble. The earth roared. Clover was clinging to Leven's neck and watching out behind them all as he bounced up and down. He could see great mounds of rock and earth surging from the ground and galloping toward them. There were too many avalands to count. Some stood on their back legs and roared as others lowered their heads and charged after Leven, Winter, Geth, and Clover. It looked as though the whole planet was rolling toward them.

As the avalands reached the trees some blasted through, snapping entire trees and sending splintered limbs and branches everywhere. Most of the beasts dived deep into the earth before they reached the trees and burrowed swiftly in the direction of Leven and Winter.

"Where are we going?" Geth hollered to Winter.

"I don't know for sure," she hollered back. "There's a cliff out this way. Lev used it to destroy one last night."

"Amazing," Geth commented as if this were all sort of exciting. "I don't think I've ever met someone who's killed an avaland. To be honest with you I didn't think it was possible," he yelled.

"Great," Winter huffed, sweat pouring from her forehead.

"Interesting and all," she screamed, "but we're about to be eaten by dirt!"

"Amazing," was Geth's only reply, as he tucked himself deeper into Winter's pocket.

Winter had no idea what she was doing. Her only thought was to try to do what Leven had successfully done the night before.

"Run faster," Clover yelled, still clinging to Leven's head. "They're right behind us."

Leven was now thoroughly awake. He picked up his speed, and in a few he strides passed Winter and began pulling her along.

"This isn't going to work," Leven yelled. "There are too many this time."

The world continued to mound up behind them as the avalands thundered closer, the sound of crumpling earth rumbling across the prairie. Winter and Leven could feel themselves being lifted up by the approaching avalanche of dirt.

"The cliff is just up there," Winter screamed.

Leven looked forward and could see the ridge that led to the steep drop off. He held tightly onto Winter's hand. Just before they would have plunged over the cliff they jumped to the side and rolled away from the edge, their hands and knees scraping across dirt. Winter looked up, expecting to see at least a few avalands fly past them and over the cliff. But apparently these were wiser than the one who had pursued them the night before.

Not a single beast flew off or out of the cliff. Instead, the entire herd thundered to a halt and began to circle Leven and Winter. Ring after ring of huge earthen beasts surrounded them, creating what looked to be a small, circular mountain range. The hideous beasts

stamped the ground and blew mud from their mouths and nostrils, focusing their fiery eyes on the two helpless kids.

Leven held Winter's hand and the two of them faced the raging circle. Hearts racing and breathing heavily, they stared at the unbelievable sight and the impossible odds. They were ringed in.

"We're dreaming, right?" Leven exclaimed. "Please say we're dreaming." The fear inside of him was so strong it was almost paralyzing.

"I don't think so," Winter answered, her back to Leven's as they cowered in the face of the menacing ring. Her hair was all over, and she looked paler than usual under the partial moon.

"This isn't possible," Leven insisted.

"There're too many of them," Winter said.

As if on cue, the beasts all began to groan and shake. Then, one by one, domino-like, each mound began to bleed into the mound next to it, forming a gigantic ring of earth that towered over Leven and Winter.

"Is this good or bad?" Winter asked, breathing deep.

Leven would have replied, but he became distracted by the end of the coil of dirt as it took on the shape of a giant serpent's head, displaying its massive fangs. The snake was coiled in concentric circles, and the moonlight reflected dully off its scaly skin. Rings away, the beast lifted its massive tail and rattled it. The noise was deafening.

"You've got to be joking," Leven said desperately, his brown eyes as wide open as they could be.

"What do we do?" Winter cried.

The humongous snake lifted its hideous head high and hissed. A long dusty tongue whipped out and back—Leven and Winter could

feel the wind from it as it snapped inches away from them. The snake rose higher and, like lightning, thrust its massive open mouth down toward its victims. Winter and Leven leaped to one side just in time. The snake recoiled and hissed again, its monstrous tongue flicking in and out, its beady black eyes focused directly on them.

"Let's get out of here!" Leven cried.

He pulled Winter by the hand and ran directly at the coiled body of the snake. He pushed her up and onto the serpent's back, and she pulled him up after her. The snake writhed, recoiled, and struck at them again, but they had already jumped to the next coil and the beast bit into his own dirty skin. Enraged, the giant serpent thrashed to uncoil itself, flinging Leven and Winter off its back, away from the cliff and back toward Burnt Culvert.

They hit the ground running and took off like there was no tomorrow, which certainly could have been the case, seeing as how the very dirt of the earth was out to get them.

Tucked down in the hood of Leven's sweatshirt, Clover peeked out at the snake behind them. In a few moments the snake had straightened itself out and was slithering across the prairie behind them with one objective: to devour Leven and Winter.

Leven spotted a chain-link fence in the distance, the length of it glistening in the soft light of the slight moon. It was a high fence with three strands of barbed wire running along the top of it. It struck Leven that if they could get over that fence the snake might not be able to get them. It wasn't a perfect plan, but it is very hard to think up great plans when enough earth to fill ten football stadiums is slithering after you at the speed of dirt. Leven looked behind him, amazed at how close the serpent was.

"Get ready to climb," he yelled at Winter.

She, of course, was already pretty sure what Leven was thinking and was mentally ready to scale the fence as fast as possible. Leven pulled off his sweatshirt as he ran. He reached the fence and sprang up toward the top, scrambling to get higher. He frantically tossed his sweatshirt over the barbed wire and laid his body on it. He glanced down to see how close Winter was. She was not only close, she was right behind him on the fence.

"Climb up my back," he shouted. She did so and went over him and dropped to the other side of the fence. She put up her arms to catch Leven as he followed her, but he landed heavily next to her, sprawling onto the hard ground.

"Nice catch," he grunted, trying to retrieve the breath that had been knocked out of him. He wanted to lay there and moan for a few minutes, but he had his life to worry about.

They scrambled to their feet and watched through the fence as the huge snake slithered to a stop. It raised its head and hissed madly at Leven and Winter, its fiery eyes burning in the dark night. The snake tried to roll itself over the fence but the sharp barbwire sliced its stomach and gave it pause.

It hissed violently again.

Leven wiped his forehead and tried to catch his breath. He wondered why Winter was yelling in a muffled voice and was startled to turn and see that she wasn't saying anything.

"Who's saying that?" Leven asked.

"I think it's Clover," Winter said, equally out of breath.

"Clover," Leven yelled. "Where are you?"

Winter pointed toward Leven's sweatshirt that was still snagged on top of the wire. It was hanging down, and there was a wad of something in the hood, which was swinging back and forth.

"He's in there?" Leven asked, panicked.

"He must have been in your hood," Winter breathed.

The huge head of the serpent lifted and swung from left to right. It was only a few inches away from the sweatshirt.

Leven almost asked Winter what they should do, thus opening up the philosophical debate over whether they should attempt to get Clover or try to save themselves. Leven could see decent arguments on both sides. They could be snatched off the fence by the snake as they tried to untangle Clover, making their efforts in vain. Plus, one could argue that Clover was here to save Leven, and Clover himself would insist that Leven leave him and save himself. Of course, Leven had grown to sort of like the little guy, and in all honestly he couldn't bear to just leave him for dead. These are thoughts and things that almost happened. What transpired in earnest, however, was that while thoughts such as those were racing through Leven and Winter's heads, the fat serpent shoved his huge face straight down into the ground and began tunneling under the fence. It all happened so fast Winter and Leven hardly had time to gasp.

Leven looked toward his Wonder Wipe sweatshirt as it hung there with Clover trapped inside. Before he could climb for it, the earth opened up beneath him, and the gaping mouth of the beast rose straight around Winter and him. The snake clamped its jaw shut, capturing them.

Instantly, it was pitch black and dirt filled Leven and Winter's noses and mouths. The snake writhed and moved the muscles in its throat to swallow. It felt like a tremendous vacuum trying to pull them down.

The huge serpent whipped its ugly head back and up. Then with irresistible force it shoved its face into the ground. The big head

penetrated the earth, taking Leven and Winter and Geth with it. The rest of his long body followed, slithering down into the dirt as if it were a noodle being slurped up by mother earth.

In less than thirty seconds the scene was completely quiet: quiet except for the worried questioning of poor Clover trapped in the hood of a tangled sweatshirt at the top of a fence.

"Guys?" Clover laughed. "Ha, ha, I get it. Trap poor Clover."

Silence.

"Hey, is everything okay? Very funny. Guys? Winter? Lev? Toothpick?"

The moon grew fuzzy, and the night went on as if nothing unusual had happened at all.

CHAPTER TWENTY-TWO

Swallowed Whole and Alive

In the darkness of the snake's mouth, Leven couldn't see a thing, but he could feel plenty. Winter was screaming and he could feel her kicking madly. He could also feel the muscles of the great snake working to move them deeper into its belly, massaging them into its stomach. Thick mucus coating the snake's mouth and throat made it impossible to resist and they moved steadily downward. In their struggle they had created enough air pockets to still have a little oxygen to breathe. It wouldn't last long.

Everything swirled and twisted as the huge serpent continued to bore deeper into the ground.

"He's crushing me!" Winter screamed. "I can't breathe!"

"Push out!" Leven yelled.

"It's too heavy."

The muscles surged and rolled, squeezing them deeper into the snake. Each squeeze left them with less and less of the hot air to breathe. Eventually the snake leveled out and began to slow down. At what felt like somewhere near the center of the earth it finally stopped completely. There it wriggled Leven and Winter down further into its belly to begin digestion. Leven had a small air pocket in front of him and Winter had a slightly bigger one for her. They both were struggling to even breathe. They knew their oxygen wouldn't last much longer.

"Why'd he stop?" Winter whispered, the air deathly quiet except for their breathing. The beast's hot belly smelled of sweat and dirt and decaying flesh.

"I have no idea," Leven whispered back, scared to death.

"He's resting," Geth spoke up. "It'll lay here until we're digested."

"Who said that?" Leven asked in shock, not having yet been introduced to Geth.

"That's Geth," Winter cried.

"Geth's here?" Leven asked in amazement. "Where?"

"In my pocket," Winter choked. "He's a . . . toothpick."

There is nothing quite as painful as a truly awkward silence. If you have fallen in love and you tell the object of your affection how you feel and she simply stares at you, the air still and empty, that's awkward. Perhaps you finally get up the nerve to ask your boss for a raise and after you muster the courage to blurt out your request he lets it just hang there in the open air. That can be an awkward silence as well. But for some reason both those examples pale in comparison to the kind of uncomfortable silence a person might

experience when trapped in the stomach of a colossal earth snake, miles under the ground, where there is nothing but total darkness and the sound of your own self taking your final hot breaths of musty, stale air, after you've just received news that the one person who you believe could save you because he is so big and powerful is hiding out in the pocket of a friend as a . . . toothpick.

"A toothpick?" Leven gasped.

"For the time being," Geth replied. "I won't always—"

"The Geth we were searching for is a toothpick?" Leven interrupted, still in complete shock.

"He is," Winter breathed hard.

Leven wished he could turn his head to scream, but the walls of the snake's belly held him so tightly he couldn't even wiggle his toes.

"A toothpick is going to save us?"

"Fate will figure this out," Geth said without emotion.

"Fate?" Leven came undone. "That's your plan, to wait for fate?" The claustrophobic conditions were too much to bear.

"There is wisdom in—"

"There's no air," Leven yelled. "I have got to be dreaming this," he rambled, anxiety now totally overcoming him. He began talking to himself. "It is impossible for giant dirt clods to turn into a snake and swallow me and take me to the center of the earth with a toothpick and a girl who can . . ." Leven stopped himself to think. "Winter," he whispered, "Can't you freeze this thing?"

"What good would that do?" she moaned. "We would just be really cold and stuck in a frozen snake."

Leven closed his eyes, which really wasn't necessary due to the dark, and thought. Nothing came to him. He tried to manipulate

the will of the snake, but no matter what he thought or concentrated on, nothing happen. Then, it hit him. His eyes jumped open.

"Freeze me!" Leven blurted.

"What?" she said in disbelief.

"Freeze me solid."

"No way, I can't see how—"

"Listen," Leven interrupted again. "You and your half-brained attempts are part of why we are in this mess and if you can't do what I ask just say so, and you and your dumb little toothpick and ratty blond hair can live happily ever after in this grave."

Leven's tactic worked.

"If you're going to be a jerk about it, I'll gladly freeze you," Winter seethed. She simply thought it and it was done.

Leven was now a block of human ice.

"I hope he knows what he's doing," Geth commented.

Winter began to cry.

"It'll be okay," Geth tried.

She was about to point out how hopeless their cause was, but she was stopped by the snake's movement. It twisted a bit and rolled its stomach. The chunk of ice inside of it was making the poor beast uncomfortable. It slithered and rocked, turning Winter upside down.

"It's working," Geth whispered. "That boy's pretty smart."

The uncomfortable snake couldn't take it. It angled its head upward and began to frantically slither its way to the top, moving at a speed that was at least double the one they had been going on the way down. The movement threw Winter against Leven, who was still frozen solid.

The serpent burst from the earth and opened its huge mouth. It

rolled around and began working its muscles as if to gag itself, constricting its body from its tail forward in an attempt to eject the chunk of ice in its stomach. Winter and Leven were squeezed forward.

"I think we're going out," Geth observed needlessly.

The snake gave one last gigantic heave, and Winter and Leven were spewed out of its mouth and onto the ground. Leven's frozen body slammed up against her, remaining intact but giving her a huge bruise up her left side. The two of them were smeared with mud and mucus.

Free of its victims, the snake shook its giant head and whipped its tongue, creating small whirlwinds of dust. It glared at Winter and Leven and hissed loudly, then lifted its huge head and thrust it down into the earth, returning to where it came from.

"We're free?" Winter coughed, standing up and inhaling as deeply as she could.

"You two did it," Geth smiled. "Can you unthaw him?"

"I think you mean, *thaw* him," Winter said, flipping her hands and flinging gook around. "But not yet. I don't appreciate people calling my hair ratty."

Geth liked that.

Winter wiped some of the gunk from her face and spit more dirt from her mouth. She looked down at Leven under the quarter moon and smiled. He wasn't exactly in a very dignified position. Thanks to being crammed in a snake's belly he had been frozen in a rather grotesque way. One leg was bent up toward his stomach and the other was sort of twisted and bent back. His hands were in front of him as if he were a very uncoordinated person about to play peek-a-boo. His facial expression was the most unflattering thing. He was

bug-eyed, and his mouth looked like a goldfish's out of water, trying to suck in air.

Winter took Geth out of her pocket to give him a better look. She had never seen a toothpick laugh so hard.

"Should I thaw him now?" she asked.

"Unless you want to carry him."

Winter touched Leven on the arm, and he instantly thawed. He stretched out and moaned. In a few moments he was a limp body lying on the prairie floor. He coughed a couple of times, opened his eyes, and looked up. He blinked. Winter was leaning over him with her hands on her knees and her ratty hair hanging down toward him.

"It worked?" Leven shivered, looking around in amazement.

"It worked," Winter smiled, extending her hand and helping him up.

"Sorry about the hair comment," Leven said. "I just needed you to want to freeze me."

"Don't worry about it," Winter grinned. "I haven't given it a second thought," she lied. "So, what now?"

"Is there really a toothpick?" Leven asked.

Winter took Geth back out of her pocket and placed him in the palm of her hand. She held him out for Leven to see. Geth bowed.

"Leven Thumps," he said formally, "I am Geth."

Leven didn't know if he felt worse being in the stomach of a snake miles underground or being on top of the soil and realizing his future was dependent on a talking toothpick.

"You're so small," Leven said in shock. "You can't be Geth."

"I am," Geth reconfirmed, giving no apology for his state.

"You're a toothpick."

"At the moment."

"Clover said the fate of our world depends on you."

"In a sense that's true," Geth said humbly.

Leven looked at Winter. "I can't do this," he complained to her, his mind still under the influence of the memory of the shadows. "I barely believed in myself when I thought Geth was a great and powerful king. Now, we're supposed to save the world with the help of a sliver? What are we going to do, poke people? Clean their teeth for them?" Leven's thoughts were still black.

"Lev—" Winter tried.

"I'm sorry," he waved. "This is all wrong. Someone is playing a joke on me. Where are the cameras?" He looked around as if this were all some elaborate scam.

Leven turned back to Geth. "Aren't you supposed to be the one to take us to . . . Foo?" he said sarcastically. "I'm sorry, but I don't see you being capable of taking us anywhere. If it were up to you we would still be in the stomach of that snake, waiting for fate to figure things out."

"Fate did," Geth said strongly.

"*I* did," Leven pointed out.

"With the help of fate," Geth added.

"Fate did nothing. If fate is so great why shouldn't I just lie here on the ground and wait for it to carry me off to Foo?"

"That would be foolish," Geth said honestly.

"Arrgh!" Leven hollered, throwing up his hands, the white in his hair bristling. "I can't do this."

"Lev—" Winter tried again. "Sabine is—"

He waved her off. "I need to think." Leven looked at both of them, his brown eyes full of hurt and confusion. "I don't exactly like

being chased by shadows and swallowed by snakes. I told you, I'm not the right one. I'm sorry." He shook his head sadly and walked off.

"Should we follow him?" Winter asked Geth, her head throbbing.

"No, he'll find us," Geth replied casually.

Winter put Geth in her pocket and looked out toward Leven as he slouched away. She sighed and turned to walk in the opposite direction toward town.

ii

"A toothpick?" Leven asked himself as he shuffled across the prairie. "A toothpick? Not even a stick or a log, but a *toothpick?* The world's in jeopardy," Leven mocked. "I know, let's send an orphan and a toothpick. That should take care of the problem."

The ground crunched beneath Leven's feet as he walked across the moonlit prairie. He looked up at the fuzzy moon and twisted to see if he could still spot Winter walking away from him. She was long gone. As he turned back to face forward he practically ran into the tall chain link fence they had scaled earlier. He had been so busy dwelling on his misfortunes, he hadn't even seen it coming.

"Clover," he said, remembering.

Leven followed the fence toward the east, wondering if Clover had been able to get himself out. Before long he began to hear the muffled sound of someone singing.

"Forty-seven thousand, eight hundred and ninety pretty nits on my mind. Forty-seven thousand, eight hundred and ninety. Take one out? No! Too full of self-doubt. Forty-seven thousand, eight

hundred and eighty-nine pretty nits on my mind. Forty-seven thousand—"

Leven ran to the sweatshirt dangling from the barbed wire and yelled up.

"Clover!"

"Lev?" Clover said, stopping his song, his voice muffled by the sweatshirt he was tangled in. "Oh, great, now I lost count."

Leven climbed up on the fence and reached up. He tugged at the sweatshirt, but it would not come unhooked from the barbed wire.

"I'm trapped here forever," Clover lamented casually, as if he were just doing what was expected.

"I'll get you out. Hold on."

Leven held onto the shirt with one hand and jumped down. He hung there for a second until his weight caused the sweatshirt to rip away, dropping Clover and him straight to the ground.

Leven got to his knees and unwrapped Clover.

"You're supposed to be saving *me,*" Leven smiled, happy to see his friend.

Clover grinned. "This makes us even." Clover bounded up as if to hug Leven, but he stopped, cleared his throat, and stuck out his hand for a shake.

Leven accommodated him.

"Besides," Clover went on. "I could have gotten myself out. I was just resting." He smiled at Leven. "Now, where are Winter and the sliver?" Clover asked.

"I left them back there," Leven said, pointing, the smile erased from his face. "I'm not going with them," he added.

"What? Are you crazy?" Clover jumped. "What else would you do?"

"I'll think of something. Something that doesn't involve dying," Leven said bitterly.

"Like what?" Clover said, interested.

"I don't know. All I'm sure of is that in the last couple of days I have almost been killed at least twice."

"Wow," Clover said, confused. "I've seen things way differently. It seems to me that in the last few days you were finally living."

Leven was silent. Clover's reasoning seemed to hit home. His head was just so full of dark thoughts and confusion. Sabine's shadows had really worked a number on him.

"I just can't do it," Leven finally said. "It's impossible."

"Exactly." Clover smiled, as if they had just had an incredible breakthrough. "It seems impossible. That, Funny Man, is why we must get you to Foo."

"Funny Man?" Leven asked.

"I'm trying to come up with an endearing nickname for you," Clover said. "Ever since Winter came and started calling you Lev. I had that first, you know."

"Well, keep trying," Leven sighed. "Funny Man doesn't work."

Clover cleared his throat. "So let's get you to Foo."

"The space between possible and impossible," Leven said, imitating Clover's voice.

"Exactly."

Leven shook his head tiredly. "You're so agreeable."

"So will you go?"

Leven sighed. "Geth is a toothpick," he complained.

"Winter is a thimble?" Clover replied hesitantly.

"What?"

"Oh, sorry. I thought we were talking in code," Clover shivered. "We have to get back. You're confused, but you will see clearly someday."

Leven sighed again. He picked up Clover and set him on his shoulder.

"So we're going?" Clover asked again, wanting to be sure.

"I guess so," Leven said unenthusiastically.

"That's the spirit," Clover cheered, his robe sparkling under the slight moon.

Leven looked at the moon, gauged where they were, and began working his way back to a girl he still barely knew, and to a talking toothpick that claimed he could save the world.

CHAPTER TWENTY-THREE

THE STRENGTH OF SHADOWS

Winter walked quickly through the trees. She had wanted to go around the grove, but Geth had assured her that they would be fine. The landscape was a mess. The ground before her was the very place where the avalands had risen out of the earth and run after them. Trees lay strewn about and dirt was heaped up in mounds all over.

"Where did they come from?" Winter asked Geth as she walked nervously through the trees. "The avalands, I mean."

"This was the work of Sabine and his shadows. Their touch brought them to life. Sabine understands earth."

Winter stepped over fallen tree limbs and made her way around the jagged holes in the ground. Moonlight filtered through the blasted trees, creating a pattern of shadows in the dark grove. She

looked to the moon, and when she glanced forward again there was someone or something standing in front of her.

Winter gasped, placing her hand to her heart.

In front of her hovered a single shadow, thin and black, wearing a cloak and a hood. Though his face was dark, his evil features were visible—a long, narrow face, a nose that twitched as if smelling something foul, and deep, sunken eyes that glowed against the darkness of its hood. His stance suggested superiority.

"Hello," the shadow whispered hoarsely. As he spoke his open mouth looked like a hole right through him.

"Hello," Winter responded weakly, moving to go around him, her heart thumping wildly.

"Do not be frightened," it said coldly, his voice a hollow echo. "Stop yourself." He held up a long, thin hand with slim, crooked fingers.

Winter stopped.

"That's better," it whispered. "We know you."

Winter held her eyes down, trying to squelch the fear inside of her. She was having trouble breathing.

"You are not from here," the shadow breathed. "You are not from here."

"You're wrong," she said quickly, knowing she had been recognized.

Sabine's shadow placed its hands behind its back and drifted slowly around Winter, looking closely at her.

"You are alone?" it asked.

Winter thought about mentioning Geth, but something held her back.

"I am alone," she whispered bravely, pushing her hair back so the shadow could see the strength of her eyes.

"Where is the boy, Leven?" it questioned.

"He gave up."

Sabine's shadow smiled. "He's smarter than we give him credit for. You would do well to follow his example," it exhaled.

"I don't know what you're talking about," Winter insisted.

"We think you do," the shadow hissed softly. "There is another."

"Another what?" Winter said harshly.

"Another spirit," it shuddered.

"There are thousands of spirits," she pointed out. "Billions." She turned to follow the eyes of the shadow as it continued to circle her.

It laughed, its laughter sounding like a cold, wicked confession that sent chills down Winter's spine all the way to the pads of her feet. She wanted to run away, but she felt as if her ankles were shackled to the ground.

"Not just any spirit," the shadow clarified. "This one is different."

"Well, I can't imagine what it would have to do with me," Winter lied. "I'm done with all this."

The shadow's eyes burned. Something in the last thing Winter had said to it caused its dark soul to churn.

"You are Winter?" it questioned in disbelief. "Winter?"

"I'm going," she said, stepping quickly away and picking up her pace.

Sabine's shadow didn't follow. But it watched her as she fled, then it slowly dissolved, leaving nothing but moonlight in the grove.

ii

Looking frantically over her shoulder, Winter splashed quickly across the river and ran toward Burnt Culvert. She wanted to be as far away from what she had just seen as possible. Her heart was thumping even harder than when she had been chased by the avalands.

She reached the edge of town and felt some relief. Winter could see a couple of people and lights and life going on. She ran up the street and stepped into the doorway of a new hotel. No one was near.

"Who was that?" she asked Geth quietly. She had still not caught her breath completely.

"Sabine's strongest shadow," Geth answered. "He's here for me and Leven. They give Sabine the chance to view us from Foo."

"We need to get back to Lev." Winter was panicked. "He's out there alone. Sabine will find him."

"We can't stop that from happening now," Geth said honestly. "It's out of our hands."

"But what if we—"

"Leven will be okay," Geth said calmly, interrupting her concern.

Winter had her doubts.

"I remember him," Winter whispered. "Sabine."

"You should," Geth said, "he tried to destroy you once. Antsel stopped him."

"How is that possible?" she asked.

"You'll understand soon."

"Now we're heading back to him?" Winter asked, sounding more panicked than she wanted to admit.

"And he's heading toward us," Geth said seriously.

Winter shivered. She had more to fear then she had thought.

iii

Leven's head was clearing, and he was beginning to feel a bit better. It just felt kind of normal for him to be with Clover, heading toward Winter. Clover was right that Leven was leaving nothing great behind. Leven had nothing to lose by following this adventure to the end. He couldn't understand why he couldn't get his mind to believe it.

"Want some gum?" Clover asked, reaching into the pouch on the front of his cloak.

"No, thanks."

"Who says no to gum?" Clover teased. "I'm worried about you."

"I don't normally say no, but I've been burned by some of your snacks before," Leven reminded him.

"How was I to know you wouldn't like the taste of roaches? This is different," Clover smiled, taking a chunk of gum out of a round tube. He tossed it in his mouth and began to chew.

"Stop it!" a voice rang out.

Startled, Leven looked around. Clover kept chewing.

"Help me. Oh, someone, please help me!"

"Is that you?" Leven asked, alarmed that he couldn't pinpoint exactly where the cries were coming from.

"Nah, that's just my gum," Clover chewed. "It'll stop complaining in a moment."

"Please, won't somebody help me?" the gum hollered. It made a gurgling sound.

"Is that normal?" Leven asked.

"It's Tarmarts's argumint flavored gum. In a second it will begin to apologize. It's a vicious cycle. It's noisier than complimint flavored, but I like it better."

"Oh, won't somebody please help me," the gum wailed. "I can't . . . I'm sorry. I'm so sorry. It won't happen again."

Clover continued to chew.

"Oh, that feels nice," the gum said.

"Would you please spit that out?" Leven asked, feeling like the whole world could hear them as they pushed through a corn field toward town.

"No one can see us," Clover pointed out.

"I still think we should be quiet."

Clover swallowed it. Leven could hear the gum screaming the whole way down Clover's throat. "I promise I'll change . . ." its yelling trailed off.

"See why I think your candy here is boring?" Clover asked.

"I'm not sure I want to go to Foo," Leven said, looking down at Clover. "I don't think I'm—"

"Good evening, Leven," a new, hollow-sounding voice spoke.

"What is that?" Leven asked, thinking Clover had put in another chunk of gum. "Creepimint flavor?"

Clover was too busy disappearing to answer. Leven looked up. Sabine's strongest shadow stood only inches away from him. Leven jumped at least a foot.

"I'm sorry. Did we startle you?" it asked, its voice seeping from its mouth and swirling around Leven's ears.

"Not really," Leven lied. "Do I know you?" His head fogged up, and his mind became stickier than it had been. Leven tried to fight it, but his mind went black.

"We're meeting for the first time," Sabine's shadow sniffed. "We think you need to know something." Sabine's shadow smiled.

"Okay," Leven said listlessly and as if drifting off into sleep.

"There are those out there who wish to harm you," the shadow whispered.

"People?" Leven questioned.

"That is correct. There are those who would lead you to believe in fables and fairy tales. We are here to make sure you understand how foolish that is—how *dangerous* that is. People who believe in fairy tales are foolish. Do you understand?"

Leven was silent, his brown eyes clouded over and dull. He couldn't fight the strength of the shadow.

"Understand?" the shadow whispered again, blowing his words into Leven's right ear.

"I don't believe in fairy tales," Leven said, as if in a trance.

"That's a good boy," the shadow approved. "We wouldn't want you trusting in foolish dreams only to end up hurt . . . or worse."

Sabine's shadow was a perfect example of uneasy. He didn't speak English, he spoke anguish. His vowels made the hair on the back of Leven's neck stand up, and his consonants sent shivers down his spine. As he spoke, the shadow's essence swirled around Leven, stealing any hope or confidence from him.

"You don't want to get hurt, do you?" it asked.

Leven looked at the glowing eyes of Sabine's shadow. Its narrow shoulders were crooked, and its wide, thin-lipped mouth was full of jagged, decayed teeth. It seemed to Leven as if he had seen this

vision before—maybe in a book, or in a dream, or on a napkin holder.

"Go home, Leven," the shadow reasoned. "Forget what you have heard—before you make a mistake, before it's too late."

"But—" Leven tried.

"No!" the shadow hissed. "You can affect nothing. Remember that. You can affect nothing. We would hate to see you or someone you care for hurt because of your foolishness."

It patted Leven on the head. Its touch was empty.

"Trust no one," it whispered.

A low wind blew, and Leven brushed his bangs back from his eyes. The shadow had vanished. After a few moments Clover whispered. "Is it really gone?"

Leven continued to stand there.

"That was a strong shadow," Clover said, all the playfulness gone out of his voice. "We have to find Geth and Winter and get out of here."

Leven just stood there.

"That will involve walking," Clover pointed out, motioning for Leven to go forward.

"He was telling the truth, Clover," Leven finally spoke. "I don't belong in this. Someone could get hurt."

"Truth is so subjective," Clover waved. "Besides, we've all been hurt before. Windy Stein," Clover mocked, his ears fluttering. "Who does she think she is? She didn't even try to get to know me," Clover sniffed. "I would have made—"

Leven's stare stopped Clover.

"Right, we should get going."

"You don't understand," Leven said seriously. "I'm out. Find

Winter and let her know. If she still believes in all this she can take you and that toothpick back to Foo."

"You are so fickle," Clover complained. "You're stronger than the shadows," he urged.

"I can't go," Leven replied.

"What will you do? In all honesty I'm not supposed to leave your side." Clover panicked. "I'm already going to get it for some of the things I've done here."

"Sorry," Leven said kindly. "But I didn't tell you to come."

Clover frowned. "There's no way of talking you out of this?"

"No," Leven answered, his eyes betraying his true discomfort over being himself at the moment.

"Well, I hate to do this." Clover disappeared.

"Do what?" Leven asked the air, looking around for Clover.

Clover sank his teeth into the back of Leven's neck and shook his head, releasing tiny drops of fluid that instantly knocked Leven out. A little known fact about sycophants is that they love to serve, but every once in a while, they just plain get sick of helping others. For such times and needs, nature has blessed them with a secret weapon: a venom that knocks out whomever they bite and allows the sycophants to have a little needed me-time. The truly wonderful thing about the venom is that it doesn't actually cause its victims to sleep, it just puts them in a trance where they are shown pictures and scenes of sycophants and learn how wonderful sycophants are.

Clover released his bite, and Leven dropped to the ground like a sack of potatoes.

"Sorry," Clover said, pushing on Leven to roll him behind a thick stretch of tall corn. "Pleasant viewing."

Clover jumped away in search of Winter.

iv

Winter and Geth weren't too terribly hard to find. Winter had planted herself at the main bus stop on the main road into town, hoping whenever Leven did wander back she would see him. She was sitting there wishing she had something to eat when Clover showed up. Actually, he didn't exactly show, but he drew near to her and spoke.

"Miss me?" he asked.

"Clover," Winter said with excitement, to nothing but air.

"Save the gushing," Clover smiled, his blue eyes materializing. "I have Lev."

"Where?" Geth spoke up from within her pocket.

"I sort of bit him."

"Sort of?"

"I mean, it's not like I took a chunk out of him. He's all right. Just sound asleep."

"He shouldn't sleep," Geth said with concern.

"Um," Clover hesitated. "It's not exactly sleep. He's kind of under a spell."

Confused, Winter shook her head.

"Let's go get him," Geth ordered.

Clover hopped on top of Winter's still-shaking head and gave her directions. It was dark, but they found Leven lying there on the ground, peaceful and quiet.

"He looks so young when he's resting," Clover cooed. "He's growing so fast."

"What happened?" Geth asked. "Why'd you bite him?"

"He wanted to leave again."

"Again?" Winter questioned.

"When he got me down from the fence he was ready to dash. But I talked him out of it," Clover said proudly. "But then he changed his mind."

Leven shivered and shifted. He muttered something about sycophants being great.

"Oh, I wish I had a blanket," Clover said in a motherly tone. "Silly me," he said, slapping his furry forehead. "I do." Clover reached into his void and pulled out a pretty pink blanket with lace around the edges. Winter smiled.

"It's my sister's," Clover explained defensively.

Winter smiled wider.

Clover laid the blanket on top of Leven, and the lace contracted and worked itself until Leven was wrapped snuggly. Clover continued talking.

"Anyhow, Lev and I were working our way back across the prairie, and we ran into a tall shadow with really bad teeth. I'm sorry. I think even if you're going to be sinister you can take five minutes a day to floss and brush. I had a short spell when I was a kid when I wasn't exactly the best sycophant, but I always—"

Winter cleared her throat to bring Clover back to the conversation at hand.

"Oh, yes. Anyway, this shadow was tall and spoke uneasily."

"Sabine's shadow," Geth said softly. "We saw him, too."

"He started talking junk to Lev about fairy tales and not trusting people. Lev seemed to buy into it, said he was done, and that I should tell you two to go on without him."

Winter and Geth stared at Clover.

"So I bit him," Clover added nonchalantly. He gazed dreamily at Leven. "I hope he's seeing good things."

"We have got to get him out of here," Geth said authoritatively. "I think it will help him change his mind once we are on our way. Besides, the time is getting short."

"Where are we going?" Winter asked.

"To the gateway."

"Is it far?"

"Only halfway around the world," Geth said casually.

Winter shrugged as if it were no big deal to travel halfway around the world with a toothpick, a sycophant, and an offing who didn't want to be there. I suppose if a person had been through what she had been through, they too might not see any great challenge in simply traversing thousands of miles to make their way to the mysterious gateway.

"How are we going to carry Lev?" Winter asked.

The ground began to lightly vibrate and then rumble. Winter's face turned as pale as new paper. She probably would have passed out, figuring it was a new herd of avalands coming to get them, if it had not been for the low whistle that accompanied the vibrating.

Somewhere in the distance a train was coming.

"Do you think you can drag him to the train tracks?" Geth asked Winter.

"Sure," she replied. "But there's no way we're going to be able to get him onto a moving train."

"I'll take care of that," Clover promised, evaporating into the air.

"I'd help you drag him, but . . ." Geth smiled apologetically.

"Don't worry about it," Winter said. She pulled Leven's arms out of the blanket and took hold of his wrists. She began walking backward and dragging his limp body toward the sound of the approaching train.

CHAPTER TWENTY-FOUR

All Aboard

Bennett Williams was a train engineer. He had been one for just over seven years. In high school he had wanted to be a biologist who lived by himself out in the wilderness, observing the living habits of wolves. But then he met a nice girl who didn't share his dream, so he became an engineer. It wasn't a bad deal. He got to spend a lot of time by himself, watching the world fly by, and still go home to a wife and family.

At the moment Bennett was hurtling over the state of Oklahoma, pulling fifty cars and two additional engines and whistling a song he couldn't quite name but thought sounded mournful. He wasn't alone, thanks to Roy, his fireman, who was sitting in a soft chair nearby, snoring blissfully.

It was well past midnight, and Bennett was making good time. The cab of the locomotive was a bit warm, and it felt good to occasionally hold his head out the open window. He checked his gauges and routinely adjusted a couple of controls. When he looked up, there appeared to be a misshapen cat in a doll's dress hovering in the air and staring right at him. Startled, the engineer flinched, and the cat thing was gone.

Bennett looked around the cab, his adrenaline suddenly racing. He glanced over at his companion, who was still sleeping. He rubbed his eyes, and when he opened them again, the strange creature was flying right at his head.

"Ah!" Bennett threw his hands up in front of his face to protect himself, but the creature was gone again.

The noise had been enough, however, to wake Roy. Roy looked over at Bennett and blinked. Bennett was still holding his hands in front of him and frantically looking around the cab of the locomotive.

"Are you okay?" Roy asked.

"I'm not sure," Bennett breathed. "I think I saw . . . well, I was . . . oh, I'm sure it was nothing," Bennett waved, too embarrassed to explain.

Clover appeared on the top of Bennett's head, then quickly disappeared. Roy's jaw dropped as he pointed to where Clover had been.

"What was that?" Roy gasped.

"What was what?" Bennett asked, twisting to see behind him.

"It looked like—"

Clover showed up on Roy's head, and Bennett hollered. Clover was at the window. Gone. He was on Bennett's head. Gone. Flying though the air. Gone. On Roy's leg. Gone. On Bennett's face. Gone.

Clover was appearing and disappearing at such a rapid rate it looked like he was at least fifty sycophants in the air.

Bennett and Roy were swatting and screaming and brushing and stamping. Roy was having the most difficult time, crying and cursing and begging for whatever it was to go away. Bennett was swatting the air around his head and trying to catch his breath.

"Stop the train!" Roy screamed. "Stop the train!"

Both of them were too busy swinging and kicking at nothing to notice the big smile on Clover's face as Bennett frantically worked the brakes.

Clover's plan was working perfectly.

ii

Leven's wrapped-up heels created a wavy track in the dirt as Winter struggled to drag him across the prairie and toward the train tracks. In the distance, she could see the lights of the engine as it barreled closer. Winter stopped to wipe her brow, and Geth looked up at her from the inside of her pocket and grinned.

"I'm not sure why you're smiling," Winter said. "There's no way Clover can stop that thing."

A loud screeching noise screamed out into the night. It was high-pitched and sounded like a pack of howler monkeys being slowly squashed by a steamroller.

With its brakes locked, the train was slowing. Geth smiled even wider. Winter tugged on Leven's wrists and began straining backward again as the wheels of the heavy train screeched in protest at being slowed down.

Winter reached the side of the tracks just as the locomotive

came to a shuddering stop. Dust and steam and the smell of burning coal filled her nose and burned her eyes. Winter stopped and dropped Leven's arms to catch her breath. Her messy blond hair was wet with perspiration. Winter was standing about in the middle of the train's length, but even in the dark she could see two men jump out of the cab of the engine up ahead, frantically swatting at the air around their heads and yelling.

"What's that all about?" Geth asked, peeking out of her pocket.

"I have no idea," Winter replied, looking down the length of the train for an open car. "There," she pointed. She picked up Leven's wrists again and dragged him behind her. The boxcar was high, with an open door that Winter herself could have easily gotten up into, but she didn't know how to work Leven up. He was a couple of inches taller and weighed at least twenty pounds more than she did.

"Hang his hands on the edge and lift him from the legs," Geth suggested, apparently trying to think of a solution as well.

Winter somehow wrestled the limp Leven to his feet and stood behind him, holding him up in her arms. She managed to lean him forward and drape his hands on the floor of the boxcar in the open doorway. But they just kept slipping off.

Frustrated, she laid Leven face down on the ground and hooked his blanketed heels on the train and lifted him from his shoulders, trying to push him up and on. It was no use; his limp body just kept folding.

"Can't we wake him up?" Winter asked as the train began making noise. "They're starting back up."

"Only Clover can wake him up from his bite."

Winter looked around, wondering where Clover was.

"You could freeze him again," Geth suggested.

Winter shrugged. She laid Leven down with his face up and his feet pointing toward the train. She pulled his arms up over his head and pictured him frozen.

In an instant he was just that.

She picked his rigid body up by the shoulders and strained to carefully lean him up against the train.

The engine whistle sounded.

Winter put her arms around his legs and lifted. It felt as if Leven weighed four hundred pounds. She lowered him back to the ground.

"I can't lift him," she cried.

"You have to," Geth yelled above the noise of the train warming up.

"He's too heavy," Winter protested. "Let's wait for the next train, or for Clover."

"No," Geth said in an unusually stern voice. "We don't have the time to waste."

Winter looked around frantically. "I could freeze him to the train," she said, half jokingly.

"Do it," Geth said, as the train began to inch ahead. Winter lugged Leven to the couplings between the boxcars. With the train beginning to move, she hoisted him up and balanced him on the hitch and pictured him frozen there. Again, her gift worked perfectly, and Leven was securely attached to the train.

Backing out of the space between the slowly moving cars, she jogged alongside the moving train, glancing at Leven's face. He looked relaxed despite the fact that he was iced. The frozen blanket wrapped around him made him appear almost cozy. Winter couldn't help but smile at her handiwork.

"Jump on," Geth shouted; reminding her that all her work would be for nothing if the train got away without her.

It was gaining speed. Winter ran as fast as she could to keep ahead of the boxcar. She grabbed the door, her feet flying and her hands gripping tightly. She counted to three, bounced her feet, and pulled herself up, rolling onto the wooden floor. Her head was spinning, but except for some sore muscles and scrapes, she was still intact. She felt her pocket to make sure Geth was still there.

"I'm here," he said as she pinched him.

She rubbed her side where she had scraped it on the train and crawled to the open door of the boxcar.

"Is he still there?" Geth asked.

"I can't see him, but I can't imagine where he would have gone," Winter smiled.

There was a pile of packing quilts in the corner of the empty car, and Winter spread them out to make a half decent bed. She folded one to create a pillow.

"Where do you think we're going?" she asked Geth as she made herself comfortable.

"East," was Geth's only reply.

"Is that good?"

"Perfect," Geth smiled. "We should run into Germany eventually.

"Germany?" Winter asked.

"Germany."

"Why?"

"That's where the gateway is," Geth said, yawning.

Winter pulled a quilt over her, thinking of Leven still frozen to the moving train. "He did say my hair was ratty," she rationalized.

Geth smiled.

"Germany," she whispered, wondering what a foreign country looked like and if they would actually make it. If Sabine was there, she half hoped they wouldn't. Exhausted, she fell asleep before she could question Geth further.

CHAPTER TWENTY-FIVE

Leaving on a Midnight Train to Danger

Winter, Geth, Leven, and Clover reached the town of Cincinnati, Ohio, a day and a half later. Clover had joined the others shortly after Winter had fallen asleep. He would have gotten to them sooner, but he had wanted to hear the conversation the train engineer and his fireman had after they had stopped the train and started it up again. Clover didn't really think staying for the conversation had been worth it, seeing how the two of them had basically just bawled and agreed to never speak about the incident to anyone ever.

As the train stopped, Winter jumped from the railroad car and carefully defrosted Leven from the train. She warmed him up to his old self. Of course he was still under Clover's spell, and she thought

it might be best to tell him what was happening someplace less public and noisy than right next to the tracks.

Winter dragged him down into a ravine and into a grove of tall, leafy trees for a very pertinent powwow. At that point Clover woke Leven up.

Leven stretched and coughed and looked surprised to see Winter sitting in front of him.

"What are you doing here?" he shivered, his brown eyes clearing just a bit. "I was talking to Clover, in a cornfield at night."

"Good to see you, too," she smiled.

"We're on our way to Germany," Clover spoke up, materializing in front of Leven.

"Clover," Leven said happily, the prosycophant visions he had been shown while bitten still fresh on his mind. Clover moved closer to Leven and allowed him to scratch him behind his ears. "We're going to Germany?" Leven questioned, his face showing how odd the idea sounded.

"That's where the gateway is," Winter added. "We got this far by train."

"Really?" Leven asked, a bit of excitement in his voice now. "I've always wanted to ride in a train. I don't even remember it. Was I sleeping?"

"Well, actually . . ." Clover started to explain.

"What he means," Winter interrupted, "is that it's a pity you slept through the whole thing."

"That's not what I meant," Clover protested. "I was—"

Geth cut him off this time. He leaned out of Winter's pocket and said, "We really do need to get going."

Leven's expression changed. "I'm not going anywhere," he said

mournfully. "I don't know exactly how you talked me into getting here, but I'm not going any farther. I already told Clover I couldn't."

"Sorry, Leven, but you have to," Geth said strongly.

Winter thought that Leven would react harshly to the order Geth had given. Instead, Leven spoke earnestly.

"I can't, Geth," he replied. "I wish I were the person you think I am, but I'm not."

"Yes, you are," Geth said strongly.

"I can't put any of you in further danger," Leven sighed, brushing back his bangs. "If you knew my life you would know there is nothing remarkable about me. I can influence nothing."

"I *know* your life," Geth replied. "I have seen you every day since you were young. I have waited patiently for the time to come when you would be strong enough to enter Foo."

"You've watched me every day?" Leven questioned. "Like Clover? Where were you, in my pocket, bed . . ." he looked at Geth, "holding my sandwich together?" He tried to smile.

"No, I was the tree that stood by your home," Geth said.

Leven was shocked. "The tree? You lived in that tree?"

"I *was* that tree," Geth explained. "Your home wasn't set down there by accident. I was waiting for you."

"I don't believe it," Leven said quickly, thinking about how much he had loved that tree. "How did you . . . I mean . . ."

"As soon as you left home, I provoked Terry into chopping me down. He took me to the lumber yard. I was taken from there and cut up into a toothpick."

Leven just stared at the tiny sliver of wood.

"I know Sabine's influence on you is strong," Geth said, climbing out of Winter's pocket and leaning against a pebble by Leven.

"He wants to get here so badly, and you are the only one who can prevent him from gaining access to reality." Geth shifted on his pebble. "Leven, you need to know some things about yourself."

"This ought to be good," Clover smiled, sitting down on the ground next to Leven and putting a small hand on Leven's knee.

"Your grandfather was a man by the name of Hector Thumps," Geth began. "He made candles in a small shop in upstate Ohio. He was a quiet, kind man who enjoyed what he did, and he fell in love with a girl by the name of Katie."

Clover snickered.

"One evening after a nice meal," Geth continued, "your grandfather took his Katie on a walk though the neighborhood. His plan was to ask her to marry him and make him the happiest man alive.

"Hector and Katie stopped on the corner of Elm and Twelfth to watch the sky and marvel at what an amazing world this was. There he reached into his pocket to extract a ring and ask Katie for her hand. Unfortunately, the temperature was exactly sixty-three degrees, and the sky was filled with some pretty impressive shooting stars. They were also standing over the imperfectly joined intersection of sidewalk connecting Elm and Twelfth. The situation was just right, and before your grandfather could pop the question, he disappeared from in front of Katie's eyes and was swept into Foo.

"He wasn't exactly happy. Since its creation, many souls had protested the fact that they were brought to Foo. They haven't wanted to accept their missions. Your grandfather was no exception. He simply wanted to return to the life that had been stolen from him. His talent, his home, and his love were gone. He petitioned the powers that be for some sort of escape, but they knew no possible escape existed. Were there a known exit where beings could leave,

then Foo would eventually cease to exist. Almost everyone would run back to what they were snatched from, leaving Foo empty and unable to create dreams. With no Foo, those on earth could no longer dream. With no dreams there is no hope, and mankind cannot survive without hope. Ultimately everyone would perish."

"I can't dream without Foo?"

"It's impossible," Geth said kindly. "When you sleep or when you focus on what you dream to be, Foo picks that up and makes the imaginable possible. Your dream is caught by a resident of Foo, and he is responsible for bringing it to life. It is a remarkable place, but not all inhabitants want to accept being there. Your grandfather traversed the entire realm, determined to find a way out. No way existed."

"That's all true," Clover said, as if his reassurance would comfort Leven, "I've heard this story millions of times."

"So if my grandfather was stuck there," Leven asked. "How did I end up here?"

Geth held up his single arm as if motioning Leven to be patient. "After almost a year of searching and hoping, your grandfather finally discovered a way to get out of Foo."

"How?" Winter asked.

"He gave up," Geth stated plainly. "It wasn't a new idea, others in the past and since have tried, but your Grandfather Hector was the only one to ever succeed at it. Somehow he got his brain to believe he wasn't there. He refused to believe that Foo existed. He just lay on his back and closed his eyes. He wouldn't sit in a chair, because that would be admitting that chair existed. He wouldn't eat food or visit with others because in his mind they did not exist. He did not believe, and something in his brain's chemistry allowed him

to fully convince himself. It took some time, weeks," Geth explained, "but eventually, after everyone had forgotten about him, his body drifted back into reality.

"Your grandfather awoke in the same spot in Ohio he had been taken from. It was almost fifteen months later, but he was thrilled. He ran to his small home only to discover it had been sold at auction some months before and now belonged to a big Italian family. He hurried to his candle-making business to find a closed sign and an empty building. He ran to Katie's house and there discovered she had married two months previously and was already expecting her first child.

"Your grandfather was devastated. He had been gone for just over a year, but in that time everything had changed. He had nothing left in reality. He knew then that he had cheated fate by leaving Foo. He had escaped his destiny and messed up the plan. He felt he had nothing in reality and began to long for the very place he had just abandoned."

"He wanted back in Foo?" Leven asked, in amazement.

"He was an interesting person," Geth answered. "His mind worked differently than most. Suddenly for him Foo seemed to be the only answer he could see. He knew the impossible was obtainable in Foo. And since he felt it was impossible for him to ever be happy without Katie, he believed he could only be well again with the help of Foo. Of course, he had no way back, and as I have mentioned before, getting to Foo is not easy. And it is almost always accidental."

"So what did he do?" Winter asked.

"He would stand on street corners that didn't match up for

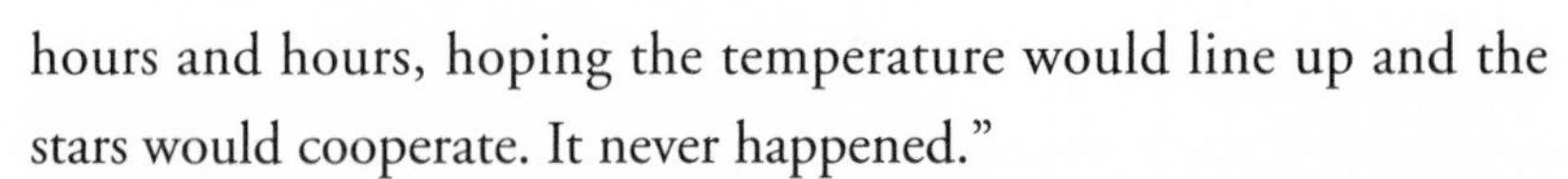

hours and hours, hoping the temperature would line up and the stars would cooperate. It never happened."

Geth stopped talking to scratch a small itch on his backside.

"And?" Leven asked, wanting to know more.

Geth looked at Leven and smiled. "You look so much like him," he said, "your dark eyes and the streak in your hair."

Leven touched his hair, looking confused.

"He was a brilliant man, Leven, but his confusion and desire drove him mad. He did nothing but whisper and think about Foo. It became his obsession. He wanted to return to the very magic he had once abhorred. He studied the things that made a trip to Foo possible. He built mismatched roads and learned all he could about shooting stars and how they occurred. He delved into weather and temperature and tried to determine if it is possible for a temperature to remain constant."

"Amazing," Leven whispered.

"Sad, actually," Geth added. "In his madness he discovered that certain bodies of water had the potential to maintain exact temperatures at different depths. In chasing and detailing shooting stars he formulated a theory that it wasn't so much the stars that cause the reaction, it was the way the earth responded to them—as if the earth were in awe and humming happily. That hum, he theorized, might be possible to recreate in other ways. This was his most important discovery. He just had to make the earth as happy as it was whenever a shooting star went off.

"Then came his masterpiece. He built a large box out of stone and cement. At the base of the box he placed the dug-up portion of misaligned sidewalks from Elm and Twelfth street, the same piece

he had stepped on all those years before. He extracted the pieces and inserted them at the bottom of his gateway.

"He then positioned that box deep in a certain body of water at just the right depth to achieve a correct temperature. Once it was set up, he simply swam into it and stood on the mismatched ground."

"Did it work?" Clover asked, so caught up in the story he forgot he already knew the ending.

Geth nodded.

"How do you trick the earth into being happy?" Winter asked skeptically.

"You'll see soon enough," Geth replied.

"So he made it back in?" Leven asked in wonderment.

"Unfortunately," Geth answered. "When your grandfather returned to Foo, our world went crazy. No one had believed that Hector had gotten out of Foo, but now they knew that not only had he gotten away, he had gotten back. Foo had been a place where the option of leaving didn't exist. Daily, two or three people accidentally stumbled into Foo, and they were always told there was no way out. Now, thanks to your grandfather, everyone knew it was possible to get out and to get back in. Accepting fate had been their only option. There had never been much envy and hate in Foo, until your grandfather's gateway."

Leven didn't look proud.

"It is impossible to kill another in Foo," Geth informed them, "but suddenly there were those who wanted to do just that to your grandfather. They wanted his secret. They wanted to know where the gateway was. He insisted it had been destroyed on his return into Foo, but no one believed him, not even Amelia, whom he met

and married when he returned to Foo. Even after he married her he told her nothing. Antsel . . ." Geth stopped to look at Clover.

Clover smiled and blushed at the mention of his former burn.

Geth continued. ". . . Antsel, the lead token of the Council of Wonder, came forward to point out to all that even if a gateway did exist, their role was to dwell in Foo and make the dreams of mankind possible. They had a divine purpose. Sabine, on the other hand, felt the divine purpose was a myth. He believed that mankind could dream just fine without them in Foo. 'Why should we be trapped here fulfilling people's dreams when they don't even realize we exist?' he would say over and over, convincing many in Foo that any notion of a divine purpose was outdated and foolish.

"When your Grandfather Hector died everyone figured the great mystery of the location of the gateway had died with him, but they were wrong. Antsel had been given the secret by Hector before your grandfather had passed away. Hector had whispered the secret to Antsel because he wanted him to take his child and send him back to reality where he would not be persecuted and could live a life without knowing about Foo.

"The child that Antsel returned was your father."

"How did he get him back to earth?" Leven asked.

"That is the wonder of the gateway your grandfather built. It remains open in Foo as long as the occurrences are right. If people knew where the entrance on each side was, they could travel back and forth from Foo to reality quite often and fairly easy."

"Some grandfather," Clover complimented Leven.

"So we're heading to the gateway he invented?" Leven asked.

"The very same," Geth nodded. "Sabine won't stop until he has found it. He has armies of followers searching for its whereabouts.

He wants into reality so that he can rule both. He doesn't care if the dreams of man cease, nor does he believe that if Foo falls he will no longer have any power."

"Why not just destroy the gateway?" Winter asked. "That way no one could ever come back." Her green eyes were dark and serious.

"Antsel tried," Geth said. "The gateway is protected. It is a law and fact of Foo that that which is truly created can only be taken apart by someone with the same blood."

"Me?" Leven asked.

"We're all hoping so," Geth answered. "You are the only blood relative of Hector Thumps left."

"And you're here because . . . ?" Leven questioned Geth.

"I was captured and put into the seed of a fantrum tree. Sabine thought it would destroy me, but I was rescued by Antsel. Antsel in his wisdom slipped into reality and placed me here, knowing that fate would someday see to it that your path and mine would cross, and you would be able to return me to my rightful position and destroy the gateway behind us."

"Wait a second," Winter said. "So we'll have no way back here once we enter Foo?"

"I hope not," Geth said solemnly. "We must keep Sabine where he is. Foo was not meant to have an exit."

Leven looked at Winter. Winter looked at Leven. They both looked at Clover.

"Listen," Clover said. "Don't worry about not being able to come back, I've lived both places, and trust me, you won't be getting the short end of the stick if you end up in Foo. I mean, candy alone . . ."

"How can Sabine not know his plan would be the death of everyone?" Leven wisely asked.

"Because he is a fool consumed by ambition," Geth answered. "His mind is not his own anymore. You will understand more once we are in Foo," Geth replied. "For now just know that the plan Sabine is selling is a lie that will bring about the end of all of us."

Everyone was silent for a few moments. Geth slid off the pebble he had been sitting on and climbed back into Winter's pocket. He looked toward the sun. "We have to go," he finally said. "I figure we have no more than five days before it's too late."

"Five days?" Leven laughed. "We're supposed to get to Germany in five days?"

"If we do our part, fate will help us," Geth said. "So, are you coming, or does Clover need to bite you again?"

Leven looked confused. "Clover bit me?"

"Only because I care," Clover explained.

"I can't see a way out of all this," Leven said, rubbing the back of his neck.

"Good," Geth replied as Winter stood. "Let's find a way to get to the eastern shore."

Winter began walking and Geth whispered to her. "We have to keep Leven awake."

"Why?" she whispered back.

"Sabine's shadows can only locate him in his dreams. Those of us from Foo don't dream here, but the shadows know Leven's dreams now. They'd find him instantly."

"Keep him awake for five days?"

"At least," Geth said seriously. "Clover can bite him again if we get desperate."

"This should be a fun trip," Winter whispered.

Leven and Clover caught up. The four of them climbed back up the side of the ravine and walked toward the railway station.

It was up to fate now. Of course, it always had been.

CHAPTER TWENTY-SIX

Boats Are Too Slow and Planes Are Too Complicated

They were lucky to find a train going further east, and fast. They climbed aboard a weathered red boxcar and rode through Pennsylvania, New York, and Massachusetts.

The landscape was beautiful, but a blur, especially for Leven and his poor eyesight. The boxcar they were in was dark and cold and it rattled uncomfortably as the train flew across the country. Any conversation they had was jittery and shaky. Geth explained to Leven the necessity of him staying awake and how Sabine's shadows could easily find them all if Leven ever slumbered. It was Leven they knew. Leven was willing to do his part in all of this, but staying awake for so many days seemed almost too much to ask, if not impossible.

Thankfully, the cold, vibrating metal floor of the train car helped him remain conscious a lot easier.

In Massachusetts they got off the train they were on and snuck into the car of another heading into Maine, a boxcar full of mattresses.

"This isn't fair," Leven complained.

"Obviously fate has a sense of humor," Geth smiled.

Leven stood up through New Hampshire and was contemplating lying down, despite the shadows, as they crossed into Maine and they all got off. From there they caught a ride in the back of a produce truck, which moved them all the way to the shore and a nice town called Cape Porpoise.

Their spirits were pretty high, what with fate helping them out so generously, but when they reached the actual coastline of Maine and looked out at the endless ocean they suddenly became more than a little discouraged. The water stretched out forever.

"It's huge," Winter gawked.

"You can't even see the other side," Clover worried.

"It's impossible," Leven said. "All that water, and, I've got to tell you, I'm tired."

"None of that," Geth chastised. "There has to be a way."

The four of them had done nothing but discuss what their options were for the last two days, that and work to keep Leven awake. They couldn't take a plane because they didn't have money. Leven suggested he try and manipulate fate so someone would give them some money, but that still left them as minors trying to buy tickets to cross the ocean. It was also true they didn't have passports or the papers and time to procure them. So flying seemed out of the question. The option of getting on a boat was considered, but that

had some of the same problems as flying. Even if they were able to stow away on a ship it would take too long to get there and, according to Geth, time was of the essence.

Leven always got just a little frustrated when Geth talked about time running out. If time were so incredibly important, why didn't the great toothpick offer suggestions that might speed things up, instead of sitting back and waiting for fate to take a hand?

"What are we going to do?" Winter moaned. "Two kids, a toothpick, and a stuffed animal against the entire Atlantic ocean."

"Maybe we should eat something," Clover suggested, ignoring the crack about him being a stuffed animal. He had been making that same suggestion for the last half of the day.

"Maybe we should sleep a bit," Leven said.

"I don't think so," Winter and Geth said together. "I wouldn't mind eating, though," Winter added.

Leven could feel the air thinning. He rubbed his eyes, hoping he might be able to see something. His mind cleared. His gift of being able to see and manipulate things was not all that dependable, and he felt he made a rather pathetic offing. At the moment, however, his gift seemed to be kicking in. His eyes burned gold. He could see lights and movement. A large picnic was in full swing. He could see Winter and him filling their plates with food from a table and sitting down to eat. He could also see a church next to a flagpole and flag.

"I know where some food is," Leven announced. "Look for a church around here with a flagpole."

They all turned from facing the ocean and wandered into Cape Porpoise. Winter spotted the steeple of a white church, and in no

time Leven and Winter were helping themselves to food served by a noisy bunch of Baptists at their October-blessed celebration.

ii

Sabine was agitated, and his brain raced, and his body twitched. His shadows had lost Leven. He had called them all home to assess how their search was going, but when he sent them back out, Leven was gone. They searched the entire state of Oklahoma. Nothing. They were now working their way through the surrounding states, but so far there had been no sign of Leven's dreams.

"Where are you, Leven Thumps? You can't stay awake forever. And Geth?" Sabine seethed. "*I* thought *I* destroyed you long ago, yet here you are again." Sabine twitched. "And Winter," he slurred. "It looks as if we will meet again."

Sabine ran his thick bumpy tongue over his small teeth. He knew there was a possibility that Leven had truly given up, but he could not take that chance. Sabine also knew that if Leven had not given up he was probably heading toward the gateway. But since the gateway's location was unknown to anyone besides Geth, that information did Sabine little good.

Sabine inhaled, and like bats returning to their cave, his shadows filled the arches and open ways of his castle, cramming the halls and ceilings.

His spirits whispered, "We've failed. We've failed. Nothing." They swirled around, hissing hideously and berating themselves.

No good news. The only hope Sabine now had was to find the gateway himself. The very idea seemed impossible, which was quite a contradiction to the spirit of Foo. But creatures and men of all

breeds, under Sabine's command, had searched high and low for the opening in Foo, and nobody had ever discovered it. The search had revealed nothing. Sabine was still no closer to knowing where or even what the gateway was. He glowered, his evil mind searching for the solution. Only Leven Thumps possessed the power to destroy his dream.

A strong dark dream pushed in from reality and caught Sabine's attention. It jolted him up and backlit his features. His breathing slowed as he closed his eyes. Someone in reality was dreaming the foulest of dreams, and Sabine's soul had intercepted it. Sabine could see everything this person was dreaming. He manipulated the images to make the plot and outcome of the dream even more selfish and to satisfy his own greed. Sabine took the things he saw and twisted them into thoughts he could use. Then he opened both his hands so that his palms were facing upward, flipped his hands over, and sent the sordid dream flying back into reality.

The images Sabine had intercepted and manipulated had given him pause. A thought struck him, and his face broke into an evil smile. He stood, threw on his cloak, and stormed from his chambers. He needed to visit someone immediately.

iii

Leven had never tasted anything better than the food the First Baptist Church of Cape Porpoise had put out for their third annual October-blessed celebration. The corn on the cob was so buttery, the potato salad so tasty, and the pie so thick that Leven felt as if he had died and gone to culinary heaven. Likewise, Winter was helping herself to as much food as she could get her hands on. She had

an entire half a watermelon and two of the thickest, most scrumptious burgers she had ever tasted. Clover circulated invisibly, snacking off everyone's plate. Geth pouted and complained about how fate should have given him a form that could digest food. He also went on and on about how time was growing short. Enjoying their feast, Leven and Winter ignored him.

"This isn't so bad," Winter smiled at Leven as she prepared to gnaw on a huge, butter-soaked cob of corn.

"I've never had food like this," he replied.

The folks putting on the event seemed like pretty nice people; they just kept cooking food and putting out more chips and soda. The bowery next to the church was packed. Leven felt like nobody would notice him and Winter in such a big crowd. He was wrong.

A tall woman with big hips and pushed-up hair noticed them and approached.

"Well, hello," she said. "Are you two getting enough to eat?"

Leven and Winter nodded, fearful of being discovered to be intruders.

She studied Leven's face. "You look familiar, young man, but I'm not sure I know who you are. Are you two members of our congregation?"

Leven shook his head no. "We go to the Fourth Baptists," he lied.

"Oh, I see," the woman smiled. "Well, I can't help but think how I've seen you before," she said, pursing her lips. She looked closely at the white streak in Leven's hair. She reached out to touch it and then stopped herself.

"I have a really average face," Leven tried.

"What do they call that?" she asked, ignoring his response and pointing at the stripe in his hair.

"It's a skunk spot," Leven answered. "I got it when I was four."

"I think I've seen your picture on TV," she said.

Leven began to panic. To the best of his knowledge he had never been on TV, but his knowledge was off. He didn't realize that his picture had been on a number of TV stations just recently. Apparently his house being frozen and dropped to the ground was of some interest to some people. There was even a reward being offered for finding Leven. *National Inquirer* had picked up on the story and spread it across the entire country.

The woman's tiny eyes widened. "Do you have family in Oklahoma?" she asked.

"No, ma'am," Leven lied nervously.

"Well," the woman said, retreating and wearing a strained smile, "you youngsters enjoy yourselves. There's plenty of food."

Once she was twenty paces away she took off quickly.

"I think I must have been on TV," Leven whispered to Winter, squinting and trying to see what the woman was doing now. "That lady seemed to recognize me. We'd better get out of here."

Winter looked at her remaining food and frowned.

"Take it with you," Leven insisted, watching the woman talk to a couple of men over by the church. They all looked in the direction of Leven and started to walk over.

Leven pulled Winter up and glanced around for the best way out. The men started moving faster toward them. "Let's go!"

"That's what I've been saying," Geth said.

Leven dragged Winter through the crowd and directly across the

path of some children having a sack race. They jumped over a low hedge and into the church parking lot.

"Hold up!" one of the men running after them yelled.

That was their cue to stop holding back. They dashed out onto the main street and in the direction of the shore.

"Where are we going?" Winter yelled.

"I have no idea," Leven yelled back.

"That's the spirit," Geth cheered, happy that Leven was simply traveling by fate.

"Clover, are you here?" Leven hollered.

"Right on top of your head," he hollered back.

"Is anyone following us?" Leven yelled.

Clover turned to see the two men still pursuing them. Behind them a couple of other people were piling into a car.

"Yes," Clover said. "Quite a few actually."

Leven glanced back. "Run!" he hollered to himself as much as anyone.

The four of them ran—well, actually, the two of them ran and Geth held tight in the front pocket of Winter's blue shirt while Clover bounced up and down on Leven's head.

"Around there," Leven pointed, indicating a narrow, empty street to the left.

They turned the corner, hopped two fences, and crawled under a long semi-truck that was parked, delivering cheese to a tiny café. Leven stopped behind the store to catch his breath.

"What did she mean she saw you on TV?" Winter asked, fairly breathless herself.

"I have no idea," Leven huffed and puffed. "Maybe Terry and my Aunt have a warrant out for me or something."

A nicely dressed young man in a red convertible pulled to the curb on the street next to where Leven and Winter were resting. He checked out his reflection in the rearview mirror, then hopped out of the car. He glanced over at Leven and Winter and sneered as if they were trash. Leven looked at himself and wondered how anyone could think anything else. His dark hair was a mess and hanging in his face, his clothes were dirty and ripped, and his hands were filthy. It's not easy trying to stay clean while on the run. Winter looked even worse than Leven. Her blond hair was always a mess, but now it was the kind of mess other hair would tell horror stories about. Her dirty shirt was also ripped in a couple of spots, and her jeans were torn at the knees.

"I can't believe what's happening to our town," the snooty young man said, loudly enough for them to hear. "It's a shame." He walked off and into a store just down the way.

"What a jerk," Winter said.

"Look at the positive," Geth spoke up. "He left his keys in the ignition."

"What good does that do us?" Leven asked, exasperated.

"I'm not sure," Geth admitted. "It just seems sort of fateful."

One of the men who had been giving chase peeked over a wall and spotted them. He hollered to those with him, and people began climbing over the wall and working their way closer to Leven and Winter.

"Do you know how to drive?" Winter asked.

"I've seen a few movies," Leven said, scared.

"Then let's get out of here!" Clover yelled.

Leven jumped into the front seat of the convertible, and Winter

leapt into the back. He turned the key, and the engine started right up. He pressed on the gas but nothing happened.

"You have to put it in drive!" Winter yelled.

Leven couldn't hear her so he just kept pushing on the gas petal and revving the engine in hopes that it would do something. Those chasing them had cleared the wall now and were just a few feet away. Winter reached over from the backseat and pulled the lever into drive. With the engine revved, the car shot forward like a bullet, tires screeching and smoking. Leven turned the wheel and barely avoided crashing into a small truck that was parked on the other side of the road. He slammed on the brakes and glanced nervously in the rearview mirror. He squinted. It looked like half the town was running after them.

"Go!" Winter yelled.

Leven pushed on the gas again and the car flew forward. He grabbed the wheel and tried to simply keep it going straight. A big bus going the same direction blocked his view and caused him to have to swing onto a side street. The sounds of sirens sang through the air.

"We're dead," Leven moaned.

"Just keep driving!" Geth ordered.

Leven flew over the road, his tires screeching and wailing. The sirens got louder as two cop cars roared up behind them.

"What do we do?" Leven hollered.

"Don't worry," Geth screamed. "It'll work out."

Leven strongly wished that Geth was lying on the road in front of the car so he could run over him. Here they were, flying down a seaside road, going eighty miles an hour, and being chased by cops, and Geth's way of helping was to suggest that he shouldn't worry.

Leven blew through an open toll booth and into the beach area. A few people hanging around the shore took notice and pointed.

"I'm running out of land," Leven said with concern, realizing he could only drive so far. "Even I can see that."

"Just keep driving," Geth hollered.

"But—"

"Keep driving!" Geth ordered.

The police cars had also entered the beach area and were breathing down Leven's tailpipe. Leven steered onto a narrow street and found himself driving onto a wooden pier.

"Seriously," Leven cried. "We're out of land!"

"Keep going!" Geth shouted.

Leven looked at the ocean in front of him. His vision wasn't the greatest, but he could clearly see where the pier ended. His heart plummeted into his shoes. He hated water, and there was nowhere else for him to go.

Clover appeared long enough to scream, "Are you crazy?"

Leven's reply was to step on the gas even harder. He closed his eyes and prepared to get wet. He couldn't imagine a worse ending. Geth looked at Winter, and she nodded. The car flew off the end of the pier and down toward the water, but there was no splash. Instead, they landed with a small bump on a long patch of ice that had suddenly appeared.

Leven opened his eyes and smiled in awe, his heart pounding and sweat dripping down his face. Winter kept the path in front of the car frozen, but the area behind she let drop off. One of the two police cars screeched to a halt on the end of the pier and the other slid into the water, lights flashing and siren wailing.

The surface of the roadway of ice was rough, not smooth, as

though Winter had textured it for traction. Leven pressed on the gas and the car shot forward on the frozen highway into a bank of dense fog.

In a few moments they were miles out from shore. Leven kept his hands on the steering wheel in the ten o'clock and two o'clock positions, looking as if their very lives depended upon him holding the car straight.

"Amazing," Clover said, hanging his head over the side of the car, staring at the narrow frozen stretch they were careening along. He could see fish and other objects from the sea frozen in the trail they were traversing. He looked up ahead, seeing nothing but a thin white roadway that stretched out directly in front of them and disappeared into the fog bank.

Winter sat back in her seat, impressed with herself and smiling.

"You couldn't do this without me," she pointed out, her blond hair whipping wildly in the breeze.

"That's why I sent you," Geth added.

"You sent me?" Winter asked.

"We knew Leven couldn't get back by himself," Geth smiled. "And we didn't know just what kind of shape I would be in. So we used the dreams of those on earth to help you revert back to an infant. We then came through the gateway and switched you with another child.

"Janet's not my real mother?" Winter said with shock and glee.

"Nope," Geth said. "We didn't want to displace anyone, but we needed you to be here. So we located the worst parent we could find at the time and switched her child with you. Janet's real little girl ended up in a nice home out in the country with a pony and caring

parents. Sorry for all the heartache you suffered, but we could think of no other way."

Winter didn't smile, she sighed deeply.

"You *chose* to do this," Geth added. "In fact, if I remember correctly, the child swapping was *your* idea."

"I suppose I'm happy someone else didn't get stuck with her." Winter said, the headache that had been coming finally taking hold.

"Family history is so interesting," Clover said, butting in.

Winter looked at Leven, who was still holding tightly to the wheel, his foot firmly pushing on the gas petal. The speedometer needle was as far to the right as possible, indicating that they were going at least one hundred and twenty miles per hour.

"We're going to run out of gas eventually," Leven hollered.

"We'll worry about that when it happens," Geth said, staying true to his character.

"Just don't let the ice end," Leven begged Winter.

"Just don't fall asleep," she replied. "It's going to be a long drive."

"How wide is this ocean?" Clover asked.

"About twice the size of the Lime Sea," Geth answered.

"Wow," Clover said. He turned to Leven. "We really are going to run out of gas, Dog."

"Dog?" Leven said.

"No good?" Clover asked, referring to the nickname. "I heard someone on the radio use it. I thought it sounded important."

"Keep trying," Leven smiled.

Clover disappeared, and Leven sped like the wind farther across the surface of the Atlantic Ocean.

CHAPTER TWENTY-SEVEN

Closer

Sabine had to stoop to get through the crooked, old doorway. As he stepped into the ancient house, a handful of his shadows swooped in after him. It was the home of Amelia Thumps, the woman Hector Thumps had married after he returned to Foo. She was also the mother of Levin's father, whom Antsel had returned to reality shortly after Hector's death.

Amelia had been a beautiful woman in her youth, a somewhat attractive woman as an adult, and almost an eyesore as an old woman. Her hair was thin and scraggily, and the tip of her lumpy nose had for some years drooped down over her top lip. She wore thick glasses that made her eyes look huge. She was one hundred and fifty-three years old, and she planned to live at least three hundred more. People often wondered what she would look like then.

Sabine had come to visit her, hoping he might extract from her

some bit of information regarding the location of the gateway. She had been questioned many times before, but Sabine had the feeling she might be withholding something she knew. The dream he had intercepted and manipulated earlier had given him reason to visit this house again.

Amelia offered Sabine a seat but he declined to sit, choosing instead to pace as she sat uneasily on a worn velvet couch.

"How nice of you to meet with *me*," Sabine said, affecting a civility that was not natural to him.

"I don't see that I had any choice," she complained. "Your shadows kept at me until I gave in." Amelia tried to keep her voice even. She had a lot to hide.

"*I'm* so sorry," he said, trying to keep from becoming angry. "Their manners are not always the best."

"You cast them," she smiled rudely. "Now what do you want? I'm meeting friends in a short while to make splotch."

"*I* won't keep you but a moment," Sabine began. "*I* was wondering if you would mind answering a few more questions about Hector's gateway."

"Ha," she laughed. "There is nothing else to say. I've told you everything I know," she said, hoping he would just go away.

"In a moment," Sabine snapped. "Perhaps there is something you forgot to tell *me*," he coaxed.

"I don't know where the gateway is," she lied. "I wish it had never existed. I wish he had never returned and that I had never fallen in love with him. He was trouble from the start. It took me losing my son to know that."

"Yes, your son."

"Hector couldn't bear to think his son would grow up here, never knowing life outside. Antsel snatched the baby from me after Hector's death. I should have never let him take him. At the time I didn't want the reminder. I know now I was wrong."

"Of course." Sabine tried to sound compassionate. "But certainly Hector spoke of the gateway."

"That's all he did," she said irritably, knowing she wasn't admitting anything that most in Foo didn't already know. "He was mad. He thought he had created the greatest thing since sliced splotch."

"And after he took your son back, he never used the gateway again?" Sabine asked.

"He claimed he destroyed it," she whined. "I wish he had never found a way out of Foo in the first place. Lying on the floor like a fool. Disbelieving the very place he later fought to come back to." Amelia was trying to keep her voice emotionless, but it was obvious she missed Hector.

Though he tried not to show it, Sabine was angry; the few shadows around him swirled and spit. He had one remaining question. "Is this the house in which Hector originally escaped from Foo?"

Amelia looked surprised by the question. "It is," she said, obviously bothered but trying not to show it.

"Where is the room he laid in?" Sabine asked, a wicked excitement rising in him. "The room he stopped believing in?"

"Why?" she asked, more quickly than she should have.

Sabine's shadows fluttered. "Show *me,*" Sabine demanded.

Amelia got up from the couch. "You come into my house and start asking to see things. I suppose if I say no I'll wake up perched on the Cliffs of Dwell with small children playing behind me—small children who might accidentally knock me over and to my death."

"*I* suppose that's a possibility," Sabine said, confirming the threat. "Now show *me.*"

Amelia looked disgusted and confused. Sabine followed her down a dark hallway into the far corner of her home. He knew he was on to something. He had heard the story many of times of how when Hector had returned to reality after losing his belief in Foo, he had gone to the exact spot in Ohio he had originally been taken from. It only made sense that upon coming back to Foo, he might have reentered in the exact spot he had slipped away from. Sabine cursed himself for not putting the pieces together sooner. He had been trying to make the solution too big and too mysterious. But, if what he was now thinking were true, then that spot—in this

house—was where he would find the opening to the gateway from this end.

Sabine's small, coal-like heart burned with excitement.

Amelia was frightened. She pointed to a doorway at the end of the hall. "It's just a dumb little room," she said. "He never let me even clean it. I've left it just as he left it." She stopped, hoping Sabine would just look in and then leave. "That's it," she said.

Sabine looked at the door. He breathed in deeply, drawing the hairs beneath his nose back up into his nostrils. He breathed out and they reappeared. The door opened without a sound.

The room was brightly lit, illuminated by seven large candles. In the center of the floor was a shaggy thought rug. Sitting on the rug was a table with a clear glass top with thin gold edging. There was nothing on the table, allowing a person to see the entire rug beneath it. The color and design of the thought rug shifted and changed as the thoughts of Amelia and Sabine entered the room. Part of the carpet grew dark while the other yellowed with long orange streaks.

The room was dusty and filled with books, stacked in piles on the floor and spilling out of the tall shelves against the walls. A number of the books lay open. In one corner an old clock struggled to tick, and the only window in the room was open, letting in the scent of a Foo afternoon and adding even greater light.

Sabine's shadows danced about the room. They had searched this house many times before. As Sabine moved deeper into the room, new, smaller shadows formed as he passed each candle.

"Have you read these books?" Sabine asked Amelia, wondering if perhaps there were clues in them as to the whereabouts of the gateway.

Amelia looked nervous. She pushed her heavy glasses up on the

bridge of her nose and stuck out her chin, "I'm lucky to read the headlines on the *Scroll*."

"What a waste. Books are for fools," Sabine said casually. Two of the books that were lying open snapped shut and scurried off as if insulted. Sabine walked slowly around the room, touching things and looking for some indication his thoughts had been correct.

"He spent a lot of time in here?" Sabine asked.

Amelia didn't answer. She sniffed instead, the tip of her ugly nose twitching as she did.

Sabine touched the walls and listened. Nothing.

"Look all you want," Amelia said irritably. "What do I care if you take anything. Crazy fool. Just leave the candles burning so your shadows don't start knocking everything over," she added. Without excusing herself she stepped from the room, leaving Sabine alone.

"Where is it?" he said aloud, knowing he was closer to the gateway than he had ever been before. He could feel the answer was here. His black soul was sizzling. "You're here somewhere. You exist," he proclaimed. "Show yourself," he challenged, as if the gateway were a being in hiding.

Nothing.

Amelia stuck her head back into the room. "When you're done talking to yourself, just let yourself out. I'm going to make splotch at Caroline's. Don't let the cat out."

It is hard to feel sinister when a nervous old woman with a lumpy nose is telling you not to let the cat out. But Sabine had enough sinister self-esteem for ten beings.

"All right," he sneered.

Amelia closed the door and walked to the front of the house. She knew that the cause was in big trouble.

CHAPTER TWENTY-EIGHT

Blown Away

Leven, Winter, Geth, and Clover had a lot of things working against them. For starters, they were hundreds of miles out to sea in a car, driving on ice across an ocean that was beginning to act up, *and* they were running out of gas.

The car began to buck and shiver as it choked on the final drops of gasoline. Geth and Clover had been asleep for the last couple of hours, and Winter had been telling Leven any stories she knew in an effort to keep him awake. It had been days now since he had closed his eyes, and he was beginning to show real signs of sleep deprivation.

"The car is stopping," he cried. "Please, let me sleep. Please."

"No," Winter said, pinching him on the arm to keep him awake.

The ocean around them was moving and lapping up against the bridge of ice that Winter had so ingeniously created.

"I think a storm is coming," Winter said.

The car emitted one last gasp and rolled to a stop, in the middle of the Atlantic Ocean.

"We're here," Leven tried to joke.

The ocean air blew and rocked the car.

"Should we wake up Geth?" Winter asked, looking down at the snoring toothpick in her pocket.

"Why?" Leven asked. "He'd only tell us to wait and see what happens."

"It's worked so far," Winter defended.

"This is working?" Leven asked, opening his arms to indicate the vast body of water they were now marooned in. Mist from the choppy sea began to spray them in the face, making everything wet and miserable.

"Do you think we could get this top up?" Leven wondered aloud.

"We could try."

Leven and Winter cautiously got out of the car. The ice had amazing traction. Lev inched slowly along the side of the vehicle and back to where the top was folded down. He looked at the ice and marveled. He spotted a sea turtle frozen in the path. Winter was on the opposite side of the car, pulling on the top.

"All this water," he sighed nervously. "So if you wanted to, you could make this ice go away?" Leven asked her.

"Sure," she shrugged.

"Don't you think it's weird?" he asked, looking around at the ocean.

"What do you mean?" she asked, tugging on the canvas covering the collapsed convertible top.

"Look around you," Leven motioned.

Winter gazed around at the vast and endless sea. The wind was picking up, and the blue sky was taking on massive gray clouds that looked like fat smoky marshmallows. In the distance, she could see large swells forming. A huge purple swordfish leaped from the water, arched over the ice path, and dove back down into the ocean. Winter glanced across the car at Leven and realized how completely unbelievable it was to be right where she was.

"This is a turn I never saw my life taking," she laughed. "I was in school a couple of weeks ago, wishing I were a different person." Winter twisted her long hair and wrung out some water. "I remember when I was about nine," she said, "my mother . . . well, Janet, took me to a movie. I was so surprised and happy. We had never done anything like that together. Then, we get there and she has me buy a child's ticket at a child's price and makes me go in and open a side door so she can sneak in without paying. The worst part was once we were both inside she didn't even want to sit by me, and on the way home she told me, 'Get used to opening doors for people. It's about all you're good for.'"

Winter's green eyes looked sadder and prettier than Leven had ever seen them.

"Now look at me," Winter finally said, hoping to lighten the mood. "Stranded in the middle of an ocean." Winter smiled.

"She was wrong," Leven said. "I mean, look at you now. We'll find a way out of this," Leven said confidently. "I don't know just how we—"

Leven stopped to pay attention to the image suddenly playing in his head.

His brown eyes burned gold. Lights and shadows began to fill his mind. Leven envied Winter's ability to use her talent on cue and with efficiency. He couldn't even think clearly most of the time, much less put his skill to work. Now, however, his tired head was suddenly clear, and he could see the future. Brighter lights burned within him. He saw they were driving across the ocean with the wind pushing them. They were moving slowly, and Leven let his mind tell the wind where to blow and how fast to push them. In his thoughts they were suddenly racing across the ice faster than they had been going before.

"Lev," Winter interrupted. She was still pulling on the cover. "I can't get this roof up without you."

Leven looked at the car top and thought of what he had just seen. "Kneel on the trunk," he said excitedly, climbing up on the trunk himself.

They both got on the back and started to pull the top out and up. As it extended it naturally wanted to angle forward.

"We need to bend it back," Leven shouted above the wind. The waves and the noise were quickly growing louder.

"It won't close if we bend it," Winter said, baffled.

"We don't want it to close. We can use it for a sail that will help blow us the rest of the way."

Winter instantly understood and began working to free the top. As it came up out of its storage compartment, Leven and Winter stood up on the trunk of the car, and pulled the top back in a direction it was not designed to go. The two side bars bent, and the entire

top stood straight up. The vehicle bucked and shivered from the wind.

"We need to bend it back just a bit more," Leven instructed loudly.

The waves in the ocean were beginning to splash up against the car, making the back end they were standing on slippery.

"Pull!" Leven yelled, struggling to keep his footing.

Winter pulled. Together they were able to bend the top back. It stood at an angle slanting slightly backwards.

"That should work," Leven said.

They climbed back into the front seats just as a huge wave crashed down and watered them all. Geth woke up and inquired what was going on, as casually as if he were someone asking what time it was on a lazy summer afternoon. Clover woke up complaining. Leven concentrated and could see the wind growing in large gray sheets from the west and flying toward them. Another wave rocked against the car and pushed the vehicle so close to the edge of ice the back left tire slid off.

"We're going to slide in," Clover shouted.

"Don't worry," Leven hollered back, "hold on!"

Geth popped out of Winter's pocket, looking excited. Just as Leven had seen earlier, a terrific wind came rushing across the water, from behind them. It caught the jury-rigged sail and began to move the car forward.

"It's working," Winter shouted happily, her hair flying wildly.

"Of course, at this rate it will take us a year to get there," Clover complained, the gray fur on his body wet and funny-looking. He was wringing water out of the bottom hem of his cloak.

"Don't worry," Leven said again. "The real wind is coming."

The air surged, and in a second the car was flying over the ice path.

"Impressive," Geth complimented Leven.

The wind was so strong they could feel the back wheels of the car lift off the ground. Leven kept his mind on the wind and the future to give them thrust the entire rest of the way there. Winter, in her wisdom, curled the sides of the ice so as to create a half pipe and made the path smooth. The vehicle surged ahead.

"Can you keep the wind up?" Winter yelled.

"If you can keep the ice in front of us," Leven replied, closing his eyes to better concentrate.

"You won't fall asleep, will you?" she asked, concerned that he had his eyes shut.

"I've never felt more awake," he yelled. "But when we reach the shore I might be a little exhausted."

"We'll deal with that then." Winter smiled.

Geth drifted back to sleep as Clover sang to himself until he too was sleeping. Leven looked over at Winter as she rested her head, and he glanced in the rearview mirror at Clover. The sound of the wind pushing them was noisier than the car engine had been, but amidst the noise he couldn't help but marvel at his life. The waves bulked up and crested all around, and the sky darkened as night came on.

Still, the wind pushed them speedily across the ocean.

ii

Sabine sat, the candles burning bright, each one growing taller as it burned. The old woman had returned and since gone to bed.

Still Sabine sat.

He was more convinced than ever that he was onto something. This room held the answer and he knew it. He stared at the walls and mumbled about the wait and the value of his time. Books shifted and moved about cautiously, taking care not to come in contact with him.

As the night deepened he began to grow angry. He stared at the candles, their light filling the room. Amelia had instructed him to keep them burning, but Sabine had a sudden feeling in his thick hard heart. He wet his forefinger and thumb with his coarse tongue and reached over to the candle closest to him. He pinched the wick to extinguish the flame. There was a soft hissing sound as a thin stream of smoke drifted up. Sabine stood and did the same to another candle and another until they were all out. The room was dark except for what little moonlight was filtering in through the window. The pale light rested on the thought rug in the center of the room.

He was onto something.

Sabine lifted the glass table off the rug and pulled the rug aside. He stepped to the window and pulled the drapes closed, blocking out any trace of light.

The room was pitch black, yet there on the wood floor, a dim light shone through the cracks in the wood. Sabine dropped to the ground, his hands fluttering maniacally over the floor, his dirty long nails searching for something to grab or pull. He wedged his fingers into a thin crack and yanked. To his surprise the plank came up in a thick, long, rectangle-shaped piece. The dirt beneath the flooring glowed. Sabine's mouth went dry, his eyes on fire. The dirt was moving, smeared with blotches of red, orange, and green colors, swirling wildly around in circles.

Sabine stared at it in dark awe.

He had found the gateway.

iii

Good things come to those who wait. Patience is a virtue. In time all things are possible. You cannot rush perfection. Blah, blah, blah. Winter thought the drive across the ocean would never end. She was usually the one with the best of spirits, but this was just one long stretch of nothing. Her head hurt. Plus, the wind working at their backs was so loud, a person couldn't have a calm thought if she wanted to.

Leven had stayed conscious due to his need to stay focused on the future and the wind, but Winter was worried about how much longer he could hold out. Clover had complained and complained about how hungry he was and then they discovered him eating some actual humble pie back behind the seats. They wouldn't have caught him if they hadn't heard the extremely humble pie loudly apologizing for its flavor and promising it would taste better next time.

"You have food?" Winter scolded. "I thought you said you were hungry."

"I'm hungry for other things besides what I have," he argued back, his leafy ears twitching.

"Well, could you share some of the stuff you're sick of?"

"Here," Clover said, handing her what looked to be a square cracker.

"This is it?" she complained. "A cracker? I'm starving."

"Just eat it," Clover insisted.

Winter bit off one half and chewed. It tasted good. She stuck

the second half into her mouth and did the same. "Do you have any more?" she asked.

"Trust me," "Clover said, rolling his blue wet eyes. "You don't want more than that. You really shouldn't have eaten the whole thing. I thought you'd just nibble a corner."

"Why would I just . . ." Winter's stomach started to sound.

"I'd get out of her pocket before you're penned in," Clover said to Geth.

Winter suddenly looked frightened. Heeding the warning, Geth quickly clambered out and onto the dashboard. Leven had his hands on the wheel and was driving with his eyes closed, concentrating on keeping the wind coming. His arms were locked into position so that the car traveled straight down the path. He was focusing so intently on what he was doing that he didn't even hear Winter and Clover talking.

"What was that you gave me to eat?" Winter panicked.

"A Filler Crisp," Clover said, his eyes seventy percent concerned and thirty percent mischievous. Now even Geth looked frightened.

"You gave her a *whole* Filler Crisp?"

"I thought she'd nibble the corner. I didn't think she'd be so greedy."

Winter's stomach began to expand and her arms and legs started to swell. Then suddenly, as if someone were inflating her with an air pump, her whole body expanded. Even her hair got fatter. She could feel something coming up in her throat and all at once what looked like shaving cream burst from her mouth and nose, filling the front seat of the car and oozing everywhere. The foam rushed out of her with such force it knocked Clover back and flung Geth up against the front window, where he remained pinned to the glass.

Winter wanted desperately to scream, but her mouth was too

busy competing with her nose to see which orifice could shoot out the most goo.

Clover screamed enough for the both of them, causing Leven to take his mind off the future for a moment and open his eyes to join in the scream-along.

Panicked by what was happening to her, Winter momentarily stopped managing the ice path. The frozen road came to a sudden end, and the car rocketed off and slammed into the water. Winter flew out of the vehicle and bounced across the water like a bloated beach ball. She finally settled on her back, bobbing, swatting, and kicking as the white goo continued to ooze out of her mouth and nose. Clover grabbed Geth from off the car's window and climbed on top of Leven, who was frantically swimming up and out of the now sinking car. In no more than a few seconds the vehicle had completely disappeared under the water, and the four of them were bobbing about on the surface of the ocean.

Even Geth looked a little concerned.

Leven splashed his way over to Winter as she bobbed up and down on the waves. She was on her back, flailing her bloated arms and legs about wildly, while white foam continued to spew from her mouth and nose, making her look like a marshmallow fountain. Her green eyes were wide with panic and disbelief. Leven grabbed onto her ankle, surprised and happy to find how buoyant she was.

"What happened?" Leven yelled.

"I didn't think she'd eat so much," Clover explained. "She'll stop doing that in a few minutes."

Leven looked at her as she continued to spout. "I sure hope so."

"I think the more important question is, what should we do now?" Clover asked.

Leven looked into the distance and wondered how they would ever get out of this. He wanted to simply hold onto Winter's ankle and go to sleep. He was so tired and too spent to go on. He wasn't sure he would even care if a shark began to nibble on his legs, as long as he could go to sleep.

Winter's mouth continued to spew white foam as she kicked and swatted the water like mad. Leven couldn't blame her. She looked terribly uncomfortable. She kept slapping the water and oozing foam. Each time she turned toward Leven she sprayed foam in his face. Fortunately, the white goo immediately dissolved when it came in contact with the seawater.

"I think it's biodegradable," Clover said.

Winter glared at Clover, who was holding Geth in one of his hands while clinging tightly to the top of Leven's head.

"He didn't think you'd eat the whole thing," Leven said, sticking up for Clover, still slightly indoctrinated by his bite. "Besides, Clover says it will wear off before long."

"Thanks for backing me up, chief," Clover said kindly.

"Chief?"

"No good?" Clover asked.

"Keep trying," Leven insisted.

Winter splashed and kicked as if she were trying to say something. She gestured awkwardly above her head with one of her bloated hands.

"What is it?" Leven asked, treading water. He spun Winter around and pushed her up-ocean a bit. He could see instantly what she had been trying to point out. In the not-so-distant distance was a big fishing boat. Winter's swollen body had been hiding it

completely from his view. Leven began to holler and wave as Winter finally began to deflate.

The ship had seen them and was heading their way.

Winter's stomach began to contract and her arms and legs hissed as they shrank back to size. She was still burping up foam and having a hard time speaking, but by the time the boat got to them she was almost back to normal—well, as normal as a person could be after having thrown up foam for half an hour.

"*Bonjour,*" a tall dark man on the bow of the boat hollered, then began jabbering in a language that sounded like French. He could tell by Leven's blank stare that he had not understood. "Can we be of assistance?" he asked in English.

"Please," Leven hollered back.

The crew helped Leven and Winter up onto the boat and asked them where their raft was.

"We don't have a raft," Leven said.

"I thought I saw you with one when I first spotted you," the captain said.

Leven smiled, knowing that what he had spotted was a bloated Winter. Winter frowned. They both, however, were amazed to discover that they were only fifty miles off the coast of France. They were questioned about how they had gotten where they were, but when they hemmed and hawed a bit with their answers, the captain simply said, "I'll make you a deal. I won't ask you what you are doing fifty miles out in the ocean if you won't ask me why I am fishing in an area I shouldn't be. *D'accord?*"

"Deal," they agreed.

The captain fed them some soup and bread that tasted marvelous to Leven. Winter didn't eat any due to her recent history, so

Leven gladly had her share. Two hours later the boat docked just outside the town of Granville, and Leven and Winter set foot on the shore of France.

"So do you know any French?" Leven asked as they walked along the dock.

"No important words," Winter replied.

"How about you, Geth?"

"I've always wanted to learn," he replied.

"Clover?" Leven asked.

There was no answer.

"Clover?" both Leven and Winter asked in unison.

Nothing.

"When was the last time you saw him?" Leven asked.

"When we got on the boat," Winter said. "That's when he slipped me Geth."

"Clover!" Leven hollered, attracting stares from the waterfront crowd.

"Don't worry, he'll show up," Geth said. "We have to keep going."

"This is France," Leven pointed out needlessly. "Clover has no idea where to go."

"He's a sycophant," Geth said calmly. "They always return to their burn. We have to keep going."

"He wouldn't leave you," Winter said. "I know he'll show up."

Leven looked around hopelessly. "Clover!" he yelled one last time.

Nothing.

The three of them walked down a cobblestone street, two of them worried about Clover and all three of them waiting for fate to point out what their next ride would be.

CHAPTER TWENTY-NINE

PHYSICAL AGAIN

Sabine could not possibly have been more surprised by the sudden rush of freezing water. He had stepped into the colored dirt in Hector Thumps's room thinking he would simply walk out into the world and begin his final quest. Instead, he plunged into water so cold it took his breath away. He tried to scream, but his mouth filled with water. He pushed out of the gateway and swam toward the surface as fast as he could. His dark, wet robes were no longer just a dreary fashion statement, they were suddenly a death trap. He pushed them up over his shoulders and frantically thrashed upward.

It is true that in the eternal scheme of things, Sabine was one of the truly bad seeds. He was totally selfish and as power hungry as anyone could be. He cared not a whit for the soul or salvation of anyone other than himself. He was cruel, looked frightening, and was feared by thousands. His only concern was his own self-interest.

All that aside, he looked pathetic, frantically trying to swim to the surface, like a baby squid flailing its tentacles for the first time.

Sabine came up gasping for air but in a beautiful setting, in the middle of a large lake, surrounded by forested mountains. He looked around. The sun was shining in a perfectly clear, blue sky. In the distance he could see a small boat gliding away from him. It was a scene as picturesque as any that might be imagined. Of course, Sabine hadn't come to take photos.

He had come to take control.

He dogpaddled his way to the nearest shore, his face a perfect picture of disgust. He hauled himself out of the water and onto dry ground and shook himself like an uncoordinated dog with no rhythm. He bent over to touch again the physical world he had been snatched from many years before. His teeth were chattering so violently he couldn't fully exult in his triumph. Wet to the bone, he glanced around, trying to get an accurate idea of where he was so he could easily return to the gateway when needed.

He was a stranger here, but he felt invincible. He looked around, understanding that all he saw was real. In Foo, Sabine had control and power over the elements and beings; here he had none of that . . . yet. With access to the gateway he would be able to move freely between reality and Foo—and enjoy the ability to achieve the impossible in a world where all others had limits.

Sabine looked at his own hands. He had not been real for many years now. He was only nine when he had been snatched from reality and sent to Foo. He had been out playing with two of his friends late one autumn evening. He could still remember the sound of crickets chirping and the sweet coolness of the fall air. He could hear their mothers calling them all to come in. They had pretended not

to hear, in hopes of playing just a bit longer. So they ran farther down the road, kicking a ball and talking excitedly like nine-year-old boys do. The only interruption was when the dark sky showed off a beautiful shooting star. All three boys had looked up at it in awe.

"Maybe it's a rocket," one of them said.

"I bet it's an alien spaceship," the other suggested.

They turned to get Sabine's take on it, but he was gone. There was nothing but empty space above where a sidewalk and a side street came together in an imperfect junction.

That was the last Sabine had ever seen of reality for himself. For years his shadows had scoured the planet at his direction, but their vision and reports were only two-dimensional.

This was what Sabine had longed for. He breathed in deeply, expecting his shadows to rush to him. Nothing happened. He inhaled as deeply as he could and still not a single black patch of shadow came to him. He positioned himself so he could cast a new, earthly shadow. The sun did its part, but the new shadow just lay there, two-dimensional and black. It also vanished the moment he stepped out of the sun's rays. Apparently his shadow thing didn't work in reality.

This was a concern. Sabine had anticipated being able to use his castoffs here. Now he would have to make an adjustment. He wondered where his shadows were if they were not responding to him. He worried about it for a moment, then brushed his concern aside, smiling, his tiny numerous teeth clicking against each other. The possibility of ruling everything was finally in his grasp. He could always slip back into Foo and create more shadows. Only one thing could stop him now, and that one thing was a boy by the name of

Leven Thumps. Only Leven had the power to destroy the gateway leading in and out of Foo. Sabine knew what he needed to do. Leven Thumps had to die.

Sabine drew his wet robe about him and moved silently through the thick forest of trees and along the shore. He could feel Leven and Geth and Winter drawing ever closer.

ii

Leven was exhausted. He had not slept for days, and his mind was spent from the effort he had focused on conjuring the ocean wind. He could barely walk straight, and Winter constantly telling him to stay awake put them at odds with each other. So far he was not enjoying France.

Plus, they needed money, so Leven decided to try out his offing gift. He spotted a woman in a shop about to buy a few expensive dresses. He closed his eyes and manipulated fate to the best of his ability. Somewhat to his surprise, she actually decided not to buy the dresses, and when she walked out of the exclusive store into the street, she spotted Leven and simply handed him the money she had saved. Once again Winter was impressed. Sure, it was a neat trick, but Leven didn't exactly feel good each time he did it. Nor did he have any real accurate control over it.

In all honesty, he had really only been trying to manipulate the woman into just offering them a ride. Instead, she had handed him all her cash. He kept thinking he would someday repay the lady who had bought them food in the diner, the snotty young man whose car they had driven across the ocean, and this woman who had given

up her shopping spree to provide for their needs. But he knew that would not be an easy thing, seeing how he didn't know any of them.

Leven purchased a new shirt with some of the money, one with a pocket in front for Geth to ride in and no Wonder Wipes logo. The shirt was on sale and had the words *essuie-tout* stenciled on it. Leven figured it was the name of a French rock band or something cool. Winter also got a new shirt and some pants for herself. They felt rich, pulling out all that money and paying the bill. The French clerk had been very rude to them, probably because of their appearance and the fact they couldn't speak French. But when they showed him the cash, he started treating them nicely.

After purchasing new clothes they took a few minutes to eat at a French McDonald's. It looked just like an American McDonald's except the Grimace statue was wearing a beret.

"We're in France eating at McDonald's," Winter said with astonishment, her green eyes becoming increasingly alive each mile of their journey.

"I'm still not sold on this being more than a dream," Leven replied, his eyes partly cloudy.

"I could pinch you again," Winter offered.

Leven tried to smile back.

Clover was still missing. Leven wanted to go back to the docks and search for him, but Geth had insisted there wasn't enough time. After eating, they hailed a taxi, showed the driver the money they had, and told him to drive them as fast as he could across France and into Germany. He insisted on seeing their passports. When they told him they had misplaced them, and was there any way he could get them out of France and into Germany, he asked to see their wad of money again.

He then said yes.

The ride across France seemed to take forever, even though they were speeding a hundred miles an hour across the surface of the earth.

Leven wanted more than anything to go to sleep, but Winter kept him awake by continually poking him and pulling the hair on his arms. He would beg her to let him rest, and she would pinch him in reply. To distract him, Winter constantly pointed out the villages and landscape they were flying by. On a good day Leven couldn't see very clearly, now as the taxi blew over the road he could make out even less. Everything his eyes took in at the moment was a blur.

The large, happy taxi driver seemed to be enjoying the unusual trip across his country. He laughed and smiled as he listened to French music and sang. Shortly before reaching the German border, he pulled off the road and helped Winter and Leven into the trunk of his cab. He acted as though he might have done this before.

"No talking," he said, right before he slammed the trunk closed.

"I hope this works," Leven whispered, scrunched up against Winter in the dark trunk.

"Me, too," Winter replied.

Geth was tempted to say something positive, but he wisely stopped himself.

It was incredibly warm in the trunk of the cab. It was also obvious, from the stench, that the taxi driver had carried many rank and odorous things in there before. The floor of the trunk was covered with a fuzzy material and worn in spots like knee holes in trousers. Winter hated it, but Leven couldn't help being lulled to sleep by the steady hum of the tires and the darkness. He had stayed awake as

long as he could. Winter kicked and pinched him, but the trunk provided insufficient room for her to really get at him.

"Lev," she begged, "please don't go to sleep."

"Just for a second," he pleaded.

"Leven," Geth said authoritatively. "You must stay awake."

"Sleepy," Leven mumbled. "Very sleepy."

He was beginning to drift off when the taxi started to slow down just outside of Strasbourg, France.

"We're stopping," Winter hissed.

Leven opened his eyes. As tired as he was, he knew they were probably crossing the border of France into Germany. He also knew that if the border patrol opened the trunk, they were all done for.

"Be really quiet," Geth whispered.

They could hear their driver get out and slam his door. He said something loud, in French. He laughed and another voice responded back to him. They could hear the sound of keys rattling, and suddenly the trunk popped opened. Light flooded in. Leven and Winter laid there staring up at the driver. He was looking in another direction and motioning to someone to come and check the trunk if they really wanted to.

Leven and Winter stayed perfectly still.

The border guard said something, and the driver shrugged and closed the trunk. He called out something loud in French and got back into the car and slammed the door. The engine roared to life, and they pulled forward.

Leven and Winter finally breathed.

"That was too close," Leven said, his heart still racing.

"So, we're in Germany?" Winter asked, obviously short of breath herself.

"I hope so," Geth answered. "We are running out of time. In a short while the lake's temperature will change, and we will have to wait two months to return to Foo. That's the very next time the temperature will be right."

"Two months?" Leven moaned. "What do we do until then?"

"If we don't make it back now, it's over," Geth said. "Sabine's shadows are too strong. You won't last another week with them knowing about you. We have to succeed now."

"We will, won't we?' Winter asked urgently. "I mean, fate will make it happen, won't it?"

"Fate might have something else in mind for us," Geth answered honestly. "We've done our part."

"Great," Leven lamented, his right arm asleep in the cramped quarters. He was actually jealous of the sleeping limb. "Now that we are nearing the finish line, you're admitting that fate isn't the answer to everything?"

Geth was wise enough not to answer. Winter remained quiet as well. Her head throbbing, she could feel both the ending and Sabine drawing nearer.

iii

Clover was too curious for his own good. He loved looking in places he knew he shouldn't. It was a trait shared by most sycophants. So, when he saw the locked door with the big man in front of it at the bottom of the boat, he couldn't resist taking a peek.

He had waited and waited until the captain came down and unlocked the door. Clover slipped in with him. The room they had entered was small, with no windows or vents, which made it extremely stuffy. Two metal cabinets sat closed against the far wall. The captain opened one of the cabinets while singing a song in French.

Clover gasped.

The captain quickly looked around to see if someone was in the room with him. When he was satisfied he was alone, he shrugged and continued to open the cabinet doors.

Clover's gasping was called for. The cabinet shelves were piled with jewelry, coins, cups, shields, and other objects made of gold. It was clear to Clover that these men weren't fishermen afraid of being caught—they were *treasure hunters* afraid of being caught.

Clover was captivated by the glitter. He stared at it in awe, wishing he could materialize and touch it. The captain closed and locked the cabinet doors and left the room still singing. Clover could have followed, but he wanted another look at the gold.

Once he was alone in the room, Clover messed with the locks on the cabinets, but he couldn't get them to open. He pushed and pulled to no avail. With no other option, he decided it might be best to just let it be. He needed to get out and find Leven. Unfortunately, the door to the small room was locked. He banged and banged, but the walls were too thick for anyone to hear him.

Taking a page out of Geth's book, Clover just laid back and decided to let fate take care of him. After half an hour of waiting for fate to do something, Clover fell asleep, and by the time he woke up the boat had already been back out to sea for an hour.

"I bet they're just sick about me coming up missing," Clover said to himself, thinking of Leven and Winter and Geth.

A key finally sounded in the door. Clover stood invisible in the middle of the room as the captain came back in whistling. He

walked to one of the cabinets and opened it up. It too was full of gold and jewels and all kinds of sparkling things that sycophants are so fond of.

Clover pulled a pout from his void and looked at it in his hand. Pouts are small, bumpy, stone-like creatures. They are the texture of wet clay, with their only real feature being a tiny, wrinkled hole on the top of them. Pouts are native to the Swollen Forest. They are shy little things that are almost impossible to find and catch unless you accidentally step on one and cause it to begin pouting. Clover had found this particular one years before when he inadvertently sat on it. He had tucked it away in his void for just such an occasion.

Clover set the pout on the floor behind the captain's back. He closed his eyes, whispered an apology, and then kicked the poor little creature as hard as he could. The pout flew up against the wall and fell down between the desk and the wall. It instantly began to pout, filling the room with the sound of sniveling.

The captain immediately turned to locate the source of the noise. As he did so, Clover slipped into the cabinet, picked out a couple of nice pieces of treasure, and shoved them into his void. Invisible, he rolled under the desk, pushed his skinny arm up behind it, and retrieved the pout. He shoved it back into his void just before the captain pulled the desk away from the wall. The sniveling immediately stopped and, finding nothing, the captain stood there scratching his head and wondering if he had gone crazy.

Clover dashed from the room and climbed the stairs to the open deck. He was surprised to not see any land. The sea was blue, and a cool wind filled his tiny nostrils with the smell of saltwater. A small boat roared up alongside the big boat Clover was on. In the little boat was a short, orange-haired man.

"I think this is the spot," the man yelled up to some crew members. "I'm getting positive readings."

"Perfect," a tall, dark man standing near Clover yelled back. "Let's get the gear and get down there."

The short man with the fiery hair left the engine of his little boat running and put his foot on a ladder, preparing to climb up to the deck of the bigger boat. At that exact moment the engine of the small boat he was still halfway balanced on suddenly roared and the craft shot ahead.

As his boat pulled away, the astonished man was dumped into the water. The crew of the bigger ship hollered as the seemingly empty little boat made a broad turn away from them and headed toward the French coastline. Their hollering did little good as the boat continued to speed farther away.

Clover smiled as he skillfully captained his first vessel. He turned and looked back at the men still hollering, then faced France and joyfully pushed the throttle down for more speed.

iv

The black French taxi stopped at a park just outside of Munich, Germany. The fat, friendly driver took all the money Leven handed him and then gave him a few bills back.

"For food," he said in broken English. "One must eat." He smiled, patted his stomach, and then drove off.

"What now?" Leven asked Geth.

"We need to get to the town of Berchtesgaden," Geth answered. "Our destination's not far from there."

"Can't I just sleep for a few minutes?" Leven begged, eyeing a large patch of grass.

"No," Winter insisted.

"What about Clover?" Leven tried. "Shouldn't we just lie here and wait for him?"

"Our time is almost up," Geth said. "We need to keep moving."

Winter took Leven's elbow and helped pull him down the street to a train depot.

The train station was large. Inside the depot, huge posters written in German hung on all the walls. Tall tiled columns and long wooden benches occupied the center of the large, open building. A short man was busy mopping the floor in front of the escalator going down to the trains.

"I can't stay awake anymore," Leven moaned. "I'm falling asleep on my feet."

"Just a little while longer," Geth begged. "This is the last place we want Sabine to know we are."

They stopped and counted the few bills they had left.

"I have no idea how much this is," Winter confessed, staring at the Euro money. "It could be ten dollars or ten thousand."

"Just go to that window," Leven pointed. "Ask the man for tickets to Berchtesgaden and see what he says. I'll be sitting right here."

Winter sighed, folded the money into her palm, and approached the ticket booth. Leven sat down on the long wooden bench and tried to keep his eyes open.

"Stay awake," Geth warned.

"I will," Leven slurred.

As she waited in line, Winter glanced back at Leven and could

see him fighting to keep his eyes open. She waved to him but he was too glazed over to notice her.

"*Guten tag,*" the man at the window said, letting Winter know she was next.

Winter stepped up to the booth, trying not to look too nervous.

"Do you speak English?" she asked.

"Yes," the man replied coldly. "How may I help?"

"I would like two tickets to Berchtesgaden," she said firmly.

He punched a few buttons on his computer and tapped his fingers. Winter tried not to let her anxiety show, but she knew if the man asked to see her passport she would be caught. She was purchasing tickets to a destination within the country, but she wondered if he might ask to see her papers anyway

Winter smiled and tried to look at ease as he typed.

"Two tickets to Berchtesgaden," he said, pulling the tickets up.

Winter felt great relief at simply seeing the tickets.

He told her the cost and held his hand out, waiting. Winter slid all the money she had through the slot at the bottom of the window.

"I'm not good with your money," she apologized.

He looked at the bills. "It is not enough," he declared.

Winter felt like crying. Her head had been aching for hours, and she was almost as tired as Leven. She wanted desperately to tell the impatient man behind the glass that she was homeless and had been chased by big clumps of land and eaten by a snake. She wanted to describe to him the fear she had felt as they had driven across the Atlantic Ocean and how uncomfortable she had been, both as a swollen girl with foam spewing out of her mouth and as a deflated girl trapped in the trunk of a taxi. She wanted to tell him about Sabine and how frightened she was. She knew once he had some idea what she had gone through he would simply hand her the tickets, and she could be on her way to the finish line.

But of course she couldn't tell him.

The German ticket master looked at her in confusion. "Are you all right?" he asked sharply.

"I'm fine," Winter lied, wiping her eyes and reaching through the slot to take her money back.

He didn't buy it. "May I see your papers?" he asked, grabbing her hand as she reached in.

"That's all right," Winter panicked. "I just need to go recount what I have."

"Your papers please," he said more firmly, squeezing her fingers tightly.

Winter was in trouble.

V

Leven simply could not stay awake any longer. His head bobbed and his eyelids felt like they weighed two hundred pounds apiece. He could barely see Winter off in the distance at the ticket window, and he wasn't sure if she was a dream or reality. He closed his brown eyes and that was it.

He was out.

Geth heard the snoring and instantly started poking Leven. Geth pulled his legs together to give him a sharper form and began jabbing Leven as quickly as he could. He climbed up Leven's face and pushed up his right eyelid. Leven gazed at him as if in a trance. He was completely checked out.

"Wake up!" Geth ordered. "Leven, wake up!"

It was no use. Leven slouched over in his seat and slid down on the bench, snoring with his face in the wood. He began to drool.

"Leven," Geth begged. "Get up." Geth thought of Winter and pulled himself up to see if he could spot her. She was still at the ticket booth, talking to a man behind the glass.

"Winter," Geth whispered, knowing his voice would never be heard above the noise of the train station. "Winter."

They were in big trouble.

vi

Sabine's shadows were confused. One moment they were under control and being driven by the very master they had desired to escape. Now, they could feel no pull. Sabine's departure into reality had cut them all off and left them to be their own beings. They were now free to do as they chose. Of course, shadows aren't the greatest free thinkers. All they knew was their command to find Leven Thumps. They flew around the earth wild and free, making whatever mischief they wished, happier than they had ever been, and still searching for Leven. Freed from Sabine, their forms became bulky, filling with air and dimension as they swirled wildly. They were no longer only two-dimensional, and they found themselves able to touch and destroy things in ways they had never been able to before. Soon after they were freed, sleep finally overtook Leven, and his location immediately became known to the shadows. Normally they would have reported back and been given instruction by Sabine. But with no master controlling them, they knew only one thing to do.

They needed to get Leven.

vii

"Your papers, Miss," the German man insisted for the last time. "I must see your papers." He was hurting her hand.

Winter panicked and turned toward Leven just in time to see thousands of shadows pulsing though the windows and doors of the train station. They looked like black waters flooding the entire place. She screamed, jerked her hand free, and ran toward Leven.

The small German behind the glass signaled two guards standing nearby and they moved toward Winter. She had already reached the bench where Leven was asleep in a pool of his own drool. She glanced over her shoulder and could see the two guards walking quickly toward her. She could also see about ten thousand black swatches of evil swooping through the station. The shadows began knocking down people and tipping over trash cans and tearing down signs. Papers were flying all over the station and people were screaming in terror.

Of course, people weren't absolutely sure what they were screaming at. With no connection to Foo, people were unable to see the shadows, only the effect they were having as they flew joyfully through the depot, discovering the thrill of having no master other than their own will. Who knew how satisfying it could be to swoop up behind an unsuspecting person and knock him off his feet? Or what about the great thrill of snatching the wig off an important-looking woman and terrorizing her poodle?

The shadows went wild, all of them swirling and working their way toward Leven.

The two guards who had been after Winter turned their attention instead to the hysterical crowd. The taller of the two guards was

suddenly picked up as if riding on a horse. He was lifted to the high ceiling and dumped with precision into the large fountain in the middle of the room.

"Lev, wake up!" Winter screamed. "Get up!"

Leven stirred, mainly because the whole station was in utter chaos and sounded a bit like a bomb going off in slow motion.

"Run!" Winter yelled, grabbing him by the collar and pulling him to his feet. He had been standing for no more than a couple of seconds when a huge shadow slammed into him from behind and sent him sprawling face-first across the tile floor. Leven knocked over at least ten people before he came to a stop. He looked up to see Winter soaring across the room on the backs of two shadows, her hair flying wildly about and her eyes as big as dinner plates.

As Leven tried to stand, hundreds of shadows leaped on him and pushed him down. He kicked and hit, but they just kept piling on top of him.

"Help me, Geth!" Leven screamed in desperation.

"There's too many!" Geth yelled back, trying to work himself out of Leven's pocket.

Leven slammed his fist into a shadow and it dispersed. No sooner had that one gone than hundreds more jumped at his wrists, pinning him to the floor. Leven kicked and bucked with his legs, but there were just too many.

Meanwhile, Winter was being bounced across a crowd of shadows, like a beach ball above a crowd of concertgoers. She flew up and down, up and down, and was becoming sick to her stomach. Tiring of the game, a cruel shadow seized Winter by the ankles, spun her around, and let go of her. She flew across the depot and might well have been seriously hurt had it not been for a group of

twelve large women heading to Innsbruck for a quilting convention. Their fat bags of quilting material as well as the extra pounds they were carrying around made for a rather awkward (but soft) landing.

All over the station people were screaming and crying and covering their faces in fear. Many attempted to flee, fighting to get through the exits, but those who couldn't get out continued to be harassed by the invisible shadows.

The chaos made some sense to Leven and Winter. They could see their attackers. But those who were blind to the shadows had no explanation for the madness of the scene. They didn't know if they should bob or weave or simply drop to the floor and pray for an earthquake to cover them. If someone had just walked up to the station and looked inside through the glass doors, they probably would have been more amused than frightened. Without being able to see the shadows, it would have just looked like a bunch of Europeans practicing some extraordinarily physical mime act.

Leven was buried by shadows. They held him to the floor and jumped up and down on his stomach. He struggled, but it was no use. There were too many, and they were too strong. A few of the shadows who were holding down his arms became jealous of those who were jumping up and down on him. It just looked like so much more fun than what they were doing. They let go to have a jump on him. With less resistance Leven was able to wiggle his wrists free. His hands flew up and came together, creating a clapping noise. The shadows directly above Leven disappeared. The other shadows close by realized what had happened and began to panic. Leven clapped again, and more vanished.

"Winter!" he shouted. "Clap your hands!"

At that moment, Winter was upside down, being carried by her

ankles in a circle in the air. She couldn't hear Leven, but she could see him. He was clapping, and the shadows around him were popping like soap bubbles into nothing. She clapped, and the huge black spot holding her was gone, along with about a hundred others. She landed on the floor and skidded across the tiles into a row of lockers.

A few other people in the crowd figured they would try clapping and began doing so. The shadows immediately began to vanish. Finding the chaos subsiding, others began applauding as well. Leven watched the room empty of shadows as he and the entire gathering clapped madly.

It made for a peculiar sight. It is one thing to arrive at a train station, look through the glass doors, and see people flying across the room and tripping over each other. It's another thing entirely to arrive at a train station, look through the glass doors, and see people applauding wildly, their faces panic stricken and tear stained, their mouths screaming in fear as they clap.

Winter got to her feet and went back to the ticket window. The two tickets that had been printed up for Leven and her were still lying on the counter behind the glass. She tried to reach in and grab them, but the opening was too small for her arm to reach. She looked around the room at all of the clapping people and at the few remaining shadows that were still flying around frantically and without purpose.

The ticket agent who had earlier been behind the glass, wanting to check her papers, was running to get outside when a shadow caught him by the ankles. Another shadow grabbed his wrists. The two of them flew across the room, carrying the wide-eyed man in the direction of Winter. A police officer was applauding at thin air

near Winter, and his clapping caught the two shadows off guard. They disappeared, leaving the short man flying through the air. His momentum carried him toward Winter. She ducked while imagining that the glass blocking her from the tickets was ice. The man slammed into the ice, shattered it, and bounced backward onto the floor in front of his booth.

Winter reached through the opening where the glass had been and picked up the two tickets.

"Thanks," she said calmly to the dazed agent. "Fate is really depending on these."

By the time she reached Leven, only a few shadows were left. A couple of travelers in the far corner clapped and got rid of those.

"Are you okay?" Winter asked, out of breath and amazed to still be alive.

"I think so," Leven replied.

"Geth?" Winter said, looking in Leven's pocket.

He was not there.

"Where is he?" she asked.

"I have no idea. He was there yelling at me earlier."

They began to look around.

"Geth!" Winter shouted.

"Geth!" Leven copied.

They dropped onto their hands and knees and began searching the floor. Trash and debris were everywhere. People were walking over everything, trying to get out of the station or to their trains.

"He could be a million places," Winter cried.

"Just keep looking."

They looked everywhere Leven had been thrown or beaten upon. They checked the fountain and under the benches. Geth was

nowhere. This was not a good thing, seeing how he was the only one who knew where the gateway was, and well, to be honest, they had become quite attached to the optimistic little toothpick.

"What should we do?" Winter asked.

Leven looked at her and sighed. "We have to do exactly what he would want us to," he answered. "We have no choice."

Winter's green eyes were sad. Leven stuck his hand out, and she placed hers in his. They walked together through the debris and subsiding chaos toward the platforms.

The stationmaster addressed the crowd and tried to make the disruption sound as though it was due to some new pipes that had recently been installed in the station's heating system. No one really believed that, but they all accepted it due to there being no other explanation. He announced they would quickly get the trains running on schedule.

"Did you get the tickets?" Leven asked.

"Of course," Winter replied.

"How much money do we have left?"

"It didn't cost us a thing," Winter grinned.

When they got to the platform their train was there and waiting. They showed their tickets, climbed on board, and found an empty compartment toward the end of the train. They pushed open the door and fell upon one of the seats with both exhaustion and relief.

"We did it," Winter whispered.

"So far," Leven added.

"What about Geth?"

"Fate will work it out," Leven said, trying to sound as though he believed it.

"We should have looked for him a bit longer," Winter moaned.

"We looked everywhere we could," Leven rationalized. "I know he'll show up."

Leven remembered how tired he was as his body gently reminded him by shutting down. Not only was he tired, but he had been pummeled by hundreds of shadows.

"Is it okay if I sleep now?" he pleaded.

"I guess so," Winter said, too exhausted herself to stay awake and watch him. "But if you hear clapping, join in."

A well-dressed man looked through the glass in the compartment door, then opened it. "Excuse me," he said, "but is this seat occupied?"

When Leven said no, the man nodded and sat down on the empty seat across from them. Leven and Winter were a bit saddened to share the compartment, but they were also too tired to really care.

It was lights out for both of them.

viii

Clover had really enjoyed driving a boat—so much in fact that when he got to the shore he decided to try out a car. He waited around on a busy street, looking for someone to leave their keys in their vehicle. Clover had always wanted to drive, but he knew it would be difficult due to his size. He was too short to reach the gas pedal and still see over the dashboard. So he borrowed a large stone from a rock garden, which he thought he might use to weigh down the accelerator. He planned to sit on the steering wheel and maneuver by twisting his body.

A man wearing a worried expression pulled to the curb and got

out of his car with the engine still running. He took a stack of papers off the backseat and hurried up some stairs into a building. Clover hustled to the car and hopped in through the open window. He pulled the stone from his void and dropped the heavy rock on the gas pedal. The motor roared. He jumped up onto the steering wheel and craned his neck up so he could see through the windshield. If his friends back in Foo could have seen him, they would have been so jealous. Clover kicked the gear shift lever and the car popped into drive and shot off much faster than Clover had anticipated.

He had thought he would be able to handle the wheel so professionally he wouldn't need the brakes. He could see now he was probably wrong. The car flew wildly down the street, with people gaping at what looked like a vehicle driving itself. Pedestrians dived out of the way, and people on bicycles and automobiles swerved to avoid Clover's first-time attempt at driving. He threw his body weight to the left, and the steering wheel turned, sending the car into a tight spin around a corner. A policeman writing a parking ticket spotted the screeching vehicle and jumped on his scooter to give chase.

Clover straightened out the wheel and weaved his way between slower-moving cars—which happened to be all the other vehicles on the road. He was sweating and hanging on for dear life, with his toes wrapped tightly around the bottom of the steering wheel and his two hands gripping the top. The line of cars in front of him had slowed down, so he threw his weight to the right. The car bounced over the curb and flew up onto a walkway, scattering the tables in a sidewalk café. The bump caused Clover's belly to honk the horn.

Clover liked that. He moved his stomach in and out to warn those in front of him.

People were diving and jumping out of the way as he flew honking down the walkway. His big blue eyes were as wide as saucers, and he was laughing giddily. Tires screeching, he turned a corner onto a less congested street. He flew down the road, beginning to wonder how he was ever going to stop. His plan had seemed so perfect, but in retrospect it had more than a few flaws.

Clover leaned to the right and directed the car onto the highway. He merged into the traffic and began to pull ahead of all the other slowpokes who were casually going eighty.

The traffic cop on the motor scooter had been left far behind, but seven speeding police cars were now on his tail.

Clover heard the wailing sirens and glanced behind him at the flashing lights and smiled. He honked the horn a couple of times just for fun and set his sights straight ahead and toward Leven.

ix

Winter woke Leven up by pulling at the hair on his arms. She had been awake for some time, worrying about Geth and Clover, and she wanted Leven to share her concern. Besides, they were only minutes away from their destination.

Leven didn't want to wake up. After going without sleep for so many days, the small amount of rest he had just gotten wasn't nearly enough to make him feel refreshed or even normal.

"What?" Leven said irritably.

Winter shushed him, pointing to their fellow passenger, asleep on the seat across from them.

"We're almost there," she whispered, "and we have no idea where to go."

"We'll wait at the station until Clover or Geth show up," Leven said groggily. "We can sleep on the benches there."

"We can't sleep," Winter complained. "Geth said we don't have time. We have to finish this or it's all over."

"Well, we can't go any farther without knowing where to go," Leven pointed out. "Isn't it Geth who's so big on fate? Well, let's see if he's right."

The sleeping passenger shifted in his seat and crossed his right leg.

"He could be anywhere now," Winter sighed. "He's probably still back at the train station. We shouldn't have left without him."

A slight buzzing noise sounded in the cabin, and Leven looked around for something to swat at. He couldn't see anything so he kept his hands to himself.

"It's not like I don't wish he was here," Leven said honestly. "I would feel much better about things if he and Clover were around."

Again something buzzed, and this time Winter heard it as well.

"Is there a fly in here?" she asked.

"I thought there was," Leven said, staring closely at the window and ceiling. As he was glancing around he noticed the sole of the sleeping passenger's right shoe. Near the center of the sole there was a flattened out gob of gum the man had stepped on. Leven would have thought nothing more of it, but the gum was wiggling just the slightest bit. Leven looked at Winter and pointed.

"Do you see that?" he whispered.

Winter leaned across the space between the seats. She could see

a tiny sliver of wood sticking out of the gum stuck to the bottom of the sleeping man's shoe.

"No way," Leven whispered.

"I think it is," Winter said with excitement. "And he's trying to yell at us."

The train was pulling into Berchtesgaden.

"You've got to pull the gum off," Winter told Leven.

"But—"

"We're almost there," she said.

Leven got down on his knees and scooted closer to the man. He used his finger to poke lightly at the dirty gum. He put his fingernail beneath one of the edges and tried to peel it off, but it was stuck tightly to the sole. The sleeping man didn't seem to even notice. Leven boldly dug into the gum and pried at it. Nothing. It was still stuck, and the man hadn't stirred.

"You've got to pull harder," Winter whispered as if they were robbing a bank and Leven was trying to figure out the safe combination. "We're stopping."

Leven could feel the train slowing and knew that in a few moments the man would be awake and getting off. It was now or never. He seized the man's shoe with his left hand and pulled as hard as he could on the gum with his right.

No one could sleep through that.

The man woke up and hollered. Leven screamed too as the gum popped off of the shoe and into his hand. The man jumped to his feet. He glared down at Leven, who was still kneeling on the floor.

"What do you think you are doing?" he asked in English, taking Leven by the ear. His face was red and flustered. "Were you trying to steal my shoes?"

"No," Leven said quickly. "Honest, I—"

"I think we should talk to the authorities," the man huffed.

"No," Leven said, even louder. "I dropped my gum, and it got stuck to the bottom of your shoe." Leven held out the gross gob of chewed and stepped-on gum with the end of a toothpick sticking out. Little bits of grit and hair were mixed in the gum as well.

"You were retrieving your chewed gum?" the man asked indignantly, staring at the dirty gob in Leven's hand.

Leven looked at Winter and nodded slowly.

"Why?" the man asked.

"I wasn't finished with it," Leven said sheepishly.

"Really," the man smiled meanly. "Well, then, if you really weren't stealing my shoes, let's see you chew your gum."

Leven looked at the pink, already-been-chewed gum that had at one time been on the bottom of someone's shoe and was now in his hand. He could see the tip of Geth's head sticking out and wanted nothing less than to put it in his mouth.

"Just as I thought," the man barked, motioning to hail a conductor.

Leven had no choice. He popped the gum into his mouth. Both Winter and the man were shocked. Both winced.

"Chew it," the man said, wanting to teach a life's lesson to a young man whom he perceived to be a thief.

Leven chewed slowly, making sure he didn't bite into Geth. The gum tasted like dirt and floor and mud, with a hint of cherry. His brown eyes didn't look happy.

"Yumm," Leven said weakly.

The man smiled. "Let this be a lesson to you."

He stepped out of the compartment as the train came to a

complete stop. As soon as he was out of view, Leven spit the gum out onto the seat, gagging. Winter picked up the gooey wad and peeled it away from Geth, who was also gagging.

"That was disgusting," Leven and Geth said in unison.

Winter held Geth in her palm. He was dirty and covered with splotches of gum. He also had a new crooked bend in the middle, which made it difficult for him to stand completely straight.

"What happened?" Winter asked.

"I flew out of Leven's pocket as he was getting tackled by shadows. I tried to work my way back to one of you, but that clod . . ." he pointed after the man who was gone, "that clod stepped on me with his sticky shoes. I've been trying to get myself out of that gum for hours. My face was pressed into it so tight I couldn't even yell.

"Well," Winter smiled. "We're here."

Geth glanced out the window of the rail car and then back at Leven and Winter. He smiled. "We are, aren't we?"

"You didn't doubt fate, did you?" Leven asked.

"Not for a second," Geth answered. "Well, at least not for a *full* second."

Winter put Geth in her shirt pocket, and the three of them got off of the train, in Berchtesgaden, Germany.

X

Clover had a total of seventeen police cars behind him by the time he started to run out of gas. It had been a long, exhausting chase. No one had dared run the vehicle off the road because for one thing, it was driving itself rather well, and for another, the police feared it might have explosives on board.

As soon as the car began to slow down, the police cars circled and boxed it in. Clover threw his weight one last time and turned the car off the road and down a grassy embankment. The car rolled slowly to a stop. With guns drawn, the police flew out of their vehicles to come and investigate the car that had given them chase for so long. They threw open the doors, ready to pounce on whomever was inside.

Clover slipped unseen out of the car and walked between their legs and around their vehicles as they all talked and scratched their heads in confusion, all of them wondering how in the world the car could have driven itself.

Clover climbed into the open window of a vehicle whose driver had stopped to gawk. The driver was a thin man, wearing suspenders and smoking a pipe. As soon as the thin man realized there was nothing to look at, he put his gas pedal to the floor and drove Clover the rest of the way across France and over the border into Germany.

When the thin man stopped just inside Germany to use a pay phone, Clover didn't waste any time. He secretly hitched a ride with a nice German couple and their new baby. That didn't last too long. The baby kept crying and keeping Clover awake. Clover appeared to the child so as to be a delightful, soothing surprise. Well, the child did like Clover. In fact, she held him and cooed. When the parents turned around to look at her and saw their child holding a furry, living creature, they needlessly panicked. The car swerved and rocked as the parents practiced their parental screaming skills. Disgusted with the noise, Clover climbed out through the half-open sunroof and jumped into the bed of a passing truck with an open back. He settled into a roll of insulation it was carrying and rode, somewhat peacefully, closer to Leven.

CHAPTER THIRTY

The Occidental Tourist

Leven liked Germany. At least the little bit of it he had seen. It was beautiful and green and vaguely reminded him of someplace he had been before. Berchtesgaden, however, was even prettier than the rest. It was a lovely town with quaint-looking buildings, beautiful flowers, and friendly people. Thousands of tourists filled the streets, and he could hear polka music coming from two different directions at once. There were a lot of men with moustaches walking around.

"I wouldn't mind getting something to eat," Leven said as they passed a gasthaus and the smell of cooked sausages and onions filled the air.

"No time," Geth insisted. "See that sun?" he pointed from Winter's pocket.

Both Leven and Winter nodded.

"When that sun goes down we have to be ready. If we don't make it tonight, it will be too late."

"Too late?" Leven said in amazement. "Too late for what?"

"They have gotten through," Geth replied.

"Who's gotten through?" Leven said, so hungry he wasn't speaking clearly. "How could you know that?"

Geth smiled. "It's fate. Don't worry."

"So you're saying if we had not made it here right now we would have been out of luck?" Winter questioned.

Geth nodded.

"What if we hadn't found you on that shoe, or a boat hadn't picked us up, or—"

"What-ifs are for fools," Geth interrupted. "We are here because we are meant to be. Now let's hurry."

Leven was always tempted to point out how easy it was for Geth to say hurry. After all, he was riding along while they did all the walking. He also knew that Geth wasn't compelled to stop and get something to eat because, well, he had no digestive tract. And Winter wasn't about to help him fight for a meal break because she was still full from the cracker Clover had slipped her in the ocean.

Leven sighed and inhaled the aroma of cooking food as they walked along the tourist-packed street, heading toward the Konigsee, or the "King's Sea."

"So what do we do when we reach the Konigsee," Winter asked.

It was a silly question for Winter to ask. She knew from the pain in her head and the fear in her soul that the time was finally here to face Sabine and step into the gateway.

"We wait," Geth answered.

"Well, can't we stop here and wait and eat at the same time?" Leven begged.

Geth smiled as if Leven were joking, and it was obvious to Leven that he was going to have to take getting something to eat into his own hands. They were passing dozens of tourists, many of them eating as they strolled along the quaint streets. Leven spotted sausages and pretzels and ice cream. He decided to try to clear his mind in an effort to manipulate fate just enough to make one of those passersby offer him food. That way he could just keep on walking, and they would have lost no time.

He spotted a woman wearing a large hat, carrying a huge pretzel in her hand. He willed fate to have her reach out and give it to him. Instead, she patted him on the back, looking very surprised that she was doing so. Leven kept walking. He saw a man with a thick, delicious-looking sausage sandwich. It was made out of dark bread and had sauerkraut on it. Leven tried really hard to manipulate fate, but as they passed, the man just handed Leven his used napkin.

Leven tried one last time on a woman who was enjoying some bread and cheese. As she got closer, she smiled, made a fist, drew back her hand, and punched Leven on the chin.

She was as surprised as Leven was.

Leven staggered backward and tried to right himself. His brown eyes saw bleached white stars. Winter turned to see him stumbling and ran to his side.

"I am so sorry," his assailant said, displaying both her remorse and her American accent. "I have no idea what came over me."

Leven eyed her bread and cheese. "Is that mine?" he asked in fake confusion.

"Well, honey, actually . . ."

"I only remember being hungry, " Leven added.

"Well, you just help yourself," the woman said, handing him her food.

Leven smiled weakly as she walked off, shaking her head in disbelief, wondering with her friends about the strange thing she had just done.

"Way to use your gift," Winter scolded.

"I'm starving," Leven defended.

"That doesn't make it right," Winter insisted. "I could think the whole world besides us was ice and we could simply skate to the lake without interference, but that wouldn't be right."

"I can't skate," Leven admitted, taking a welcome bite of his newfound food.

"You know what I mean."

Leven smiled smugly at Winter, his bangs covering his right eye. "I won't do it any more," he chewed. "At least not today. Besides, I still haven't gotten the hang of it. If you hadn't noticed, I just got myself punched."

"Serves you right," Winter said nicely.

They reached the shore of their destination.

The Konigsee was a large, beautiful, blue-green lake surrounded by impressive, pine-covered mountains. It was a jewel in the lush German landscape and a favorite vacation spot for government dignitaries and military officers. On the far shore was St. Bartholomew's, a church that had stood for thousands of years. Day in and day out visitors came to take a boat ride across the lake.

When they reached the center of the lake the motor would be shut off, and absolute silence would descend over the scene. Then a solitary musician would stand on the deck of the craft and play his

trumpet. The mountains encircling the lake produced an unbelievably clear and rich echo, which allowed the trumpeter to play a duet of sorts with himself. The performance never failed to move those who heard it. Even the most jaded individuals could not resist the serenity of the setting and the beauty of the music.

Years before, Leven's grandfather, Hector Thumps, had discovered the soothing effect music has on the planet. As he searched for a lake with a constant temperature, he had been delighted to discover the Konigsee and its remarkable mountain echoes. This extraordinary coming together of natural beauty and beautiful music created a mood similar to that a shooting star might stir up.

It was fate.

It was also the most beautiful place Leven and Winter had ever seen.

"So what do we wait for?" Leven asked, looking up at the mountains and taking in the entire view.

"We need to get on a boat," Geth instructed. "It will take us across the lake, and from there we can walk to where we need to go. You can both swim, I hope."

"No!" Leven quickly said.

"Not at all?" Winter questioned. "You swam in the ocean."

"That wasn't swimming," Lev insisted. "That was panicking."

"Well, you'll need to panic yourself down to the gateway," Geth said seriously. "We have no choice."

Leven looked at the huge lake and let the panic begin.

They bought tickets for the boat ride, and with the few Euros left over, Geth had Winter purchase a small pocket knife in case of an emergency. The price of the tickets and the knife added up to the exact amount of money they had left.

It felt sort of fateful.

They boarded the next boat and were soon on their way across the lake. The scenery was spectacular, but as the small boat glided across the green water Leven kept his eyes down, hoping to see the gateway. Unfortunately, the green water didn't reveal anything.

As advertised, halfway across the water the captain turned off the engine and the boat glided to a stop. The passengers quieted themselves and prepared for what was about to happen. It was so still, it was almost as if the entire planet were holding its breath.

An authentic-looking German with a long mustache and lederhosen stood on the deck of the boat and put a trumpet to his lips. He played, and the clear notes drifted across the water. As if answering back, the mountains replied in perfect tune.

The effect was so beautiful it gave Leven chills and caused Winter to tear up. It also left them speechless.

After a couple of songs, the boat started back up and carried everyone to the far shore where St. Bartholomew's stood. Leven and Winter got off and walked back behind the old church. The crowds weren't as dense as those on the other side of the lake, and as Leven, Winter, and Geth moved farther into the woods, the little group soon found itself quite alone.

"So, how does this work?" Leven asked Geth. "What do we do?"

"See those bushes?" Geth pointed to a clump of thick growth farther down the faint trail they were on.

They both nodded.

"We need to wait there until the last boat of the day makes its return trip. On the way back we will get into the water and wait. When the timing is right, we will swim under water toward a very faint glow. That glow is the gateway. Swim in, touch the mismatched floor, and you will be in Foo."

"That's it?" Leven asked. "No secret knock or challenge?"

"That's it," Geth answered. "You have nothing to be afraid of. Actually, that's not really true. The water is near freezing. The multiple of seven is not always some balmy temperature. Your lungs probably have just enough capacity to make it down. If you don't make it into the gateway, you will most likely not pop back up alive. You can't stop swimming, understand?"

Leven took a moment to inventory his life. Being warned of your potential death by a toothpick can make a person quite reflective.

"What if the gateway is not working?" Leven asked. "What if we get down to it and it's out of order? Or what if the earth's no longer happy?"

"As long as we get in before the effect of the music fades, the gateway will work," Geth said. "If it were breakable it would have been destroyed by Antsel and me years ago. The gateway is unchangeable. It is a perfect creation made unbreakable by the will of your grandfather. It is also the one thing that can destroy Foo and eliminate all dreams. With no one in Foo to bring dreams to life, everyone here would be without hope. This existence would be dark and completely full of despair. Sabine has no idea what his selfish scheme will ultimately bring about."

"So I guess I can't back out now?" Winter asked.

"Back out?" Geth asked, surprised Winter would even say such a thing.

"Well," she said defensively, her head pounding, "I have no idea where we're going. Clover showed me some images, but . . . what if we swim through that gateway and it's worse than this?"

"It's not perfect there," Geth conceded. "It is filled with turmoil and confusion now, thanks to Sabine. But it is a place unlike any

you have seen before. You belong there," Geth reminded her. "You chose to come here, but it was only with the promise that you could come back."

"I just wish I could know." Winter's green eyes darkened.

"Listen," Leven said, "I have no idea what's going on. A few weeks ago I was in school, worrying about my aunt's temper and Brick picking on me. Now, here I am, after crossing the world, listening to a toothpick tell me I had better swim fast enough or I'm dead. So, I'm a little confused. But the one thing I'm sure of is that I couldn't have done it without you," Leven said to Winter. "If not for you, I would have been digested by a giant snake or drowned in an ocean. I wouldn't have even made it across the Oklahoma state border without you, Winter. I can't imagine what we'll find on the other side, but somehow I think it will be okay, if you're around."

Winter and Geth stared at Leven in astonishment.

"Are you okay?" Winter asked, reaching out to touch his forehead.

"Seriously," Geth added. "Maybe that cheese you ate was bad."

"Oh, knock it off," Leven said defensively. "See if I ever say anything nice again."

Winter smiled. "Thanks," she said, her face red. "I couldn't have done this without you and Clover . . . he should be here now."

"It's odd he hasn't caught up to us yet," Geth added.

"I wish we could wait a bit more," Leven said. He looked to the sky as the sun began to settle behind the nearby mountains. "It doesn't feel right to go without him."

"He'll make it back to Foo," Geth said confidently. "If he doesn't, then it is his design to remain here."

The three of them moved into the bushes Geth had indicated

and made themselves comfortable on the ground. They were all silent and deep in thought about what lay ahead. Leven looked at everything around him with new eyes—eyes that understood he might never see any of this again.

"You okay?" he finally asked Winter.

"I've never been more scared in my life," she answered.

"Good, me neither," Leven smiled.

ii

Clover had no idea where fate was leading him. He was simply following the feeling inside himself. Sycophants are naturally drawn to their burns—there is a constant pull for them to return to those to whom they have been assigned.

The insulation truck had taken him quite a way. When it began going in a direction contrary to his feelings, Clover had abandoned the truck and hitched a ride in a tour bus filled with American senior citizens. As fate would have it, they were on their way to the Konigsee so they could take some pictures and prove to their friends back home that they were really living. The problem was, Clover felt they were going way too slow. He figured he would help them all out by squeezing in next to the driver's feet and pushing down on the gas pedal.

Clover had never heard such sustained, high-pitched screaming.

The bus flew as the driver frantically tried to slam on the brakes and stay on the road. Clover positioned himself so he could push the brake pedal up with his legs and hold the gas petal down with his hands. The poor driver had no choice but to accept his fate and simply steer in an effort to keep the bus on the road.

It was a new model bus with a huge engine and lots of power. It sped down the autobahn at breakneck speed with everyone inside

screaming and praying. An elderly gentleman with flowing white hair, wearing baggy shorts and dark knee socks, fought the g-forces and worked his way up the aisle of the bus, pulling himself forward by clinging to the seats.

"Stop this bus!" he yelled at the driver.

The driver was too occupied to reply. His main concern was trying to keep the bus on the road. The old man figured the driver just didn't understand English, so he got out his English-to-German dictionary and, while hanging on for dear life with his left hand, tried to look up the words with his right.

"Stopen die auto!"

The driver looked up at him as if he were crazy. "We're all going to die," the driver said in perfect English.

The old man turned back to the rest of the passengers and conveyed the message. Clover once again was amazed by the volume of noise the nice group of senior citizens was able to make.

As they barreled down the road, Clover grew jealous of the others, who were able to look out the window and see the passing scenery. He had grown quite fond of seeing the world fly by while driving himself earlier, and now he wanted to take just one look. When he took his weight off the gas pedal to squeeze out, the driver felt the bus slow and began frantically stomping and kicking at the pedals beneath him in hopes of stopping the vehicle. Caught in the fury of the attempt, Clover took quite a thrashing before he was able to crawl out from under the driver's feet and haul himself up onto the dashboard.

The driver was finally able to get the bus under control, and the passengers began to fan themselves and put their hands to their hearts instead of just screaming.

The bus came to a stop directly in front of a small sign that read: Berchtesgaden.

"That feels right," Clover said to himself. He waited for the driver to open the door and hopped off as if he didn't have a care in the world, happy they had made such good time.

iii

Leven and Winter could do nothing but wait. The last boat would not be leaving for an hour, and Leven was anxious and scared. Wanting to be alone for a moment, he left Winter and Geth in the trees and wandered back down the lakefront and to the small white church with the funny red roof.

St. Bartholomew church was hundreds of years old. It was a small, white cathedral, with big red onion-like domes on top of it. Originally, it had been used as a hunting lodge for great kings. Now, it was more of a photo opportunity for wealthy tourists. Leven wished his eyesight were clearer, but from what he could see he loved the look of St. Bartholomew against the lake and wished his life could be as peaceful as the scene before him. Going to Foo would seem much less of a sacrifice if the gateway had been in a barren desert or in the middle of a congested city.

Leven slipped into the dimly lit chapel and sat down on the back row of pews. A number of tourists wandered about, looking over everything and whispering. Leven turned from gazing at a family with two young kids and noticed a dark being sitting right next to him. He was so startled that he hollered out and jumped in his seat.

"Hello, Leven," the voice low and menacing. "*I've* been waiting for you."

Leven's heart was suddenly racing. It was not hard to recognize

the rat-like features of Sabine. He looked just like his shadows, only bigger. There was also a dark aura around him.

"You're Sabine," he managed to say.

"Smart boy," Sabine's oily voice dripped. "But not smart enough to take the advice of *my* shadows and forget all this. Now look where you are."

A pair of tourists walked by, conversing loudly.

"Do you mind," Sabine glowered at them. "We're in a church."

The couple gave Sabine a strong look and walked away.

"How did you get here?" Leven asked, trying to keep his mind clear of Sabine's voice and thoughts. "Or are you just a shadow?"

"Oh, *I'm* quite real. *I* came here the same way all of Foo will soon arrive," Sabine said clearly. "Think of it, Leven. With Foo here, there will be nothing you can't do."

"That's impossible," Leven said. "You'll destroy everything."

"There is no impossible," Sabine snapped. "Geth and his self-righteous belief," he scoffed. "The dreams of man are not my concern. If you destroy that gateway, Leven, you will be destroying the possibility of perfect lives for everyone. Geth doesn't want you to know this. Geth wants Foo just as it is, so that he can rule over everyone."

Leven was silent as a few nearby tourists conversed quietly, examining some of the church artifacts. He could hear people outside and knew that life was going on as usual while he had to make decisions that would affect everyone.

Leven squinted. He could see the light from outside as it rested against the far wall. It was dimming quickly. Soon it would be time to swim.

"Think of it," Sabine twitched. "With Foo here, you will have it all. Geth wants to trap you, cut you off."

Sabine's words were not going unheard. Leven had many concerns and fears, and part of them were things Sabine was now addressing. It didn't feel totally right to destroy the gateway and trap himself in Foo forever. What if Sabine's plan were possible? What if the dreams of man were not dependent on Foo? Quite frankly, it scared the life out of Leven to think of destroying his only way back. His time here had not been charmed, but something inside him had given him hope that he could someday become more than he was. It was that hope and dream that had enabled him to go on each day. Leven couldn't let Sabine eliminate that belief for anyone else.

"There is no killing in Foo," Sabine said softly, as if he were sharing bad news. "Here, however, is a different story." A few more tourists filed in. "The moment you swim toward that gateway," Sabine continued, "*I* will kill you. *I* don't care if you have the great Geth with you or not," he mocked. "You touch that water, and *I* will kill you."

The church emptied a bit.

"It's not hard for you to stay alive," Sabine smiled enticingly. "Simply . . . don't swim."

Sabine stood up. "*I* know where the gateway is," he warned. "*I'll* be watching. You go into that water, and *I* will kill you and Winter."

In a sense Sabine was lying. He had no intention of letting Leven live. He contemplated taking care of the problem now, but the church was full of people: Sabine didn't want any further complications.

He smiled a wicked smile at Leven and drifted out.

Leven could hear a woman telling people in broken English that the last boat would be leaving soon and everyone needed to gather at the dock.

Leven slipped out of the church and back into the forest, Sabine watching his every move.

iv

It was October, and the day had been unseasonably warm, but Winter was unusually cold.

"Are you okay?" Geth asked her as the two sat on the ground beneath a couple of beautiful pine trees near the water's edge. A gentle, warm breeze descended on them, coloring the moment beautifully. Water lapped against the shore, and the reflection of the setting sun shimmered across the smooth water.

"I think so," Winter said. "Just frightened beyond belief." She took out the small pocket knife Geth had earlier instructed her to buy. She turned it over in her hand, looking at it with her green eyes.

"It's your home you'll be swimming toward," Geth said kindly. "You made me promise that you'd get back."

"I know," Winter smiled sadly. "At least that's what you've told me."

"I'm just keeping my promise," Geth teased.

"So will we make it?" Winter asked. "What if Leven can't swim fast enough?"

"Oh," Geth waved. "That's not the problem. The problem now is Sabine."

"Sabine?" she gasped.

"He's here," Geth said. "I knew he would get through. I could feel it earlier."

"Where is he?" Winter asked, not surprised in the least.

"Talking to Leven," he said without concern.

Winter stood up quickly. "Let's go," she said frantically.

"Sit down," Geth ordered nicely, patting the ground with his one little arm. "We've done all we can. It's now up to fate. Leven needs to be sure about what he is doing."

"How did you know Sabine is here?"

"We lithens travel by fate. It's important to know what roadblocks might be standing in our way. A soul as deep and dark as Sabine's is not easy to ignore," Geth answered. "Being from Foo, you probably felt him as well."

Winter was silent, her thoughts on so many things. She flipped the knife, turning it over in her hands.

Geth looked at Winter. "There is a little something I was wondering if you could help me with," he said. "I'm a bit embarrassed even to ask, but it seems as if fate moves me to do so."

Winter stared at him with a quizzical expression.

"I had you buy that knife for a reason." He cleared his little hole. "I was wondering if you might slice me another arm. If anything happens I would be much better off with two of them."

"Another arm?" Winter asked.

Geth looked pitiful.

"I guess I could," Winter said reluctantly.

"And could you sharpen my head?" Geth threw in.

"Sharpen your head?"

"It might come in handy," Geth shrugged.

Winter shook her own head. "You had me buy this to cut you up? Won't it hurt?" Winter asked.

"Just a bit," Geth said. "But I'd put up with a lot to have another arm."

"And a sharp head," Winter smiled at him.

Geth climbed up on a large boulder and lay down. Winter

picked him up by the feet, and he turned his head to look away. "Are you sure?" she asked one last time.

He nodded.

She sliced slowly and calmly as Geth's body tightened in pain. The wood was hard and there wasn't much to work with. Winter feared she might cut right through. Geth bit down and looked away. Winter finished cutting, and Geth turned back. He moved his new arm and smiled weakly.

"Perfect," he said. "How about some fingers?"

Winter went to work on Geth's fingers and forehead. In a short while Geth was a whole new toothpick and the sky was almost dark. Leven came through the trees with a concerned look in his eyes and the weight of two heavy worlds on his shoulders.

"So," Winter said. "Are you all right?"

"I'm fine," Leven waved.

"The last boat is all ready to set sail," she added, folding up the knife as Geth wiggled his new fingers.

"I know," Leven said sadly, still thinking of Sabine's last words.

Geth stretched and sprang off the rock and onto Leven. His new arm and fingers made the move considerably easier than it had been before. He flexed his tiny muscles and looked at Leven.

"You spoke to Sabine," Geth said almost reverently.

"How do you know?" Leven asked with shock.

"That's not important," Geth replied. "What matters now is what you believe."

Leven looked at Geth on his arm and then at Winter. Along with Clover, they were the only friends he had ever known. They had done nothing to cause him to disbelieve in himself, but his heart still ached to somehow know for sure that what he was about to do was right.

"I think I believe in you," Leven said. "I just hope I'm right."

"There will be none of that if Sabine gets his way," Geth said, referring to the destruction of hope.

Leven understood.

"Sabine said if I touch the water he will kill us," Leven said, his mind finally made up to do it.

"Sabine says a lot of things," Geth smiled, knowing that what Leven had just uttered was a declaration of his resolve. "We'll get you to the gateway."

The bell of the last boat leaving sounded.

"I'll push you through the gateway if I have to," Winter added. "I know . . . ," Winter stopped what she was saying to rub her head. "I can hardly speak, my head hurts so . . ."

She would have said more, but she had been turned to ice.

She stood there baffled by her state. She thawed herself and looked over to see that Leven was solid ice. Geth dropped from Leven's frozen shoulder and down to Leven's feet. Winter thought for a second there had been a glitch in her own thoughts and that she had turned Leven and herself into ice by accident, but that thought evaporated quickly when she saw Sabine standing there.

"Sabine," she whispered.

"*I* forgot you were a nit," Sabine said to Winter, referring to her ability to thaw herself. "Where is Geth?" he demanded. "*I* heard him speaking."

Winter froze. Not because she was ice again, but because she realized Sabine didn't know what shape Geth was in. She felt pretty certain Geth's current size would not discourage Sabine, so she kept the truth to herself as she looked down and saw Geth standing behind Leven's frozen left foot.

"He's coming," Winter said, her head burning.

"Coming?" Sabine asked, looking around with concern.

Winter pictured him in ice and Sabine froze. She ran and touched Leven, who instantly thawed. She could hear the sound of the trumpet being played on the last boat of the day out in the middle of the lake. They needed to get into the water.

"Let's get out of here," she yelled to Leven as Sabine began to shake off the ice she had encased him in.

"Not so fast," Sabine sneered.

Leven and Winter turned to face him.

"So you've decided to ignore *me* again," Sabine seethed. "That's a decision you will not live to regret, Leven Thumps."

"We'll see about that," Geth shouted triumphantly.

Sabine looked around, suddenly scared. "Show yourself," he challenged, thinking that Geth was hiding somewhere in the trees.

"I'm right here," Geth answered.

Sabine directed his attention to Leven's sleeve, where Geth was clinging in all his toothpick glory.

"Geth?" Sabine questioned. "Geth? Surely the fates are playing with *me*," Sabine laughed scornfully. "*I* am up against a sliver of wood?"

Geth climbed up to Leven's shoulder and stood as triumphantly as a tiny piece of wood could. "You are up against *fate*."

"Fate?" Sabine scoffed. "You will never reach the gateway. That is your fate," he spat. The joy in his eyes over Geth's current state was very apparent. "Foo and reality will be one. And *I*," Sabine said pompously, "will rule them both."

"Flick me," Geth whispered into Leven's ear.

"What?" Leven whispered back.

"Flick me!"

Leven snatched Geth from his shoulder and flicked him as as hard as he could toward Sabine. The little toothpick struck Sabine in the left cheek with his newly sharpened head, piercing Sabine's skin and flying past him onto the ground beyond the dark figure. Sabine threw his hand to his face and obviously thought of Leven and Winter in ice because they were now just that. He tried to picture Geth in ice, too, but lithens are unaffected by nit tricks.

Winter defrosted and saw Sabine in white, frozen stiff. She held her thoughts there as Geth worked his way back over to Sabine. The concentration became too great. She turned from Sabine to Leven, touching his arms. Geth was already on the now defrosted Sabine. He didn't have much size, but he was creating a pretty good distraction by zipping over Sabine's body and jabbing him over and over. Sabine danced as he swatted with his hands and tried to grab hold of Geth.

The last rays of the sun were touching the edge of the lake. The earth would not remain in a good mood for much longer. Leven ran toward the water, knowing what he had to do. He was too slow, though, and Sabine turned him into ice again. It was like a vicious game of freeze tag, and Leven was always It.

Winter imagined not only Sabine as ice but the trees around him. They froze, and she moved as quickly as she could, slamming into a tall thin tree and breaking it down. It cracked and fell toward Sabine, who was now thawed and moving. Geth was keeping at Sabine just enough to distract him from repeatedly freezing Winter. Winter ran to Leven and touched his shoulder. He thawed in a running stride, heading for the water. As Leven's foot reached the edge of the water, Sabine froze him again. Now a solid chunk of ice, Leven fell forward into the water with a large splash.

"Lev!" Winter screamed before she was suddenly ice again.

Leven drifted out into the lake as Winter returned to form. She looked at Sabine with her eyes burning.

"You can't stop *me*," Sabine sneered at Winter. "You couldn't in Foo, and you can't now."

Images of her life in Foo began popping into her head like slides thrown onto a screen. She could see Sabine smiling. There was the girl with the long red hair. There was a strong-looking man with fire in his eyes.

The thought swept over her. This was not a new fight she was fighting. Her head cleared and her mind relaxed.

Winter shot ice from her being and froze Sabine. She thought hard and long, coating him over and over with thick layers. She wrapped him up until he was nothing but a giant block of ice, as stiff and frozen as his heart.

"It won't hold," Geth yelled.

"I know," Winter hollered back, "but I've got to get to Lev before he starts melting in the water."

Leven had drifted out quite a way from shore. His body bobbed up and down in the emerald green water. Winter turned to run but was ice again. Sabine was melted and at her already. She thawed and faced him once more. Geth was doing everything he could to be a distraction, but his attempt was thwarted by the sudden grip of Sabine.

Sabine smiled and looked at Winter. He glanced deliciously at the toothpick in his hand.

"The great Geth," Sabine sneered. "*I'd* prolong your death, but you being a lithen would simply accept the pain as fate."

Winter lunged forward and froze Sabine. She flicked Geth out of his hands and into the lake before Sabine could thaw and freeze her again. He then did just that and held her in his concentration until her will overpowered him and she was normal once more.

"This is pointless," Winter said, breathing hard. "Let us be."

"Impossible."

"That's not a word," Winter said as naturally as if she really knew it.

"Your precious Leven is melting," Sabine said, an evil smile flickering across his dark face."Soon there will be no reason for our quarrel."

Winter thought the entire lake ice so as to preserve Leven, and it was.

"Impressive," Sabine hissed, looking out at the frozen body of water. He thought the mountains around them to be ice, and they were.

"Big deal," Winter said, changing the entire landscape around them into ice.

"I will not be outdone by a foolish child," Sabine seethed.

It was at that moment that Winter first saw movement up above Sabine and behind the trees. Sadly, it was too late for Clover to be of any help. Clover looked down from the top of a steep trail, wide-eyed and determined.

Sabine closed his eyes and froze the entire world.

Under his thoughts the whole planet and all that it had on it became solid ice. The earth groaned and the sky lit up with fuzzy stars and color as the planet wobbled. The ground creaked and shuddered as the wind howled painfully, the world crackling in pain.

"You can't defeat *me*!" Sabine roared.

Winter flashed back to the conflict in Foo. She could see Sabine and remembered the struggle she had fought there in her old home.

She remembered having to run from Sabine and hide, so she could play the part in retrieving Leven that she was now playing.

Winter's evergreen eyes burned ice cold. The earth was screaming as it struggled to revolve as it was supposed to. The sky grew smeared and wavy. It was to humanity's advantage that Clover was not of this world. Being a sycophant, he was impossible to freeze, thus making him the only thing on the planet that wasn't solid ice. Winter shook herself from her thoughts and watched Clover leap onto the slick trail and slide quickly toward her and Sabine.

It was now or never.

"I'm done with all this," she said aloud, using words she had used before somewhere else. She thought it, and Sabine was ice. Her thoughts were more cold and concentrated than they had ever been.

It was perfect timing.

Before Sabine could return to form, Clover barreled into him from behind. His small amount of weight, combined with his speed, knocked Sabine over and sent him quickly to the ground, where the demon shattered into a thousand pieces of ice. Winter covered her head to avoid the storm, as bits of ice rained down everywhere. She stared at the spot where Sabine had been standing and marveled. She glanced down at Clover as he stood there, looking guilty.

"Oops," Clover said.

The earth creaked and groaned, as if it could not possibly make one more rotation. Winter quickly fell to her knees and touched the ground.

The world was green once more.

No history book has recorded the fact that at one point the entire earth was ice. But those who would argue that point were frozen as well and simply can't recall it. The doubt of anyone doesn't make it any less true. In fact, on those days when it's warm and you suddenly

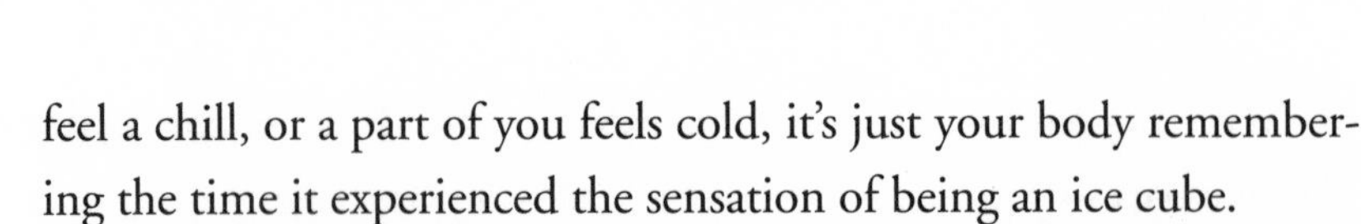

feel a chill, or a part of you feels cold, it's just your body remembering the time it experienced the sensation of being an ice cube.

"I really didn't mean to do that," Clover said, looking at the thousands of tiny pieces of Sabine. "I was just trying—"

"Don't worry about it," Winter spoke. "You may have just saved the world."

Clover smiled.

"So, can you swim?" she asked him.

"Came in second place in Sentinel Fields my senior year," Clover bragged.

Winter would have stood there congratulating him, but instead she took off running toward the lake. She flew into the water and almost lost her breath due to the coldness of it. She held her head above water and gasped for air. Leven was a good distance from the shore, coughing and thrashing. He had thawed upside down and with freezing water rushing into his nose and mouth. Winter swam to him and grabbed him under the right arm.

"We have to swim," Winter hollered at him. "Before it's too late."

"Where's Sabine?" Leven asked, confused, struggling to stay afloat.

"Gone."

"Gone?"

"It was an accident," Clover apologized, while swimming effortlessly up to Leven.

"Clover!" Leven cheered. "You're here."

"Of course," Clover smiled and spit, his forehead covered in goose bumps.

"We need Geth," Winter yelled.

"Right here," Geth answered, paddling over, his new arm working swimmingly.

"Toothpick," Clover said affectionately.

Geth smiled, swam to Clover, and climbed on. "We have to go now the sun is gone. Are you ready?" Geth asked Leven.

"No," Leven replied, smiling tightly and with chattering teeth. "I'm not sure I'll ever be. But I'll do it for the candy alone."

Clover smiled.

V

Sabine was no longer. Actually, he was no longer the personage he had once been. The shattered bits and remnants of who he was lay upon the still earth as the soil turned from ice back into its normal self. The tiny pieces of Sabine melted into the dirt and dripped down deep into the ground. He was now a countless number of shadowy bits. Every piece of him hissed and surged, scurrying through the dirt like a horrid stream of fluid black ants. He could feel the influence of Leven and Winter. They were still here, in the water and swimming toward the gateway. He had no form, but all was not lost. Every particle of him whispered and pushed forcefully under the earth and into the lake, breaking out from the soil and into the Konigsee. Like an explosion of deranged tadpoles he blew out into the water, swirling and pulsating. Leven was in the distance, swimming toward the gateway. Sabine collected every bit of himself into the shape of a rod and shot through the water like a torpedo toward Leven.

VI

Leven took a giant breath and swam down underwater. Geth had been right. The moment his head was below the surface he could see a faint light glowing in the distance. He pulled and kicked

as he worked his way deeper and deeper. His lungs burned as a heavy anxiety smothered him. He turned to his side as if to try and resurface, but Winter was there pushing him downward. His chest felt like it was going to explode. He could see the gateway now, its corroded gray sides covered in rust and algae. It glowed bright and ominous. Winter swam by him and into the gateway. He watched her stand on the bottom of the box his grandfather had constructed and in an instant she was gone. Leven pushed forward in an effort to follow her, but before he could get there, his legs were struck by a streak of blackness.

The force of the blow propelled him away from the gateway and toward the surface. Leven spun like a rolling log as he twisted uncontrollably upward. Geth had warned him about not being able to make it back to the surface before his lungs gave out, but at the moment Leven wanted nothing other than to get some air. He was propelled at speeds he had not thought possible, forced upward by the impact of whatever had struck him near the gateway. Leven broke the surface of the water and shot twenty feet into the air. He made a terrific arc through the sky and splashed back down into the lake.

Leven kicked and thrashed, trying to right both his mind and his body. He had no idea what had just happened. Winter was gone and something had expelled him from the water.

Geth and Clover were no where to be seen.

Leven would have taken a few moments to seriously contemplate his state of affairs, but his earnest reflection was interrupted by something seizing him by his ankles and dragging him irresistibly down, back under the water. Leven screamed, and his body went rigid as it was hauled downward, deeper into the lake.

Leven willed his mind to concentrate. His eyes burned gold and he could suddenly see the recent past: there was Sabine's dark soul, each tiny fragment melting into the earth. Then Leven's mind showed him the present: millions of fragments of Sabine wrapped around his feet and dragging him to his death. His thoughts shifted, and he got a glimpse of the future: there he was, floating face down on the surface of the lake, his life over.

Never! Leven's mind screamed.

His eyes sizzled as he forced the vision of his death to reverse itself. He wrestled with fate and the future to will himself to live. The future was changing. Leven looked down at the millions of bits of Sabine and used his gift to manipulate them away from his ankles and into oblivion. With one incredibly strong thought, Leven blew Sabine's leftovers away from him. They were dispersed through the water like buckshot from a shotgun blast.

Leven had never felt his gift so strongly. He clawed at the water in an effort to get back to the top, but he was too deep. He would never reach the surface without air. His mind caught hold of fate, and the wind above the Konigsee formed itself into a giant vortex, revolving and boring its way down into the water, creating a funnel of air directly above him. The funnel picked Leven up, filling his lungs with air and spinning him out of the water and into the sky.

Leven was now thirty feet above the lake, twisting like a being in a blender. He might very well have been amazed, but his mind was too busy watching the pieces of Sabine gather and regroup. Like a thick black cloud, Sabine raced in from the north, surrounding the funnel and reaching in with thin, sharp limbs to slice and grab at him. Leven's mind raced with fear. He opened his eyes wide and manipulated the funnel cloud into lifting him higher.

The wind surged upward.

Sabine's remnants followed, swarming like black bees in the funnel around him. Every particle of Sabine hissed and screamed in confusion and hatred. Leven focused his thoughts, his eyes burned, and the tornado exploded, the wind hurling itself into the clouds and peppering them with Sabine's leftovers.

Leven dropped like a rock into the lake.

He hit the water headfirst and shot like a bullet down toward the glow. In an instant he could see the gateway. He twisted his body and plummeted straight toward it. There was no time for hesitation. He reached the gateway and stepped into the bottom of the box his grandfather had made.

Instantly the water disappeared, and Leven was lying on the wooden floor of a small room. He coughed and inhaled as deeply as possible. He couldn't seem to catch his breath. A single candle burned in the far corner. He looked to his left and there was Winter, smiling at him.

"I'm glad you made it," she said.

"Me, too," Geth added, jumping from a nearby table onto Winter's right shoulder.

Clover materialized next to both of them, his big blue eyes almost sparkling. "Welcome home, Lev," he said.

Leven was still breathing hard. He glanced around in amazement, wondering if what he saw was real. "So this is Foo?" he asked, realizing that as solid as everything looked, it did have a different appearance than what he had just left.

Leven got to his feet just as the door opened and a smiling Amelia Thumps stepped into the room.

"You made it," she praised. "I was afraid Sabine might have

stopped you. I had no way to keep him from this room when he finally figured out the entrance."

"We made it," Winter smiled in amazement.

"Winter," Amelia said affectionately, taking her in her arms. "Foo has not been the same without you."

Winter's memory came rushing back. Her life in Foo was suddenly an actual memory she could recall. The pieces all fell together. She saw her childhood on earth. She saw where she had been standing when she was snatched and brought to Foo. She saw her home here in Foo and the people and friends she knew. She saw Geth as the king that he really was and Amelia as the kind and unknown defender of true Foo.

Amelia stepped from Winter to look closely at Leven.

"So this is the boy?" She asked Clover, eyeing Leven suspiciously. "Are you sure he's the one?"

"He is," said Clover. "We've seen him do all sorts of odd things."

"I've seen a lot of people do odd things. That doesn't mean they're the one."

"It's Leven," Geth spoke forcefully, ending any doubt.

"Geth?" Amelia asked, bowing slightly as she said it. "You're back?"

"I am," Geth answered.

"You're a little shorter than I remember," she smiled.

"Age has touched your memory," he laughed.

"Well, I must say this is a great day for Foo." Amelia turned to focus on Leven. "We've been waiting for you," she said kindly, opening her arms. "I've been waiting for you. You are my only family."

Leven yielded to her embrace, feeling for the first time in his existence the love of family. Despite all the doubt and confusion and fear he felt, it was right to be here. She held him at arms' length and looked into his eyes.

"I have something for you," she whispered, her voice quivering with emotion and her eyes shining.

Leven envisioned a watch or a photo or some treasured family heirloom. Instead she handed him a round, ceramic-looking pot with enough potch powder in it to blow up the entire house they were standing in.

"This looks like a bomb," Leven said nervously.

"It is," she smiled, patting him on the shoulder. "I've been saving it for years. You need to go back through the gateway with it. Just drop it in the gateway and stand on the crack. You'll be back here, and the gateway will be destroyed," she said casually.

Leven looked at the ceramic pot in his hands. It was red with a purple band spinning around it. On one side there was a one-inch nub sticking out. Above the nub there was a bit of unreadable writing.

"Hurry," Geth whispered.

Leven glanced at the gateway. The colors swirled and spun across the dirt. Leven looked again at the ball in his hands. He glanced at the others. It was one thing to have the courage to travel to Foo, but it was another thing completely to destroy the only exit he had.

"Hurry," Amelia said, echoing Geth's order. "There isn't—"

Amelia's warning was cut short by Clover's sudden scream. Everyone looked to the sycophant to find him pointing toward the gateway. Oozing out of the light were thousands of black dots. They hissed and cackled wickedly, swarming up out of the gateway like a thick virus. In an instant they were on Leven, clinging to him, entirely covering his body. Leven thrashed and stamped his feet, trying in vain to shake them off. Holding onto the explosive, his hands were useless.

Sabine was not done.

vii

Sabine had only one objective. If he could set off the explosive inside of Foo, Leven would be gone and the gateway would be safe from destruction. His thoughts were not clear as millions of crawling pieces of his once-self tried desperately to detonate the ball.

Winter tried to freeze Sabine, but there wasn't enough of him left for the spell to take. Clover leaped onto Leven's head and began kicking and swatting at the swarm of gnat-sized particles of black. The darkness covered Leven completely and then began to subside as every bit of Sabine swarmed over the ball, trying to make it explode. Sabine's remnants clung to the ball, beating it wildly. The detonator sank into the sphere, activating the explosives.

Clover yelped.

Leven dropped to his knees and dove headfirst into the gateway. His head was instantly in the lake, his legs still remaining and kicking in Foo as Winter tried to get hold of them. His mouth filled with frigid water, and the coldness was a vivid reminder of what he had so recently left. He glanced at the walls of the gateway and down at the floor. He could see the piece of sidewalk and road that didn't match up quite right—the very same spot his Grandfather Thumps had stood on when he started all this. Leven looked at the explosive as he hung upside down with only half his body visible. The ball was covered with what was left of Sabine, every particle of it vibrating frantically. Leven dropped the pot as a noise louder than any he had ever heard shattered his mind.

Darkness engulfed him.

CHAPTER THIRTY-ONE

Foo

Leven felt strange. His body was relaxed, settling like liquid on the floor. His ears were still ringing, and he couldn't see anything but black. He wiggled his fingers to see if he were still alive. He could feel the wood floor. He opened his eyes, surprised to see light. Winter was there smiling at him again.

"Are you okay?" she asked. "We pulled you back."

Leven looked up at Winter and at his grandmother. Clover was on the floor next to Geth. Leven glanced at the dirt of the gateway. There was no glow. Clover approached him and put his hand on his arm.

"Are you okay?"

"I've never been more scared in my life," he answered, getting to his feet, and repeating the words all of them had used at least once.

Winter hugged him as his grandmother did the same. Geth was

caught in the middle so he considered it to be fate and hugged Leven as well.

You may question the importance of what Leven did, but truth be told he made it possible for every dream to continue and every hope to go on—all without a single thanks from anyone.

As Clover cheered, a large gold platter slipped out from his void and clattered noisily onto the floor. Clover blushed and tried to pick it up quickly.

"Where'd you get that?" Winter asked.

"I, uh . . . I sort of borrowed it from those French guys who picked us up in the ocean," Clover said, looking at everyone guiltily. "Is that wrong? Because if someone would have told me that's wrong, I never would have taken it."

Leven smiled again, amazed at where his life had come to.

"All right then," Geth clapped. Of course it wasn't much of a clap, seeing how he had only two little sliver arms. But it was a pretty good click. "We've got to get going."

"Going?" Leven asked. "We're here."

"We've just started," Geth said seriously. "We must get to the Turrets of Foo, and you are the only person who can return me to my rightful state. Did I not mention that before?"

Leven did not smile.

"Sabine may be gone, but the division between good and evil grows. We have to stop those who would destroy Foo," Geth insisted. "Or all that we've done is in vain."

"So we're no better off?" Leven complained.

"Sabine's gone," Winter pointed out, "and the gateway is destroyed."

Leven didn't look as though he was impressed.

"I thought destroying the gateway was our mission," Leven questioned. "Didn't we—"

"Oh, it's just the beginning," Geth interrupted. "Maybe it would help if you take a look at what we'll be saving," Geth said. He jumped off Clover and onto Leven's shoulder.

Leven stood and moved out of the room and down the dark hall. The front door to Amelia's house opened without anyone touching it.

"How did—?" Leven asked.

"Doors know what to do here," Geth explained.

Leven stepped out of the house and into Foo and knew, without a doubt, that he was dreaming. He had never seen anything like what he now saw. Not only that, but he could see it clearly; his sight was perfect. Mountains and valleys and rivers and foliage filled his view, but they were nothing like those he had just left behind in reality. The sky was bright yellow near the ground and purple at its crown. Creatures he had never seen, and would have been unable to imagine, ran across prairies of long orange grass that blew in the wind. He could see incredible darkness to the north, and behind that darkness, thin pointed mountains that looked as if they were moving. A river of deep blue water spilled across his view, creating waterfalls in at least twenty places. The clouds were shaped differently, the air seemed to glisten, and if Leven wasn't completely wrong, he could have sworn he saw a person flying in the distance.

"Wow," he gasped.

"Not a bad view," his grandmother said, putting her hand on his shoulder. "But it's nothing compared to some of the other sights you'll see here."

"I can see everything so clearly," Leven whispered happily.

Geth cleared his wooden mouth. "Now what we must do is get to the other end," he said kindly. "Of course, that should be no big deal to you."

"Is Winter coming?" Leven asked, still looking out at the miracle landscape in front of him.

"Of course," Winter said.

"And Clover?"

"You are my burn," he replied, a gold goblet slipping out of his robe.

He blushed.

Leven took another long, clear look at his new home and his next journey.

"Can I sleep before we begin?" he pleaded.

"I think we can fit that in," Geth answered. "Heaven knows you're going to need to be rested."

Leven went back into Amelia's house and to a short couch that sat in front of a huge roaring fire. The fire was not only burning, it was also singing softly. The couch wasn't long enough to sleep on, but Leven didn't care. He lay down and stretched out his legs, and as he did so the sofa lengthened to accommodate him. He looked at the couch and then back at all those still standing there.

"Pretty cool," Leven admitted, closing his eyes as he said it.

"That's nothing," Amelia whispered, stepping up and laying a blanket over him.

Leven would have said thanks, but he was out cold.

Clover tisked affectionately. "That's my little human."

Geth smiled at Clover. "Keep trying."

The fire sang softly and the windows dimmed nicely as Leven experienced his first dream in a place where there was nothing but.

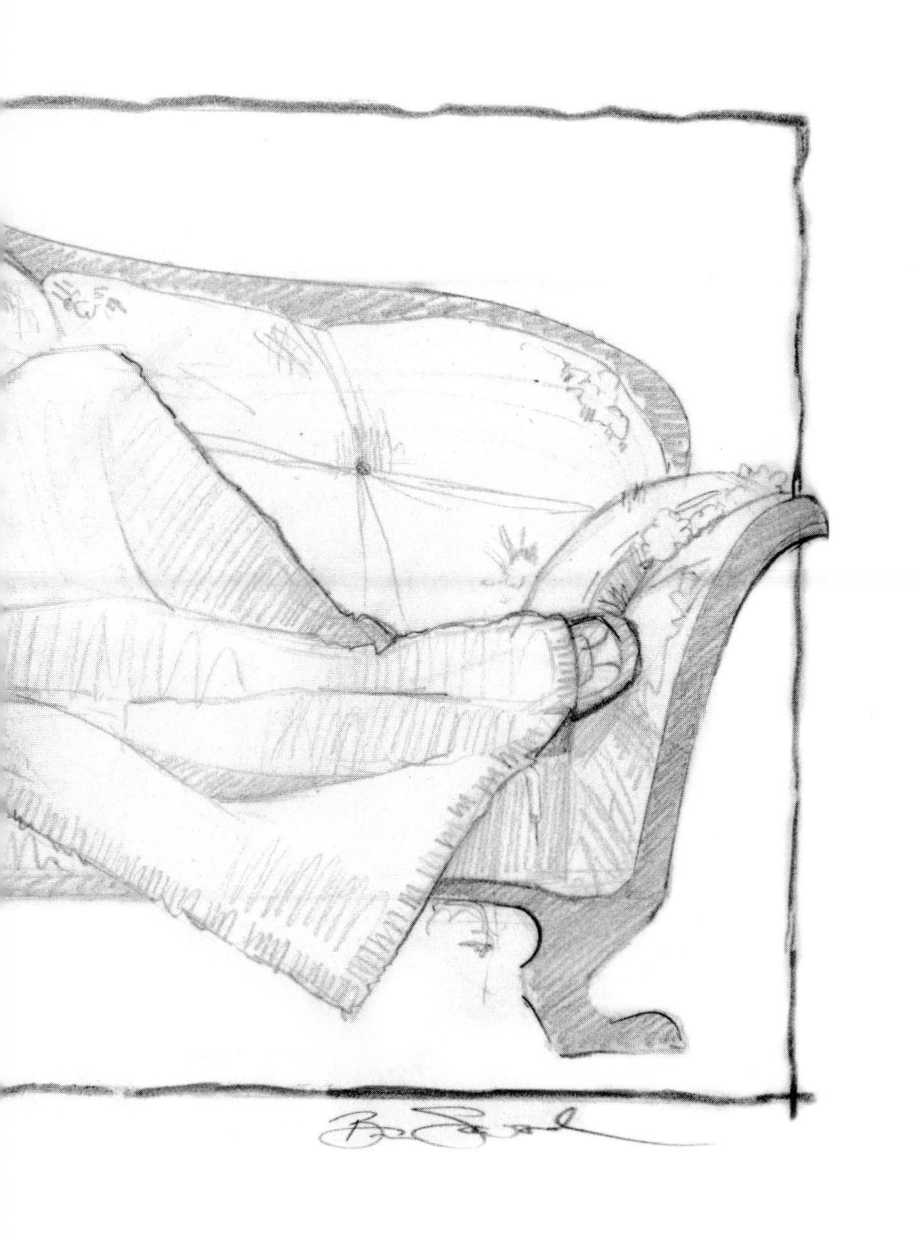

INVISIBLE VILLAGE
FTÉ
CINDER DEPRESSION
RED GROVE
THE DEVIL'S SPIRAL
VEIL SEA
HIDDEN BORDER
CUSP
THIRTEEN STONES
LITH
WET BORDER

GUARDED BORDER
PILLARS OF RANT
GREEN POND
SUN RIVER
MORFIT
SWOLLEN FOREST
FUNDRALS OF FOO
LIME SEA
ALDER
HARD BORDER
FISSURE GORGE
SENTINEL FIELDS
NITEON
CORK
UP
U
B
BACK
O
OVER
D
DOWN
VEIL SEA
THE LAND OF
FOO
SYCOPHANT RUN

GLOSSARY

WHO'S WHO IN FOO

LEVEN THUMPS

Leven is fourteen years old and is the grandson of Hector Thumps, the builder of the gateway. Lev originally knows nothing of Foo or of his heritage. He eventually discovers he is an offing who can see and manipulate the future. Lev's brown eyes burn gold whenever his gift kicks in.

WINTER FRORE

Winter is thirteen, with white-blond hair and deep evergreen eyes. Her pale skin and willowy clothes give her the appearance of a shy spirit. Like Sabine, she is a nit and has the ability to freeze whatever she wishes. She was born in Foo, but her thoughts and memories of her previous life are gone. Winter struggles just to figure out what her purpose is.

GETH

Geth has existed for hundreds of years. In Foo he was one of the strongest and most respected beings. Geth is the head token of the Council of Wonder and the heir to the throne of Foo. Eternally optimistic, Geth is also the most outspoken against the wishes of Sabine. To silence Geth, Sabine trapped Geth's soul in the seed of a fantrum tree and left him for the birds. Fate rescued Geth, and in the dying hands of his loyal friend, Antsel, he was taken through the gateway, out of Foo, and planted in reality. Geth is one of the few beings who knows the location of the gateway.

SABINE (sub-bine)

Sabine is the darkest and most selfish being in Foo. Snatched from reality at the age of nine, he is now a nit with the ability to freeze whatever he wishes. Sabine thirsts to know the location of the gateway because he believes if he can move freely between Foo and reality he can rule them

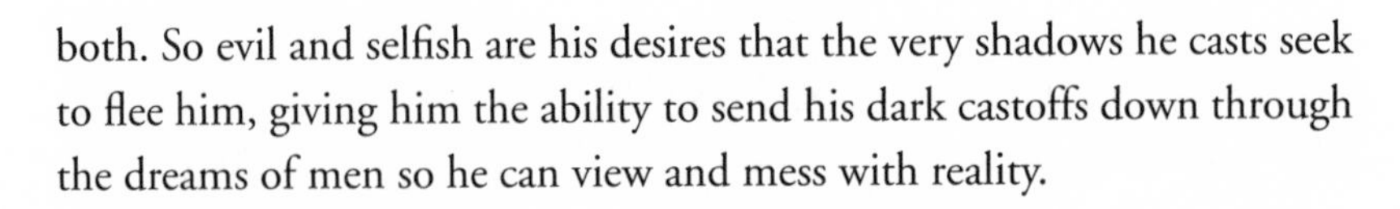

both. So evil and selfish are his desires that the very shadows he casts seek to flee him, giving him the ability to send his dark castoffs down through the dreams of men so he can view and mess with reality.

ANTSEL

Antsel is a member of the Council of Wonder. He is aged and fiercely devoted to the philosophy of Foo and to preserving the dreams of men. He is Geth's greatest supporter and a nit. Snatched from reality many years ago, he is deeply loyal to the council and has the ability to see perfectly underground.

CLOVER ERNEST

Clover is a sycophant from Foo assigned to look after Leven. He is about twelve inches tall and furry all over except for his face, knees, and elbows. He wears a shimmering robe that renders him completely invisible if the hood is up. He is incredibly curious and mischievous to a fault. His previous burn was Antsel.

JAMOON

Jamoon is a Sabine's right-hand man as well as a rant. Being a rant, half of his body is unstable, transformed continually into the form of the dreams being entertained by humans. He is totally obedient to Sabine's wishes. Jamoon believes Sabine's promise that if he and his kind can get into reality, the rant's unusual condition will be healed.

HECTOR THUMPS

Hector Thumps is Leven's grandfather and the creator of the gateway. When fate snatched him into Foo, he fought to find a way back to the girl he loved in reality. His quest nearly drove him mad.

AMELIA THUMPS

Amelia is old. She is the woman Hector Thumps married after he returned to Foo a second time. She is Leven's grandmother and lives between Morfit and the Fundrals of Foo. She is the protector of the gateway to Foo.

The Order of Things

Cogs

Cogs are the ungifted offspring of nits. They possess no great single talent, yet they can manipulate and enhance dreams.

Lithens

Lithens were the original dwellers of Foo. Placed in the realm by fate they have always been there. They are committed to the sacred task of preserving the true Foo. Lithens live and travel by fate, and they fear almost nothing. They are honest and believed to be incorruptible. Geth is a lithen.

Nits

Niteons, or nits as they are referred to, are humans who were once on earth and were brought to Foo by fate. Nits are the working class of Foo. They are the most stable and best dream enhancers. They are given a powerful gift soon after they arrive in Foo. A number of nits can control fire or water or ice. Some can see in the pitch dark or walk through walls and rock. Some can levitate and change shape. Nits are usually loyal and honest. Both Winter Frore and Sabine are nits.

Offings

Offings are rare and powerful. Unlike others who might be given only one gift, offings can see and manipulate the future as well as learn other gifts. Offings are the most trusted confidents of the Want. Leven Thumps is an offing.

Rants

Rants are nit offspring that are born with too little character to successfully manipulate dreams. They are constantly in a state of instability and chaos. As dreams catch them, half of their bodies become the image and imagination of what someone in reality is dreaming at the

moment. Rants are usually dressed in long robes to hide their odd and unstable forms. Jamoon is a rant.

SYCOPHANTS (sick-o-funts)

Sycophants are assigned to those who accidentally step into Foo. They are there to help those who come in, adjust and understand. Their entire lives are spent serving their assignments, who are called their burns. There is only one way for sycophants to die, but nobody aside from the sycophants know what that is.

THE WANT

The Want is the virtually unseen but constantly felt sage of Foo. He lives on the island of Lith and can see every dream that comes in. He is prophetic and a bit mad from all the visions he has had.

THE ADVENTURE CONTINUES
IN BOOK TWO,
LEVEN THUMPS AND THE WHISPERED SECRET